TIME LOVES A HERO

Other Books by Ben Greer

SLAMMER

HALLOWEEN

Ben Greer

TIME LOVES A HERO

DOUBLEDAY & COMPANY, INC.
GARDEN CITY, NEW YORK 1986

The characters and the events depicted in this book are fictitious. Any resemblance to living persons or actual events is unintended and entirely coincidental.

Library of Congress Cataloging in Publication Data
Greer, Ben.
Time loves a hero.
I. Title.
PS3557.R399T5 1986 813'.54
ISBN 0-385-19662-8
Library of Congress Catalog Card Number 85-10328

PRINTED IN THE UNITED STATES OF AMERICA

To *Franklin* and *Dottie Ashley*.
Without your care and direction
I could not have finished this work.

B.G.

TIME LOVES A HERO

Prologue

When he finally did make love to Greta Garbo, she wore a glove. A white cashmere glove on her left hand. Even now he remembered the orange spot of Merthiolate between the thumb and the index finger. She had not told him why she wore the glove and he had not asked. Afterward, she had gone into seclusion, forever.

The old man tried to sleep, but he could not. He was lying in his bed, in his house, on his island and he could not sleep.

Four hours ago he had returned from Boston. The doctors seemed certain. He was dying. Emphysema had complicated his recent coronary. He reached for a pack of Lucky Strikes on the walnut nightstand. When he struck the match the blue spark woke a shadow in the chair.

"Pop?"

The old man wheezed and sucked the cigarette.

"You shouldn't. You'll make yourself worse."

He pulled down the hot smoke as deep as he could. The ash glowed weakly.

"Pop, there's a new bran treatment. Just natural grains and mineral baths."

He looked at him. "I want Chivas and soda and two ice cubes."

"You could get off all the medicines and let your body heal itself."

"Two ice cubes and exactly two ounces of soda."

His son left the room and he propped himself in bed. The

smoke had no taste and it would not go down deep enough. He crushed the Lucky in an ashtray on the bedside table. Beside the guttering cigarette lay his journal and the new pages he was still writing. He set the book in his lap.

It was here, his whole life. Every woman he had loved, every deal he had made. He flipped through the pages: Ethel Barrymore, Mary Pickford, Garbo, Stalin and Perón and Joseph Kennedy. He had listed over a thousand names. Each one had a story, a story in which his bank had lent money or his film company had gambled or his mind had constructed a campaign which devastated or beguiled his opponents.

He set his hand on the journal and maybe that was when he finally decided. Oh, he had thought about him many times, many years, but now he decided to reach out for him—for the boy. The Southerner. The one he had never seen, never touched.

His son walked back into the room and handed him the drink.

"Write a letter."

"You're too weak, Pop."

"I said write a letter."

"To whom?"

"He calls himself Walker. Cody Walker. Make it sound warm and friendly. Make it sound like you've known him all your life."

Maybe this was the way everything started, I'm not sure. But I am sure about the letter because when it came, it came to me.

1

I was called Dooley Rice Codele Walker and baptized by total immersion in a muddy river named Tiger. My mother and her family were Scotch-Irish, teachers and preachers and clerks. We lived in Glenn Springs, South Carolina. Our town had one stoplight, one store and one miraculous well whose water every July turned into sweet, sour-mash bourbon. Wearing straw hats and white shirts and pleated pants, the men would line up on the morning of the Fourth. They tossed the rusted tin bucket down into the well and then cranked it back up. Carefully each man submerged a yellow gourd dipper into the bucket, then raised it to his lips and drank. Their faces turned ruddy and red as new pennies.

I was twelve before I discovered the well was not miraculous. The sweet, sour-mash bourbon was a gift of Mr. Hiram Owens, who owned the store beside which the well stood. For thirty years every night of July the third he went into his store's freezer, took out four five-hundred-pound blocks of ice and dropped them into the well. Then he added two fifty-gallon barrels of a bourbon called Wild Pig. Mr. Hiram Owens didn't like parties and it was his way of settling social debt. The whiskey and the ice and the hangovers lasted a month.

Below the store the tar-gravel road and the red earth descended into the flat. Mules lived here. Red-dust mules and mosquitoes and black ticks and possums and indestructible chinaberry trees. Our house sat above the flat: two stories, painted white, ten rooms, more like a barn than a mansion.

I still dream about that tall house and its slow, damp life. I dream about the endless summers when my nanny Teresa would wake me at seven, hug me to her white and scratchy apron and carry me downstairs, the smell of Bumblebee snuff sweet upon her lips. Poached eggs on wheat toast, the yolk carrot orange and just a little runny. Then I would go out to the woods. My game was the Civil War. Day after day I arrived in the nick of time to save Lee at Appomattox and kick the Yankees back to Boston—where, I assumed, all Yankees came from.

Dinner (we never called it lunch) was at one. Green beans and yellow cream corn and tomatoes and fried chicken. Then the nap. I loved the nap. Pulling down the brown shades, revving the clacking fan, descending into bed, sleeping beyond the range of the meat-eating sun. Generally, I was roused at 4:30 or 5:00 by a blustery thunderstorm. It lasted twenty or thirty minutes while I drank a glass of sugary iced tea. A couple more hours of play: catching green chameleons or grabbing brown-shelled crawfish from the creek or rooting in the cellar for oily toads.

Supper was simple. Vegetable soup or Rice Krispies, maybe chicken wings and noodles. Then I tried to teach my chameleon tricks or forced two crawfish to fight in a jar of spring water. At nine o'clock Teresa caught, dunked and scrubbed me in a cast-iron tub. She dried me off and dug at my ears and took me to bed. She sang me to sleep while the katydids buzzed and the wind nuzzled the curtains and somewhere in the dark a bobwhite called against a whippoorwill.

My father was named Joe Walker and he was our mysterious link to wealth. Raised in an orphanage in Aiken, he kept his early life, the years before the orphanage, a complete secret. Neither my mother nor I knew anything about his parents or his childhood. For us my father's life began on his fourteenth birthday when a wealthy couple who often visited the orphans brought along a friend. An incredibly rich friend. A financier from Boston, Massachusetts, whom they said was worth a billion dollars—Mallory Beale.

Beale never formally adopted my father, though he might as

well have. One week after he met Joe Walker, the billionaire took him from the orphanage and sent him north to a prep school called St. Georges.

After he graduated from St. Georges, Joe Walker went one semester to Yale and then left school to work with the Beale family. The primary family business was banking. The Beales owned outright the multibillion-dollar Boston International Bank. In addition, Daddy told me that the Beales owned a percentage of every major banking chain in the United States and several in South America.

The Beales also possessed fifty thousand acres of industrial parks, high-rise apartment complexes in Japan, Brazil and the Netherlands. A film distribution company, restaurants, hotels, a hockey team, a football team, a shipping line, twelve radio stations, sixteen newspapers and somehow in all of this Daddy said they had acquired many other smaller businesses which simply generated four, five, six million dollars a year, including a national chain of hamburger stands which exploded in profits and wowed the blue-chip analysts on Wall Street.

My father worked in the Beale world for a number of years. I saw his scrapbooks. Pictures of Joe Walker being congratulated by Vice President Alvin Barclay; shaking the hand of union organizer John L. Lewis; posing for a snapshot on a Malibu Beach with Walt Disney. Then suddenly, inexplicably, it was over. In 1950 he abandoned the magic world of the Beales, went south, married a redneck country girl and lived off stocks and memories.

For the rest of his life my father told himself that the day would come when he would return to Mallory Beale and they would put together the biggest deal that America had ever seen. Even as a boy I knew it was self-deception and I promised myself that I would never be guilty of such a distortion. I would look at life honestly, not as I wished it to be, but, rather, as it was.

Still the mystery haunted me. Why had my father left the dazzling society of the Beales? Why would anyone choose a barren hamlet in South Carolina over Paris and Rio and New

York? At the age of ten or twelve my questions were vague and erratic, but when I turned seventeen something happened which fired my curiosity and filled me with incredible expectations.

Nine o'clock on a cold night in December. My father had downed four or five Budweisers and a wedge of ripe Brie. We sat in the parlor before a fluttering gas heater as he finished a story about one of his flamboyant business partners and "an airtight deal" which had actually worked.

". . . and both of us were happy as the devil. Thinking five ways to invest the money and a thousand ways to spend it—and then, all of a sudden the car stopped. Just quit. A brand new Cadillac. One mile out of downtown Manhattan. Right in the middle of the Brooklyn Bridge at five-thirty on a Friday afternoon. Punky tried the engine. Half a crank. Horns were blowing. He pumped the accelerator, turned the switch. A death rattle. Truck drivers pounded their doors. He waited a second, pumped and turned at the same time. Nothing. Not even a click. Then ole Punky Waller—I still can't believe it—ole Punky Waller turns around to me and he says—let's go. I said, what? He says let's go. Time to move on. And then he just grabbed those car keys, slammed the door behind him, wound up like Whitey Ford and pitched the keys right off the bridge. Laughing? Why he was laughing to beat the band."

Daddy. Black hair and blue eyes and a Gable mustache. Daddy. In his boxer shorts and long black socks, hooting at the memory.

He became quiet, then confidential. "It's timing, son. Timing. Knowing when to go and when to stay. Every great man has it. Punky Waller did. He was a great man. Made millions. Millions. There's only one fella I knew who had better timing. Only one."

"Mallory Beale, Daddy?"

"Yeah. Him."

"Why'd you leave him, Daddy? Why'd you go?"

In the semidark room I could just make out the gold crowns

on his white boxers. The sigh expanded his thin stomach, then whistled from his lips.

"I need to tell you something about Mallory Beale, son. About Mallory Beale and me. It could affect you one day. It could even change your life. Change it—completely."

"Tell me now."

"No. Not now. When you're a little older. When you're ready."

For the next few days I was visited by every kind of wild, fantastic, harebrained hope, dream and desire. It is recess at Glenn Springs High, and I'm talking to a few friends when the black Mercedes limousine with European fog lamps and opaque windows and silver, real silver, hubcaps turns—no, slinks—into the driveway. A chauffeur clad in a papal white suit exits, opens the back door, points—to me. In unison I hear my friends say, Ooo-hhh crap. Inside, a leather wall divides the limo in half. A small screen opens. The voice says, "Cody Walker, you're too good for Glenn Springs High. Come with me and I'll show you how to build—an empire."

There were a thousand variations on the Mallory Beale theme: bankers appearing at my door with million-dollar checks: "Cody, Mr. Beale and your father set this up. Of course, it's only the first payment." Naked Hayley Mills climbing a tree, creeping into my room, my bed "just to spend the night with the richest boy in America"; at 4 A.M. a phone call:

"Cody Walker?"

"Yeah?"

"Please hold for the President of the United States."

They were fun, all these fantasies, these fairy tales, but they lasted only a week. I did not daydream about Mallory Beale again for some years. Some years after I had buried my parents.

Joe Walker was killed in a car crash. He had a blowout at sixty miles per hour. The car was completely crushed, and so was he. Everything but his brave face.

The day after the accident, and due to shock and grief the doctors said, my mother died of a cerebral hemorrhage. They lay side by side in cherry-wood coffins in the lonely light of a country church. I still remember how beautiful their hair looked and wondered (still do wonder) how the morticians knew to comb it so perfectly.

In his will my father left a small amount of money, enough for living and for college. He left something else too. The ring. The turquoise ring, which was as blue as his eyes and which he had worn all his adult life. It fit, exactly.

But nothing else did. Death: For a year I was thick, cumbersome, slow. I felt nothing. Not even the expectations about Mallory Beale, about how he might "affect me." Just before I started college I found that I could not afford the house at Glenn Springs. I had to sell it.

At school I discovered writing. I crammed two notebooks with stories. It worked for me, filling my loneliness and lending me purpose. But imprisoned in my thoughts, I grew shy and went out only once in a while. Eventually, I did meet a girl in a bar. She turned out to be a catalyst, propelling me into a novel which I had been planning for months.

She sat down in my dark corner. Two pale and silent faces in the dark. She was wearing a red tam and a yellow flour-sack dress. It was 1969. "Are you a writer?" I asked. "No, I'm a poet," she responded. She bought me a grenadine. I threw the stuff down over my Jack Daniels. Fortunately, she didn't ask me to dance. We never danced in the late sixties anyway, we *discussed.* She asked me to go home with her. She said she had a psychedelic pad. I asked her name. She replied that she was not into names. I said that I wasn't either, of course.

Her "pad" lay in the basement of an apartment house called Nada. The walls were painted bright pink and festooned with multicolored plastic fruits and posters and peace signs. Her furniture was a mattress on the floor. She led me there and pushed away *Soul on Ice,* two boxes of animal crackers and a gas mask. She asked if I was into oral sex. I said yes, thinking somehow that oral sex was French kissing by another name. When she went for my belt buckle, I sensed the distinction.

An hour later I lay beside her. I still wore my shorts. She

was beautifully nude. Her brown hair was waveless, deep, having a blond patina on the exterior layers. Around one thick ankle she wore a wooden peace symbol tied in leather. Each china-doll foot bore a tattoo: on the left, a rosebud on a green stem; on the right, a rose blossom. We had kissed and handled, but the liquor had worn off and I was terrified. I had never seen a girl with hairy legs. I sat up and said that I wasn't into sex. She said that she admired my position. We talked about the TET offensive and the poetry of Senator Eugene McCarthy, both national disasters. She asked me to go to Washington for a protest, but I said I had to finish a novel I was writing. We said good night and I did not see her again and I began the novel.

In my senior year I finished the book. Like me, the hero had brown hair and hazel eyes and a pretty good build. He was sensitive and bumbling and funny, just trying to grow up. I knew it was not an original story, but I liked it—and so did a New York agent, Lesly Combers. I had randomly selected his name from a handbook of New York agencies. I sent him *Tiger River* and a month later he mailed back a card that went something like this: Dear Cody Walker—like book, probably won't sell, will handle anyway. More later. L. Combers.

I was exultant. It was then that I began to think about Mallory Beale. He was the closest thing to a relative that I had. All through college I had spent weekends and holidays alone. During that time writing and class and solitary Swanson TV dinners had been enough, but now I felt the need for something more, for somebody who cared. Obviously, Mallory Beale had cared about my father. He had taken Joe Walker from the orphanage, sent him to school, etc. Maybe there was something special between them. Maybe that's why my father had said, "It could even change your life. Change it—completely." The line sounded wonderful and promising. But there was another possibility. Maybe my father's abrupt departure from the Beale world meant that something ghastly had happened. Something dark and horrible. I had to find out.

Living on the last of my sparse inheritance, I decided to find a way to approach Mallory Beale. I had to come to him well off. No one wants to see a stranger bleating hungrily at the door. I decided to write movie scripts. Dollars from these would propel me grandly toward the Beale family.

In six weeks I wrote five scripts. Absolute trash. Horrible stuff. Then an idea. The idea. While I was reading through a history book I ran across the story of Billy Browning. He and his missionary parents were sailing to their first station in the Pacific when a storm beached them onto an island called Lohai. The natives ate everyone but Billy. The fourteen-year-old boy was taken by the island king. Eventually he became the king's favorite, married his daughter and ultimately ruled Lohai. It could be filmed in Hawaii, set to Hawaiian music. I'd make a fortune.

Incredibly, the letter came just after I had finished my research.

At first I thought it was a bill or a bounced check. (I was now completely broke.) I opened the envelope and read.

> Dear Cody,
>
> I know we've never really been in touch, but I've often heard your name. As you may know, my father, Mallory, is not well. When he was more active Father devoted his summers to family friends and distant relatives. I guess all this will be up to me now. So—please come up on May 1st to see Black Island. Stay a month. It will be nice to finally meet you. Bring some boots.
>
> Peace,
> Chip Beale

At the bottom of the letter he left his address and phone number.

I called Chip, nervously thanked him, accepted the invitation and then told him about my movie script. He said that he had backed several films and was interested in my idea. He said perhaps we could work on the project together.

Dizzily, I packed my bags.

At twenty-two I was poor, an orphan and a virgin and felt as if my whole life waited somewhere in the North.

One week later, on May 1, 1973, I boarded Delta Flight 777. Two fingers into my first bourbon and looking down at the last green earth of the South, Chip Beale's words returned: Family friends and distant relatives. I sat back and wondered.

Who is Cody Walker? Who is he really?

2

Boston. Two o'clock in the afternoon.

The city curbs lay dirty in spring soot. The engines of yellow taxis shivered. Coal-dust buildings, ashy sills of lofts, broken lentils and black steeples and gargoyles and spent light finished a factory sky. Distantly, a fog swallowed the wharves. Brick upon brick businesses sat stacked to the river. Dry goods, hosieries, shipwrights. Sicman and Son Warehouses, Stregga and Sons Barge, Miglioresi's Shoes, Popincheck's Trucks and Watches. Curling from the river, the fog was devouring the city. Slowly streetlamps ignited while the first floors of department stores and groceries disappeared. Those few who walked pulled hats lower or closed collars or stepped into the rye darkness of bars. Monoxide flooded the alleys and climbed the grates. Horns muffled, smoke stacks clogged.

I opened my arms and laughed.

When I had arrived at the airport, I had called Chip Beale. He sounded friendly and cheerful. He told me to catch a cab and meet him in downtown Boston on the corner of Pilgrim and Done streets. I was waiting there now, my father's worn leather suitcase beside me, the one he'd taken to Yale, a present from Mallory Beale.

At seven-fifteen that evening I was still waiting. I had called Chip three times. No answer. I was beginning to feel abandoned, and then a mud-covered, dented and barely blue Ford station wagon chuffed into a no-parking zone.

The driver stepped out in patched galluses, work boots and a red stocking cap. He approached in a distant and cool arc, his face sunburned and misplaced in the steelish city, his eyes cool and reserved above a black beard. At last he smiled. "Cody, I had a meeting. Sorry. Did you nearly die of pollution?"

We shook hands, talked about the plane flight while Chip Beale found the trunk key.

For the first hour or so Chip was talkative. He asked about the movie script. I gave him the main plot line, then told him about my novel. He said that he was creative too. He said that since his father's illness he had been trying to redirect his family. It took a lot of creativity. He said he was also looking for God.

In the last three years he had studied with an Indian guru, a Shinto monk, a hand reader, a back reader, a Bangkok snake charmer and two Mississippi Holiness preachers, one of whom had reportedly raised the other from the dead.

I didn't say much after that. Neither did he. We traveled north until we reached the rim light of a town.

Cedar Point. I opened my window. The air felt sharp and cold. The fog here smelled of sand and minerals. In the darkness a church steeple tolled nine o'clock. The bell hammered the new world: Republicans, icy manners, eaters of bluefish, real Catholics and gin and birches. And now I saw the moon higher than the fog. Abolitionist moon, harsh and pocked, far different from the honey melon down home. No, this was not the same sweet body at all, but here sent light which was scrubbed, short, stiff and white as any Puritan's collar, unrelenting in brightness and mean size. Yankee moon, cold and small as the heart of Cotton Mather.

At the first gate of Black Island, Beale stopped the car and slipped a card into a metallic box. The wooden arm raised. We bumped down a broken paved road. Sand dunes and brown sea grass. We passed through two more gates. Across a bridge. The fog was thick, stubborn, as if pushing us back.

The house sat beside the sea. Oddly, the fog did not touch it. Two stories, gray shingles, blue shutters. Red geranium boxes along the sills. Stars above, sea below, porch lights burning.

Chip opened the back of the car, took my bag, walked me to the front steps. "You'll like this place. It's one of my favorite houses here." When he pulled off his red cap a cascade of red hair fell and flared upon his shoulder tops, the striking color irradiating his face and black beard, the bright hair smelling of herbs and soap.

"Aren't you staying?" I asked.

"I'm across the lake."

"I don't want to wake anyone."

"It's quite yours. The place."

"The whole house is mine?"

"There's food prepared. Some really fine salad. Will you be afraid by yourself?"

"No."

"Black Island has only good vibes."

"I'll be fine."

Beale's face turned pink in ocean air, blue circles below his eyes. His beard curled in the humidity. Buck teeth broke through the horseshoe mustache.

I wanted to ask him when we would start work on the script. What were the plans. Had he ever met my father. But I felt that now I should not ask these questions. I waved good night.

The dirty station wagon chugged into the woods. Car lights became a golden sphere in fog.

I listened. The sea fell carefully on the beach. A small wind rattled the woods. Crickets. The ringing of a distant buoy.

Inside, I turned on a lamp. The base was fired clay and indented by a vast handprint and date—Cumaquid 1931, M.B. A living room of old wicker furniture. White walls. One new grass rug sprawled before a black fireplace laid in seasoned oak for fire. At one end of the room a glass door etched in sea gulls led to a porch. Just beyond the fireplace, a dining area. Scratched oak table and chairs. The kitchen was warm and small. Drawers full of stainless steel and cheap utensils. Many wine openers. Cabinets stocked in Green Giant canned mushrooms, wild rice, pickled partridge eggs and Earl Grey tea. I opened the refrigerator. A 1971 bottle of Gatannara wine and red-breasted roast chicken. A covered salad: lettuce, avocados, mushrooms and almonds. I pulled off a chicken leg and went into the living room and saw it. A figure in the darkness.

Waiting on the back porch a few feet from the glass door, it was apparently a girl. She had not seen me yet and moved forward. Reaching out a finger, she touched the glass, then hung hands at narrow hips and cocked a leg. She stepped to the door and pressed her whole body against the glass. She was naked; brown muscles, dimples and striations. I saw her shudder, back away, then gently settle against the designed sea gulls, hands shading her eyes as she peered inside.

When I moved she saw me and darted away.

From the door I looked out toward the yard. The small, glassed porch held puddles of water and watery footprints lay on the steps and brick walkway. I waited. The sea seemed to be moving from side to side, as if shifting weight. As if watching. I pulled the porch door tight, locked it and ascended the front stairs. I chose one of three bedrooms. New towels were waiting on a pine washstand. The navy blue bedspread was turned down. Three windows framed the starry sea.

Beneath the starched sheets I lay somewhat stupidly. The day was a haze in my head. The image of the girl arose; her black eyes, soft lips and the trail of water which followed her. My heart slowed and the bedroom dimmed. The sea wind pummeled the house and I saw the girl slip into a thicket on lovely calves.

When I awoke I was still thinking about the beautiful girl. I wondered if she were a Beale.

I propped in bed and looked through the three windows. The early sun turned the sea pink and blue. Gauzy whitecaps broke the surface. I listened. Only the sound of soft waves and wind which rushed and pushed pops and creaks from the house. The air felt fresh and cold and healthy.

I grabbed my suitcase and opened the sliding door to a closet. I hung up two sport coats—a blue blazer and a checked green tweed. I didn't have any more formal clothes. My suitcase held jeans and knit shirts and underwear. I had brought my dress-up shoes: one pair of black wingtips.

Downstairs, I made instant coffee and went outside.

Brambles and wild rose bushes crowded the backyard. The rose bushes did not yet have opening buds, but the brambles glittered in new leaves and chlorophyll. Two maples at the yard edge stood bare and gray in the sun. A brown dirt path led through the brambles to wooden stairs and the beach below. From the beach a boulder rose to eye level. The boulder was pink and gray and cedar seedlings grew inside fissures but not on the top, which lay flat and red except for panes of sea water which reflected the sky. The horizon fell evenly on the sea, as if I faced a blue wall. I could not tell the difference between the blue of the sea and the blue of the horizon.

I had thought that the island was small, but standing on the beach I could see two miles of shoreline to the left and over three to the right. No houses, no boats, no sign that anyone else lived here. Chip did mention another house. Perhaps there were only two.

I walked into the front yard. Here stood green holly bushes and brown-rooted crepe myrtle. The gravel driveway connected to a narrow tar road which disappeared around a curve of white birches. Beside the tar road stood a rusted sign: Beale Street.

I returned to the house. On the glass back porch I sat in a ratty wicker chair and read old Sierra Club magazines for a couple of hours.

At one o'clock the house was beginning to feel bleak and so was I. Where was Chip?

In the kitchen I wolfed down two pickled partridge eggs, a mouthful of "crunchy style" Peter Pan and stared at two cans of green turtle soup. Ah, these people knew how to eat. Absolutely bored, I began rustling through the other kitchen cabinets. I found a typed list of names attached to an inside door: Abercrumbie, Allan . . . Ledge, Lowell . . . Simpson, Tufts. . . . There were thirty-six names and each had a phone number. Did all of these people live here? If so, where?

I gave up and went into the backyard and sat in a weathered oak chair. The sun was warm and the wind was still. I dropped off to sleep.

"Hey!"

I jumped.

In yellow waist-waders and a ragged plaid shirt, hair black and wild, the kid sloshed closer.

"Jeez, I know I smell like crap. Been fishing for stripers. Fell in. Got water in my boots. Chip said to come get you. We got to make Uncle Mallory's cove. Right away. Name's Doug Summers." He held out his hand, red knuckles below a large forearm vein, acetylene blue eyes, a half-smile, skin windburned and powdery in salt. When I took his hand he hauled me from the chair.

"Come on, buddy. We're late."

In the front yard Doug hopped on the fender of a blue 1949 Ford pickup equipped with a snow plow, huge yellow fog lights, two six-foot radio antennas and a flatbed of tools, rusted fish scales and a large and dangerous-looking winch and hook.

Doug threw open his arms. "Hey, class, huh? You know what I paid? Six hundred American dollars. Good deal, huh? Hop in. I brought some coffee."

In the cab were tackle boxes, fishing gear; along the visor, colored pictures of baseball players; on the floor a red hockey mask and rusty skates.

The engine chewed and pinged forward. From a red thermos Doug poured a cup of hot coffee and stuck it into my hands. Stripping gears, coughing smoke, we rode off into the island.

The bad suspension and acid coffee woke me. "Have you ever seen a naked girl running around here?" I asked.

Doug blew his coffee and watched the road.

"I just saw this gal last night on the back porch. She was buck naked."

Doug observed me in a refined way, then slapped my shoulder, spilled coffee. "Wow, Southerners!" He gunned the engine. "You know, I've never known a real Southerner before." He gargled a mouth of coffee, dashed hair from his eyes.

"My father—"

"Hold it! Sorry! Hold it." Doug attacked his shirt pocket, flipped out a battery-powered radio, yanked the aerial with his teeth. Crackles and static and the last lines of a song. "Christmas! Missed it. I called in a request. Dynamite song. Ever hear it? 'Time Loves a Hero.' It's my song this summer."

"My father went back to South Carolina twenty-five years ago," I said.

"Jeez, I've never been there. Florida. Now I snorkel a lot in Florida but negative on South Carolina. What's it like?"

"Some warmer than here. We—"

"Still got moonshine down there?"

"In the hills there—"

"Hey, you still have lynchings I bet, huh? How's that coffee?"

Doug swerved off the road and blasted down a dirt lane. The truck roared across a bridge and slid to a stop before an immense house of white boards and climbing roses.

The house was three stories and the red and white roses climbed the side to the third set of windows. Below, two people stood in a semicircle of boxwoods before a table holding a Playmate cooler and two bottles of wine. The red and white roses turned the air a dappled pink. Doug raced from the truck, hurriedly introduced Marlow Smith and Harding Wicks. "Now let's get moving. They'll be gone." Doug grabbed the cooler and bolted, Marlow behind him.

When Harding Wicks smiled, so did my heart. She was beautiful. She wore a collarless, white cotton dress which opened below her neck to expose brown collarbones and below them high breasts. When she turned for the wine her auburn hair flew about her shoulders. It was feathered, parted in the middle, and framed a classical face: violet eyes, high cheekbones, patrician nose. She approached me quickly in white canvas deck shoes and handed over two bottles of claret.

I just stared at her without breathing.

"Um, you need to run these down the hill," she said.

I took the bottles and ran, looking over my shoulder at her, bottles tucked into my belly.

A sudden collision. Hard fall. Dull burst of a claret bottle, quick pulse of aromatic wine. Harding laughed and sprinted by.

The lanky Marlow Smith lay sprawled in gray blazer and plaid gabardine trousers. He was older, around thirty. From freckles and white pallor, his brown seal eyes blinked. "Isn't this simply grueling?"

"I'm sorry. I—"

"Oh, it's Doug. Doug must rush everywhere. Dashing about is the perennial plight of his family."

"Run!" Doug yelled.

With one surviving bottle, Marlow and I raced down a dirt trail beneath cedars and then across a plateau of spring grass which rose above a blue harbor and docks and brown beach.

3

We crashed through scrub oak and sprang to the weathered boards of the dock. Two motorboats bobbed in the tide.

"Can you drive a launch?" Doug shouted at me.

"I used to sail."

"Can you or not?"

"Sure, I guess."

"Here, you take the Mercedes. I'll handle the Chrysler." Doug grabbed my arm, towing me to the wooden launch, badly painted blue and white. He jumped into the boat.

"Here's your starter. Your throttle. Let me check gas."

The launch was fifteen feet long. Yellow water flooded the deck boards, which were dented, bashed, broken and seemed totally unseaworthy. "Why is this called a Mercedes?"

"Have a look," Doug said. He lifted the top of a wooden well in the stern.

The engine looked as rusted and miserable as the rest of the boat. "Can I pass on this?"

Doug caught me by the shoulder, put his head close to my face and said in solemn tones, "Do you know what this is, buddy?"

"A leaky engine," I said.

"A 230 SL Mercedes. Runs like a thoroughbred."

"Yeah, but will it start?"

When Doug turned the switch the boat shuddered and died.

"Think I'll take the Chrysler," I said.

Again the starter whined and this time the Mercedes kicked, then purred as if newly delivered from a shop.

I felt disappointed when Doug went to Harding and Marlow jumped aboard my boat. Harding did not even look at me.

"Where on earth are we going?" Marlow yelled.

Doug pointed to a large rock at the mouth of the channel. "Seals! The last ones of winter."

Three or four animals slipped out of the water. On the rock they shook black fur, sparkling whiskers.

"The engines will scare them off," Marlow said.

"No way. Seals love boats. They think boats are—porpoises! Yeah, the seals think we're just big porpoises."

Marlow shut his eyes.

I threw the lines from the Mercedes. Across the dock Doug's Chrysler cranked instantly.

Throwing a white rooster tail twenty feet into the air, Doug roared into the harbor. I edged out more slowly. Marlow sat in the stern elegantly smoking a cigarette.

Behind sat large white houses along the central and higher parts of the island, leafless ash trees and green cedars, new grass, short bramble cliffs and scrub oak, the beach, the harbor. Doug was ripping across the water. I noticed the seals had left the brown rock. Doug drove around us twice in narrowing circles. I found some courage, hit my throttle and felt the wind come harder.

"Give it to him, Cody," Marlow said. "Let's show Doug our mettle." He tore a crisp handkerchief from his coat pocket and tied it about his head and gave a nasal squeal.

"What was that?" I asked.

"One of your rebel yells, isn't it?" Marlow said with something like a British accent.

"Hell no," I said. "Goes like this." I screeched out a holler that probably had not been heard in my family since Chickamauga.

The Mercedes roared after Doug and we were screaming and hooting in the charge. We zigged broadside, hit Doug and Harding with a two-foot cold wash. At once Doug pulled beside us and yelled, "Throw her into neutral!"

His Chrysler paralleled my Mercedes. Doug looked severe, quiet.

"Chinese fire drill!" he yelled, salt drying on his face, wind lines cutting beneath his eyes, teeth white and beautiful.

Harding and he stormed our boat. I ducked the bounding Doug. Marlow groaned and lumbered aboard the Chrysler.

We dodged and chased awhile. I found myself glancing at Harding, who laughed and tugged at Doug. The cold wind of the sea had made her even more lovely. Disheveled, her auburn hair shimmered sunlight. She had slipped into a yellow canvas slicker, rolled the white dress's blue-flowered hem above her knees. She sat in the pilot's chair and gripped the wheel by pink toes, dress stuffed between long legs. She sat close to Doug. I wondered if they were close in other ways.

There was another fire drill and we all ended up in the Mercedes, rolling across the shallow water that formed the channel, bouncing in cold spray toward the Cedar Point beach.

Harding stood above the launch's windshield and pointed to a sailboat about half a mile away. "Isn't that Teddy?"

Doug came up into the wind. "You bet."

"He's a terrific guy," Doug said to me. "My dad and he were at St. Charles together."

"Who's Teddy?" I asked.

"Kennedy, Kennedy."

"Senator Kennedy?"

"Hey, you want to say hello?"

I couldn't even answer.

As we splashed closer I felt obligation arise. The feeling that somehow I, and perhaps every American, owed at least respect and probably silence to a Kennedy.

"Doug, maybe we should just leave the man to his sail," I said.

"Don't be so pontifical, Cody," Harding said.

I winced and shut my mouth.

When we pulled alongside, Edward Kennedy stood, leaned forward to tie the two boats together. There was no hesitation, no surprise. (Did Doug know him that well?) He was a tree. Bigger than I remembered from television. A muscle-crammed jaw, stew-bone chin, a face hard and sunburned, a rugged, big-boned face, though the eyes had humor and green fire and dare.

"How's your father?" he asked Doug, his eyes quickly sweeping all of us. I shivered hearing that voice which was so vital, the vowels broad and held long and the ending syllables drawn through the nose, but mostly a ball of consonants at the roof of his mouth. A muscular smile. A rough hand swept through the curling, mythic, stellar hair and tendril wrinkles bloomed about his eyes; wearing a red Southey windbreaker, blue jeans, soiled blue tennis shoes, a red- and green-striped shirt whose white collar framed his redwood throat.

Harding darted over to him and hugged. They broke apart and Doug introduced us as Harding posed against his shoulder. I wanted to shake his hand, but did not have the courage.

"Say, Eunice may come over to fish a couple crabs. That okay?" Kennedy asked, a hand patting Harding on the stomach while a leg planted on the Mercedes helped to hold the boat steady.

"I think there're some in Reedy Creek," Doug said.

"Blues?"

"Yeah, big blues."

"You don't think Mallory will chase her off?"

"Tell him I gave you permission," Doug laughed.

"That I will," Kennedy said. He gave Harding another pat. She stepped back aboard. The Mercedes cranked.

I wanted to communicate. I wanted him to know how his family had inspired me as a boy. I wanted to say that I was in the fourth grade, Senator, when your brother came into office and John Kennedy was my hero and I'll never forget him. But I kept silent. We were preparing to leave. I had to do something.

As the Mercedes shuddered, as Doug said last good-byes, suddenly I threw myself toward Kennedy feeling the gray sea spread, distance shorten. Kennedy's face broke from care to joy as his hands caught, steadied me, now on his deck. Face to face, I could only manage, "Sir, my second cousin's a Catholic."

Kennedy clipped my chin. "South Carolina," he said.

"That's right," I yelled.

Doug was alongside again. He pulled me back to the Mercedes.

"Good luck to you," said Kennedy.

"Incredible!" I yelled at Doug and the others. "Absolutely incredible! He knows I'm from South Carolina!"

Doug blasted the engines. We were away.

I turned to look at Kennedy: the chiseled jaw and blarney smile and shrapnel hair bleached by American light. He waved and turned toward the south and sand dunes and the beaches of home.

The sun was a great red cell descending in the dark sky. Exactly over the island, the sphere dissolved the upper branches of cedars and reddened the high roofs of the highest house: Mallory Beale's.

Doug had pointed out "his uncle's" place. As we drove toward the docks my eyes riveted one lighted window. Was this the old man's room? Was he there now? I heard my father's voice: "It could even change your life. Change it—completely."

We docked the boats, tied them down. Harding led the way to her summer place—Stone House. Inside, Doug built a fire and Marlow made Bombay gin fizzes and I just sat before the fire, cold hands and drying salt, thinking of Beale and Kennedy. Toying with my father's turquoise ring. Thinking.

The Bombay gin took me by stealth. The vertebrae of my spine, the bones of my feet disjointed and warmed. There was some talk about Chip and his plan for taking over the family business, but I was dumb in liquor and fire. I felt as if I had found my place to begin, as if I were at the base of an escarpment, ready for a beautiful climb into the starry night.

With our drinks we huddled around the fire and everyone asked me about the South: what was barbecue, did I know George Wallace, didn't most southern cities have electricity now and when would Southerners finally forget about the Civil War?

"As soon as Yankees stop reminding us," I said.

We laughed, finished our drinks. Doug and Harding went to fix more.

I turned to Marlow. "I noticed your accent. You must be English."

"God, no. Welsh."

"Sorry."

He leaned toward me. "Have you ever seen such bombastic wealth? This family is positively stupefying."

I felt almost at ease. "You're probably used to it."

"Alas, not. I'm just Doug's poor cousin."

Seriousness suddenly took Marlow's face. He motioned me closer. "May I ask you a personal question?"

"Sure." My father came to mind.

"Which do you prefer, Wendy's or McDonald's?"

"You're talking about hamburgers?"

"But they are much more than hamburgers. They are the stuff of which the States are made."

"Yeah, well—Wendy's, I guess."

"Do you think we could sneak away to have one?"

Was he kidding?

"I've been in this country for two weeks and I've been working very hard on becoming an American. I want to drink A&W root beer on a Saturday night, wearing thongs and Wrangler jeans and an 'I Love N.Y.' T-shirt with a big red heart. I want to grow my own bean sprouts for salad and smoke dope before I get out of bed in the morning and buy condoms in Exxon stations. I must do these things! I will be an American! I'm switching my citizenship and everything. Do you know I'm planning a tour? From Cedar Point to Atlanta, Houston to L.A., Chicago to New York."

I studied the fire, changed the subject. "When Chip invited me up he said his father wasn't well."

"Not at all, I'm afraid."

"My dad called Mallory Beale the greatest American tycoon that ever lived."

"In spades. He advised seven of your Presidents. He knew scores of world leaders—Stalin, Tito, Perón. Business deals everywhere. He had a fight with Joe Kennedy over this very island. Seems that in the late twenties Beale and Kennedy were friends. Worked in movies together, Venezuelan oil. Their families spent one Fourth of July on Black Island. The stars changed then. Bad blood. A Beale cousin was found in a Kennedy bedroom. He died shortly afterward. A suspicious car crash, some say. Beale and Kennedy came to hate one another. They fought to buy the island. Beale put up more money. The day after his purchase, as Mallory drove into seeing distance of the island, a private security guard stopped him. 'Private property,' said the guard. 'That's my island over there,' Mallory explained. 'You'll have to find another way of getting there,' the guard said, smiling. 'Mr. Joseph P. Kennedy has bought all access roads for fifty miles around.' For the first five years the only way Uncle Mallory could get to his home was by boat from Providence."

"I'd like to meet him," I said.

"Rather difficult," Marlow said. "They say Uncle Mallory's dying."

Ten o'clock. Everyone was tired. When Marlow offered me a ride home, I accepted. Black-haired and red-cheeked, Doug was hunched asleep in a patchwork quilt. Harding waited at the door. She had pinned back her hair. Her arched neck rose above those long collarbones and in the firelight her violet eyes looked round and soft and the lashes seemed silk. Wearing no makeup, she was glorious.

She hugged Marlow good night. To me she extended a hand. Her grip was warm but quick. Disheartened, I turned to go. She stopped me. There was a soft curiosity to her face.

"Would you like a present?"

I was feeling hurt and had too much booze in me. "Goodnight kiss?" I asked, trying to sound funny.

Harding smiled and climbed a set of stairs. She returned carrying a book.

"Uncle Mallory's notebook. He gave it to me to read. It's a borrowing present, Cody. Chip said you're a writer. I think you'll appreciate it."

Quickly she brushed a cheek against mine.

In Marlow's car, riding to my temporary home, I felt as if I never touched the seat.

In the white and blue room I set the book on my bed. Quickly, I showered. I turned the water hot. The sea steamed off me. I dried, then damply plunged into bed. The wind whistled through the window screens. From my pillow I could see the ocean, black sea to moonlight horizon. Stars pulsed quick light. I set the book between my legs. The notebook was black cloth and a foot square. Tattered red piping decorated the outer rim. Its center was embossed with an engraving: a kingfisher. At first I did not want to open the book. I had no right. I should meet Mallory Beale before I peered into his private thoughts. I set the notebook on the bedside table, snapped off the lamp.

For an hour or so I turned and wallowed, arranged and spread the sheet wrinkles with my toes. Recollecting, I saw Kennedy and Harding and Beale's lighted window. Finally, I cut the lamp back on.

The first three hundred pages were mainly a tattered collection of handwritten notes which had been pasted onto the pages of the journal. The notes were written on napkins, brittle stationery, torn envelopes, even a yellow scrap of handkerchief. These initial entries were dialogues or brief character descriptions. On one dialogue that began with "J. P. Morgan was in a lousy humor" I saw a note scribbled in red ink by another hand:

> Mallory I was not in a lousy humor. She was in a lousy humor because of what you asked me to ask her. Now get this: He bit her. He actually bit her—Jack

> Gilbert. On top of that, her hand got infected. Can you believe it? Movie stars!
>
> J.P.M.

Toward the end of the notes the handwriting became large and strong. I read a few paragraphs about a bank merger, an expedition down the Amazon and some lines about the tattoo of a red and blue angel with golden horns which lay on the inside of Eva Perón's thigh.

On the final pages a style emerged and the beginning of a story—a story in which I saw the first glimmer of Joe Walker's startling destiny.

4

I was not born broke. I wish I could say I was, but I wasn't. My old man held a professorship at Cornell. He was a brainy guy. My mom came from Quakers. Her heart was a bucket of ice and maybe that helped me more than brains. Until I was thirteen I went to Thompson Public High School outside Ithaca. The kids at Thompson were tough and I liked them. They liked to fight and so did I and we had a hell of a time. Then my father got a raise and sent me to Choate. The guys there had these faces. A blue little aura. It said rich. They looked rich, acted rich and when you punched one, they cried rich. I really hated those guys. I always felt like an outsider. When I went home with them to their Long Island beach palaces, I always got kind of low. Servants and wine at lunch. I thought it was stupid to let a fifteen-year-old kid get plastered at noon. I ran away from Choate twice. My old man refused to take me back when I came home, so I said okay. I decided I'd be richer than any of those jerks. I decided that in twenty years I would buy and sell that rich-boy crowd. Yea, I had my father's Cornell brains and my mother's deep-freeze, Quaker heart and when I looked at Joe Stalin forty years later—I knew I could play any hand that he could deal.

People have asked me how I started out. I never thought about it much, but when I did I went straight back to the first deal I ever saw put together. It was a peach—President Grover Cleveland and J. P. Morgan and my old man. In 1893 my father (Mathew Beale) was chosen as Cleveland's top economic advisor. It was a bad year that got worse. By the winter of 1894 the country was in a depression. There was talk about the government actually going broke. Defaulting loans and stuff like that. My old man had an idea. He went to see "Birdy"

Morgan. He had met him five years earlier when the old man gave a commencement speech at Cornell. They became friends and collaborated on several investments, out of which my father ended up with a small bank.

After he talked to Morgan my father paid a visit to President Cleveland and said that he had a plan to avoid an economic catastrophe. Cleveland said he wanted to talk, but not at the White House. The President wanted the meeting held on an island where he spent his summers—a place called Black Island. Cleveland said it could be both business and pleasure and told my father to bring his family—that's how I got to see the greatest deal since the Louisiana Purchase.

I was ten years old when I first saw Black Island. It was winter and the woods were as bare and white as a birch. I remember my family were the first ones there. I spent the whole day chasing black seals, discovering coves of blue ice, racing through acres of frozen brown reeds and pure stands of white birch. When I got back to our house my father grabbed me by the neck and told me to come with him to the meeting.

When we got to Stone House a butler directed us upstairs. The President was taking a bath.

We went up and passed a telegraph operator who sat by his key in the hall. Just outside the bath door, my father stopped and handed me his briefcase.

"Now, son, I want you to listen. I want you to make notes in your mind, and I want you to remember. Always remember. This meeting, this moment, is what life is all about."

When my father opened the door the steam poured out, a huge rolling steam, like a bright fog, and in the midst sat an enormous man in an enormous tub.

The two men greeted one another, shook hands and more than anything else I remember the sight of all that presidential flesh—it was bologna—pink and hairless and thick. When my father introduced me Cleveland snorted cigar smoke.

J. P. Morgan arrived and my father took him into a parlor beside the bathroom.

"Mathew, are you sure the President will back you?" Morgan asked. His face was as gray as his wool suit, his wool scarf.

"Birdy, I worked it out. First we buy up these folding banks. I

propose we split them. Half to be purchased by your bank, the other half by mine. If we hold the banks we can stabilize the market."

"If the market goes to silver the dollar will drop sixty cents."

"I'll nail Cleveland to gold."

"I don't like this."

"Yesterday I nudged the Secretary of the Treasury into buying some wood for our new Navy."

"How did you manage that?"

"Letters. I've got some letters which talk about the Secretary playing roll the bat with a little boy."

"So what?"

"The little boy wasn't wearing any clothes."

"My God, Mathew."

"Yesterday the United States Treasury wrote my bank a check for twelve million dollars. Ought to come through this afternoon."

"You'll bust the country."

"Will you back me? Will you get the Rothschilds?"

"I don't know. I doubt it. What can we possibly offer to keep the country from going bankrupt?"

"A raffle."

"What?"

"Birdy, I plan to raffle off—the United States of America."

In the bright bathroom the President was spouting water.

Exchanged pleasantries.

The telegraph operator was waiting by his key in the hall.

"Mr. President, Birdy and I have a plan," my father said. "The government will sell bonds."

"To whom?"

"Our banks. Mine and Birdy's."

"Oh, Mathew, how much could you raise?"

"Three million, five hundred thousand ounces of gold."

Morgan coughed.

Cleveland lumbered in the water. "How many dollars?"

The telegraph began to click.

"Seventy million," Morgan said.

"Mathew, there's not that much gold in the world."

"Yes, sir. There is."

"Where?"

"Birdy and I have driven a bargain with the Rothschilds and Steins in Europe. They'll sell us gold."

Morgan's face whitened.

"For what?" Cleveland asked.

"A percentage of U.S. bonds."

The telegraph began to beat faster.

"I don't like it," the President said.

"Why?"

"It's rather like we're selling the nation."

"We're retrieving the Republic through a European loan."

"It's sticky to me, frankly."

"The Treasury's going down the drain."

"I still have nine million in reserve. I stopped payment on all national debts."

The telegraph clacked. Cleveland looked into the hall light.

"My proposal is that you sell our banks sixty-five million dollars in four percent bonds to be valued at 104½ points per share market price."

"I thought you said you would put seventy million into the treasury."

"I will, sir."

"But the bonds will be worth only sixty-five million."

"Initially."

"How much profit will you make when you resell the bonds, Mathew?"

"A good one."

Cleveland thought about it. He went down and bubbled in the tub. Rose. "I'll wait. The government will pick back up. I know it."

The telegraph operator came into the room. "Mr. President, the Secretary of the Treasury has telegraphed to say that the country is, ah, well—overdrawn."

"Impossible! No further exchange was to go on."

"A check was paid at two o'clock today for twelve million dollars. The U.S. Government is now three million dollars in the red."

"Who authorized that payment!" Cleveland yelled.

Morgan looked radiant. Banker's smile.

Cleveland buffed in his tub. He pointed at a humidor, called for a cigar.

My father nudged me. I went over and opened the humidor, which looked like a round, leather hatbox. The aroma was warm and sweet as a fresh loaf of bread. I picked out a soft, black cigar and handed it to the President.

"When can you have this—transaction—arranged, Mathew?"

"One week, Mr. President."

Cleveland looked at his cigar and he looked at me and then pulled his huge pink body from the water and stood in the tub.

"Young man," he said. "If you could have anything in the world, anything at all—what would it be?"

I felt all of their eyes then. My father's and Birdy Morgan's and the President's.

I went to the window beside the tub. I rubbed away a circle of frost and looked out.

"I'd like to have this," I said.

"You'd like to have what?" asked the President.

"This. The island. I'd like to have Black Island."

They laughed. All three of them. They all laughed and lit cigars and then handed one to me.

I still have it.

One month later my father and Birdy Morgan sold the bonds at 115 points for a profit of seven million dollars.

What a marvelous deal. It's the sort of deal J.W. constructed fifty years later. It was the kind of deal he loved—complex. I was never complex, but J.W. always was. It's what brought him right to the edge. To the edge of everything.

I set the book down and moved to the windows and looked at the black sea. Was J.W. Joe Walker? All my life my father had talked about Mallory Beale, but now for the first time Beale had mentioned him, or at least J.W. And if—if J.W. was Joe Walker, then my father's stories were validated. It made his past real.

For the next few days I tried to work on the script, but couldn't. I kept thinking about J.W. coming to the edge of everything. What had Beale meant? And when J.W. stood on the edge, did he fall or did he climb even higher? I had to be careful, very careful, but soon I had to talk to someone.

In the evenings Doug and Marlow came over. We drank beer, took a few hits off Doug's bamboo bong and ate supper. Once we all went to a place on the island called Straw Hill. Doug lived there in a squalid cabin, without electricity or water. He said he was roughing it and that he was tired of living in his family's thirty-room summer house. I could only smile.

One evening when I asked Doug about Chip's whereabouts, he laughed. "He should be in Boston working out the details for taking over the business, but he's probably hiding on the island somewhere. Eating bean sprouts and smoking dope. He hasn't got the guts to run this family."

I wondered if he had the guts to produce a movie.

On Sunday morning I rose early, looked at the script and decided not to attempt work until I heard from Chip. Generally anxious, I called Lesly Combers in New York, asked if he had sent my book to any publishers. He said that he had not, but would soon. I gave him my new phone number and address.

I returned to the glass porch and sat at the picnic table. I had made the porch my writing room. I looked at the white-capped blue sea and listened to the wind. I felt lonesome.

Then I saw something in the distance. Something gray and long near the horizon. It came closer, then veered toward the west end of the island. A ship. Painted gray and white, it looked like a destroyer: menacing and angular and deadly.

Just as it disappeared, Doug walked into the backyard.

"What was that?" I asked.

"Uncle Mallory built her in 1941. He'd made some big bucks. I think he sold Cuba or something. Say, do you know the story behind her?"

"No."

He winked a blue eye, set a finger on his big chin. "Uncle Mallory had a huge fight with Aunt Townsend—his wife. She didn't speak to him for a week. Finally he said he was sorry and that he had bought her a special present. A new dog. A real pedigree. He took her out to the harbor, pointed to the channel and she steamed in—*Ole Blue.* Aunt Towny was furious."

I tried not to look dumbfounded.

"Hey, you going to choir? Doug asked.

"Choir?"

"We do it every Sunday at the chapel. Jeez, it's a pain, but they expect me there. Besides, it's a good place for you to meet people."

The chapel sat deep in the birch woods. Ten or twelve cars lined the rugged tar road before it. The cars were not Jaguars or Rolls or even Cadillacs. They were old, faded Buicks and Dodges and Fords. The chapel itself was covered in green ivy. It had a slate roof. A triangle of daffodils gleamed by the battered front door. The interior looked barren. The oak-paneled walls were washed out, dusty, split. The black tiled floor had several squares missing. In the rough-hewn pews the twenty or so family members sat in clothes which looked as frayed and worn as the surroundings. Each of the eight clear-paned windows had a small American flag posted over the frame.

No one noticed Doug and me. Just as we sat down a woman in the pew before us stood. She wore a blue skirt and white oxford shirt. The sun had hammered her face to something like burlap.

"Now, everyone. Everyone? You are all invited to our place after Choir for Bloody Marys. That's all we have today. No scotch. No wine. We need to talk about the summer parties and of course we can only do that just a little tipsy. So—afterward. Also we're selling rides on our new Hinckly this afternoon. A dollar a person. All proceeds go to, go to—well, some relief fund. I think it's Biafra."

"Five dollars," a man shouted.

There was a big laugh.

"Oh yes, dear, five dollars a ride and supply your own sun screen."

Another laugh.

"All right, all right. Now I thought we'd start with—'A Mighty Fortress Is Our God.' "

The woman led off as the family came to their feet and followed. I was amazed. They sang four verses by heart. Next: "Out of the Ivory Palaces," "Crown Him with Many Crowns" and "America the Beautiful."

Afterward the same woman began speaking again. Doug whispered that her name was Aunt Bosey and that she was Mallory Beale's only sister. The instinct was quick: Should I ask her about my father?

"Right now, I would like to welcome the only Southerner on the island. Recently arrived. He's been down in Dixie planting cotton and grits or whatever . . ."

Doug poked me. I felt blood sting my face.

". . . so I want a polite, churchy welcome for—Bob Sims."

A short, portly man stood up. I felt relieved.

Outside, I shook several hands. The people seemed distant. I looked for Bosey Beale, but she was gone. Then I saw him. An old gentleman standing alone by the wedge of daffodils. White hair and purple jowls. Wearing a pinstripe suit, blue tie and a crisp crown of handkerchief, he was the best-dressed man here, and he was the one I decided to ask.

I introduced myself, spoke about the weather, about the beauty of the island, then carefully approached the point.

"You know, I think my father used to come here, oh, twenty-five years ago."

"Your father?"

"He worked with Mallory Beale—Joe Walker?"

"Hmm." A pause. The meat of his red cheeks hollowed. "I think not, really."

"Sir?"

"I knew everyone who came here regularly in the forties. There wasn't a Joe Walker."

The old man shifted his gaze to someone else.

I excused myself and stepped back toward the chapel. My stomach churned. He was too cool, too aloof. I looked at the turquoise ring on my finger. Something had happened here, I could feel it. I decided that I would have to be less obvious in my search. I would wait. Wait and listen.

I was feeling low and told Doug that I needed to get back and write. We left the gathering and Doug said that Harding had put together a badminton game and didn't I want to come along? I said no and he left me with a cheery slap on the back.

For the rest of the afternoon and into the evening, I read and walked on the beach, walked on the beach and read. I had three drinks, showered and went to bed supperless at ten. A land breeze was blowing from the other side of the house and I could hear the leafless spring woods creaking and blown leaves clipping the roof and the house popping and settling in the wind. Soft stars. Moon on sea. Sleep.

Sometime later, I started. I looked at the bedside clock—12:20. Something bumped downstairs. I listened, almost went back to sleep. Another dull knock. I slid into my jeans, eased down the stairs.

I could feel something moving in the house.

5

The moon was flooding silver into the living room. There must have been a storm somewhere over the sea because I could see sheet lightning and hear rough waves strike the beach. There was another sound too. It came from the kitchen. A rattle, a tapping.

Barefoot, I crept toward the kitchen. No lights except the moon. I held my breath. Someone was sorting through a cabinet. The figure edged into moonlight—the naked girl. The moonlight silhouetted her like a black and faceted piece of glass. Broad shoulders and a lithe neck and bushy, short hair and hips small as a young boy's.

Breath suddenly gone, I gasped.

The girl slammed the cabinet and raced down the kitchen hall.

I ran after her. "Hey! Wait. Wait!"

Like a brown shadow, she dissolved into the black woods.

I waited, watched. Nothing.

In the kitchen I turned on the overhead light. The floor held several pools of water. The cabinet was wet and so was the counter. I felt myself shudder. Maybe this wasn't a human being at all. Maybe this was something else. I recalled a story I had read as a boy, a story about an apparition that possessed a house. Each time the ghost was seen it would dissolve into air, leaving behind nothing but vapors or unnaturally cold puddles of water.

Absurd, I said to myself. I went back upstairs. It was just some kid having fun. Nothing more. Just some island kid.

Just before dawn I heard something else. A shudder and thump. I did not go downstairs.

At 6:15 A.M. the phone rang. Chip said to meet him immediately. He said we had to reach an agreement on the script. He said lawyers had to be consulted. He gave directions to his house. I was ecstatic.

Chip's place sat on a road called Bloop Street. The bungalow balanced on a hill above a choked and strangled lily pond. The house's front windows faced bleak cedar trees, a knobby knoll and below the knoll a dun marsh. The house was squat. It peeled in a peculiar polka-dot pattern: white spots on a blue background. In the yard lay a disheveled wood stack, a bent two-handed saw, a yale ax hopelessly stuck in an oaken log, a battered Moped. Rotting plywood stairs led to the front door. Beside the door hung pea-green waist-waders whose purple suspenders had yellow flower blossoms and a patched denim jacket on which was painted "Stop Bombing the Dikes." Just to the side of these clothes glittered what seemed to be a lighted joss stick. I came closer. A sweet smell became more pungent. It was indeed a fiery and smoking joss stick. Above, something squeaked. I stepped to the house's corner.

A small windmill. The blades seemed to be feathers and wood. The outer blade edges were painted red, the blade shafts alternating black and white. Half the tower was wooden, green lattice, but midway down, the lattice became rusted iron. The windmill worked fitfully.

I tapped on the door and did not use a large brass knocker which was cast in the form of a laughing Buddha. The god's skirt was carved in half moons and stars and lotus leaves. The brass had tarnished to dark green. Above the skirt protruded a huge, round belly of a lesser green into whose black navel fit the tongue of the knocker and over the belly grinned the bald head, apparently newly polished for the brass here was sparkling and golden.

I knocked on the door a bit louder. "Chip?"

When there was no answer I pushed the half-opened door.

Inside, a large picture window overlooked the blackened lily pond. Beyond the pond stood a grassy hill where two donkeys romped. The room was crammed and cluttered—snowshoes and skis, two or three crates whose ripe oranges sweetened the air, a Magnavox turntable and two clumsy homemade speakers, a mattress on cement blocks spread in a tie-dyed sheet, American Indian tapestries on the right fir-wood wall, dry geraniums and African violets and philodendron before the window. Upon the floor scores of internationally postmarked letters marked "Urgent," empty vitamin bottles and a yodul stove on a brick foundation in one corner, and beside this a large collection of fishing poles, baseball bats, slickers and boots, Frisbees, umbrellas, guitars, and scattered beneath the boots five or six books by Ram Dass and Paramahansa Yogananda. On the left wall hung a ten-foot Japanese woodblock print which portrayed a young prince receiving irises from several young courtesans.

From an open doorway I heard a mechanical click and then the sound of a flute. The flute was low and gentle, vaguely seductive. I listened awhile, then went to the doorway and looked into the small room.

A large video screen covered one wall. Below it sat a machine flashing red and yellow lights. On the screen the black film slowly lightened and I recognized the room behind me—the large glass window and small couch.

I felt as if the film was none of my business and was about to leave when someone very tall stepped into the scene. He was six three and wore red wooden shoes, a kimono and a yellow velvet skullcap. A high black collar sported scarlet butterflies. The kimono had vertical golden dragons which belched blue flames. In voluminous purple sleeves, the man sat down on the couch. Hair bobbed, only his nose seemed American, owlish and red and peeling. It was Chip Beale.

A moment later a young girl entered. She was a buttermilk blonde and wore what looked like a maid's uniform. She approached Chip and slowly began to unbutton her blouse. The flute music became more sensual. The girl pulled her blouse off and dropped it. Her flesh was white as a dove's, her young breasts high and the nipples were pink and puckered like the tip of a rosebud.

Chip Beale sat cross-legged on the couch and did not move. Another girl appeared. She was a brunette and also wore a maid's uniform. Carefully she went through the same ritual until she stood bare-chested. Her skin was dark and her breasts large. Neither of the girls moved until Chip nodded, then they faced one another and began unfastening the white, pleated skirts.

Entirely naked, they turned to Chip, who again nodded, and they sat down beside him. The blonde opened his kimono while the brunette gently took down his hair. His chest was brown and muscular and the brunette began massaging his muscles while the blonde worked at the purple pants. With the brunette at his chest and the blonde at his feet, Chip extended himself on the couch and the film faded to black, leaving only the seductive flute, until that, too, was extinguished.

"Well, how was it?"

I spun around.

Red hair on his shoulders, Chip Beale wore faded jeans and no shirt. He held an Arm & Hammer soda box.

"Sexy stuff, huh?"

"Yeah, uh . . . it, it . . . was."

"I must have left the timer on. Hey, are you blushing?"

I felt my face scald.

"That's wonderful, man. Good for you. I haven't seen anyone blush in years. It's a sign of purity, you know, and purity is one of the great virtues of the Japanese warrior. You see, Cody, I'm following the way of the warrior—Bushi Do."

"Who's Bushi Do?"

"Not who, what. A way to live. A way to be strong and disciplined. In order to take over my family, I must be a warrior."

"It sounds like a good . . . a good regimen." I was still so embarrassed that I couldn't look him in the face. He rubbed the soda into his armpits and stared and the burning blush would not leave my face.

It was then I noticed that his left ring finger was missing, and shining upon the stump was a small tattoo. It was a golden bar which lay parallel to his knuckle. From that day until this I thought of the tattoo as a minus sign.

"I guess you want to talk about the script?"

"I've already started writing. Really excited about it. I need to get accustomed to things here, but when I do, I promise I'll write twelve, fifteen hours a day until I finish."

"That's a bit heavy, isn't it?"

"I'll work hard for you."

"Listen, okay. I'm just really bummed out by hearing my own voice now, you know? I was talking all last week at an est training seminar. I adjusted two hundred trainers. They were confused, but I think I set them straight. But right now I'm just really sick of my own words, so our conference will have to be a short one today and then I'm going to get into the island for a while."

"I don't mean to press you, Chip. I'm just excited about the idea, about this place. My whole life seems different."

An ice web swept across his face. He looked at me as if I had touched some inviolate and private place. Everything shrank back from his surface. His face and eyes lost the faintest evidence of warmth. He spoke slowly.

"Once we do the script, we have to sell the idea to three of my uncles. My best advisers. If they like it, then we look for investors. My family has intimate contact with John Huston, Preminger and others. I'm thinking Huston, or maybe Wells, to direct."

I sat and tried to show no real emotion. "Wonderful." I moderated my voice. "Huston may be a bit old, but Wells . . ."

"I really just don't want to go into all of that, man. I mean, we may never get that far. *Billy Browning* is wait-and-see pudding."

The front door squeaked and a lady stepped into the room. She was short and craggy, her face without makeup. Ruddy lines and cracks and fissures in her skin, beaten by sun, trace of red lipstick, sweet-pea eyes, lashes stubby and short.

"Baby boy," she said looking at Chip. He introduced his mother, Townsend Beale.

When I shook her hand she said, "Aren't we related somehow?"

"I don't think so," I said.

"Oh," Townsend Beale replied. She wore a canvas, brown wrap-around skirt, denim shirt, no stockings, blue rubber boots. On her head sat a yellow rain hat.

"Well, I'm here to ask you a question, Chip. Monday I'm off to Scotland."

"Walleyes?"

"They were lousy a couple years ago. But . . ." Uncomfortably, she glanced at me. "I simply don't know how much to take."

"How much what?"

"Do-re-mi."

"On the trip?"

"I'll be there four days."

Mother and son looked at one another. Townsend put her hands along her spine.

"How much did you take last time?" Chip asked.

"I let Day arrange things last time."

"Maybe you should let him again."

"No, I'm through with servants. Breaking away. Making my own decisions now. Do you think fifteen thousand?"

"Fifteen thousand dollars?"

"Well, I don't know. Yes."

"What part of Scotland are you buying, Mother?"

"I feel awfully silly about this. Cody, what do you think?"

"Ma'am?"

"Ten thousand?"

"A lot of money."

"Oh."

"No. I mean—well, ten thousand certainly seems—serious."

"Serious?"

"In the sense that ten thousand dollars—is serious."

"Well, I don't know exactly what you mean, Cody." Townsend Beale pulled off her hat and held it against one hip. She set her lip between her teeth and painfully looked out toward the lily pond. Her left wrist held a three-inch-wide bronze bracelet in whose center was set a silver scarab.

"Well, then," she said.

"I don't know. Ten thousand seems steep, Mother. It's your decision though."

Townsend shifted her bony weight, still chewed her lip, blinked sweet-pea eyes, thinking.

"Five thousand," I said decisively.

"You think so?"

"It's a good, hard figure. You can always bring some back."

Townsend stuck out her chin. "That's true. Well, that certainly makes sense. I could bring some back." She turned rather abstractly and waved toward the door. "Oh, Chip, why don't you and Cody come up for luncheon sometime?"

"I'll bring us some fish," said Chip.

Townsend glanced at me. "I just didn't want to be foolish about this trip."

"We could grill lobster," Chip said.

"I wanted to plan this, to carry this out myself."

"Sounds like a ball to me," I said.

"You think the money's right, Cody?"

"Plumb right," I said.

"So do I. I just wanted to be correct. Well, you boys come when you can."

I liked her. She possessed a toughness, an honesty which broke through her blue-chip exterior. She had humor and vulnerability. She actually wanted communication. She was the first older Beale who seemed interested in my existence.

Chip apologized for his mother, saying that his father's illness had strained and weakened her. He said that while I worked on the treatment that he would pay me a hundred dollars a week up to a thousand and that his lawyers would design a contract shortly and that New House was mine rent-free.

He kicked through blue-painted herb jars near the stereo, found a lump of shiny keys tossed into the corner. He pulled off a triangular key and shook it warmly into my hand. "This is yours too. It belonged to Great-aunt what's-her-name. You need some wheels. I think you'll like these. Just don't open your garage until after four this afternoon, okay?"

6

At three in the afternoon I stood in New House at the kitchen window drinking my first cup of Earl Grey tea. The sea was still and flat and blue. The paraffin moon sat primly in the sky. I still held the key. I had not set it down since the morning, neither had I done any work. Too excited. What kind of car? Probably a heap. Most island cars seemed to be heaps. Nothing flashy, nothing extraordinary. Still my stomach was all nerves.

Something slammed the outside of the house. I jumped. Odd, when you listen, how much you hear. Crickets, a buoy, the wind through screen, birds, the sea below. Another crash.

I stepped onto the glass porch. Arching over a hedge, a basketball struck the house and then bounced back. When the ball hit the house again I pulled the sliding door, eased onto the slate patio.

"One on one?" a voice shouted from behind.

I managed not to flinch, turned.

She possessed the brownest tan I had ever seen. Black hair, black eyes. It was the naked girl in clothes. Cockily, one leg was straight and the other bent. She wore red running shorts, green barrettes in her hair, red sweat bands on wrists.

"Naw," I said. "I don't play."

"Nuts," she said and dribbled the ball past me. She made a perfect arching shot through a netless hoop on the side of the house.

Her legs were angular and tight. She wore a white tennis shirt which had been cut off just below her breasts. Her ribs were brown and separate as slats. She had rectangular stomach muscles and a flat navel.

"Have you been poking around my house at night?" I asked.

"What's it to ya?"

"It's my house."

"It's my stomach."

"I'm not following you."

"Yeah, I scammed some food outa your joint."

"Why?"

"I was hungry, man. You ever been hungry?"

"What about the water? There was water all over the floor."

"Skinny-dipping. I'd go skinny-dipping on your beach at night, every place else it's too rocky. So, I'd swim, then hit this joint for food. I don't have much to eat right now—but I will. You wait and see. I will."

I sat down on a step. The sun polished her tan. Her black eyes were set wide apart and she looked at me with her chin down and her eyelashes long and black and touching her eyebrows. She had a chipped front tooth, which added to her boyishness.

"Do you live around here?" I asked.

"A friend of mine worked this place last summer. I was sick of Boston. Sick of being poor. Sick of everything. She helped me get the job, then she got pregnant. I came anyway. They gave me a cabin down the street there, but I don't get paid for another week. I'm busted."

"Look, I've got lots of food."

"You think I'm a bum, don't you?"

"No."

"Sure you do. 'Cause I need food, you think I'm a bum—go ahead and say it."

"I'm a bum."

She looked at me. "Want to feel my tooth?" She took my finger.

"I saw it," I said, feeling embarrassed as she drew my middle finger around the sharply broken tooth.

"Busted it just before I left the city. Fell down jogging. Makes me look sexy, huh?"

"Actually, it does," I said. "What's your name?"

She sat down by me, her chin on her knee. "Hey, tell me about men and women."

"How about a bologna sandwich?"

"Maybe it's boys and girls. But I'm not a girl anymore, you know. I'm really not."

"You're right. I'm Cody—Cody Walker."

"And I'm not doing Rico's laundry anymore either."

"Certainly not."

"He was my boyfriend in Boston. Used to make me wash his laundry. Used to make me do everything. No more. I'm gone, man. I'm gone."

I just sat. We were close. The sun was warm. We were a millimeter apart.

"I lied to you. I've never jogged. Least not till last week." She stuck a finger in her mouth, touched the tooth. "But, I been jogging a lot since I got here. Catching rays and doing all the stuff I never done in the city. And you know what?"

"What?"

"I'm going to marry somebody on this island. Somebody rich."

"That will be tough."

"You think so?"

"I think so."

"But I'm a catch."

"Yep."

"A real catch. Don't you think?"

"Don't do anybody's laundry though."

She sank back against the door. "Sometimes I think I'm not a catch."

"Sure you are."

"Hey, let's play some ball."

The square patio had natural boundaries. I tossed the ball to her and she dribbled. The short hair blew about her face. She had the grace and the competence of a good ball handler. When she turned her back I lightly placed a hand on her hip. I was a lousy ball player, but I knew some tricks.

She drove to my left and made a perfect lay-up. She threw me a hard pass.

I dribbled in, but not well. When I moved right she kicked the ball away. I tried going left and she slapped my hand. I barely kept control, clumsily went toward the basket and sprawled. She grabbed the ball and dunked.

I rose feeling oafish. "Come on, babe," she said, directing me to the steps.

We sat and sweated. She pulled off a red wrist band and slipped it over my hand.

"You family here?" she asked.

"No."

"You could be. But you got to work at it. You got to bust your buns to belong here."

"I don't care about belonging here."

The black eyes studied me. Her black hair was rudely cut, as if along the lines of a bowl. The chipped tooth appeared in a grin. "Look, I need a jogging partner."

She held out a hand. I shook it. She raised my shirt and touched my belly. "Wow. Hair. Run without a shirt tomorrow. See you at seven in the morning." She jumped from the steps and sprinted away.

I sat and looked at the sea, feeling sorry for the girl. She could never belong here. You had to be born into this place. It was just that simple.

Back in New House, I unpacked some pads and pens and set them on the picnic table on the glass porch. I loved work. I loved ink bottles and yellow pads and smooth pens. To set up the desk was wonderful ceremony. Ordering the elements in a way.

I flipped through my research. At fourteen Billy had been shipwrecked on the island kingdom of Lohai. To him the whole world was new and dangerous.

I looked at my watch. Four on the nose.

When I snapped the garage light switch the car spit color.

Yellow wood running boards, fat whitewall tires, filigree grill, striking red hood and the rest, black paint shining. A convertible. I had no idea what kind of car it was, didn't care. I jumped into the frayed leather seat, cranked the engine. Vibration, hiss, rattle and she woke. I wheeled outside. The black wood steering wheel turned like silk on ice. I raced to the driveway entrance, stood in the car and yelled, "Hello! Hello! Good God, hello!" I roared up Beale Street, turned left and hollered and beeped at the woods. I spent half an hour honking and hollering. I couldn't remember how to get to Harding's house, had no idea where Doug and Marlow had gone. Finally I parked my new car back at New House, a little lonely but still high. I poured myself a glass of wine and went to the garage and sat beside the car, keeping a hand on the beautiful bumper. I thought about Chip and why he had made me wait so long. The idea came slowly; perhaps there was no reason at all. I had to wait because he willed it.

In the writing room I watched twilight polish the sea rose. I made a few notes on the script, then realized the girl had not told me her name.

Thundering and thumping, Doug careened and barreled into the backyard. Yellow suspenders cinched the cavernous black waist-waders to his chest. Black hair frizzy, face stung red by wind, his one left dimple crimped and pitted and ballooned a huge smile. He held two blue fish. He kicked open the glass door and slammed them on the table. They were big.

"Holy Christmas sakes, you got Aunt what's-her-name's car!"

"Where have you been?"

"My whole life I've wanted just once to drive that machine. My whole life. Come on. Let's go. Move."

"What about the fish?"

"Here!" Doug tossed one fish to me, then addressed the other: "Fish, you have earned this ride."

He gunned the Bugati down the tar road, zoomed through the open island gates, then double-clutched the access road and entered Cedar Point, where we buzzed a small shopping center. At a stoplight I was flapping my fish overhead when the cop car pulled next to us.

"Oh, crap," Doug said, his face fading from red to white. "One more ticket and I'm finished."

All at once I found myself bounding from the Bugati, rushing toward the policeman's large bumpy face, fingernail mustache, doorknob chin.

"Hello, Officer, are you a Catholic?" I asked respectfully.

Cop's eyes narrowed.

"Are you?"

"I am."

I thrust the fish at him. "Here you go. Fresh fish. It's St. Kalinas's feast day. Patron saint of fishermen. Celebrate it!"

The cop's face gave a smile. "Menhaden?"

"Caught not an hour ago. Fresh as the dew."

"She's a beauty."

"Doug—the other one."

Doug had sunk down in the car to his eyes, but reacted, tossed the fish.

I stuffed the stiffening body through the cop's window. "For your wife, your kids. Happy St. Kalinas Day!"

I dodged back to the Bugati. The happy cop waved us forward. Doug made a hectic U-turn and the cop laughed and we raced back down the shore road toward the green cedars of Black Island.

"Who's St. Kalinas?" Doug asked.

"Don't know. Just made him up."

"You got nerve."

"Naw."

"You got real nerve."

"Maybe you're right."

"We're pals."

He threw an arm around my shoulder. "Hey, want the grand tour?"

We roared through the island. The tar roads were broken and narrow and standing in black water, the roads not at all a highway, but rather belt thin, rough and shoddy like a hundred country roads that I had traveled. The trees stood so close that you could reach out and touch green cedars and scrub oak and shining holly stands from these perfectly rugged lanes—jostling, rutted, bumbling country roads.

Down the northeast road the sea rushed rocks and laid foam on the boulders. Farther out black ground swells rolled, the wind hard at them. First we passed a lighthouse. Next came the beach club: sprawling walls, shingles and windows. Weathered and old. Nothing belonging to the rich seemed new. Doug said that in two weeks all the family's children would be sent here and taught how to tie knots and cleat, to be instructed in tennis-court protocol, correct English riding style, basic watercolors and the complete stanzas of all hymns performed at Choir. Below the classroom, at twelve-thirty, luncheon was served. Crab and fish and fresh fruits on occasion, but mostly beans and hot dogs, cold salad, hamburgers and tuna fish. No alcoholic drinks offered here. Outside the beach club, I noticed the sand looked different. Far too white, too fine. Doug said the sand had been shipped from the family's compound in Miami.

Now up the eastern shore road, I saw seven or eight houses. (According to Doug the island had thirty major homes of ten to twelve rooms or more.) Gravel driveways neat as salt and pepper. Sprinklers set in the grass wrapped a spray over the houses and window ivies and discolored stone chimneys absent of television antennas. In each front yard stood an apparently obligatory original sculpture, rusting metallics of mating ducks or stylized whales. Each yard was different, distinct. Balding putting greens (the yellow flags of miniature pins soggy in spray), a wooden bird bath carved in turtles and snakes, an old teak mast made into a flagpole, a white beehive, a blue wind sock full of sea breeze.

We turned right and stopped before the harbor. It was one mile deep into the island and half a mile wide. In full summer one hundred boats waited here for the families. Dinghies, launches, rowboats and forty-foot Hincklies. Beyond the harbor and the sound lay the bare faces of the houses in Cedar

Point, below them a gray rock bank, stocky pilings rambling out into the sea. Three Morgans raced in whitecaps. They had gennies out and trimmed tight and their hulls threw rainbow sprays. Inside the harbor the surface was still as a pond. The sand of the beach was coarse and brown, littered with stones and wood, and the beach itself was narrow and quickly turned into reeds, then scrub oak and finally the brown vines of sea roses.

An old man exited a nearby boathouse, walked toward the car. He was white-haired, short, wearing khaki pants and shirt.

"It's Johnny Day," Doug said. "He's worked for Uncle Mallory for fifty years."

Day never came any closer than twenty feet. His face was brown, grainy as sandpaper. Even from a distance he seemed shy, deferential.

"Johnny, how are you?" Doug asked.

"Well, and yourself, sir?"

"How's your love life?"

"I'm working on a summer sweetheart. But it's getting harder all the time, you know. Like the fellow said to me the other day, 'Getting any on the side?' And I said, 'Hell it's been so long, I didn't know they moved it.' "

Doug roared and so did I. We waved and pulled away.

Farther down the road we raced by hammering shops where the new May crew was welding boats and oiling lawn mowers. We passed a faded red barn which housed the island fire truck. Next was the chapel where I had attended Choir. Doug took a left up a hill of ash trees.

He stomped the brakes and threw his back against his door to look at me. His black hair was wild and his eyes lake-water blue. "Let me tell you about my family. If you're my buddy, you need to know."

It took half an hour for Doug to give me the history of his extraordinary family.

When I let him out at Straw Hill, I was stunned at the Summers's wealth.

7

I sat in my backyard on the wooden steps that led down to the beach. Between my legs I cradled a bottle of Pouilly Vinselles and drank the wine without a glass. The sea was as blue as my turquoise ring. After two big gulps of wine I went over Doug's history.

The Summers's money had been made by McFarland Summers, who had immigrated from Ballymane, Ireland, in 1820. He was a blacksmith who, at thirty-five, had invented a machine that turned out horseshoes at one hundred per hour. When the Civil War erupted he received an exclusive contract with the Union Army. He moved from horses into oil in Pennsylvania and then started buying coke mines. McFarland met Henry Clay Frick and formed a coke cartel. Later these two men built a company with Andrew Carnegie. Since those days the Summers had grown ever more prosperous. They moved into stocks and bonds and shipping. They supported and encouraged artists. Painters and sculptors were often kept in spare houses on their estates. They loved horses and sailing and the fast beautiful jets that were supposed to be used only for family business and on occasion were. They held estates in Bermuda and Long Island and Maine, the Adirondacks and Sri Lanka. They wore perpetual suntans. They courted actors and musicians and even associated and played with the Kennedys. They were a people who laughed. A family who gave to the world joyously.

Thinking about the Summers, I drank some more wine, returned to the house for a sweatshirt.

The girl greeted me at the door in cutoff blue jeans and a red halter top.

"I decided I like you."

"Oh?"

"Well, kinda. Anyway, come rub my back."

She towed me upstairs and plummeted into bed. She pulled me down beside her.

"Nervous?" she asked.

"I don't even know your name."

"Lisa Kraskawitz."

She reached her hands under my shirt and stroked my chest, pinched my nipples. My hands trembled, eyes twitched, neck bones creaked. Her tongue swirled into my mouth like something alive. When she broke the kiss I was breathless.

"Where did you learn to kiss like that?" I asked.

"C.Y.O."

"What's that?"

"Catholic Youth Organization."

"Oh."

She pulled off her halter top, twisted out of her cutoffs. She sat and stared at me.

I couldn't move. I wanted to start, but I didn't know how.

"You're not queer, are you?"

"Listen." I swallowed. "You're beautiful."

"You *are* queer." She threw a blanket over herself.

"I like you, Lisa. I want to, but I . . ."

"There was a time when I was into bondage. Not heavy. Do you know about that kind of stuff?"

"Uh—sure."

"So you like to slap girls around, huh?"

I raised my hands. "Would you like a glass of wine?"

I went downstairs and opened the refrigerator. I touched ice trays and tried to collect composure.

A minute later I handed her the white wine. "I thought I'd just say this straight out—I've never—done this before."

"Had a glass of wine?"

"No."

"How old are you?"

"Well, twenty-two."

"You playing some kind of game with me?"

"I'm no good at this."

When I rose she caught my hand and placed the back against her cheek. "Southerners are different, aren't they?"

"I'm sorry. I'm a slow learner. Real slow."

"I lied about the bondage."

"Me, too."

She pulled me down next to her and swept black hair from her face. She blinked and held her eyelids shut so the lashes spread below her eyes like small violet fans. "Sometimes I'm full of it," Lisa said, looking at me. "You're really a—virgin?"

"I reckon so."

She slid fingers into my hair, then withdrew her hand and pulled the blanket to her chin. "I feel creepy."

We drank the wine silently. I was shaking. I could feel the bed mimic my nerves. Carefully I reached for her hand.

"You know what I really want?" Lisa asked. "I want to be somebody. I want people to know my name on the street. Know me, talk about me, when they go to bed at night think about—me. Is that awful?"

"No, ma'am."

"You're lying."

"Yes, ma'am."

"Why?"

"To give myself a little more time."

She laughed and hugged me and did not let go for a long time.

We drank and talked the night cheerfully late and through the bedroom windows watched the moon arc across the sea, until the first paling presence of dawn told the time and sent us arm in arm to sleep.

Sometime later I woke and found that Lisa had gone. I slipped into jeans and sandals and a baggy T-shirt. Halfway down the stairs, I smelled coffee.

She was sitting in a wicker chair in my writing room. She had tucked her brown bare legs under her chin. Her morning hair was not combed and lay in dark wedges to each side of an irregular part, the longer hair strands pulled back behind small ears, a ducktail fanning the back of her neck. In cutoff jeans and the red halter top, toenails mischievously painted violet and sharp chin over her coffee cup, she was the soft soul of morning. I touched her shoulder. She pinned my fingers between her shoulder and face, then spun around.

"Start writing," Lisa said.

"What?"

"You said you're a writer. Get a pen."

"I haven't had any coffee."

"Are you a poet?"

"Oh, God."

She sat me down in her warm chair. "What a great idea. Now you look at the sea and write some and I'll fix you breakfast."

"I can't write yet."

Lisa scrambled my hair, pushed it into my eyes. "Wonderful. You look wonderful."

"Coffee. I want coffee."

"And a bagel?"

"My daddy used to hunt with beagles."

Missing the joke, she skipped to the kitchen.

After breakfast Lisa ran upstairs and brought down both pairs of our worn Adidas running shoes. On the patio steps we laced them up, shoulder to shoulder beside the brown brambles which ran over the short cliff to the beach and the pink boulder and the green sea.

We jogged the gravel driveway and then started down Beale Street. We passed several houses landscaped behind cedar and tall holly hedges. After two miles I gave out and Lisa humored me and we sat down in a valley beside the road. I situated her between my legs, pulling her sweating back and brown ribs close to my chest and folding my hands across her stomach and she sighed and crossed her hands over mine.

From black and gray winter leaves, new ferns rose and ran down a hill to the edge of two black ponds separated by cattails. The ponds held fallen trees. The dead wood was black near the shallows, but white and skeletal deeper in the water. Below the ponds, in the midst of reeds, stood a short spruce tree, then sea grass which spread to a brown sand dune and beyond the sand lay the blue sea.

Lisa slipped my hand across her warm stomach and down into her shorts. She worked my hand against her slowly and when I tried to go inside she said no and rubbed my fingers against her faster until we beaded sweat and she groaned and shuddered.

I held her for a while, then she got up. "I got some work to do."

"Wait a minute . . ."

"Not now. I'm not into pills, you know?"

"Okay."

"Do you know what I'm saying?"

"You don't take birth-control pills."

"I'm saying—you got to take care of things. I like you. It'd be neat to get off with you, but I don't do pills. So you take care of it. I'm not going to get pregnant. At least not by you."

Lisa bent down and kissed me. "I'll come by tomorrow. You gonna have what you need?"

"I'll have them."

" 'Bye."

She jogged down the road.

I watched her until she rounded a curve. I felt hurt. She had acted so cold and crude. She had satisfied herself and I got nothing. And I didn't like being told that she didn't want to get pregnant by me. Anybody else was fine, right? Not that I wanted her pregnant, God knows. But why did she have to say it? Hell, maybe I would get her pregnant. Twins.

I lay back in the leaves and smelled the spring pushing through the damp forest floor. I was captivated by her caprice. Early this morning she had been warm and cuddly and cute. After the jog, hot and sexy, then cold and conniving, and finally faintly motherish with her peck on the lips. Woman. What a construction. What a marvelous construction.

I walked back home. In the kitchen I put the teakettle on. I was thinking about Lisa when I saw the bundle lying on the counter. A sheaf of papers.

8

They lay in a new manila folder. I opened it and turned off the whistling kettle.

It was more of Beale's writing. I glanced at my watch —nine-fifteen. Harding had probably found some more pages and brought them over while I was jogging. I poured a cup of hot water, dunked an Earl Grey tea bag and sat down in the living room.

There were no longer notes, just straight narrative.

Spadefish *motored beneath the moonlight sea.*

I was sweating. Glad to sweat. Most of the crew was sick. Influenza. High fevers. The captain was down and delirious. I was in charge. We were after something big. We'd been out on three patrols and it was November now and we still had nothing.

I remember I left the bridge to check the new torpedoes. I had a feeling for them. A taste for them. I held the torpedoes in my gut, just like the sub. I walked below the dim light of the conning tower: barometers, steel casing, gyros, the scarred periscope, glass-faced dials of radars and radio. Down the black-hole stairs to the control room of headphones, fire control boxes, chain lockers, oil valves, electric meters, hum of small black fans, ticking operating levers and three men, sallow, thin in T-shirts and jeans and fever. Down still farther and forward to the battery, holding hot static humidity and whizzing air compressors, black boxes of batteries, each cell weighing a ton, stills generating fresh water, air-conditioning, air purifying. Finally, the forward torpedo room, larger than any other compartment. Cleaner, light, cool. My beauties were racked two by two along the hull. Each torpedo a ton and a half. Ten feet long. Range nine thousand yards.

Each head carrying a quarter ton of TNT exploding on impact or as they entered the magnetic field of a steel ship.

I touched the new Mark 18 electrics. I had argued for them. Put money into their design. The old Mark 10s and 14s were lousy. Exploded too soon. Sometimes not at all. Six shots from Whalefish *had thudded into one Jap destroyer and never gone off. I drew my hand down the length of the fish: warhead, air flask, midship, afterbody, tail. I patted the afterbody.*

The perfect part. This was the heart of the torpedo and the heart of the sub and my own heart. Mechanical perfection. Hear the elements of death: oil tank, turbines, depth engine, gyro steering, immersion mechanism, starting level, depth index and these aligned in only a two-foot section of the weapon.

*With a chalk stub I wrote the name on four electrics—*Shinyo. *Sister ship to the* Yamato *and* Musashi. *She was a twenty-nine-thousand-ton aircraft carrier. She had been out only ten days.* Shinyo *was what we wanted.*

Back on the bridge, I decided to surface the Spadefish *for air. I gave the order to Johnny Day.* Spadefish *stole to the surface.*

Three healthy lookouts climbed with binoculars into the observation towers beside the high and low periscopes. It was still dark, just before dawn. I opened the forward and after catches to let air down into the sub. I walked the narrow deck. Water ran off steel sluices. The metal deck had smooth scars and dents. Then I saw them just below the three-inch gun. The whole deck beginning to glow. Just above the engine rooms and stern tubes. The hull and the black surface suddenly lit by dim light. Anemones. Hundreds. Five inches wide. Clear, jelly-like globes. White and blue nerves through their heads and crimped red tissue and, beneath this, their yellow light rising. All the ship behind the deck gun was glowing.

I ordered up a fire-ready crew and hosed down the deck. The anemones would easily give away position. Several kids worked at them with scrub brushes and putty knives. They laughed, squirted one another with the hoses. I put an anemone in a cup of water and ordered it taken to the captain's quarters.

On the cigarette deck below the lookouts, I leaned against the fifty-caliber. Johnny Day came up.

"Think we'll find her, sir?" Day asked.

"I got that feeling."

"Boys in COMSUBSAC are giving us the devil for sinking no tonnage."

"Yep."

"Captain's compliments on the anemone. Says same thing happened to him. He says we should go back. Fever's 104 degrees on some of the boys."

"Why do you think we can't sink something, Johnny?"

"There's fate, sir."

"Bloody hell there is."

"I'm thinking there is fate or luck."

"I want the Shinyo. *She's bought and paid for. She doesn't even belong to the Japs anymore."*

I remember thumbing the smooth hammer of the machine gun. "Got a radio message from Townsend. Maybe I'll marry her."

"She's from a lovely family, sir. A Beacon Hill family."

"Give me some class, huh?"

A sailor approached.

"Radio contact, sir."

"Where?"

"Bearing 028 T."

"Time?"

"2048."

"Stations," I said.

In fifteen minutes the ship was identified as an aircraft carrier. Thirty thousand tons. The course 210 and zigzagging at twenty knots. I stayed on the surface. Kept the lookouts up.

At 2130 the lookouts spotted an escort on the target's beam. Range to the escort was 6,100 yards. The carrier was nine thousand yards beyond this. I stayed on the bridge, but sent the lookouts below. I had to play catch-up. I redirected the course.

Luck. At 2232 the carrier and escorts changed course.

At 2240 I came to course 100. Five thousand seven hundred yards away from the target, I ordered the Spadefish *down.*

In the conning tower the sponge eyepiece of the periscope pressed into my eye socket. Squatting down. Knees popping in ligaments. Thighs parallel to the floor, palms beneath the belly of the handles, feeling the Spadefish *in my back and hands, eyes searching out the horizon. Then I saw her.* Shinyo. *Four thousand yards away.*

She broke the sea like a plateau of land. Superstructure black squared against the northern horizon. Two cube stacks beneath the moon. Her decks were perfectly ordered—aircraft backed nose to tail to nose.

I set coordinates. Bearing changed to the left. Spadefish *came to normal approach course. The three escorts held their position.* Shinyo *zigged out. I ordered a contact report sent out to any other subs in the area. I held the* Shinyo *in the clear glass of the periscope.*

The bow tubes open and ready. Two hundred yards away a destroyer passed close to starboard.

"Range?"

"2,100 yards, sir," said Day.

"Easy now, baby," I said. "Bearing?"

"016 T."

"Come take some of Daddy's medicine. Gyro 53 degrees to 37 degrees right."

"Aye, aye."

"Track 108 to 120 port. Torpedoes at twelve feet. Spread one and three quarters percent right, one and three quarters percent left. Fire one."

The gentle push of the projectile.

"Fire two."

The Spadefish *recoiled in the torpedo's wake.*

"Fire three. Hard port. Stern tubes to bear."

The crew waited. The Mark Electric 18s slashed wakeless through the water. I kept the periscope on Shinyo. *Ten seconds. Fifteen. Twenty.*

At the carrier's stern the first torpedo hit. A black propeller slivered the air. A triangular flame leapt the vessel's side. The second shot hit amidships and the concussion keeled the Spadefish *to port. The sky and the carrier suddenly exploded in light.* Shinyo*'s magazines blew. A big fire. Shining metal flashes. A stack shot like a missile. Planes blew and fired and careened and tumbled into the sea. Then one streaked from the deck. One plane trying to labor aloft. Explosions on the deck. Black gas whirlwinds. White foam, burning mechanical liquids. The fighter reversed, looking for distance. A white fissure broke amidships. Internal* *steel, white as opal. The fighter raced down the flattop, leapt at a high angle into the air. Up and gone. Driving high to sixty degrees, seventy degrees, eighty degrees toward the safe sky. Then a flame, burst of gas, and she fell until she crashed into the furnace of the ship.*

I slapped down the periscope handles. "All ahead, full. Right full rudder. Take her deep."

Spadefish*'s radar picked up the three escorts driving for our position. I ordered the sub rigged for depth charges.*

In six minutes we sat two hundred feet down in the black of the sea. Depth charges went off in the distance. So far I had shaken the Japs. The diving officer handed over earphones. "Get a load of this, sir."

I set the warm cone to my ear. Shinyo *was nine to ten thousand yards away. On other patrols I had heard ships breaking up below. Their death was frail and popping like the whine and static of a late-night radio. But this death was different. There was below other noise a great groaning, like the roar of substrata in an earthquake. And above this was a sharp crease of sound which now I felt in the* Spadefish *herself, ringing a hum from the hull as if from a rubbed wineglass.*

The first depth charge hit three hundred yards to port. The blast blew out a barometer in the conning tower. The attack team sat down on the iron deck plates. They were breathing hard. The second and third explosions came quickly. The explosions slammed your ears hard and quick, like a firecracker gone off too close to the head. The escape trunk ruptured and began to leak. I sent two teams to repair the damage. A report from the forward torpedo room said that the torpedoes had been knocked one foot off their skids. The line from number six air bank had blocked off. Air became thicker. No real work could be done. Any metallic sound would spot us for the enemy. The crew sat in the hiss of compressor leaks. For two hours the depth charges went off. One hit so close that a compartment decompressed. Nursing little air, perhaps only in arteries, five men sealed off the blown compartment. Spadefish *waited in darkness holding only pocket air, cold spray, the smell of Freon and oil and busted bottles of shaving lotion.*

We waited, shivering, ears stuffed with tissue, eyes fixed overhead. The depth charges grew more distant and finally went silent.

The crew in the conning tower gave thumbs-up and smiles, but I still looked overhead. I didn't give the order to resume stations. There was something out there. I clicked on the silver sonar switch. Put the phone to my ear. There was a movement in the water toward the ship. I motioned to Day. The Irishman listened, whispered, "Torpedo?"

I cupped the sonar again. Silence. Then a soft vibration, set of vibrations, as if something was circling Spadefish. *I ordered the sonar off, the men quiet.*

"Third torpedo, sir? Come back for us?" Day was shaking.

"Not circling."

"A mine. Some new kind of mine?"

A tapping sound came from the right hull above the periscope. Something had settled on the deck.

9

The thing ground across the bow.

"Depth charge," the firing officer whispered. "Shinyo *could have targeted us. Fired it from a lower battery."*

Above, the grinding sound continued. I set my ear to the hull. The sound leapt through the iron. A buzzing. I sat back, felt my own smile. "I need a volunteer."

"What the hell are you saying?" Day asked.

"Me and you are going outside."

"What's out there?"

"I-18."

"New weapon?" the firing officer asked.

"A Jap minisub," Day said.

In the dim, aft torpedo room, me and Johnny got cinched into heavy diving gear. Four crew members worked us. Suits, heavy green hoses, black iron weights.

"How did you know?" Day asked.

"They captured one at Pearl. She was twenty-nine feet long. Hundred-mile range. We trained against her in Newport. I remembered the buzzing sound—Jap electric engine. They buzz and click."

"Does she have torpedoes?"

"No. They carry demolition. An iron chest. Three hundred pounds of plastic. The crew exits the sub, unbolts and attaches the charge. Me and you are going to welcome them."

I climbed the aft hatch. Someone offered a heavy spear gun. When the trunk door opened, the sea hit hard. The icy current stabbed my bones. I crawled, half swam, from Spadefish. *Free from iron and weight, I floated in the night-green sea. Bulky head and arms and legs moved lightly in the gloom.*

Before me was the black form of Spadefish. *Day slugged from the hatch, then sprang into the dark. Sounds here: blunt air bubbles, breathing, suit creaks, clunking hoses.*

I tucked the spear gun into my chest and made the aft decks, bumped over the engine room, passed the starboard machine gun. At the base of the conning tower I stopped, saw the Jap sub.

Thirty feet long. Rust brown. Blunt-nosed both fore and aft. Three black rising suns below the conning tower. Kills? The dark-blood periscope seven feet high—triangular at the base, it rose to a flat head and black eye-slit. A spine lay down the craft's midships. Triangular teeth here, dragon iron. Way forward, below the spine, lay the chest. The plastic explosives.

Behind the Jap conning tower lay a single hatch. Not open yet. Pounding though from below the hatch, a heavy hammering. Damaged? Stuck? Good luck for me.

I waited. Day alongside now. More pounding, then silence.

Slowly the Jap hatch began to screw open. A bulbous head emerged in bubbles and half-light. Red hose and a blue diving suit.

Day and me waited behind the forward deck gun.

Tiny Jap in blue suit and yellow shoes. He stiff-legged the deck toward the large iron box. He held a wrench.

When he bent down toward the box I went forward, kicked his head. From my right I saw the shot coming, a small spear cutting through the water. No time to duck. It struck my helmet. I lost balance, fell.

A second Jap diver stood in the hatch, held a spear gun to his shoulder.

With a knife Day bobbed to the Jap I had kicked. He cut the red hoses. Air whirled and fizzed. The sea wheeled in silver bubbles. The diver grabbed at the hoses, then leapt toward the surface. Fifty feet above, the blue form doubled in size. Flesh balloon. Arms extended, legs split perpendicular. Dully the helmet popped off. A red blood funnel spread into the sea.

At close range another silver spear just missed Day. Then the Jap slammed a wrench against Day's helmet, drove him down.

I butted the second Jap square in the head. He sprawled, still held the wrench. When I grabbed him his knife struck fast. A dull blow. My suit deflected. I blocked a second stab and slipped my knife under the soft webbing of the Jap's helmet—first bubbles, then a warm, oxygen current. I sawed through. I thudded my glass plate against his. The Jap's face now a yellow scream. The eyes plunged from the sockets looking down toward the throat. He shoved his fingers into the widening hole and I tried to pry them away, but no use. So I cut through. Sawed fingers. Soft blood veil. The Jap's legs kicked, struggled as if climbing.

The blade completely broke into the interior. A sucking noise. Gentle, peristaltic tremble through the knife's handle into my hand. I pushed hard. Black blood began to stain his face glass. Within, water and blood rose from his chin to fill the horrified mouth and nostrils and gaping eyes. The legs stopped. The head collapsed upon the wound.

The helmet had no face but blood which steamed the glass. I let the body loose and signaled Day to secure the explosives.

I approached the Jap sub. I had to get her off the Spadefish. *Big hoses clunked behind. I eased down into the outer hatch, used my feet to feel the safety trunk wheel. Feet in spokes, I twisted. A bursting illumination, ten-foot air bubble. Suction pulled me down into the small compartment: three feet wide, five feet deep. Battery lights burning in salt water. Tiny fish glowed and flashed, their bodies and blue hearts transparent before dials, gauges, compasses. Two reclining seats. Everything miniature, thin and hard. Barely room to maneuver the red steering stick. I set the mechanism at seventy degrees. Punched the ballast pedals, pushed several switches before the engine groaned. The sub shifted.*

I tried to break away, escape the sub, the explosives. Legs pinned. The submarine was moving forward, grating across the deck of Spadefish. *I grabbed two handles above, yanked. Through a dim porthole I saw* Spadefish*'s aft fifty-caliber pass. The minisub was screeching ahead. Speed increased, then a sudden lightness and tilt and the metallic screaming finished. Off* Spadefish *and into the sea. I yanked again and one leg broke free. The interior lights popped off. Blackness now. Only faint sea light through the porthole. Yanked my right leg and felt something tear under my knee, pull all the way to my groin, hot pain there. I went dizzy, saw blinking lights, like broken oxygen particles,* *fractured moons. I looked overhead, saw the hatch had fallen across my hoses. Air was blocked, no good air to breathe.*

I felt the submarine pointing me down, descending toward the dark. The pain glowed from my leg to my gut; somehow I didn't care anymore. Dropping into the blackness, I recalled a boyhood fever. Didn't a thermometer break? Didn't something shatter?

A tugging on my shoulders and I came partially free, but boots caught, hung again. Quickly they were pried loose. Arms around me, towed upward, more light, warmer.

In a few seconds I landed back on Spadefish. *Through glass, Day's face peered into mine. The pain was still bad, but my head was better and I sucked good air. Below, the Jap submarine dove steeply, red hoses dragging the dead man in the blue suit and the minisub diving so quickly now that she was only a shadow whose wake pulled the diver, arms and legs gently waving, as if only taking a carefree walk above the endless black swallow.*

10

For a week I was affected by those pages. I had nightmares about being trapped with Beale in the minisub, gulped by the abyss.

There was no new reference to my father. To make sure, I reread—nothing at all. My patience was growing, however. I thought of Chip's phrase: wait-and-see pudding.

One evening while I was studying the newest section, the front door flew open.

"Let's play," Lisa said. She grabbed my hand.

"Look," I said. "It's not a good time."

"Well, it's a good time for me. I bet you didn't get any toys, did you?"

"Toys?"

"You know. Balloons."

"Oh, no."

"Doesn't matter. Let's go."

Upstairs, Lisa pulled off her pink halter top and cutoffs and slipped beneath the sheets. She stacked two pillows behind her head, pulled the blue spread to her neck. Her mouth was open, wanton. The chipped tooth made her look sexy.

Nervously, I edged down beside her. She welded her mouth to mine and I tried, but somehow just couldn't go straight at it like this.

"You wouldn't believe what I just read. You wouldn't believe what kind of man Mallory Beale is."

"Who cares."

It hit me wrong. "I care, damn it. I care. Maybe you can

handle all this money and society. Maybe you can handle it because you've decided to climb and claw your way inside. But I can't do that. Look, I'm a middle-class Southerner. My family took a two-week vacation once every year. A big deal for us was when Daddy talked about Paris while we ate fried chicken and spaghetti at Fuzz and Teetat's Italian House in Spartanburg, South Carolina. I mean that was a big deal. A crummy ten-dollar meal which mostly came out of a Chef Boyardee box 'cause there ain't no real Italians in Spartanburg, South Carolina, and never have been. And the first time I ever kissed a girl was when I was stopped in a cotton field at a train crossing with one and she kissed me; I was eighteen years old and if you think I'm getting nekkid in front of you, you're nuts."

Lisa started to laugh.

I turned around.

She laughed harder.

When I stared at her she pulled the sheet over her face and shook.

"Ain't no Eye-tal-uns," she said.

"Shut up."

"Eye-tal-uns."

"Vye-eena sausages," I said.

"What?"

"Come in a little can. Look like midget hot dogs. The word's spelled Vienna, but all my life I said Vye-eena sausage until I took the trouble to spell out the label."

Lisa screamed. She still had the sheet over her head. I was trying to act hurt, but my stomach was cramping from holding back my own laughter.

I pulled down the sheet to see her face and touch her soft, mussed black hair. Her kiss came gently on the center of my lips. The second and third to the corners of my mouth.

"I want you to do me a favor," she said. She brushed back my hair. "I want you to start off in that bed."

I looked at the cold single bed. "Start off there?"

"It's fun to begin this way. You get your clothes off and get in the other bed. I turn off the lights, then in a little while you come over here real quiet and slip into bed with me."

"Reminds me of camp."

"It'll be neat."

"Listen, don't you think we ought to kiss a little more or something?"

"Don't start off fast, either. Let's feel each other in the dark. Let's explore, you know?"

I went to the other bed, began to unbuckle my belt. "Well?"

"I like to watch guys."

"Listen, I'm no stripper."

"Just a peek."

"No way."

"Chicken."

"Turn the light off, will you?"

The room went black. I got out of my clothes.

"This is insane."

"Don't come over for half an hour."

I climbed into the cold bed. The sheets went over me like frost. I propped my arms behind my head and thought briefly about pretending to snore. I ran a finger around my navel for lint, worried about a few hairs on my shoulder blades. On the sea, the orange moon sent dappled light. A mist lay beneath the moon and just above the sea. Two buoys were ringing in the shallows. One was high, the other low. They sounded as if they were courting.

After what I thought was the proper time, I left my now warm bed and reached for Lisa's. There was enough light to see her. I lifted the covers and lay down. She had her back to me. I did not move, did not touch. I lay as closely beside her as I could without touching. I could feel heat from her body. Still we were not touching. Between us something sparked like an energy, a static field.

My left hand touched her shoulder, paused. Her breathing was so slow. I felt for her breast. The flesh there was soft as dawn. I had never touched like this before. I had never sensed such softness. My middle finger circled the nipple. I eased my palm over her ribs and down onto her stomach. When I pulled my body close against her, a sigh trembled from us both.

Sometime before dawn I awoke. Lisa had her legs tangled in mine. Her face lay blunt-nosed into my ribs. We had made love twice. My legs felt weak, every muscle radiant. There was a warm scent of salt and breath. I had dreamed about Mallory Beale again. I left Lisa's warmth. The moon was gone. The sea was black. There were no stars. Out the window and fifty yards away I could see the blue fog. An imperturbable presence upon the sea.

How incredible Mallory Beale's war story had been—and he had lived it, he had been made second in command because of his wealth, his position in society. I had never cared about money, even less about society. Somehow I had never thought that money and the right name could bring you adventure. But they could. They really could.

I heard Lisa turn. I pretended preoccupation.

"Penny for your thoughts," she said.

"They ain't worth it."

"They ain't?"

"They ain't."

"You were not bad in bed last night."

"I was real good."

"You were?"

"Yeah."

She looked wonderful in bed. The white sheets provided a perfect canvas for her black hair and onyx eyes and olive skin.

This time I was more relaxed, but still did not have the needed timing for good lovemaking. I felt and recorded everything: tissuey, kissing sounds, soft air sucks, a sudden light and funny burp, the first hard embrace and inhaling moist female breath. She put hard nipples against my chest, her fingers pinching my own nipples, cupping the dents and rounds of my shoulders, palming vertebrae and jamming my buttocks forward and deep.

In lover's perspiration, breathless, we lay wonderfully entangled—hair and arms and legs and hands jumbled together. The sun rose and the wind blew through the screens and the sea held the pink blush of new light.

"I think I've found somebody," Lisa said.

"What do you mean?"

"I've found someone to date on the island."

"When?"

"A day ago."

"What's this fellow like?" I knew she was talking about me. I felt proud. Like a man.

"He's not that good-looking."

"No—but charming, intelligent, tender."

"Terrific in the sack. A regular Houdini."

"Houdini was a magician."

"Really. Yeah, well, that's what I'm saying. This guy's got a hell of a wand."

"Thank you, ma'am."

"Thanks for what?"

"On behalf of my wand."

She patted my head and sleepily rolled onto her side. "It's not you."

I pushed close to her, curved around, stuck my nose into her soft hair. "It's not me?"

"Are you kidding?"

"No, but you are. It is me, right?"

"You're just as broke as me."

"I might be rich. One day."

"I wanna sleep."

I shifted under the sheets. Already asleep, Lisa had turned to face me. I pulled the spread down, touched one warm breast. Reflexively, she shuddered. I gently dialed a nipple, watched the softest flesh blink hard. My thumb edged down the long muscle dimple of her stomach. In her membranous eyelashes and sweet breath and pouting lips, she looked vulnerable and I went hard and let myself sketch the same route, stopping somewhere below her navel, not entering, because she seemed so open and tender.

My blood went down. I felt depressed, but noble. I propped on a pillow. The sun was yellow. Small waves tapped the beach.

Who was Lisa seeing?

During the next week Lisa started disappearing in the evenings. Sometimes we were all together. Doug, Marlow, Lisa and I. We'd be drinking Black Horse ale, our stomachs fat with Doug's freshly caught and fried yellow tail. Around ten o'clock, even in the middle of a hilarious Doug Summers tale, Lisa would quietly rise, go to the kitchen as if for a drink, then slip out the back door into the dark.

One night I followed her.

A car was waiting on Beale Street. When she opened the door the light momentarily exposed the driver. Silver hair and wrinkles.

Two days later I trailed her once more. The same situation, ten o'clock, New House, Marlow's story this time. Lisa drifted toward the kitchen. I waited, then rose.

"What are you doing, Cody?" Doug asked.

"Grabbing a beer."

"Oh baloney."

"Following Lisa."

"Look, she's a maid. She's probably putting the moves on somebody. She tried it on me and I told her to forget it."

"Thanks, Doug." I left and crept into the dark.

Just beyond my driveway she sprang from the bushes.

"Yeah?"

"Jesus!" I yelled.

"Are you following me?"

"I want to know who you're meeting."

"A very rich man."

"Family?"

"You bet."

"He's just playing around."

"Well, I'm liking it."

"What's in it for you?"

"He'll make me rich."

She paused, looked toward the dark road. "He's met everybody in the world. Presidents and kings and movie stars. He's met them all." Her voice became conciliatory. "Look, he's what I've been waiting for. Don't screw me up. You're my buddy."

Lisa kissed my chin.

I walked back to New House. For a while I resisted the thought, then it assailed me: Was Lisa seeing Mallory Beale?

11

Spring was delicately rising through the island now. I had never seen such a soft and fragile arrival. The bleak winter woods turned pink and green. The harsh breeze softened and warmed. Even the blue barrel waves seemed to break more gently upon the beach, the sand now mushy in a billion different jellies. Black and pink boulders reared fir seedlings and lichens and white-stemmed mushrooms. At the edge of the birch woods and before the shimmering ivy chapel and alongside the new grass of the white clapboard houses, wildflowers opened and blossomed—tiny, exquisite cups of violet trimmed in green, or yellow vases supported by blue striations or shiny red stars whose faces waved upon thistle stems. On the lakes the great blue heron hunted minnows. Fuzzy bevies of mallard ducklings cheeped and scurried across island paths. Fat squirrels spilled young beneath apple trees, king snakes littered black and blue ribbons, baby jays thumped and hopped in greening reeds. Foxes and rabbits, chipmunks and birds, raccoons, even deer, surged and rustled in the blazing, sappish and omnipotent spring.

Some days after I had accosted Lisa I was walking the west side of the island, trying to collect my thoughts about the movie script. As I passed by Lisa's cabin I saw her lying in the sun on a blue blanket. She was brown sex. She raised from the blanket and unfastened her red halter top. She swept black hair from her face and reclined. A glass bowl sparkled oils and limes. She dipped a hand into the bowl and smeared the concoction over her bare breasts and thin waist. When she stretched, stomach muscles and rib cage striated and glistened.

Seeing her buck naked did it. I was determined to find out who she was meeting.

In New House I poured a Molson's Ale and composed the plan. Today was Friday. Lisa was sure to meet him. I knew their routine. They drove off the island, returning in a couple hours to her place. The idea was quick and sexy. The bedroom closet. Aha! The perfect place. When they drove away I would sneak into her cabin. (She had given me a tour a week earlier.) I would pry one louver of her closet door wider than the others, so I could see her bed completely. I would hide and wait.

At seven o'clock, having downed six beers, I crouched in a dewy clump of oak saplings beside Beale Street. Across the road, lights burned in Lisa's place. At seven-thirty an old Ford Fairlane pulled before her cabin. A light horn toot. I strained to see the driver, but it was too dark. Lisa bounded from her front porch and threw open the car door. Again I saw him—a bent form, silver hair—the door slammed shut.

As the Ford huffed past, I knew it had to be Beale. Who else on this island had met Presidents and kings? I was furious. How dare he go out with a girl so young, so sexy? Besides, he was supposed to be sick, dying. I stormed the cabin and stomped into the bedroom. A big double bed and patchwork quilt. On a nightstand sat a bottle of Mogan David and two Welch's jelly glasses. Gee, that's real class, Lisa. In the kitchen I found a coffee cup and a spare Lucky Strike. I lit up, poured a cup of Mogan David and surveyed my hiding place.

The big closet was crammed. Tennis shoes, white socks, blouses, shorts. A Mickey Mouse hat hung from a nail. I set it on my head. Quickly, I repacked clothes and blankets and a host of bras. I touched the bras lightly. The cups felt like cold pancakes. Bras were those things that your mother wore, that class of articles that you never handled. I tossed the bras on a shelf. There must have been three pairs. What did Lisa do with them? She certainly never wore them. Somehow a bra fell from the shelf, flopped upon my right shoulder. How could women abide these things? Hmmm, what the hell. I tucked my shoulders, pointed my arms and made the swimming motions I had seen my mother use. There. Actually it felt rather comfortable. An odd sense—addition, increase, self-esteem. Too much beer.

I looked through the louvered door. I could see only the foot of the bed. I tried bending a wooden slat. No good. Nerves trembled and twitched my hands. Finally I just broke the louver off. I sat down on a Playtex Living Bra box, puffed my Lucky and gulped the sweet wine. I felt guilty about spying, but I blamed my subterfuge on Lisa. She could have told me who she was seeing. By now I was shaking so bad I couldn't hold the cup and smoke at the same time. There was something else too: lust. Lust was shuddering my belly as much as fear. I wanted to see Lisa in bed. "This is totally sick," my right lobe said. "Yep," replied the left, "and you love it."

I heard the car skid into the driveway.

They stumbled and laughed into the front room. Silence, then giggles and silence again. Kissing, no doubt. I burned.

When Lisa entered the bedroom I suddenly closed my eyes. I could hear her brushing her hair. I opened my left eye, then my right, peered through the door. My God, she was beautiful tonight. Chicory-black hair and eyes big and black as pea-coat buttons. She wore white Levi's and a blue silk blouse. The long, pointed collar revealed her lithe neck, slashing gold choker and, below the choker, her breasts. Braless!

I was weak from beauty, then enraged. She never dressed like this for me. I was ready to open the door and tell her so when she began unbuttoning the blouse. Well, I could wait a minute. I sat back, sipped wine, blew a smoke ring. I hoped she *did* catch me.

Lisa opened the blouse cavernously. She looked at herself in a dressing mirror. "Darling?" she called.

"Darling," I muttered.

"Oh, huggypie, come on. Let's go. I've got to scrub the whole of Wedding House tomorrow."

"A moment," came the reply.

Was that voice Beale's?

Lisa pulled back the left blouse panel. Exposed, the breast was caramel, the nipple dark red and half a dollar small. She sucked stomach muscles flat. The constriction produced a beautiful squiggle. She threw her small butt to the left, cocked her head to the right, twined bare arms overhead and posed.

"You sexy bitch," she murmured, baring her teeth.

I almost choked.

She turned toward the closet door.

Cigarette in mouth, coffee cup clamped, I winced blind.

A switch clicked beside the door, and when I opened my eyes the bedroom was black.

Great. Well, I felt safer anyway. I drank the last wine. Had a warm buzz.

I listened: wet smacks, squeezes that rush air from lungs, sucks and ecstatic little groans, male and female.

"Oh no, lass. We'll not be doing that."

I strained to listen: Was that an accent?

"Why not?"

"It's a sin."

"Oh, bullshit."

"And I don't like your language."

"What do you think this is—a parish meeting?"

"Shush now. You're a lovely girl."

"Are those garters?"

"You know about my socks."

"I don't believe this. You left the garters on again? Turn on the lamp. Turn it on."

In the light I saw him. Not Mallory Beale at all, but rather his servant, Johnny Day, in shamrocked boxer shorts, purple garters, black socks and a boozy nose, red as a Christmas stocking.

Barely, I stifled a laugh.

"When we go to Rome you better not wear those things," Lisa said, her face rosy and sensual.

"I swear, luv."

"I mean it now."

"It's done," Day said. He popped off the purple garters.

"I wanna hear you promise—I won't wear my garters in Rome."

Day wiped his stocking-red nose, then set a milky hand on his milky chest. "In the Holy City, land of cardinals and corruption, with all my heart, I promise not to apply me garters."

Right then I burst out laughing so hard that I fell, sprawled into the bedroom, still clad in my bra and Mickey Mouse hat.

Lisa shrieked.

Day clutched the quilt to his chest and cried, "My God, a homosexual!"

He leapt from bed, scrambled trousers and shirt, and raced out of the bedroom door. His car squealed into the night.

"You jerk," Lisa hissed.

I laughed even harder.

She jumped from bed and glowered, dressed only in panties whose front pictured the leaning tower of Pisa. "You stupid rebel jerk!" She kicked me in the side.

I climbed onto the bed, convulsing from laughs and kicks.

"You ruined it all. I had him. He was an Irish baron. A Summers. Rich. He was mine. We were going to be married in Rome, you bastard, bastard, bastard!"

She slapped me, then clenched fists and tried to beat my face.

I grabbed her arms. "Lisa. Lisa! He's a servant. He's the same as you. Doesn't have a dime. Nothing."

Lisa bit my left hand, freed her right and socked my jaw.

I blocked the second punch and, using an open hand, slapped her. She fell into bed and began to cry.

Her blow was sobering. I rubbed my jaw.

"You dumb hick," she cried. Her face looked like a smudged ash.

"Lisa, he was lying, babe. He couldn't buy you a plate of beans in Boston. He's nothing." I touched her leg. She withdrew it. She pulled a sheet to cover her chest. I had forgotten about my bra. The Mickey Mouse hat had been lost in the struggle. "If you had told me his name, I could have saved you all this."

"We were gonna be married in Rome."

"No, you weren't."

Lisa sat up, tightened her sheet. "It was my dream—married in the Sistine Chapel to an Irish baron."

"Well, keep on dreaming, kid." I went to the screen door.

"I want a drink of water."

I stood and considered, then without glancing at her stepped toward the kitchen.

"There." I handed her a glass of water.

Her left cheek was red from my slap. Mussed hair framed her face and her long jaws were streaked in mascara, eyes round and black and the lashes trembling and perfect and lovely as the black stems of some exotic bloom. Still sheet-bound, breasts like snowcups, she seemed the most beautiful woman in the world that spring night.

"My mouf's bleeding," Lisa said.

"Let me look." I sat beside her, put a finger on her bottom lip.

She shook her head.

"Look, I'm not the dentist. Now open up."

A small cut, a little blood. I felt ghastly and closed my eyes.

Lisa circled an arm around my waist, laid her head against my chest. "I hate you," she said softly.

"I hate you too," I said.

"Nobody's ever punched me before."

"It was a slap. I slapped you."

"I really thought I was going to Rome."

"I'll take you to Rome."

"You will?"

"Rome, Georgia."

Lisa raised her face, scowled, then kissed me.

I slipped my hand beneath the sheet.

Gently she pulled off my bra.

We made love and lay for a long time in one another's arms. Out the door I could see a dogwood, the blooms white and pure, and across the road in the black woods the peepers were singing, and below the cliffs the sea sounded soft, running through rocks like silk. Eyes open, we lay in star-smashed dark, not wanting to speak, not wanting to cease from touching.

For some reason I said to her, "You know I hate to think about leaving this place. This island."

"Whatdoya mean?"

"I like it here. Things are so different, so exciting. There're so many—possibilities."

"Yeah. I know the feeling."

Maybe Lisa knew the feeling, but I did not, or at least had not until now. I had never wanted to belong to anything. Never.

Something was happening to me.

12

I had them all over me. They pimpled my ankles, spotted my calves and now they were driving higher. I knew how I got them. In those tall weeds, waiting for Lisa. Chiggers. Red bugs.

"Looks like measles," Harding said. It was morning and she had come over to New House.

"Ringworm," I invented.

"Ringworm!" Auburn hair and blue eyes and concern. She studied my splotched shins.

"Yep. They come back every year or two. You just learn to live with it, like malaria." I looked stoic.

"You poor thing. What will you do?"

I grinned. "Old country remedy."

"Yes?"

"Chanel No. 5."

"Not nail polish."

"Suffocates them. Knocks them out for a while, until the next crop."

Harding reached into her yellow canvas pocketbook, pulled out a bottle of red nail polish.

"May I dot?" she asked.

Clad in shorts, I propped my bare legs upon Harding's knees. I pointed out a bump here and a mound there while Harding daubed each chigger with the thick, bright polish.

Dotted and swabbed, my chiggers choking for air, I regretted my country doctoring, feeling like some character out of *Huckleberry Finn.*

Dressed in faded khakis and a blue oxford shirt and tennis

shoes, Harding observed, "You need one dot on your nose." She reached for the nail polish.

I pushed down her hand. "I feel silly enough."

"You do?" She spoke using a stiff, blue-blood jaw.

"You know I do."

She let me hang there. I resented her silence.

"Why don't you come over this afternoon?" she asked.

"I'm supposed to see Doug and Marlow."

"Come this evening."

"Why?"

"I've something to show you."

"Give me a hint."

"It's something rather shapely, rather beautiful, or so I've been told. Something which has caused not a few men to—divest their clothes."

I winked.

After Harding left I tried to sit and write, but couldn't. I was disturbed by her confidence and troubled by the impending date. *She* would be suave and lovely. I would be nervous and poxed. Some rendezvous. Greta Garbo meets Andy Griffith. I left New House, walked narrow and twisty Beale Street for a mile, then turned right toward the causeway. The day was glistening and chilly and the sun sparkled the clear tidal creeks and the green reeds and the sand. Someone was standing just beyond the wooden arm of the first island gate. He was sunburned and wore a purple and red Hawaiian shirt and Bermudas. Tourist, I thought.

"Can I help you?" I asked, my speech only barely touched by Harding's accent.

He hesitated, dropped his eyes.

"Is there anything I could do?" I was enjoying this new role.

"Hey, I was just looking around here, ya know? Looking."

"Are you working here?" Stiffer jaw, some nice sinus.

"Who the hell are you?"

"I? Why, I am Cody—Beale. Cody Beale, yes. Now, what do you want?" Metamorphosis. Words fell Britishly behind my front teeth, nose and eyebrows raised, eyelids fell, superciliousness bloomed.

"This place yours, huh?"

"My family's, actually."

"Yeah, okay."

"If you give us a call we could have someone show you the island. We are a generous people. Otherwise, things are rather private here."

The tourist shrugged, jumped into his car and departed.

I howled. How marvelous, wonderful. Arrogance and pettiness and disdain. For one glittering second I was a snob. Aloud, I practiced my "rather," a word the rich used often. "Raa . . . raa . . . raaatthur."

"Why didn't you let that guy through?" Standing at the edge of the woods, a workman was stripped to his horseshoe belt buckle and jeans. He held an ax upon his shoulder.

"Oh, hello. I don't know. Just messing with him, I guess."

"I've worked here three summers. I've never sent anybody off the island."

Acting unbothered, I waved him away. A blush stung my face. I was just joking. I did it for a laugh. Who would want to be a snob?

I managed to write until the afternoon and finished the first two scenes of the script. I was stacking my pens and yellow legal pads when Doug entered the living room. He wore a brown Brooks Brothers suit, black tie. His black hair was sleek with comb streaks and water. Blustery skin and blue eyes made him shine. Marlow followed, wearing a dour purple suit, carrying a bottle of champagne. They looked strict and formal, but their eyes were red and the ashy smell of marijuana spread from their mouths. I noticed a small bulge, a bump in the lower coat pockets of each.

"We've made some decisions," Doug said. "Marlow and I. It's important. You got a minute?"

We sat around the picnic table in the warm writing room. In crisp suits, my friends looked like bankers. Outside, the sea was blowing blue and white waves. The yard's green brambles shook and leaned toward the house.

Doug pulled his white cuffs. When they appeared one button was missing, the other half-cracked. Doug meshed his red fingers. "I've decided to build a fishing fleet."

I laughed.

Doug touched the perfect, dove-wing handkerchief in his upper coat pocket. He did not laugh. "Chip has an old lobster boat. The *Sasha.* He said he'd let me use it, but I told him no way. I'm going to rent the boat, businesslike. I'll buy my own pots from a fisherman I know. They're used, but good. I plan to start fishing for lobster next week. This is just the first step, of course."

Solemnly, Marlow set the champagne bottle on the table. He popped the cork, extricated a linty flute glass from his right pocket. Doug did the same. They looked at each other and laughed.

I felt relieved.

"What do you think, Cody?" Doug asked. "I'll make a fortune, huh? I'll outfish all these Ricans around here. But it'll be mucho work."

"Will you help us?" Marlow asked.

"I don't know anything about fishing," I said.

"I need two good deckhands," Doug said.

I looked at the bubbling wine and the bubbling faces and grinned.

"Outside," Doug yelled. He threw open the glass door and dodged into the darkening yard.

"Why is it that every time Doug becomes excited he must run and sport like some kind of pony?" Marlow mused.

"Outside!" Doug yelled.

Green maple buds whistled in the wind and the evening star was shining and waves were breaking upon the beach.

"Now," Doug said. "We drink a toast to a new company. The Douglas Summers Fish Company."

"To fish," I shouted. We touched glasses, drank, threw the glasses into the sea. Suddenly our hair and clothes were swept by the wind and spray as we embraced one another, bumped heads together. A night storm, whose presence we had not seen, began to throw coarse rain.

The raindrops struck the house like corks, though the thunder was distant and tinny. I got some towels and we dried off and Doug and Marlow built a fire. Having set in a mass of supplies, I decided to fix supper. My favorite—chicken wings and rice. When I announced the menu there was mock vomiting, but I knew my guests would like the dish as long as they didn't see the chicken wings in the nude. To the unaccustomed eye, boiling chicken wings resemble babies' hands. In forty-five minutes the deed was done and we ate five pounds of the stuff.

Near the fireplace, I sat in my chair like a bloated mule. Marlow had retired to a bedroom, insisting upon his "post-prandial nap." Black hair damp and disheveled, bare feet rootish and red, Doug hunched above a plateful of small bones. His dress shirt was much too large for him. The front shirttail was tucked into his ancient belt, but the rear splayed to the back of his knees. Though the front panels were adequately pressed, the remainder of the shirt resembled a crushed paper ball.

"Nice ironing job," I said.

"Thanks," said Doug, missing my sarcasm. "I've started doing my own clothes. I felt crummy about using Dad's servants. I want to take care of myself. Do you know my father doesn't even know how to shine his shoes?"

Doug left the table, slapping his belly. Curiously, he lounged beside my stuffed chair and curled into a ball, like a fuzzy black cat.

"Can I tell you something?" he asked. He was drinking scotch. Dark stubble peeked from his jaw and chin. The cornflower-blue eyes judged me carefully, then blinked, just a little drunk. "If I can get my fishing business off the ground, making money and everything—then I can work a deal with my dad. See, if I can make my own way, then he'll leave me alone, I think. I don't want Wall Street. I hate banks and brokerage houses. I hate the city, you know? I just want to fish and live near the ocean and marry some little honey and have pretty babies. Dad wanted that once for his own life. You know my dad was a genius, Cody. Smart as hell. All he wanted to do was design airplanes. When he was my age he'd already drawn four or five. He sold the plans. Made some bucks, but then the family got to him. Uncle Mallory. They pushed him into Wall Street. For a while he was pretty good, even there. Then he just couldn't take all the pressure and he broke, went bonkers. So, Uncle Mallory put him in charge of marrying and burying for the family. He plans a marriage, arranges a funeral, brings out the little Summers beauties at debutante parties and that's it. That's his life, when what he really wanted was to build planes. I'm telling you, he was so sharp, Cody. Once he was. Once. Now he's just booze and arrangements. He doesn't even fly."

We sat side by side, listening as the last rain tapped the roof, watching the fire burn down. I did feel sorry for Doug, sorry for his father, but I was also envious. I envied Doug the burdens of the rich. How nice to struggle against wealth. How much fun to force yourself to shine your shoes, wash your own clothes and live in a hovel. Perhaps later you would travel the world, invade low societies and vulgar classes, have tragic affairs and seedy trysts, knowing as Doug now knew, as perhaps all of the rich knew, knowing that if you made any serious mistake or placed yourself in any actual danger, a battalion of lawyers and butlers and ruby-jowled uncles would rush out to save you and bring you home to some blue-lawned Connecticut palace where nothing in the world would dare disturb your long and tasteful convalescence.

Head against my chair, knees fallen together, Doug snored. I looked at my watch. Just after six. I knew Harding was waiting.

The storm had chilled the evening air. I was walking down Beale Street. Far lightning lit the woods and the green leaves glimmered above branches and rocks and black ferns. Evening woods after a storm. Every bough and seedling and moss thick with rain, heavy in lingering electricity.

Light filled two windows on Harding's second floor; the rest of Stone House was black. Successively I knocked on the kitchen door, a side door, the front door. No answer. I glared at the lighted window and half turned to go when I saw a shadow.

Against the pulled shade and the light, the shadow seemed a perfect silhouette: neck and shoulders and breasts neatly sketched, as if in pen and ink. Watching, I slowly perceived that Harding was naked. She appeared and disappeared, stopping now and again before the window. At first I was enchanted, but as I focused more acutely on the shadow, it began to seem too thin and willowy. Southern gothic crept into my mind. Maybe this was not Harding at all. I observed the form carefully. The neck seemed too swannish, the shoulders too broad and the breasts too low. God, maybe this was Harding's mutant sister. Beautiful and beguiling, but horribly inbred and possessing the mind of a grub. I decided to slip into the house.

Black as a Dutch oven inside. I waited, heard the floor overhead pop and creak. Gradually I could see the staircase. Upper light illuminated the steps. I climbed quietly. The hallway: bright cedar floors and plaster walls. I wondered where Cleveland's telegraph operator had sat. A sound cracked from a room to my left and I ducked beside a tall highboy.

It was Harding. No milky mutant. Just Harding wearing a pink velour robe, her hair wet and combed straight back like a man's. She entered a small room and half closed the door. I was relieved, then angry. Why hadn't she come downstairs? She must have heard the pounding. Playing games, huh? Promenading before the lighted shade, knowing she was casting that gorgeous shadow, watching me as I watched her. She deserved what I was going to do. She deserved it completely. I pulled off my shoes, set them down, eased forward.

13

Silently, I entered the small room, steamy air. The center of the room held a circular red curtain which went from floor to ceiling. Within this red tent, water poured and splashed. Quickly, I practiced my most horrifying face—contorted mouth, protruding tongue, and then the master stroke I learned at recess in the seventh grade—I turned my eyelids inside out, my sockets now revealing only pink flesh. Half blind, I reached, ripped open the curtains and yelled, "Booooo!"

Nothing there but the deep and enormous tub, water plunging from the spigot. I shut my mouth, pulled down my eyelids, then swiveled around. Empty room. I slumped on the tub. I was leering toward another door, which led into a dark room, when something grabbed my hair, jerked and I sprawled backward.

Soaked, I rose, belly deep in water.

Harding wore a bathing suit and she was laughing.

"I knew you were there," I said.

She screamed.

"I did."

She laughed harder, then I started. We laughed until our faces hurt and I kissed her once and then a second time and this kiss was long and luxurious.

When I broke for air I wasn't sure what to do so I nodded at the tub. "What are you doing here, training for the Olympics?"

"This tub is what I invited you to see. It was especially built for Grover Cleveland. He used to vacation here. They say he weighed three hundred pounds."

I tried to act surprised, then looked away. When I glanced back at Harding, she was closer.

"Did you really think I believed your maudlin story about worms?"

"Worms?"

"Red bugs. You said your red bugs were an infestation of ringworm."

"I just wanted you to feel sorry for me."

"I felt sorry for your insecurity." Her auburn hair was bunned and lavish and damp. Her violet eyes did not blink.

"Me? Insecure?" I feigned a twitch.

"You don't feel that you fit here, do you?"

"Oh, this is serious, huh?"

"Terribly."

I left the tub and sloshed to the door.

"You needn't be so defensive. Scads of people want to belong to Black Island."

"You did say *scabs* of people didn't you?"

Walking down Beale Street, I shivered. I knew Harding was going to act superior. From the first day, I had sensed her aloofness. She was the worst kind of woman a fella could meet. She was a cold beauty.

I guess I felt the light. Something on my back. Then I saw my shadow begin to stretch and grow. Stepping around a curve, I turned. Beneath a streetlamp I saw the car, a beautiful Jag. Yellow hood and low roof and sloping trunk above three-inch white walls.

I stuck my hands into my cold pockets and kept sloshing along. I had an idea who it was.

The Jag was following, quiet as a yellow cloud.

"I will not be a victim of your feigned, artistic snit," Harding shouted.

I quickened my pace.

"Oh, I see it clearly now. The writer who is in the world, but not of the world."

I heard the Jag speed up.

"You are not Scott Fitzgerald."

"Oh, boy."

"Did you hear me?"

"How would you know how good I am?"

"I've read your manuscript."

I stopped. The car pulled beside me.

Harding was craning out of the ceramic yellow Jag, raised blood burning beneath her rouge, blue eyes tough and teeth bared.

"Lesly Combers," she said.

"So?"

"He's a family friend. I read your book at his office last week. I like it. He likes it. You're talented, I suppose."

She was angry; I was angry. We glared at one another.

"You got a cigarette?" I asked.

Harding opened her leather purse and handed me the pack. I lit a cigarette and put my back to the car and looked at a tidal creek which made a black pond in the dark night woods.

"Why are we fighting?" I asked.

"Because you are a twit."

I puffed the cigarette, then tossed it, came around and sat in the car. The interior warmed and held her scent—fresh hair and perfume and sharp cigarette breath.

We sat, said nothing, until Harding finally spoke.

"I write poetry, you know."

"Uh-huh."

"But I don't care about it really."

"What do you care about?"

"You know you should be quite excited," Harding said. "Combers is a discerning critic. He's had an agency in New York for forty years."

"I've never met him."

"Your agent?"

"Never could afford the plane ticket."

Harding looked at her watch, threw the gear into reverse and screeched backward. "We can just make it."

"What?"

"Cedar Point shuttle. We're off to meet Lesly Combers."

"Wait a minute, I can't do that."

"Why? Do you have a date with the maid?"

"I don't have any—dry clothes, any money, any . . ."

"Spontaneity. But mine will suffice."

She went by New House, put me in blue jeans and a blue blazer, called Combers.

In forty-five minutes we were airborne.

At 425 East Fifty-first Street, Harding stopped the cab. She brushed her hair, fingered rouge upon her dramatic, sharp cheeks and dotted her lashes with mascara. She was striking.

In the elevator she said, "You nervous?"

"Naw, I do this kind of thing all the time."

"You know, you're rather handsome."

I looked down at my faded Levi jeans.

"I think I'm nervous."

When Harding pushed the buzzer a tall, older man answered the door. They quickly embraced.

"Lesly Combers, this is Cody Walker."

Hair silver as a December moon, eyes like topaz, regally thin in tweeds and a pumice wool shawl about his neck, Lesly Combers gripped my hand.

"Young man, your novel is smashing."

I nearly looked behind me to see who he was talking to. I was so flustered I stuttered, "Congratulations."

Combers introduced his associate, Charles Whitman. "Let me tell you about Charles before he hyperbolizes himself. He acted once with Olivier, twice with Orson Welles and in neither case had a speaking part. He has written seven books. Three serious, three semiserious and one successful—a dictionary of crossword puzzles. He's an unproduced playwright, unpublished poet and an unholy critic who once said in this very office to Hart Crane—'Harty, you got a way with words.' "

Charles Whitman rose from a slag pile of manuscripts that sat on his desk. He was six three and theatrically handsome. A red face and brown waved hair and portmanteau stomach. He wore a suede vest and suede tie, yellow shirt, herringbone tweed trousers and gold pocket watch.

"Would you like a drink, Cody?" Whitman asked.

"Oh, you must," Combers said, sipping a dusk scotch neat.

Harding accompanied them to a small tile kitchen. A rusted Kenmore refrigerator sat there. A dingy sink held liquor bottles.

I waited in the front room. I had never really felt like a writer. I still did not. From scores of small pictures hanging on the walls people stared at me who, I assumed, did feel like writers. Boston Bull eyes, de Gaulle noses, hollow cheeks, no smiles—they looked like postoperative cancer patients.

The room held two cruiser-size desks. Each was stacked ten deep in manuscripts. On a table a typewriter presented the draft of a letter. The stationery head was designed with a blue brownstone and trees and a magic line—Telegraph Comberlitt Murray Hill-4296. An abused hutch cradled two or three new books whose covers gleamed like painted ice.

While they were making the drinks I read the letter in the typewriter.

> Dear Winslow Bosk:
>
> While your book, *The Iguana Maiden*, is entertaining in the sense of high comedy, we don't feel it's quite right for us. The novel is, after all, a story. We

Here the letter stopped, as did my breath. Did I have a story?

Whitman, Combers and I drank Johnny Walker Silver Label. Harding sipped soda and traded some island gossip with Combers. We were standing and the scotch lit our nerves and rose red in our cheeks, and then Harding slipped her warm hand into my own and leaned her lovely length against me.

Combers finished his scotch. He tied a red silk scarf about his neck. He grabbed a carved ivory cane and a topcoat. "Cody, how about supper at Elaine's?"

I pointed at my clothes. "If it's a nice place, I don't think they'll let me in."

"Nonsense," said Combers. "You're an artist. They will adore your arrogance."

14

When we entered Elaine's a young girl in dawn-blue leotards approached me. "Could I have your autograph, please?"

"I'm nobody," I said.

"Nobody's don't come here," she snapped. "Are you going to sign this or not?"

I signed and she worked Harding and the crowd behind. New York, I thought. You could find a girl like her only in New York.

Elaine's was cigarette smoke and wine breath, the air a soft, lucent tincture as if a fabric, a gauze. I had never seen so many square jaws in my life. Jackets of blue and gray, French cuts in wool and flannel or silk and cotton, narrow lapels, cuffless pockets. Shimmering blue and red silk shirts. Pink cotton trousers polished and tight as new bare skin. Silk ties thin as a silver butter knife and socks which held the luster of metallic night. The shoes were leather and canvas and snake skin and other beaded skins that I had never seen.

The women orbited the men. Willow bodies loosely hanging upon a man's arm or dramatically embracing him from behind, her cigarette raised upon his chest, her chin pouting upon his shoulder. The women seemed to be waiting for the movies, a part, a role. Here a beauty stood looking serious and intellectual, her lips perfect symmetry, hair blown to fine brass, eyes stratospheric blue, her tweed jacket having two onyx buttons, a large square breast pocket, the skirt gray wool slashed in red pockets.

We sat down at a small table. Quickly ordered. Around us

the atmosphere was noisy, excited, hot in gossip and contracts and offers. Whitman and Combers were arguing. Harding squeezed my hand. She had eyes for me and I for her. I glanced at Lesly Combers. He didn't seem quite right. He was pale. Only his red scarf colored his face. He gripped his ivory cane, whose silver head was carved in the shape of a small book. Was he trembling?

Whitman tapped my hand. "I think Ava Gardner would be a lovely choice for the mother figure."

"Ava Gardner?" I asked.

"In *Tiger River*—oh it would make a marvelous film. It's a theatrical story, really. And we need a theatrical lead."

"Oh, Ava Gardner has never set a toe on the stage," Combers said.

"Pardon?" said Whitman.

"Ava Gardner is not theatrical. She's film."

"I believe she did play *Night of the Iguana* at the Morosco in '56."

"She did not."

"Lesly, she is a Southerner and heaven knows a booze hound and she would be just perfect."

Supper arrived. Lamb chops in Béarnaise and a green salad. Dessert was fresh peaches and whipped cream.

Supper had ended the argument, but when I looked at Lesly Combers I was startled. The bright silk handkerchief had fallen loosely atop his tie. His naked neck was transparent as wax; spider veins wove through the skin. Though his silver hair still shone, his face was white, pocked. A terrible shaking had taken him. He used two hands to get his coffee cup to his mouth.

Harding was studying Lesly carefully. Her eyes registered his abrupt infirmity. She touched Combers' arm. "We should go."

After making sure that Lesly Combers would be taken home to bed, we left him standing with Whitman at the entrance to Elaine's. He was bent, broken. One eye had pulled to the left, the other was unfocused. His bare silver head had dropped to his chest, where the youthful red handkerchief lay. The palsy was vibrating his shoulders now. An old and classy agent standing outside the party of Elaine's, tweeds and silver-handled ivory cane and red handkerchief losing light and distinction in the darkness.

At the Naval Air Station we caught the last shuttle to Cedar Point. The heater was not working in the old plane. The pilot gave Harding a worn afghan. We looped around the electric galaxy of New York City, then climbed the coast toward Massachusetts. I held Harding close beneath the cover. Out the rattling window of the old plane the moon was shining like the polished belly of a silver spoon.

"You warm?" Harding asked.

"Yea."

"Poor old Lesly. Poor old darling."

"What happened to him?"

"Diabetes and alcohol."

"I like him."

"Yes."

Harding tucked her head beneath my chin. I felt her breath. She settled a hand on my stomach.

The plane bobbed and shuddered through the night as I watched white bottom sand shine through the sea. A tail wind pushed the plane. I had my arm around Harding's slim waist, felt her breast against me. I wanted to kiss her, but felt that I should not. The plane bumped along as I slipped to light sleep.

I awoke with a little heart jump. Harding was still asleep. I reached down and kissed her then. At first there was no response and then I felt her warm mouth open. The kiss was sweet. It was actually sweet. Different from Lisa's, more gentle. I did not know a kiss could taste. She pulled the warm afghan around us again and retucked herself into me. Her hair seemed to catch starlight beneath my face. We lay close to the window and our breathing made white wreaths on the cold pane.

I tried to kiss Harding good night at the door to Stone House, but she pulled me inside and offered a cup of coffee.

We talked for two hours. She told me about her family, who lived in San Francisco. Her father ran Mallory Beale's West Coast newspapers. The Wicks, Hearsts and Patricks were considered "the fabulous three" in Nob Hill society. She said she hated the obligations, the pressure, the endless affairs, endless booze and pills and suicides. She said that when she was fifteen her mother contracted a kidney disease. Six months later, when the hospital called to say that her mother was deteriorating, her father wouldn't come, so she went and held her mother until she died.

To my amazement, Harding began to cry. I hugged and held her for a while, then went to the kitchen and scrambled some eggs. At three in the morning, over early breakfast, I recited my own family history: growing up in the South, my father's business dealings with Mallory Beale (I omitted any sense of mystery), my parents' death.

"So, you're alone?" Harding asked.

"All by my lonesome."

"No family at all?"

"None that I know of."

"How long will you stay on the island?"

"I'm not sure." I paused. "I like it here."

"Stay then."

"Right."

She sipped her coffee. Suddenly her violet eyes lit.

"You know what you need?"

"A shower?"

"A patron."

"A patron."

"Actually a patroness. Someone to look after you. Open the right family doors. Why you'd be marvelous here."

"It's like you once said—I don't fit."

"But you could fit. You really could. First, we must keep you here the rest of the summer—July through September. You must meet the right family members, and—yes! You must attend some parties. They're very important."

"I don't know."

"Well, I do. And after the summer, there's the winter season. The Caymans, the Keys, Tortuga."

"Of course. I'll just fly my jet right down."

"My family has a compound in the Cayman's. Three houses. Lots of room. How marvelous it could all be. How truly marvelous."

Harding walked me to the door. She said she would begin working on some invitations. In the meantime, she instructed me to mingle with various family members, particularly Townsend and Bosey Beale.

I went home, took a shower and faced the fact: I really did want to stay. I wanted a family, a sense of security, a place to belong. Maybe it could be here.

Around eight o'clock in the morning Doug came over. He asked me to breakfast, said that he had a business proposition. We drove the Bugati to a deli in Cedar Point.

15

The Yankee deli was exotic and marvelous. The glass cases held white bagels and fresh blueberry tarts, orange cheesecakes, terraces of honeyed baclava, stacks of kaloshka (round pastries whose centers were filled with cherries or apples, blackberries or dates). Here lay cassata, a sponge cake whose thin layers alternated candied lemon peel and ricotta cheese and grated chocolate, all this frosted in whipped cream, and below the cassata was cannoli, and below these crisp tubes sat hamentaschen, looking like small three-cornered hats, the corners seeping puréed dates.

And what did I get? Ham and eggs. Ah, imagination.

We sat down at a Formica counter and ate. Doug produced a pen and pad and began figuring how much money he needed to rig the *Sasha.* He asked if he could borrow two hundred dollars. (Chip had paid me five hundred dollars down on the script.) I said sure, but thought how silly because I suspected that Doug had at least one trust fund. He insisted that we compose a contract and that I be paid 9 percent interest. When I protested against the contract and interest, Doug blushed, saying that we had to act responsibly. As I quietly agreed, she opened the door to the deli.

Aunt Bosey. White hair and amber eyes and a red hook nose. A thought flashed. If I was going to follow Harding's instructions, this was a good time to begin.

I stopped her at the bagel case.

"Mrs. Beale, I'm Cody Walker."

She blinked. "Miss Beale."

Nervously, Doug interceded. "Hi, Aunt Bosey. Uh—Cody's . . . visiting the island this summer. He's . . ."

"I'm working on a project with Chip," I said.

"Who?"

"Chip."

"Doesn't ring a bell."

"Bertie," Doug said.

"Oh, Bertie," Bosey said. "Why do you call him Chip?"

"He introduced himself as Chip."

"How absurd. We've called him Bertie since gestation. What's your project?"

"We're making a movie."

"My God, how I hate movies."

Whoops, I thought.

"In general, I dislike movies. In particular, I dislike Bertie's movies. Excuse me."

Bosey summoned a waitress, requested two unfilled, unsugared, unglazed doughnuts and left the deli.

I shook for thirty minutes.

Bleakness and gloom. For two hours after Doug dropped me off I sat around and worried about my botched introduction to Bosey. I went to see Harding, but couldn't find her. I stopped by Chip's.

He greeted me cordially and offered Morning Thunder tea. He looked remarkably groomed and conservative. The black beard was trimmed and the long red hair smelled clean and herbal. He wore gray slacks and a starched blue work shirt. Needing some reassurance, I confessed my ruined introduction to his aunt. He said that Bosey seemed tough and belligerent but that actually she was a real pal. She had always liked and supported him and he was sure she would feel the same way about me. I accepted his comfort.

"As a matter of fact, I'm going to approach Bosey very soon now."

"For what?"

"Her advice. I've decided I want to run the island. It will be my first step toward renewing the family. We've had a manager for thirty years, but I'm kicking him out. I need to personally supervise the work crews and the servants. Personally manage everything here—docks, forests, houses, shops, even the clam beds and beaches. You see, Cody, Black Island is really the heart of the family."

Chip stared out the picture window toward the strangled lily pond. When he looked back at me his big teeth were gleaming. "To start things right, I'm going to have a party. There are all these other gatherings—the Chowder Party, the Gin Party, all that meaningless crap. I'm putting together the first Worker's Party. We'll invite all the guys who cut the grass and paint the buildings and fix the broken pipes and the busted boat propellers. It'll be the first time ever. What do you think?"

I thought—great, the Worker's Party. Roustabouts and rummies and losers. "My kind of folks," I said.

Naturally, Chip wanted me to fry chicken. So, a day later I collected Doug and Marlow and Lisa. Harding had gone to Boston. We went to Chip's, where six boxes held thirty blue-skinned pullets. I set Doug to mixing eggs while Marlow and Lisa floured. After the chickens had been covered in batter, I dunked the separate pieces into boiling Crisco and fried the buggers until cherry brown.

At six o'clock in the evening Doug deposited ten shining beer kegs in Chip's front yard, along with four gallons of scotch, two gallons of rye and fifteen gallons of red and white wine. Finally the workmen arrived, not piecemeal, but in a flood. They brought wives and children and dogs and in several cases even bent mothers and gnarled grandmothers. Some wore polyester suits and ties, others sports jackets and pressed jeans. Everyone's face seemed pink and scrubbed, although the crevices of their hands and fingernails still held black grease. They were drunk within the first hour, the younger ones vomiting in three. They devoured the chicken, guzzled the beer and booze and never even sipped the wine, preferring to smuggle gallons of it into their vans and trucks.

Though a number of family members had been invited, only

two appeared—Townsend and Bosey. The latter brusquely complimented me on the chicken. The two women joked and told stories and drank and addressed the workmen they knew by the wrong names. Three hours after the all-night party had started, it was finished. Townsend and Bosey left arm-in-arm talking about Townsend's fishing trip. The workmen exited as they had arrived, in a roiling mass. Doug and Marlow and Lisa sat amid the chicken bones and clam shells and red beer cups. Exhausted, they passed a joint.

Lisa filled her lungs with marijuana, then stepped toward me. She wore a white maid's uniform. Flour dusted her short black hair.

"Sorry I haven't seen you lately," she said.

I wondered if she knew I had been to the city with Harding.

"I've been working hard. Fourteen, fifteen hours a day. Lots of new people showing up."

"Seen any more of the Irish Baron?"

The big black eyes squinted, then relaxed. Her chipped front tooth shone. "Miss me?"

"Kinda."

"Kinda?"

"Kinda a lot."

"I'd come see you tonight, but I'm beat. All this week they had me scrubbing floors. Next week too. It doesn't bother me though."

"It would bother me."

"Not if you know what I know."

"What do you know?"

"One day I'm gonna own those floors. Own them. You believe me?"

"Dare I doubt?"

She kissed me. "I'll see you in a few days—if you're lucky."

Lisa took a couple of steps, turned, hiked her dress to expose a thigh, then giggled.

I had not seen Chip in an hour. I looked behind his bungalow and found him sitting before a lit Coleman lantern. Wearing an Indian wedding shirt whose front panel was decorated in hedgehog bones, hair red and down upon his shoulders, he sat beside his lily pond. He heard my approach and pulled a large pair of scissors from his shirt and held them over his head. They flashed lantern light.

"I've made a decision."

"Hey, calm down," I said, raising a hand toward the scissors.

"It was a bust, man. Like everything I do on this island. The party was a bust."

"The workmen had a ball."

"My family, though. I invited twenty. Nobody showed up."

"Townsend and Bosey."

"So, I'm going to do it. Rather, you're going to do it, Cody." Chip thrust the scissors toward me. "Cut my hair."

"Are you kidding?"

"I can't have my hair anymore. My family hates it. Long hair indicates rebellion. If I'm going to take charge here, the hair must go."

I took the warm scissors. Chip turned his back and adjusted the Coleman. The light blazed.

When I was a kid and just beginning to consider the future, I developed a fear of ending up as a small-town, fish-faced barber, talking failed peach crops, redneck softball scores and the cancer which had started in Miss Polly's right earlobe and now was digesting her eye. I had left the South, entered the land of the rich and what had happened? Here I stood, left hand holding hair, right holding scissors, snip, snip, snipping. So when I heard my voice squawking and rasping, I was not surprised. "You know when they cut her open, they just shook their heads and sewed her right back up. Doctor told me her innards looked like a hurrah's nest."

"What?"

"Nothing, nothing."

I sheared a hunk to the right and chopped a tongue to the left. The red hair fell like a pelt. In a few minutes it was done.

Chip grabbed my hand and pulled me down. The hedgehog bones rattled. His gold eyes softened.

"Will you do me a favor?" he asked.

"I won't cut your beard."

"You've been seeing a maid. The one you brought to the party."

"Lisa."

"It won't work with the family. Just like my hair won't work. They can't handle relationships with servants. If you want things to go smoothly here"—Chip paused, discerned—"if you want to come aboard, then you must stop seeing her. Particularly if we make the movie. I know she's beautiful and maybe you're even in love, but you must let her go."

I was stunned, and felt the heat of the lantern touch my skin.

"I'll help you if I can. I know it hurts," Chip said.

"Let me think about it," I said and stepped away.

"Wait a minute, brother. You take this. I don't know, maybe it can help you in some way. Go ahead, it's yours."

I opened my hand and received a red scalp lock.

In New House I built a fire, drank a beer, opened another, sat before the fireplace and watched the flames flicker and shuttle. I liked Lisa. I liked her looks and quick enthusiasm and I liked her in bed. Chip Beale was a fool if he thought I was going to stop seeing her. Sure, I'd like to stay on the island. I would enjoy a closer relationship with the Beales—but I would not give up a friend for the sake of society. Never.

I endured a desultory, water-drinking booze-sleep. Up for aspirin and down for puzzle dreams and up for the bathroom and down again. Finally, at eleven, I rose for good and left the house.

Beale Street held blue rain puddles. Black-eyed susans sparkled at the edge. Green ferns shimmered. Cardinals and yellow-winged finches sang and shook dew from the island pines.

In the clear, harsh, pebbly light, I saw Doug and Marlow walking my way. They wore red hunting jackets etched in a black grid pattern and big, mud-covered boots. They were drinking coffee and had not combed their hair.

"Up mighty early," I announced.

Marlow pointed a thumb behind him. "Doug's truck just died. We were coming to get you."

"I buy my lobster pots today," Doug said. "Want to come along?"

"The Bugati won't hold the three of us," I said.

"I've just been looking for the chance," Marlow said and mischievously rubbed his hands together.

"What chance?" I asked.

"I adore Harding's new Jag. I just adore it. We'll ring her up. Ask her along."

"What about my two hundred pots?" Doug asked.

"We'll rent a U-Haul trailer," Marlow said. "I have yearned for years to do that."

We laughed and trudged back toward New House to call Harding.

16

Marlow was driving the 1973 yellow Jag coupe. Doug sat beside him and Harding and I had the backseat. She wore khaki pants and a pink shirt and her leather deck shoes. Every stitch was starched and precise. She was her old self, rather cool, rather distant.

"Hey, Cody, look at Marlow's slick wheel moves," Doug said.

Marlow sat perfectly perpendicular in the leather seat, his hands held the steering wheel at ten and four, a cigarette artistically gripped between index and middle fingers.

"What's wrong with my driving?" Marlow asked.

"Just use one hand," I said.

"Why?"

"Cool," I said.

"Right," Doug said, sidling closer to Marlow. "You got to be cool. You got to act like 'Yeah, I'm driving a beautiful Jaguar but it doesn't really mean anything to me 'cause I have twelve more where this came from.' "

"How garish," Marlow said, wrinkling his long and handsome nose.

"You want to be an American or not?" Doug asked.

"I suppose," said Marlow.

Doug lunged for the wheel and forced Marlow under him and into the passenger's seat.

"Doug, for God's sake!" Marlow screamed.

Doug wrestled the wheel, slowed the car. "Look at me now! Watch!" The American driver swiped Marlow's Pall Mall and let the cigarette dangle from his own pouting lips, slumping toward the wheel, left arm hanging languidly from the window.

"Doug, move out of my seat," Marlow yelled.

"You gonna drive American?"

"Absolutely not!"

Doug punched the accelerator. The Jag squealed and swerved. Harding laughed a scream.

"All right!" Marlow hollered.

Doug plunged back, quickly exchanging seats again. He turned to Harding and clucked, "Hey, babe, you want to make a little whoopee?"

I leaned forward. "You know what we ought to do, Doug?" I looked over my shoulder at Harding. "We ought to teach Marlow how to drag."

"You're a good man, Cody Walker," Doug said.

"I am not James Dean," said Marlow.

"Loosen up," Doug said.

"I am miraculously loose," Marlow said. "I was first in my class at squash."

"Look, Marlow, you've got to learn the drag signal," Doug said.

"Oh, well, all right. What is it?"

Harding presented two fingers in the front seat.

"Isn't that rather Churchillian?" Marlow asked.

Doug said, "Now you pull up at a light, sneak your fingers to the window ledge and present a V. Nothing dramatic. Then you turn your head a hair toward the other car. Don't blink your eyes. Keep your face frozen. Think ice."

Marlow's face turned white as a glacier when the jacked-up '59 Chevy coupe pulled beside us at the stoplight, just beyond the causeway. The Chevy's hood was red. The body was blue. The rear fins had been spray-painted white. On the passenger side the door was completely covered in tiny American flag decals. The closest face turned and gaped. It was yellow and unshaven.

"Oh Lord," I said. "It's the Klan."

Marlow suddenly lost his American cool. He withdrew his sprawling arm, stared straight into the windshield.

The two occupants of the Chevrolet wore green hard hats, chopper sideburns and muddy T-shirts. They chewed gum as if it were barbed wire and leered our way.

"Flash the sign," Doug whispered.

Marlow's face was dead nerves.

Doug leaned toward the Chevrolet and gave a Summers smile.

The two bristly faces lost their grins.

"Give them the sign," Doug urged.

"The hell with that," I whispered. "Just ask them to drag."

Carefully, eyes closed, our driver sneaked half an elbow over the window ledge. He opened his eyes, turned half a degree and said, "Yo . . . you like to drag?"

"Fag?" The yellow face rushed red. "You calling somebody a fag?"

"Drag," Marlow stuttered. "Drag."

"What did you call me?"

"Race. Want to—"

"Did you call me a faggot?"

Just as the hard hat bolted from his door, Doug reached over and hit the pedal and we squealed away.

The Chevrolet leapt and sprung, grated, jerked, stopped dead. The two men jumped from the car. One hurled his green hard hat. The other lit a cigarette.

We hung out the Jag windows and screamed insults and laughed. High as the new, day moon, we sailed through Barnstown and Bath, belting out cheers when Doug produced a smuggled bottle of Pinot Blanc which we drank from the cool glass neck, except for Marlow, who produced a glittering compact that expanded and louvered to form a crystal cup. We pummeled him and teased him until all had one crystal drink.

Marlow pointed ahead to the golden arches. "Here."

"No," Doug said, his black hair blowing about his face. "We've got to find a trailer for the lobster pots."

"I must have a McDonald's!" Marlow said.

"Let's wait," said Harding. The wind had teared her violet eyes and a small scar in the dimple of her chin reddened.

"Starving. Ravenous. Must have McDonald's," Marlow declared, and we zoomed into the lot.

The golden arches held no customers. Inside, the place was yellow and white, clean as a church, the plastic daisies ebullient, the Dacron ferns tall and splendid and green. A blond girl behind the counter telegraphed Teutonic eyes.

"Look at those teeth," Marlow whispered. "Have you ever seen such teeth?"

"Mighty white," I said.

"The poor louts at Wendy's or Burger King never have these beautiful features. Look at that lass. Butter-blond hair and blue eyes and Colgate teeth. I tell you, McDonald's has bred the master race. They are the S.S. of the burger business."

Marlow swept at his hair, pointed both hands at the big order board. "I would like one of each."

The scrubbed-cheek girl in the pink uniform and blue hat and yellow pigtails blinked. "Sir?"

Doug slapped Marlow on the back. "Come on, buddy. Let's just get a couple burgers, fries and shakes."

"I want one of every sandwich. Cheeseburger, fish, chicken filet, Big Mac and a Coke, *s'il vous plait.*"

Blue eyes fluttered under a wisp of mascara. "It might take a while. There's just me and one helper."

In twenty minutes Marlow sat before a steaming pile of sandwiches; he bit into a fish sandwich, then a chicken filet and finally a Big Mac. His cheeks ballooned red. He chewed, whistled air through his nose and closed his eyes. We squinted painfully as the mouthful slid down his neck like a goat down a python. When the load reached his stomach he paused and said, "In a thousand years America shall be remembered for only two things—McDonald's and rock 'n' roll."

I heard the car before I saw it. The others had their backs to the front. I nudged Marlow when the two men started walking toward the door.

17

Apparently, they had seen the Jag. One man was tall, the other short. The tall man weighed two hundred pounds. He had a dark face and square chin, brown eyes and wide eyebrows that trailed off into dusky temples. His brown hair was coarse and shoulder-long and held a young man's part through the middle scalp. He wore a muddy T-shirt, yellow salt crescents at his armpits, green army fatigues and blue thongs, which exposed hairy feet.

When the tall man came through the door he walked straight to us. Smiling, he offered his hand to Doug.

"Valance is my name."

Doug nervously rose and shook the man's hand.

"You the man who called my buddy a fag, right?" Valance looked at Marlow.

"You misunderstood," Marlow said in an indignant tenor.

Harding sat straight as a hat pin, hands clamped on the table before her. Doug looked pale and I got the twitches myself.

Valance surveyed the food before Marlow. "Eat like a damn bird, don't you?"

"What's the problem?" I asked.

"Hey, where you from?"

"South Carolina."

"Hell, ain't that something. I'm from Georgia—Savannah."

Valance had an odor about him, sour and spoiled and dangerous, like the smell of an August swamp. His companion loitered and shifted outside the building. He was short and bald and muscadine black hair framed his skull. Shirtless, his bare chest was burned red, so that a piece of flesh protruding from his belly button looked like a small tongue. He wore paint-smeared Bermuda shorts and cowboy boots decorated in metal stars.

"Yeah, well, we got to be going," I said, rising from the table.

Lazily, Valance pulled a .38 from his trousers. He set the pistol on the table. "You see, I been studying cancer and such things as that. I been trying to figure out what makes good things go bad and I declare, but it's a mystery to me."

"What do you want?" I asked.

"What do I want? Well, first of all I want the skinny man here to apologize. You can just wave to ole Froggy out there, he'll understand."

Marlow did not move.

"Go ahead, Marlow," I said.

"But, Cody, that's not what I said." He looked nervously from me to the gun.

"Apologize," I whispered. "Do it."

Marlow looked at me again and then at Valance. Finally, he turned and nodded at Froggy.

" 'Preciate it. I surely do. Now you can answer a question," Valance said. He focused on me again. "How does badness get started?"

"Oh, God," Harding said.

"Prob'ly," Valance answered her. "But it's something I gotta spend my life thinking about." He looked at me. "You know, you just don't seem to belong with these rich Yankee kids. What you doing here?"

"Some business," I said.

"Now, bisness I understand. Why, I'm in bisness myself. Selling a little dope. Grass mostly." Valance stepped to Doug. "A little coke, too, though it pains me to think of them deviated septums. Why don't you lay off staring at my pistola, sonny? You making me antsy."

"Is everything all right here?" The counter girl saw the pistol. She squealed and stiffened.

Valance retrieved the gun and cut her open with his eyes. He glanced outside. "Well, I see Froggy's got the itches. Listen, the two of us are gonna be around, so if you folks need some smoke, just ride down main street after midnight. Likely as not we'll be there." He stuck the pistol into his trousers. He turned and spread his arms and looked at McDonald's. "You know, I was always partial to the blue-plate special. But every good thing passes, don't it?"

The two men walked slowly out to the Chevy and left.

We forgot about the lobster pots and Doug drove us back toward Black Island. I put my arm around Harding. I thought she was going to cry, but she only trembled.

"You Americans have a dreadful history of such characters," Marlow said.

"What do you mean?" said Doug.

"Those desperadoes."

"Those guys were jerks. I could have handled them."

"Could you, Doug?"

"They were punks."

"You are a violent people. Brutal. You've murdered all of your great men and I think the carnage will probably continue."

"Bullshit!"

"History."

"Listen, Marlow, those two guys were scumballs. Not real Americans. Scum. We don't have anything to do with them. We don't deal with them and we're not afraid of them, you understand?"

We raced back in that awful, invisible, stinging blister of silence which rises between friends when they have clashed over some point, a point which at the moment seemed so irresistibly moot.

As we bumped over the causeway and through the last island gate, a gray Oldsmobile appeared. We pulled over. The faded Olds 98 skimmed alongside. A window opened. Townsend Beale's head emerged. "Well, hello."

Doug immediately swiped at his hair, sat straight. "Hi, Aunt Towney."

"What a super car."

"Harding's."

Townsend craned from the Oldsmobile, which was scratched and dented and in need of paint. Her craggy face looked sleepy. "Is Cody there?"

"Yes, ma'am," I said, waving a hand.

"Cody, can you come to supper?"

"Really?" I said.

"Really? Well, yes. Really. Just some fish. Scrod. Do you like scrod?"

"Never had it."

"Harding, will he like scrod?"

"I'm sure he will," Harding said.

"Oh. Okay, well, supper tomorrow night, then. The rest of you will have to come out on *Ole Blue* or something. I can't have all of you tomorrow."

Townsend waved and drove away.

"Hey! Supper with Townsend Beale!" I yelled.

Marlow and Doug said nothing.

I turned and kissed Harding on the cheek.

In New House, Harding started bacon and eggs. (We hadn't eaten much at McDonald's.) I built a fire. Marlow took a shower and Doug grabbed a slicker and went for a walk on the beach.

"You don't seem to belong with these rich kids." Valance's words. They disturbed me. Was it that obvious? I tried to think about tomorrow: supper at the Beales'. I wondered if I would get to see Mallory. The old man. The one that I ultimately had to meet, confront. I felt that too—that I had to confront him, ask him about my father. There was an old set of encyclopedias in the bedroom across the hall from mine. I decided to research submarines. Surely Beale would still have a love for them. But would I see him? Was he well enough?

When Doug stomped through the front door he brought the slashing smell of the sea. He looked better; blown red by wind, his face seemed relaxed, though subdued. Harding called for breakfast. The table was ready: a red platter of eggs and bacon, brown mug of grape jelly and a yellow steaming teapot. These utensils lay on a round, blue tablecloth. In the fragile atmosphere we poured Russian tea into white cups and spread daubs of jelly on pumpernickel bread, chopped eggs and cut crackling bacon, sugared and salted and peppered and did everything we could not to look at one another or speak.

It was too much.

"Honk-a-donk, honk-a-donk, honnnkkk-a-donkkk," I was intoning—"Shall We Gather At the River."

Harding looked. "What are you doing?"

"Honkahonkahonkahonka Donk. Church organ," I said.

"You're absolutely crazy," Doug said.

"It's my song and I like it and I'm going to sing it through. . . . Honkadonk, honkadonk . . ."

Doug threw a napkin and Marlow hissed boo and the cold wave broke.

Breakfast-full and sleepy, we moved to the fire. Harding sat close beside me, neat and precise as a Sunday purse, her auburn hair free and vital, Izod blouse impeccably tucked into creased khakis and her eyes so blue and luminous that I could not bear to look at them.

Marlow hunched beside her, otter brown, stiff and square in summer whites, hair drying, loosening and falling over his forehead and knob cheeks. Doug sprawled before the hearth, the black slicker hood pulled about his head, the blue interior framing a face hawkish and sharp and mischievously boyish.

Their conversation centered on "high school" and past summer projects. Sometimes my new friends made me mad with their understatement. My high school was in the country. The teachers were old ladies who wore Sears Roebuck print dresses and creaky sandals, from which their callused little toes protruded, perpetually separated from other, hornier toes by corn pads and iodine stains. They were good-hearted, slow and oddly intelligent old women, dull witted as ruminating cows and always married to an ex-master sergeant or ex-carpenter or an ex-third-shift mill foreman who taught history and geography and coached.

St. Charles and St. George's seemed to be a bit different from Glenn Springs High. The teachers were male, young and Ph.D.'d. Thirty-five percent of the graduating class went to Harvard, forty percent to Yale and the rest went to work for daddy at G.E. On their summer projects St. Georgians went to Sri Lanka to photograph the migration of the gray whale while St. Charlesians packed off on an expedition to Afghanistan to collect volcanic rocks.

Here were our summer projects: shoveling hog shit for the new Methodist minister; shoveling cow pucks for the old Baptist minister; picking hairy peaches and wormy tomatoes and scratchy turnip greens. Digging and clawing and hammering and toting while the sun beat and the wind died and the red dirt didn't do nothing; and the most interesting conversations ran along these lines: "You know, Cody, ole Dewitt tells me there's a old nigger lady down in the flat who does it with a donkey and don't charge but a dollar to see it all."

18

After a nap which lasted into the shimmering sun of a lazy island afternoon, we each drifted off to be alone. I spent several hours researching submarines in the encyclopedia and read about the war in the Pacific. I wanted to impress Mallory Beale.

Late that evening Chip called to say that I should wear a tie and that he was going to be at dinner also. He didn't ask about the script. I was beginning to think he had forgotten it.

All night long I dreamed about Mallory Beale. He was enormous. Thirty or forty feet high. He loomed above the island trees, now and again disappearing into the fog. He watched and puzzled over Lisa and me as we played some game like tag. Then I saw Valance, shining like a star. Sparkling in the dark of Black Island. When he touched a bloody knife to the front door of New House, I opened my eyes. Dawn.

The whole day I had a sense of dread. Would I see Mallory Beale? And if I did, what would he reveal about Joe Walker? Now more than ever I could not understand why my father had left this society. Gloomily, I spent the afternoon working on the film script. I wrote a long scene about Billy impressing the king with a juggling trick. At five o'clock I stopped. Beyond the glass walls of my writing room the sea looked as still as the sky and the sun burned a red hole into the horizon and a dark blue rectangle, pure space drove the sun below the sea. All water, all air was suddenly pink and still and soft.

I drank an inch of Early Times bourbon, took a shower and shaved. The bourbon buzz eased my nerves. I acquired a little humor. I wasn't afraid to meet Mallory Beale. He puts his pants on the same way I do, buddy row, don't you know. There was no reason to get uptight about this. If Beale didn't like me I would just slide back home to the South and sell decreasing-term insurance.

In this brown bourbon cheer, I slipped into worn gray slacks and a blue blazer and a red tie. On the back of the front door I studied a map which located main paths leading to the major houses of the island.

The summer woods were hard green. Ferns trembled upon the forest floor and briar bushes sparkled yellow flowers and above the briars bloomed purple rhododendron. I passed resiny cedars and syrup-holed live oaks, and often separating these two stands a wild phalanx of mushrooms, gray and brown and violet. I climbed several hills whose bases were black rocks. The hill summits were crowned by short needle pines and brown needle drifts. In a sweet mint valley, a creek ran clear water and brown stones lay on the banks and within the creek, minnows dashed silver against the current. Then, in a small pond, I saw him—a big, green turtle. A marvelous turtle. A forty-pounder, the black shell edged in yellow squares, orange metallic feet wide as a shovel and the anvil head four inches across. He just sat on his rock, dull heart throbbing his throat, beak face staring at me, watching, as if to say "Here I am. Take me if you can."

I ran the next hills and jumped a rail fence and spun around in the woods, drunk on possibilities.

The house occupied a hilltop. It was a large, barnlike building. On the gabled roof perched several machines whose metallic arms were turning in the wind. The green paint of the second story was fading. White curtains blew through seven upper windows. A six-foot boxwood hedge surrounded the hilly yard, the young maples and elms. In the middle of the hedge stood a red wooden gate. The house seemed so simple, so much like any old beach house at Pawley's Island. I had thought Mallory Beale would live in a palace.

Harding walked into the yard. Her hair was bunned and she wore a gold cashmere dress with beaded shoulders.

When I drew close she frowned. "Cody, you look awful."

I set my hands on my hips and glared at her.

"Don't you have a decent suit?"

I spun around and headed back.

Harding grabbed my arm.

I jerked away, stopped. "Why the hell would you say something stupid like that? I'm nervous enough as it is and you tell me I look awful."

"Well, you do."

"Gee, thanks."

"Now look, if you're going to be accepted here, you must dress properly."

"Fine. Why don't you buy me a new wardrobe?"

Her face brightened. The small scar in her chin colored. "Why it's an absolutely splendid idea."

"What is?"

"A new wardrobe."

"No. Nope. No way. I can't let you do that."

"I'll pick you up tomorrow at 6:30 A.M. We're going to New York."

"Now listen . . ."

"No arguments." She took my arm. "We're late for dinner."

I caught her warm hands. "You really are my patron, aren't you?"

"You know—I am. I think I really am."

I followed Harding inside into a hall. To the left lay other rooms and straight ahead a small, exquisite staircase of maple wood. On the right wall spread a map. Japan held the center. Instinctively, I looked for the battleground between the *Spadefish* and *Shinyo.* Not one hint. Not a circle, not an arrow, not even a small red pin. Nothing but longitude and latitude and Japan hanging there like a dried, pressed organ.

I stepped through a dining room whose glass windows looked onto a screened porch and the harbor beyond. I could sense Mallory Beale. He was a presence, a vitality, an attraction as tingling and persuasive as a great summer storm that builds and gathers just beyond vision.

Harding had disappeared and I walked out onto the porch now: wrought-iron furniture and small wooden tables whose vases held sparkling pansies and jonquils. A bar at one end, indoor grill at the other, brick floor, faintly rusting screen and, near the grill, a perfect pyramid of oak kindling. Outside, a grass plateau and then a cliff of terraced flower boxes.

The earth of the garden was black. Red bricks separated the long terraces. Lavender pansies and marigolds and red tulips glistened in the evening. Below the flower garden stood oak saplings and then a rough line of cedars and pines, and then the harbor, silver and silent. Small sailboats bobbed at gray docks, and up-shore, in a stone berth, sat the sharp, powerful form of *Ole Blue.* She even looked blue in the reflection of the water. A sleek blue dream of American steel and wood. A force. A charge. With gun turrets, she could have been the *Arkansas.*

Harding stepped onto the porch. She looked so beautiful, fit here so perfectly, that I felt like the yardman.

"Ma'am, I got to have some gas for my mower so I can get on with my job."

"Does that mean you want a drink?" Harding asked, her hair raked back, her elegant body pressed against the cashmere dress.

"Scotch and soda," I said.

"Not bourbon?"

"Scotch and soda."

Behind the bar hung a picture of a dolphin in top hat and tails. Ice and booze clunked and clucked. I rolled the turquoise ring around my finger.

"Nervous?" she asked.

"Nope."

"He's stronger today."

"Gee, that's great," I said. "Sounds like Dr. Frankenstein talking about the monster. He's stroonnggerr today."

"One jigger?"

"Four or five."

Harding brought the drink over. Delicately, her fingers touched my hand. It helped, but the drink was what I needed —Chivas, white ice and soda.

"Just be yourself," Harding said.

"If I meet him, what do I call him?"

"Mallory."

"No way."

"What do you propose?"

"You got a back door?"

Harding glanced at the dining room. "Oh my. No flowers. I will never have American servants." She stepped from the porch and went down into the garden.

Alone, I swallowed a fist of scotch. To my left something bumped, then banged. A small door stood half open. Within, I could see a dim staircase. I heard a creak as someone descended.

I looked around. Where was everybody? I couldn't meet Mallory Beale alone.

Just as I was leaving the porch, a thin voice cried out, "Halp."

I heard a thrashing sound, then: "Halp, someone. Haaallppp!"

19

When I opened the door the face looked at me fiercely. "Oh. You. Well?"

It was Bosey. She had caught her dress on a nail in the wall.

Carefully, I released her.

On the porch, she turned. "Is it ruined?"

"What?"

"My skirt. Would you look?" Her heron-white hair was combed back from the tan face. She wore a long-sleeved pumice blouse, black skirt and olive pumps.

"What's the verdict?" she asked.

"Reprieve," I said.

"How marvelous," said Bosey and flicked her head, moving to the bar. She made herself a Campari and soda. "Mallory's not coming down," she said.

I felt my face plummet.

"You wanted to see him?"

"Yes."

"He's taking a nap. I don't know why. He looks smashing."

I was disappointed, utterly. It seemed as if I had been waiting all of my life to meet Mallory Beale.

Chip appeared, greeted each of us.

"Your father will not be dining," Bosey said. "He's resting."

"I have to see him," Chip said. "I might as well go now."

"Why don't you take Cody?" Bosey looked at me. "I think he would like to meet Mallory."

A dark room still as a cavern. Simple furniture: a walnut highboy, wicker reading chair, frayed chaise lounge. I stood at the door and did not enter the room. Mallory Beale was lying in bed.

In the dark the body seemed small and bony, completely and absolutely without power. Outside, the fog touched the window.

Chip leaned over and hugged the angular frame. "How've you been, Pop?"

Silence.

Chip pulled a chair beside the bed. "They painted *Ole Blue* last week. She looks good."

Chip's voice trembled. His tension caused my own stomach to draw.

"We could dry dock her now, Pop. It's a good time. There'd be no rust. She's just inefficient. Wasting too much petrol. It's one of my new ideas for the island. You remember we talked about all this."

The match splattered sudden light. Tortoise eyes and a mottled beak nose and bone chin. Then darkness.

"I got my eyes on a super Morgan. Forty-five footer. You could sail again, you know."

A sucking cigarette draw. The glow lit the hollow face, then faded.

Chip's voice lost strength, settled to a whisper. "It's just a thought, Pop. Just a thought."

Then: "Yeah . . ."

Relief. Communication.

"Y-e-a-h-h-h . . ." and the word drawn out like a line, drawling long and phlegmy and gurgling, preparing perhaps for the next word, but no, it was still this one. "Y-e-a-h-h-h . . ." the word spinning out, a train of olfactory vowels and sinus rasping, while the mouth blew smoke and the lungs exhaled little wheezes and the esophagus hissed mucus. "Y-e-a-h-h-h . . . she's a goddamn energy crisis in herself."

The response saved Chip—and me. The silence had been

masterful and that word, "Yeah," so pure and tough and violent.

"I'm to breakfast with Mother tomorrow morning."

"Oh."

"She's concerned about you."

"She's concerned about her dogs. Where have you been all week?"

"Helping get the docks ready."

"I watched some tennis on that Jap set you gave me. I like that lousy little Sony."

"I haven't played a game in a while."

"Me either."

The old man held up a small earplug. "Swell gadget. I can get the dope on sports. Yanks are winning."

"Bosox are tough though."

"You got money on them?"

"On the Yanks, yeah."

"Shall I ring for Sanka?"

"Sure."

Mallory Beale pushed a wall buzzer. In black shadow, he tapped the butt of a cigarette against his thumbnail. He inhaled slushily and switched the cigarette to his left hand, hitching his shoulder and leaning toward his son. Baring a smile, head bobbing circles, he spoke in his high, sinus, prep school drawl. "Your mother doesn't want you to run the business. She's afraid you won't last."

"I think we'll work things out."

"Do you?"

"There's a proposal between us."

"Her lousy dogs. She even smells like them."

"I want her to sell me controlling shares of the steel company."

Mallory Beale blew some thinking smoke.

"Her people are to meet with mine."

"I just don't want any fighting."

"No fights, Pop. The lawyers will negotiate."

"Why don't you run for the Senate? Let your mother keep

the stock." Mallory Beale leaned forward, cigarette hanging from his lips. "I can still put together a machine."

"Pop, I've got good men behind me now. You wanted me to take over. It's taken me a couple years to get my head straight, but now I can do it *and* end family bickering. I can run the family like you did."

"Run for the Senate, will ya?"

Chip measured his father's face.

The maid brought in a tray of Sanka. Brown teapot, white cups. "Mr. Beale," she chimed, "you're looking lovely."

"What's for dinner?" Mallory asked.

"Scrod."

"Ya. Thanks. Good-bye."

Chip poured cups of Sanka.

"Her mother had better hips," the old man said. "You tell her I want a steak. Screw the scrod. I need meat."

"Can your stomach hold it?"

"I want a steak," Mallory said.

"I'll tell her."

"I also need some exercise. I think I'll take a good walk."

"Why not join us for dinner?"

"Dinner is not exercise. Is there someone in the hall?"

I grimaced, shut my eyes.

"Cody Walker."

"Wallace."

"No. Walker. Cody Walker."

The old man smiled. "Why don't you cancel that meeting with your mother?"

"Look, Pop, I'm ready to take charge now. But you have to back me. Make my word the final word. Give me the power. I'll always seek your guidance."

The old man said nothing. His cigarette was out. He took the butt from his lips. "The bank?"

"I need you to put it behind me after I've proven I can run the island and the steel company."

Mallory Beale shifted, rattled the brass bed. "I want no fighting. I want peace while I'm dying."

"Help me, Pop," Chip said, and reached out and touched his father's legs.

The shaky lighting of another cigarette. "I'll speak to my advisers. I'll get a letter off to you next week."

Chip kissed his father's cheek.

Downstairs, I sat on the back steps and looked at the night harbor. The stars were shining and the wind was still and the sailboats in the docks were black and sharp. I had sneaked a scotch from the bar. I had poured it from a large bottle marked "Family" and not from an even larger one inscribed "Guests." I think I was drinking Chivas. The stuff was not even touching my brain because I was so high from seeing the old man. My God, Mallory Beale. Even half dead, he was electric and solemn and majestic and stylish and so rudely practical: "Har muthar haad betta hips," I mimicked. I said it again—"Har muthar haad betta hips." Trying to get it right. Trying to relive the words, bring them back perfectly. I felt ionized, volatile, brilliantly alive. I felt as if each cell in me had been blowtorched. I drank Chivas like Canada Dry, then felt a depression. He never saw me. Maybe he never would see me. I was an invisible creak in the staircase. I looked over my shoulder at what must have been his lighted window.

Suddenly I jumped up and threw my glass at the panes. "Mallory Beale! Mallory Beale!"

A hand pushed open the screen. "You! There!"

"Yes, I'm here. Look down. Look! Look at me, Mallory Beale!"

"Cody," Chip said. "How about some dinner?"

Startled from my fantasy, I gazed at him, and then followed him into the dining room.

20

Harding was arranging white daisies and yellow tulips in a glass vase in the center of the table. Bosey sat at what I guessed was Mallory Beale's place. A rusty newspaper holder erected the Providence *Journal* beside her plate. Behind her chair towered a built-in cabinet which held miniature wooden birds. Each statue had a small light to illumine its plaque: kingfisher, magpie, teal. . . .

Townsend Beale entered the room in a new sunburn. The candlelight made her look even more rugged. She wore a yellow muslin dress which had BALI written in blue script down the right side. Tonight was the first time I'd seen her well-dressed. She even wore jewelry. Around her neck lay a necklace composed of small gold squares. Within each square sat tiny diamonds, crisscrossed and secured by a gold grid. The necklace was designed so that the largest rectangle held the lowest angles, each square retreating in size until all disappeared behind her florid neck.

"The Kennedys are building a new *Senior,*" Harding said.

"Supposed to have some kind of newly designed spinnaker," Chip said. He poured everyone a glass of Pinot Blanc.

"Ethel will beach her in a week," Townsend said, nodding toward the harbor. "Her day sailor still out there?"

"Stuck off Log Island," Chip said. "Day told me Farrah Fawcett was aboard when Ethel keeled over."

"Who?" asked Townsend.

"Farrah Fawcett," Harding said. "Miss Pin-up."

"Oh, Miss Pin-up," Townsend said and looked around the

table smiling. "I'll have to tell Mallory. I'm sure he knows her."

They laughed and I joined in, still thinking about Mallory Beale, still shaking from seeing the old man.

Two maids entered. One served broccoli, the other boiled potatoes.

Bosey ate tiny bites of food. I had never seen bites so small. She saw me watching her, looked up. My eyes ducked. She nibbled her potatoes.

"Do we have a pusher?" Bosey asked, and her eyes fired at me, reprimanding my invasion.

"What's a pusher?" I returned, trying to be chatty.

"I'd like to have a pusher," Bosey said again.

A maid handed her a utensil which resembled a small silver hoe. Bosey raked food molecules onto the fork, her head circling, silver pinging as the pusher tapped the fork. "So you're a writer, huh?"

"Oh, Cody," Townsend crooned. "I didn't know that." Her blond and silver hair gleamed.

"I've known a writer before," Bosey said. "Mallory and I bought a place down in Alabama, you know. The owner, a fairly prominent fellow, told me a writer went with the works. At the time I thought it was swanky. He ate all the food and drank all the booze."

"Who was it?" I asked.

"Some jerk. Can't remember his name. Some bloody jerk."

"Somerset Maugham," Harding said.

"Maugham. Yes. He liked boiled ham as I remember," Bosey said with a deadly smile.

"He finished *The Razor's Edge* down there," Harding said.

A dark-haired maid named Molly served the scrod. Molly had a caterpillar mustache, which made her seem wanton. When she dipped the platter to me, I almost dropped the large fork and spoon. My blood was scotch. Bombed, blitzed, blown away. I set a scrod chunk on my plate, then shut my eyes. How could they forget Somerset Maugham?

The conversation shifted to baseball and tennis, then Bosey

mentioned something called "the sail," which was two days away. I had not heard of it before. Family sailors raced to something called "the spindle" and back again. In earlier years a prize had been given to the winner, but that tradition had been stopped. Bosey was about to name some past prizes when Molly suddenly rushed into the room.

"Mrs. Beale—your husband's missing. We looked all over the house. Mr. Day's gone out into the woods."

After searching near the house for thirty minutes, I ran behind Chip and Harding down a leafy road. There was no moon. A black wind shook the trees. The air was cold and salty. Peepers cried in birches. We turned right onto Chapel Road, stopped just down from the chapel. Day stood holding a Coleman lantern. Mallory Beale lay on his elbows. Chip spoke to him and when he did not answer sent Day for a truck.

An hour later Chip and I waited outside Mallory Beale's bedroom.

The doctor joined us, closing the door behind him. "Has he had any pain?"

"No," Chip said.

"Well, I'll come out again tomorrow if it'll make you feel better."

"He didn't hurt himself did he?"

"Not at all. He seems very well. In fact, he seems stronger than I have seen him in a while. I think he just went for a walk and had a fall. I gave him liquid Valium. He's out till morning. It's rather curious really. The man seems years younger."

Downstairs, Townsend and Harding were waiting on the porch. Chip waved off questions. He went to the bar and poured a scotch. He sipped the whiskey and told them his father was weak but otherwise fine. He looked at me and I said nothing. He took a sip of his drink, nodded at the door. We went outside.

"He's different," Chip said, looking at the harbor. "My father. He's—changing."

By nine-thirty the next morning Harding and I had arrived in New York City. We sat in Joe Clancy's Bar.

"So you do *like* Lisa?" Harding asked.

"I wonder why Chip told you about her," I said.

"Because he's a cad."

"I can never repay him. He invited me up, you know?"

"And Lisa?"

"We just fool around together."

"You fool around together."

"We're not sweethearts."

"These adolescent expressions."

"What do you want me to say, Harding?"

"You could be straightforward. You could say you're sleeping with her regularly and enjoying it."

"I'm sleeping with her regularly and enjoying it."

Harding's gaze was blue ice water. She was wearing a blue muslin dress and suede boots. She reminded me of a cowgirl and I felt like Gary Cooper. I stuck a toothpick in my mouth, squinted in the barroom mirror, swigged my coffee.

"Yes, ma'am. Why, she's a little darlin'."

"Lisa?"

"Sho is, ma'am, but she can't kindly hold a candle to you."

Harding rolled her eyes.

In five hours we hit Bonwit Teller, Brooks Brothers, Burberry's and Barney's. The salesmen were bearded, coiffured and perfumed. Harding commanded. She stood before the racks of clothes, hands upon her hips, and shook the clerks from closets. She engineered assembly lines of suiters—five to the left, five to the right—and, coming straight, two fitters of shoes. I was dressed in wool, linen, cotton and silk. Scores of ties were tied about my neck. Trousers zipped up and zipped down. I tested Cesarani suits, Hathaway shirts, Bullock ties. I promenaded Alexander Julian ensembles and Givenchy breakfast attires. Von Furstenberg was rejected, Botany 500 cast aside. Southwick, Austin Reed and Jean-Paul Germain were bought and bagged. Now at four o'clock in the afternoon, deep in a paneled room at Saks Fifth Avenue, surrounded by a sweating bevy of young men, Harding delivered last orders for two brown linen shirts, one cotton-string knit vest and finally an exquisitely small DeBeers stickpin, a lapis set in gold and silver, a flash as keen and sharp and fetching as a faceted drop of rich man's blood. It matched my ring.

Finished and broke and ebullient, we caught the gin-and-tonic shuttle to Cedar Point.

Around seven o'clock we arrived at New House. Harding went inside and fixed coffee and I laid a fire and we became cozy. I kissed her and she seemed warm and willing.

"Want to make a little whoopee?" I asked.

"I'm not ready for that—yet—but I would like to—relax you. To indulge you."

"How?"

Grover Cleveland's bathtub sweated and steamed. I sank down in hot suds to my neck. The soot of the city disembarked. In a mirror above the tub I watched Harding tie the tails of a white shirt over her thin abdomen and jeans. Her rich auburn hair was parted in the middle, pulled away from her face. She wore no makeup and her skin was clear and wholesome. Her lashes were spread against eyebrows, and, numbed by the day, the blue eyes seemed soft. She knelt behind me and squeezed a watery sponge over my head.

"What happens if some of this stuff doesn't fit right?" I asked.

"Don't be vulgar."

"Maybe I could try things on again tomorrow morning. Get alterations done."

"Tomorrow's the sail. You should go with Doug. He's a marvelous sailor."

"I'm a pretty good sailor myself."

"And humble."

"Very humble."

She squeezed the sponge over my shoulders. Her hands slipped down and squeezed my chest. I caught them and pulled her half over the tub and kissed her. She relaxed and kissed back.

"Let me spend the night with you, Harding."

She sat down behind me, grabbed the sponge. "Sit up."

"We'd have a good time."

"Not tonight, I think."

I straightened my back against the warm tub. She scrubbed my neck, shoulders.

"Hey, Harding?"

"Hey," she said and kissed in that long, open and giving way which signaled a new state between us, higher and softer.

"You're not a bad kisser," I said.

"I?" She blew my neck.

I crossed my eyes and sank.

Downstairs, we loitered in the kitchen. Violet wisteria and pink roses climbed outside the windowpanes. A salty spray lingered in the night air. Owls called in the white birch woods.

Finally I kissed her good night.

"The sail starts at nine o'clock. Don't be late," Harding said.

I walked down the sandy road beneath the stillness of Ash trees. A fog horn blew somewhere in the sound. I looked for the lights of the Beale house. They shone uphill, not far. White clover grew beside the road and the blooms bordered the pressed sand and marked the road. A wind blew through the cedar stand, but here there was only starlight and the fragrance of jonquils and the white clover drifts.

I was starting to feel something for Harding.

21

Somebody had a hand between my legs. It was Lisa—naked—again.

"What are you doing?" I grabbed my bedside clock. Five until nine.

"Getting you up. Ha, ha."

I sprang from bed. "Look, I've been thinking. Maybe we should stop seeing each other for a while."

"Why?"

I attacked my chest of drawers. Threw clothes into the air. "Because you want to get ahead and if you keep seeing me you'll scare off the people you want to meet. Where are my whites?"

"Look at my body."

"Not now."

"Why?"

"I've got to find white shorts, white socks, white everything."

"Did you have sex with Harding in New York?"

"How did you know I was in New York?"

"Look at me."

I sifted two handfuls of red and blue socks, turned. Black hair and black eyes and the brownest tan. "You're gorgeous."

Her bottom lip protruded. "No, I'm not. I'm ugly. Harding's prettier."

I set my hands on her broad shoulders. "Listen, your body is prettier than Harding's body. Period."

"I thought you said you hadn't seen Harding's body."

"I give up," I said and yanked open the third drawer.

"I don't care. I'm dating my meal ticket. I found him at last."

"White shorts!" I cried, finding the worn Bermudas.

"He's gorgeous."

"And a shirt. A wonderful white shirt." I plunged into the shorts, then the shirt. A whistle bleated in the distance. "Socks. I need socks." I tore open the other drawers.

"You know him."

"Good."

"Promise not to hate me?"

I emptied the last drawer and sank to the floor. "No socks. No white socks. I can't believe it."

Several whistles went off. Nine o'clock. I pulled on red ones.

"Chip Beale."

I looked at her. "Are you kidding?"

"You're not wearing those socks, are you?"

"You're dating Chip Beale?"

"You look dumb."

I heard a horn, deep and low. I knew it had to be *Ole Blue*. She was to start the race. I sprinted for the door. "I want to talk about this. I want to see you right after the race."

"I can't."

"Why?"

"I got a date with Chip."

I gave her the finger and lurched down the stairs.

Breathlessly, I bounded across the weathered oak gangway which led over the stony beach and the green scrubs to the docks. The family was already stepping onto the decks of the boats. The men wore white, long socks pulled up mid-calf, tennis hats slashed down across their eyes, sweat bands on wrists, worn rigging knives dangling from burned necks. The women's hair was combed back from faces of plain sun and freckles, noses sharp and straight and smeared in sun screen, wearing pink half-socks with blue tufts at the heels, legs browner than the men's, shirt collars open and turned up.

Seven boats lay parallel in the windy tide. Each had a number on the bow. They were Hincklies and Morgans. Wooden. The lines were low, though broadly designed for the local shallows. The ketches had white hulls and brown decks and white masts. The cleats and brass were copper green.

Again a horn blasted the air. *Ole Blue.* She sat beyond the docks and farther up the beach in her stone berth. Four blue flags flew from her teak masts as the crew stood beneath them dressed in white trousers and short-sleeved white shirts. The brass of the decks flashed. The *Boston Whaler,* at the stern, swayed above the second deck. On the first deck, below the bridge, the white cloths on five tables blew in the wind. The captain, who was looking toward the shore, suddenly saluted.

Mallory Beale rolled into view from a copse of ginkgo. Johnny Day stood behind his wheelchair. In indigo sunglasses and a faded blue golf hat, Beale wore loafers and white pants and a frayed khaki shirt. He puffed a cigarette. A few hands waved to him from the racers below. His head bobbed in circles. Blowing smoke from his nostrils, he studied the raised hands and the racers and *Ole Blue.* Looking at his watch, he signaled Day. He was rolled down a walk and lifted to the deck of *Ole Blue.* On the bridge he hit the first of four engines. The air thundered and boomed. I could feel the power push my chest. Number two started. A small explosion echoed across the cove and drove toward the sound.

The family was blown to silence. Laughing ceased. In the huge, driving pulse of the engines we were cast into a shadow of noise as compelling and absolute as the blue unyielding gravity of the earth.

Doug Summers crashed through a stand of reeds and cedars holding deck shoes in one hand, a small cooler in the other, a red diving mask clamped upon his forehead. "Holy Christmas, Cody! Come on. We're late. Uncle Mallory's aboard *Ole Blue.*"

At the docks Chip Beale boarded his boat. He partly unfurled the mainsail, which was China red. A girl climbed from below deck. It was Harding.

I set my foot upon the bow of the blue racer—number four. Her decks were scarred. Stays somewhat rusty. She was missing a few cleats and shipping some water, but when Doug rigged her up, the promise trembled in her as if the sea itself charged the wood of her belly. We sailed out upon an edge of air.

Chip and Harding were ahead. Why was she with him?

The first fin threshed the water. I blinked, rubbed my eyes. Starboard and twenty feet away from the boat, I looked again. The water seemed still. I went below and brought up the winches. Ten feet away, the black triangle sawed the surface and vanished.

"Doug, you have sharks around here?"

"Sand sharks."

"No white tips?"

"Not in the cove. They're usually way south. Unless they smell something."

I raised the mainsail and looked at the cove. The water was unbroken.

The roar of *Ole Blue*'s diesels blurred as she backed from her berth. She came toward the center of the cove and anchored. An orange buoy bobbed some two hundred yards toward the opposite shore. The finish line lay invisibly between *Ole Blue*'s bow and the buoy. The other racers had cast off. They followed number four and we sailed past five or six of the Beales' big houses along the shore. These houses were fifteen rooms or more. Summer grass ran from screen doors to the gray edge of storm walls. Below the walls were sand banks and olive-sleek driftwood, sea grass between the cedars and the sunny water. Irish baby-sitters and blond children waved from a few of the yards. Number four sailed through the shoals and into the sound. Doug opened maps on a mahogany slab just before the wheel. On the white and blue calibrated paper he reviewed Log Island and Thump Rock. They lay in the first shallows. Looking beyond the bow, I could just see these features. Log Island was a collection of sandbars, Thump Rock a black boulder whose head was painted yellow. Beyond these obstacles was the night-blue Atlantic and whitecaps and, a mile across, the clean beach of Cedar Point. I did not look at Harding. I knew she was looking at me.

Just outside the cove, the racers formed a line. They positioned forty feet apart. The race was to the spindle (five miles out to sea) and back. Behind us a flare popped from *Ole Blue.*

Chip Beale's red mainsail bowled in the wind. Harding squatted down holding the tiller. Her white tennis visor raked her nose. She waved at me. I didn't respond. Why didn't she tell me she was sailing with Chip? Skillfully, Beale's boat tacked, jibbed, took the lead.

The wind was light and straight. I worked the winches. In high school I had been a good sailor. I wondered if I still had the touch. Doug decided to drive toward the mainland and run off the thermals there. Chip went right to the heart of the sound. The other boats were slow. Already I felt the race was between me and Chip.

When wind tightened the sails I looked back at the racers. They were a hundred yards behind now. The crews were calm. No excitement. No overt determination to win. They tugged at the rims of white hats or cleated a loose line and then elegantly slouched against the hull.

Doug sat beside the tiller, his black hair shaggy and handsome in the wind, his eyes lapis. He had patches of unshaven beard on his long neck. His legs were hairless and white and the knees red knobs. On his feet were ragged tennis shoes. He reached into a cooler and pulled up two Coors.

"All right," I said.

"Beat Chip," said Doug.

"Beat them both."

The beer tasted light and hard. I was mad at Harding, Lisa and Chip. The hell with them.

A water swirl broke twenty feet away. I saw only one at first. Then a second and third appeared. Dorsal fins hissed the waves. I touched Doug on the shoulder. I knew a little bit about sharks.

"Six-footers," I said.

Doug whistled.

"We'll outsail them," I said.

"Prepare to jibe. Let's have a look at Chip." I was skipper now. I loosened the mainsail line, handed the winch to Doug. "Jibe," I said.

The boom swung around. I went to the other side of the boat, cleated the line. We were moving straight for Chip. Harding was not on deck.

Chip squatted beside his tiller. His black beard seemed square and solid as a block of oak, and there were no eyes in him now, in the red shadows of his boat, only squinted sockets as he leaned over the side and strafed the sea with his blunt fingers.

The sharks had vanished. The spindle sat two miles ahead. I grinned at Chip. "I'll get you, boy." He gave a disaffected stare across the water.

"We'll beat him," I said.

"He's a good sailor."

"I got a few tricks."

"So does he."

In the wood of the tiller, I felt the wind. Waves were becoming larger. Spray hit the decks. Doug brought yellow slickers from below. They smelled of rotting rubber and zipper rust. My heels thumped against the deck as we hit the waves and I saw my breath.

When the wind began to change I felt the new direction on my face. I looked at Chip's boat. It had shied starboard and moved ahead. He must have found a good lift. I could hear the tight ticking of his sails and knew he had to be moving fast. The boat did not plop and pat in the water, but cut along silently.

I told Doug to get ready to jibe again. Suddenly—the wind. Not a splash of force, but a clean curve and we heeled over into the waves. The dark, blue sea ran across the deck. Doug yelled out, "Go for it, Cody!" We splashed through a wave. The coldness of the sea made my elbows ache and my eyes weep. We heeled even farther. The water was just below the hatch now, clear and hard as it snapped across the face of the racer, galvanizing wood and sails like electricity.

A quarter mile away, the spindle was bucking. Beale's boat skated another header. Harding worked the tiller. She pulled off her hat, tugged yellow goggles into place. Her hair spread in the wind. Her face was sharp and grim. Maybe she knew I was angry.

With the spindle only two hundred yards distant, I sat right at Beale's stern. I had a trick. A freshwater trick. Harding turned and shot me a cold smile. She was working. I steered to port, two boat lengths from Beale. His sails were tight. He had the lines hard and did not allow much plane to the sails. Sea weathered both boats. Ahead the iron pole of the spindle wrenched in the kicking platform.

22

Ten feet from the spindle I stood up. "Room!" I yelled.

Chip's soaked beard and blustery face weakened.

I drove closer, forcing him. "Room!"

Harding jumped up. "We were here! We've position!"

I came even closer. Decks were swamped. Masts shook and ground. The blue racer lay only one foot from the red.

Chip looked at the lines and sails, but could not move. Harding leaned out over the water, her face a growl behind the goggles. "Make contact and you lose!"

"Room!" I yelled, standing at the tiller.

Doug cupped his hands. "Easy, Cody. Easy now. We'll lose if we touch her."

"Position! We have position!" Harding screamed.

"Get over!"

"You bastard!"

"My bow broke the plane of your stern."

"No!"

"Rules."

"You're wrong!"

"Room!" I boomed again, and raced to prepare the spinnaker. I rigged the pole and came back. Doug took down the Genoa. One inch now from the red boat.

Chip hunched in his stern.

Half an inch from their boat, I began to make the turn around the spindle.

Harding tossed out her spinnaker, shouted back to Beale, "For heaven sakes, Chip, move! Get down the genny. Move!"

With the stern of my blue racer one quarter inch from the bow of the red, I whipped the tiller and finished the turn. The wind hit the spinnaker. The sail shot out blue and orange over the sea. A giant piston of wind and power. The blue racer jumped ahead and I still had not used my freshwater trick.

"We have to make a good move now," Doug said. "The wind will die in another thousand yards. Those small islands break it off."

The distance left was perfect for the freshwater trick.

Harding pulled close, three feet behind my stern.

I let her come closer, down to two feet away. It was Harding's show. Chip was balled up, sick and weary-eyed, his hands loose and empty. Harding crouched at the tiller. Her oversized foul-weather gear had fallen about her like a yellow tent. She had the slicker hood up. Her goggled face was wet, just bared teeth and flexing muscle and hair licks.

One foot away, just before she was going to throw me behind, I made the move. I grabbed the boom and began sweeping the air. Twenty yards ahead there was no wind on the water. The swells rolled clean. They had no patches or dents. I threw my body against the boom and waved the sail back and forth.

Suddenly Harding lost power in her spinnaker. She lost her heel. The red racer slowed.

"Cody!" she screamed.

"A little bad air," I hollered, laughing.

Doug clapped his hands.

"Illegal!" Harding screamed.

"Just throwing you a little spoiled air!" I yelled.

Harding worked to increase her power.

My blue racer slid two hundred feet ahead and cruised into the calm of the windless sea.

Doug grabbed me. "You did it! You beat Chip."

"I beat Harding."

"They're the best here. The best around. No mistakes now and we've got them all the way home."

I watched Harding. She still had not given up, but there was little wind. She tried to tack low toward the sandbars on her starboard side, but there were no thermals. The red sails went dead. Beale was no longer on deck.

The blue racer sailed slowly. The spinnaker was finished. We rigged the mainsail and passed the other racers, still moving toward the spindle. Hats were doffed. Neat applause. I sat down by Doug at the tiller. We drank two beers fast. The sea was spreading blue. The distant banks of Cedar Point rose portside. Down farther starboard was Black Island. The sea smelled like land.

Harding lay distantly behind now. She was still working, trying to find the lucky tack. Too bad.

Fins appeared once more in the bubbly wake of the boat. The sharks were small. They followed out of curiosity, I thought.

Starboard, two blacker shadows rose. They cut toward the boat, then away. They went down into the sea, then surfaced again. Closer. I had seen these dark shadows before. They were not sand sharks. They were big.

"I think we have some trouble," I said and pointed to the sharks.

"What kind are they?"

"White tips."

"Not up this far."

"Probably followed a warm current," I said. "White tips are bad. They're killers. I've heard of them capsizing boats."

"We've got fifteen hundred pounds of lead in our belly."

"Friend of mine killed an eighteen-foot white tip that had eaten six hundred pounds of coral."

Seven or eight more fins streaked the water. The two large sharks were twenty yards from the boat now. They glided just beneath the surface. Blue-black hide broke the water. They were eight to ten feet long.

"You got some line?" I asked.

"Below."

"Grab it."

"Why are they following us?"

While Doug was below I watched the sharks. A few circled the boat, though most of them zigzagged behind the stern. There seemed to be fifteen or twenty now. Some were only three feet long and their caudal fins barely bubbled the water. The large ones stayed out: their swimming was not jerky; their maneuvers were smooth and powerful. The great black shadows went beneath the ground swells. They swam the troughs and wasted no effort and their dorsal fins did not disappear.

I remembered a boat of fishermen off Murrell's Inlet in South Carolina. They were in a fifteen-foot Comanche which was supposedly unsinkable. They were fishing squid. A shrimp vessel had seen them. The sharks hit the boat as a pack. The first blow knocked three of the men out. They went down and did not come up. The water turned to blood. Then, like a cork in a pond, the entire boat was taken below the surface. The shrimper said she stayed down five minutes. No one survived. The sharks kept pulling the boat below until the Coast Guard blew them away with cannons.

Doug brought up rope.

"Hammer and nails," I said.

"What for?"

"Grips."

"The boat will be ruined."

"These fellas are smart," I said. "They bump just a little to test. Like you or me might shake an apple tree. If things feel promising, they hit hard. They shake loose every eatable thing."

We nailed down rope to the deck. Two or three half-inch nails went to each end of a small rope section. I put my hands into the loops and pulled to test the strength. Maybe I was overreacting.

I was below when I felt the first nudge. A soft bump. A knock just at my shoulder.

Doug stuck his head down. "Damn."

"Probably heard me down here."

"Why did it do that?"

"Just testing."

Beneath a seat I found three spear guns. Seventy-pound pressure. I brought the guns and eight spears to the deck. Doug was looking through binoculars.

"Not one shark near Harding," he said.

"Load these."

"Seventy pounds won't work."

"It better." I loaded the cool aluminum spears into the shafts and made a line of the spear guns on the deck. The black razor heads gleamed in the sun.

We were half a mile from Black Island now. The smell of pine trees filled the air. Rocks and dry beach. Safety.

The largest shadows had made a pack. The blue water frothed between the fins and the sun glistened on the cold backs of the sharks. The eyes and heads were kept low now. They were watching. Listening for warm life. Smelling. Hunting.

I tied two fifteen-foot rope sections to the lead weights below, then came back up. I tied one of the sections in a bosun's knot around my waist and gestured to Doug.

"Not for me," he said.

The nudge again. The soft rap.

"I think we're carrying something below us," I said.

"No way."

"They wouldn't be trailing us otherwise."

Doug kneeled at the side of the boat.

I felt something, a minute change in the air, and then suddenly a gust of wind hit the mainsail and the boom swung port and bashed Doug's head.

I reached for him, but he spilled into the sea.

23

I grabbed a knife, cut the rope and jumped into the water.

The sea was cold and my skin rushed blood and the freezing water stabbed my sinuses. I opened my eyes and saw Doug below. He was sinking, unconscious. I got down to him, grabbed him and was starting back up when I saw the shark.

The massive head hung before us like an opaque triangle—a white tip, its mouth black and open. The jaw was moving and the eyes were flat and black. I could feel the power of the shark. The cold water trembled as the white tip swam closer. The triangular head peered directly into my face. Huge gills gorged with blood, scarred hide, a gaping mouth of current and black teeth.

The head snaked forward and butted my nose. I held on to Doug and we rocked in a circle from the blow. The shark followed. The jaw dropped, opening the long blackness of the gut.

I balled my fist and punched. Quickly the shark darted to the left. Swam back around, flicked farther out.

I pushed Doug toward the surface and the ladder and he began to thrash, then stopped when he found a grip and pulled himself up.

I broke the surface and looked over my shoulder. The fin was sweeping behind. I grabbed the ladder and started climbing when I felt something catch me. The loop around my waist had snagged on the ladder.

"Pull me!" I yelled.

Doug caught my shoulders.

The shark was cutting through the water.

I tried to rip the rope free, but couldn't. I was waist deep in sea.

The shark was five feet away.

"Give me the gun!" I yelled.

"Get out!"

"The gun!"

Doug thrust the spear gun.

I tried to keep my legs still. They wanted to climb. I turned and set the spear gun to my chest and fired at the huge black head. The sea whirled. I saw the creature roll in blood and white bubbles. I turned my back, jerked the rope free and scrambled onto the deck.

I looked at Doug. He had a cut on his forehead. He reached out a hand and I caught it. We were trembling and out of breath and we said nothing.

A few seconds later I heard an engine. I turned and looked toward the harbor of Black Island. The *Boston Whaler* was racing toward us from *Ole Blue.* It reached us quickly and the captain jumped aboard.

"My God, I saw it all. Are you all right?"

"I think Doug's hurt."

"No, I'm okay. A little dizzy."

The motorboat pulled us back into the harbor, where twenty people waited. Doug was taken to the Cedar Point hospital. Townsend and Bosey fussed over me while I downed three fast scotches, gained a little warmth and told the story. The family was horrified and thrilled.

Two hours later Doug returned with a bandaged head. He was exhausted but okay. He had to tell his own version then. Harding returned with the other sailors and I went through the whole event once more. At the end of my story the captain of *Ole Blue* approached and said that he had found the reason for the shark attack: a live bait well was left filled with chum. The bottom of the bait well was screen and opened directly to the sea. He told me that Chip had been fishing in the boat the day before the race.

By seven o'clock I was beat and Harding drove me home. She told me I could stay at Stone House and that she was worried about me, but I wanted to be alone.

When I walked through the front door of New House, Lisa was waiting.

"I heard about it," she said. "Are you okay?"

"I'm fine. I just need a shower."

"So do I."

Beneath steaming water Lisa and I lathered in Lifebuoy and drank sudsy scotch. My skin pulsed with sun and windburn beneath the thistle shower. My nose was sore, bruised from the shark.

"Your face looked so funny," Lisa said. Her chipped front tooth made her look wonderfully childish.

"Your face would look funny, too, if you'd just seen a thousand-pound shark."

"Cody, that thing could have eaten you."

I pulled Lisa against me. She felt slick and warm and I kissed her. "Tell me about Chip."

"What's to tell?"

"Are you sleeping with him?"

"Not yet."

"But you will."

"You gonna worry about it?"

"I'm gonna worry, yes."

I tried to take her, but she pushed me away and jumped from the shower.

We dried each other off, then went into the downstairs bedroom where I had stashed my new wardrobe. I was trying to act funny and light, but I was still angry at Chip, shaky from the shark.

"I would have picked out better junk than this," Lisa said, sorting through the closet of new clothes.

"Harding has good taste," I said, and then realized my mistake.

"I hate her."

"Just forget about Harding."

"Why don't you forget about her?"

"Do you know Chip told me to stop seeing you? Said the family couldn't handle it."

"And you were going to do that?"

"Somewhat."

"What a faggot."

I ducked away into the walk-in closet, looked at my splendid collection of new clothes: linen sport coats and blue oxford shirts and striped school ties and yellow checks and deep red weaves. "Ah, the simple life," I said, trying to diffuse the argument.

"Is the bag going to the Chowder Party?"

"What's that?"

"It's the next big party."

"She may, I don't know."

"Oh, that's just great. I'll be handing out cheese and crackers in my maid's uniform and she'll look like a queen. She's going to make me feel awful. I know it. I just know it."

I put my arms around her. Her black hair was still damp. She wore my old terry-cloth robe. Her dark face was moist and soft, her black eyes wet and deep. At the corners of her eyes a few wrinkles shot toward her temples. Her face hardened.

"Don't hug me."

"Why?"

"Just don't."

I pulled away. "You know, there's a song, Lisa. If you want me to get closer to you, you got to get closer to me."

"I don't want to get closer to you."

"Fine."

"I'm not in love with you. You're a bum just like me. We're bums living with rich people. I'm not going to get anywhere by hanging around you."

"But we continue to screw each other, right?"

"I get off; you get off."

"That's fine with me. How about right now?"

Lisa stripped off the robe. "Which way you want it?"

I stepped back and clipped her behind the knees and we hit the floor. "Should we kiss or can we forget that too?"

"Just go for it."

I was ready and went into her hard, the way she wanted. The sex was sharp and brutal.

Finished, we lay side by side, backs propped against the bed, looking at our red faces in the closet mirror.

"You're getting good at this," Lisa said.

I didn't hear her. "You know, I may go to the Chowder Party."

"So you can hobnob with Harding?"

"So I can establish myself a little."

"I thought you didn't care about society."

"Well, maybe I've changed. Maybe I do."

"Maybe you care about Harding."

"So?"

"So—good-bye."

Lisa stood, pulled on her jeans and T-shirt and left without a word.

I lay on the floor awhile, feeling guilty about not having said good night. When I went upstairs the pages were lying on my bed; more of Mallory Beale's memoir. Immediately I picked up the island phone directory, found Harding's number and called.

She asked if I was sure I was okay. We talked about the shark, about the race. She told me I was a dirty sailor. I laughed and then asked if she had been delivering Mallory Beale's writing. She said that she had given me his only notebook and that Beale had not written anything else. I said good night and did not mention the memoir.

In bed, I began to read. Who was bringing me this stuff?

24

Adolph Zukor was a Jew. I didn't like Jews. I always thought they were smarter than me, that they could skin me alive. Jews gave me the heebie-jeebies. But somehow I did get on with Zukor. He was kind of a sweet guy in a way and he knew his business. He knew pictures, the flicks. In the beginning he needed a hundred thousand dollars. None of the big banks would touch him. My bank, the Beale Bank, was coming on strong. He came to me. He was quiet, had a funny accent and a quick mind. I lent him the money for a goof. Good fun, and I thought maybe, just maybe, he could make this picture business work. After that, he came to see me a lot. He wore baggy brown suits and Stetson hats. In 1915 he had formed his movie company, Famous Players. A few years later there was a fire, burnt his company, burnt everything to the ground. No insurance, but Zukor was smart. He had put all his film in a fireproof vault. Mary Pickford was working for him, bringing him lots of dough. Her two new films survived. One day he called me up. He said he needed money to buy another place to house Famous Players. He needed something else too—revenge. He wanted to bloody up a competitor, guy named L. J. Selznick. So we met for lunch at a Jewish diner on Twentieth Street and Eighth Avenue. I remember he ate matzo and eggs and I ate Cream of Wheat. It was 1922.

"So two hundred thousand dollars I need, my friend. A lot of money, I know," said Zukor.

"What's the security? What can I sell if the picture fails?"

"How about America's sweetheart?"

"Mary Pickford?"

"She's gold."

"I want a twenty percent lien against the profits of her new picture."

"A deal."

Adolph Zukor and I shook hands.

"Now," Zukor pointed to his stomach. "Here's my problem. There is someone in my stomach. Someone who is trying to poison me. Louis Selznick. He was a competitor. I made him a partner and took him into Famous Players so I could control him, but he's busting everything in my business apart. He's got marquees all over the city saying L. J. Selznick presents this, L. J. Selznick presents that. But now he's really found something, Olive Thomas. A beautiful girl. She's money. She's a Pickford and he's drawing customers away from my business—of which he is still a part. He's even got his own theaters again. I want to belch him out. I want to vomit him. Then I want to stomp his guts out of the movie business forever."

"What's his greatest asset?"

"His greatest asset? His ego. My God. He sullies everything he touches. I let him open, I let him premiere Pickford's last movie. What does he do? He brings half-naked hoochie-coochie girls riding elephants to the theater. He has spotlights and military bands. He brought prostitutes to work the crowd. My God, he's destroying me."

"Sure, I'll help you, Adolph—if."

"If?"

"If I get a percentage of your next five films and if—you get me Mary Pickford for one night."

"She's got a will, my friend."

"Get me Pickford."

Zukor raised a palm. "Do you like matzo?"

"No."

"A shame."

In bed with Mary Pickford, I was blowing smoke rings from a Havana cigar that Zukor had left at the Plaza desk. We were drinking Izarra from crystal glasses. It was Pickford's favorite drink. After sex, she was talking business. Her blond curls glowed on the pillow.

"You know, Chaplin's getting a lot more money than me," she said.

"He's funnier than you."

"Sweetie, I'm not supposed to be funny."

"Good, 'cause you're not."

"When you see Zukor, you tell him I want as much as Chaplin. Four hundred and fifty thousand a year."

"I'm not your agent."

"What are you then?"

"What do you think?"

"A stud."

"I'll talk to Zukor."

Mary Pickford was the best kisser I ever kissed, period. She wasn't bad at a couple of other things either.

I did a little detective work on Selznick. Found out he was a bankrupt jeweler from Pittsburgh before he got into the movie business. When he went broke he pocketed a few stones and gambled big. He made a few pictures, did pretty good. Then he met Zukor. The result was a flashy movie business. In two years, in 1920, he was pulling down seven million a year net. He had a twenty-room apartment on Park Avenue, seven Rolls-Royces (each one a different color for a different day of the week), twenty-five servants and fourteen French poodles, seven black and seven white. The black poodles he called Adolph, the white ones—Zukor. He liked gags.

I had my office call Selznick about estate planning. I guess my name had gotten around the city some. Selznick said he would talk estate planning if I came over personally. There was no real reason to meet Selznick; I knew how I was going to bag him. I just wanted to look at his eyes before I ruined him. I wanted a little—friendly conversation.

When I pushed the buzzer at 506 Park Avenue, the door opened and a gramophone automatically began playing Mussorgsky's "Great Gate at Kiev."

While the music blasted, Selznick and I just stared at one another. He was dressed in a purple silk Chinese smoking jacket and wore a white ascot. He sat behind a ten-foot semicircular desk.

Finally the crescendo was reached and the scratchy music stopped.

I spoke first. "Catchy tune."

"Zukor must be worried, very worried."

"The appointment was about estate planning."

"Mr. Beale, you come into my office. I welcome you with a great

piece of music. Don't play games. What does my dear friend Adolph Zukor want?" A perfect, black beauty mark highlighted his left eye.

I took my time. The dramatic pause. I walked to the left wall. An enormous zebra wood bookcase. Every great book here: Tolstoy, Dickens, Balzac, Thackeray, etc. I pulled at one, then another. Fake books.

"Nice library," I said.

"The originals I keep at home."

The beauty mark had disappeared from his cheek. Later I figured out it must have been fake, too.

"Zukor wants you out of his business."

"I'm getting out of his business. Already I've purchased twenty theaters. My own."

"He wants you out of his business, then the movie business. He wants you finished."

"And your small bank will push me out?"

"More or less."

"You're a man with a future, Mr. Beale. I've done some homework. So, you and Adolph Zukor, why?"

"Now look, why don't you just sell out. Leave the city. Go start someplace else. There's talk about the West Coast opening up."

"And if I don't?"

"Then in six months you won't be worth spit."

"Your bank hasn't got the clout."

"You're right."

"So?"

"So, in six months you'll be chopping up your fancy desk to feed a fire in a third-floor room on a Hundred and Tenth."

"You can't touch me. You ain't got the dough."

I went to the door, turned and said two words:

25

"Olive Thomas."

She was more than a beautiful girl. She was a knockout, a killer, a Yankee Doodle sweetheart. You've heard about rockets going off and bells ringing; well, that all happened to me when I pushed the buzzer in the Yale Club and she answered the door, Olive Thomas.

Red hair and eyes blue as robin's eggs and a smile—a smile that puttied your knees.

"You know, Mary Pickford's gonna hate your guts," I said.

Lovely eyes opened wide and blue. "Mary Pickford?"

"You know her?"

"I know her movies. Do you know her?"

"Never had the pleasure. Lemme in."

"Are you Mallory Beale?"

"You didn't hear?"

"Hear what?"

I pushed through to her apartment. "Mallory Beale checked out last week. He gagged on Cream of Wheat in a diner on Twenty-sixth Street. Terrible loss."

"Oh, I'm sorry. It's just that Mr. Selznick said to stay away from Mallory Beale. That's why he moved me here, so nobody could find me."

"Selznick's a brainy guy."

She wore a violet double-skirted, cotton gauze dress, pale, mauve shoes.

I knew things about Olive Thomas. I had done my research. I had a file on her. You've got to keep files on everybody and everything. I had over two thousand files: people, businesses, restaurants, resorts, sham-

poos, soaps, nail clippers. I had files, and in Olive Thomas's file I had underlined the surprising vice to which she was addicted: opium. At nineteen she was a dopehead. Smoked like a steam engine. Funny that a sweet girl from the coal mines outside of Pittsburgh should acquire such an exotic pastime, but she had. Selznick had kept her tied to him with opium. Just feeding her a little along. My plan had been simple: introduce myself as Selznick's brother, then immediately offer her dope. Give her a stellar high, whisk her away to a flat on Central Park West and have my boys feed her the stuff until she was mush. After she got over the kidnapping, she'd become totally addicted to me. She would dump Selznick. Without "the new Mary Pickford" Selznick's picture business would begin to fail, and when his rents and bills mounted, my bank would close him down. This was my plan, until I saw the dame. Until I saw her beautiful face.

"I'm afraid I'll have to ask your name," Olive Thomas said, a gap between her two front teeth.

"My name?"

"What is your name?"

"Sorry, I thought you knew. I'm Hillel Selznick, L.J.'s brother. I got a jewelry store in Harlem."

"I should have known. You even look like him."

Funny how some things work out. "Why don't we blow this joint and get a nice lunch?"

"L.J. doesn't like me to leave."

"Hey. He sent me to get you."

Blue eyes blinked and the luscious red hair tossed.

"If you don't trust me, Olive, I'll call him. You can talk to L.J. himself."

I moved to the black phone, gripped the column, touched the receiver.

"I trust you. I trust you, Hillel."

Good gamble. "Chink food, Olly. You know I just got this craving for something Chinese."

So we went to lunch, Olly and me, and for the first week I was Hillel Selznick to her and managed rather artfully to escape any detection from L.J. By the second week it was springtime in New York, piebald sparkling April, and I'd fallen for the girl and I didn't give a damn about Selznick or Zukor. I guess she had gone down pretty hard for me too. I told her I was the nefarious Mallory Beale and she laughed her mild, baby laugh and said that she had known all the time anyway. I don't know if she had or not. Now, it made no difference. With Olly my days and nights were light as down.

But she still had the habit, and what was worse, she was shooting now. She never shot up when I was around, but I could tell. For a while I paid no attention, but then one day, as she stood waiting for me on Lexington Avenue, I saw the opium eating her. Her hair had thinned to threads and even with makeup the blue eyes looked like gutted candles, pupils thin and black as wicks. I had heard of a doctor in Paris who could break the addiction. Besides, L.J. was hot on my trail.

We rented a cottage in the Rue Neuve-Sainte-Geneviève. Climbing red roses completely covered the egg-white house. The first day in our bungalow Olive said she was pregnant. I remember that when she told me I kissed her and went out into a small bower of roses and sat there and cried. The only time I had done this. Nor would I again, even when they buried her.

After some months in Paris, Olive was gaining weight, down to one fix every two days. The drug doctor knew his stuff. Meanwhile, Selznick had released Olive's second film in the States. It was a boomer. In the first two weeks it had grossed over three hundred thousand bucks. When I asked Olive if she wanted to go back, she smiled that day-star smile and said she was my baby and that was all that mattered. I've never had a soft heart, but that line turned me sloppy.

The roses bloomed brilliant and soft and sweetly over the house. White and red and pink. I was going to my office once a day to check telegraphs and the market. My business was cracking. When I came back one afternoon about four, Olive was not there. The front door was open, a note attached to the handle: "Why you and Adolph Zukor?"

For two weeks I had everybody I could buy and bribe in Paris looking for her. I think every room in the city was entered. In the States I had some boys hunting Selznick. I spent over fifty thousand dollars. I didn't sleep or eat much. I even started drinking scotch. I had never touched the hooch before.

Then, on a chilly day, a police inspector came by egg house. He took me to a sooty hotel called Rouge et Noir near Notre Dame. He opened a door and stood back, his eyes flat and tarnished as his blouse buttons.

Olive was lying on the bed. Naked, she seemed almost alive. When I touched her, she was soft. The syringe lay beneath her swollen and blue arm. The vein was flat and green. I lay down beside her and held her hand. There was a noise then. Something out in the hall. The police inspector called me. I didn't want to leave Olly.

In the doorway the cop was holding the kid.

"Monsieur Beale, is he yours?"

I turned to Olly, expecting her to say something.

"The lady was going to the airport. But it was time for the baby, so a man brought her here. The child was born and the mother died one hour later. Is he yours?"

I reached out a hand, parted the blue blanket. The crying stopped. Face like a red tomato. My eyes, my hair.

"No," I said. "He's not mine."

The inspector's face fell.

I looked one last time at Olly. I hurt and I hurt bad and I decided that I would never again love anything that could be taken away from me. Then the kid cried and when he did a place popped into my mind. I'm not sure why. A pink house on the corner of Whiskey and Easy streets. A place far from business, far from my heart.

"He's not mine," I said again. "But you know what? I'm gonna name him. Call him—Joe."

"What shall we do?"

"I'm the girl's uncle. I'll take responsibility. Call my house in fifteen minutes. Someone will tell you what to do."

The inspector extended the bundle toward me. "Monsieur, just once hold him."

"I don't hold what I can't keep."

After the funeral I sent five quick telegrams. I jumped the Queen Elizabeth. *I was going for Selznick. I had some connections with a guy on Christopher Street, guy named Genovese. He was awfully good at doing bad. But, sailing over, I decided that murder was too simple. Maybe murder later, but first I wanted ruin. I wanted ruin passed down from generation to generation in Selznick's life.*

I was patient. My brain worked cold and quick. In one year I collected fifty-seven files on Selznick, his wife and kids and all his business. Lucky for me his entire fortune was based on movies, and his most successful—in fact his only successful—movie venture in the last year was Olive Thomas. Every other flick failed. Unknown to Selznick, I acquired the mortgage to all three of his houses, including the twenty-room Park Avenue apartment. I also got the liens against his thirty-odd theaters.

With all of his new movies bombing, Selznick started floating loans. I went to my buddies at the banks—Hanover, Citizens and First National. I influenced them to let me handle Selznick through their facilities. I would deny Selznick two loans at First National and then give him a small one at Hanover. (He didn't know I was calling the shots, of course.) One loan would keep him going a week or ten days. Then I'd close a couple of theaters. Squeeze him a little more. I foreclosed and auctioned his forty-room Tudor house in New Jersey, sent notice of foreclosure against his Federal-style mansion in East Hampton.

Six months later Selznick was selling off everything. All seven of his Rolls-Royces, thirty-seven Ming vases, the mink off his Park Avenue apartment floor, every last star sapphire and turquoise and opal that he had been holding back, finally even selling his wife's forty-two-carat diamond engagement band, which had been fashioned by Fabergé for a cousin to Czar Nicholas II. He sold his furniture and left his swank apartment. He and his wife and three kids moved to a third-floor walk-up on Ninety-third Street.

Two years later, on the exact day of Olly's death, I finished Selznick. In one afternoon I hit all three banks. I closed down Selznick's remaining theaters, confiscated his nineteen movies and called his seventeen loans due for payment (over $3 million).

I remember, the day was cold. I went down to the ashy tenement on Ninety-third Street. I wore a nice suit—a handmade pinstripe and red silk tie. The pistol felt bulky in my pocket. When I knocked on the rusted tin door a small boy answered.

"Sonny, is your father here?"

"He's not feeling good."

"Oh?"

"Who is it, please?" asked a man's voice.

I pushed past the boy, patted his head, felt something from him.

L. J. Selznick was slumped behind a scratched desk. Behind him, one last Ming vase. A fireplace burning oily coal. He wore a white shirt and blue suspenders and purple linen pants. On his head sat a small blue yarmulke.

"Yes?"

"Mr. Selznick. I've come about your loans."

"Behind, I know. Just a little patience. I'm doing a new movie. I'm putting together the deal."

"You're no longer behind."

"What?"

"It's over. Come up with $3 million plus a hundred and fifty thousand for late charges or you're finished."

"Who are you to say?" Selznick set his glasses upon his nose.

We looked at each other. He rose in his chair, then settled. His sallow face decomposed. Thin hands touched the stubbly chin. "For Adolph Zukor?"

I said nothing.

"Everything I am, my business, my houses, my beautiful vases. Everything gone—for Adolph Zukor?"

"Olive Thomas."

"Of course, of course. The overdose in Paris. You blame me."

I took the note that had been left on the door handle in egg house. I balled the paper in my fist, flipped it at Selznick. It struck his head. He opened the paper ball and read.

"Yes, I came for her. She was mine, not yours. She was property. I tried to convince her to come back to New York. She would not, so—I left her. I gave her no dope. My hands are clean. You have destroyed an innocent man."

"Now listen"—and I said this soft and quiet—"I've been to everybody in the picture business. I've talked to Goldfish and this kid Mayer. I talked to Bill Hart and Chaplin and Pickford and Zukor. I touched every bank and lending institution in the country. You will never make a movie again. You will not be able to borrow a penny for a pay toilet. You're finished and not only you, but your children. Finished. For two generations, anyway. Finished, Selznick."

When I pulled the pistol from my pocket, Selznick raised his hand, but it was too late. I squeezed the trigger and the gun exploded.

The last Ming vase shattered. Selznick jumped from his seat and crawled on the floor. He began scraping together the shattered pieces. I tossed the gun to him.

"There's nothing left. Why don't you do something honorable? Why don't you blow your brains out?"

He said nothing. He just held the Ming fragments to his chest and cried.

I walked to the door. The boy was standing there. He was crying.

"What's your name, sonny?"

"David."

"What?"

"David O. Selznick."

I knew he would amount to nothing.

I reread a section, then rose and opened my chest of drawers. Carefully I stacked the new pages of the memoir against the other sections. I closed the drawer and lay down on my bed.

So Beale had another son. I wondered if he was still alive, and if he was—where did he live? What did he do? And wouldn't it be wonderful if Mallory Beale had not yet revealed to the boy that he was his father. Of course now the son would be middle-aged, say fifty or so, about the age of my own father had he lived. Delightfully, I shivered. How marvelous to suddenly discover that your father was Mallory Beale.

Thinking these thoughts, I dozed. Sometime later in the evening the address that Beale had recalled floated into my mind. I reopened the drawer and checked to see if I had remembered imprecisely. No. There it was—a pink house on the corner of Whiskey and Easy streets. I knelt at the windows, propped my chin on the cool sill and squinted at the sea.

In Aiken, South Carolina, a town not twenty miles from my home, there were two streets I had often traveled. Two streets whose names had always caught my fancy.

Whiskey and Easy.

I wondered. Had Joe Beale lived in Aiken?

26

The next day I spent two hours trying to call friends in Aiken. Finally about twelve-thirty, I got one—Vic Ballentine. We had gone to high school together.

After a few minutes of obligatory reminiscing, I asked him if Whiskey and Easy streets crossed one another, intersected. He laughed and said, yes, and that there were a lot of local jokes about living on the corner of Whiskey and Easy streets.

"Vic, do you remember—this is kind of important—is there a pink house on one of the corners beside those streets?"

A hesitation. "Pink house on the corner . . . hmm, well . . . I really don't know. Let me call you back. . . ."

I waited by the phone for almost an hour. Nothing. Even if there was a pink house, so what? Obviously, Mallory Beale had had friends in Aiken. My father had told me that. Perhaps Beale had sent his infant son there for a while. There was nothing else. There was nothing mysterious. And yet, I felt something.

About three-thirty in the afternoon Vic called back.

"Cody?"

"Yeah?"

"Grocery store."

"Pardon?"

"There's a grocery store on one corner. The others are empty lots. No pink house."

"Oh." I felt a little disappointed, then talked to Vic awhile and forgot about the whole matter—until a week later, when he called back on the night of the Chowder Party.

"It *was* there," Vic said. "Until about twenty years ago. In fact, they used to call it the Pink House. Sometime in the fifties they tore it down, built the grocery."

"You didn't happen to find out who owned it?"

"Took me a while, but yes, I did. Guy named Beale. Real rich. A Yankee."

So what. Mallory Beale had owned a house in Aiken. True, I had not known that before. My father had not told me. But that was not earthshaking. My father didn't tell me a lot of things. Particularly when they concerned Mallory Beale. Apparently, Beale had sent his newborn son to Pink House about the time my father was born in Aiken, 1923. It's funny how people's lives intersect—Joe Beale and Joe Walker. Fate.

I poured myself a drink and tried to control my imagination. I did a good job, until four hours later at the Chowder Party. There I discovered another—coincidence.

Around seven o'clock in the evening the phone rang.

"Cody, could you bring ice?" It was Townsend.

"Uh—bring ice. Where?"

"Where? Why, the Chowder Party. You didn't forget, did you?"

"But I didn't get a, that is, I don't . . ."

"Well, never mind. You sound awfully confused. I'll ask Chip for ice. You will still come though?"

Perhaps Townsend had intended to ask me, forgotten and then simply assumed that she had. Or maybe Harding had gotten to her. It made no difference. I was excited.

From my new wardrobe I selected a white cotton suit and light blue shirt and pastel blue tie. Just as I began dressing, the phone rang again and Doug said that he and Marlow were going and would give me a ride.

Right now I did not want to question either the abrupt invitation or the literary installments. I was afraid to break the spell: I felt as if the Beale family was beginning to accept me.

As I finished my tie a horn blew outside. I turned on the porch light and opened the door. Marlow and Doug sat in the blue pickup truck.

As soon as I squeezed into the truck I smelled the hash. From the looks of them, they had already smoked a couple of bowls. They greeted me cheerfully and then told me that Mallory Beale was not coming. Paranoia. I was sure the old man was avoiding me.

Marlow parked the truck before a great house whose windows framed soft yellow light. Having finally donned his shoes and socks, Doug led the way to a path between several blue spruce trees. I could hear the party somewhere: glasses colliding and laughs and yips and the human murmur, a soft resonance that trembled from the very heart of the party. Although I was excited to see what awaited me there, somehow this gentle sibilance stopped me—the voices traveling out into the night, disembodied and frail, tender and painfully separate. For a quick second I saw that these people were no different at all from me and that their frailty was as certain and as inexorable as my own. Then the illumination failed.

Low lamps lit the brown needle ground. Just beyond the stand of spruce stood a pink stucco wall. White roses climbed the wall and changed at its summit to a rouge color, which brightly ran along the ledge.

The gate to the rose garden was massive—two-inch oak hung on eight rusted hinges—and in the center of the door was a small window with six black bars which afforded a view inside. The three of us stuck our noses to the bars. We saw the family and a few visitors and I knew that if I didn't make a move soon, I would lose the courage.

"Let's do it," I said to Doug and Marlow.

"Oh dear, dear, dear, dear," Marlow said, holding his eyes shut with his fingertips.

"I don't think I'm ready for this," Doug said.

With a quick move I flung open the gate, which immediately crashed against the interior wall, showering us with white rose petals.

Marlow had snapped to impeccable attention while Doug slapped and daubed his hair into neatness, his eyes batting and bulging like a rudely awakened sheep.

As soon as we walked inside, Marlow turned to Doug. "Dope," he said.

"Not now," Doug said.

"One bong hit or I shall perish over the pâté."

Doug slouched, stuck out his chin, dug knuckles into hips. "We'll be back, Cody. I've got to fry Captain America's brains."

I looked around. There were about twenty people. So far I didn't know one. Where were Harding and Chip?

The grass of the rose garden was smooth as green moss. In the center, sunken in weathered bricks, sat a small reflecting pool and a water fountain. Thirty yards to the right stood a white- and green-striped canvas, and below it a long table held shining glasses, several silver ice buckets, liquor bottles. The crowd stood before the table. They were served by four waiters who, as usual, had black hair and blue eyes and milk-of-magnesia skin. Beside the pavilion and tables lay more manicured grass and then two white wicker sofas and seven or eight deep wicker chairs.

I nudged into the sunburned crowd, got a scotch and soda, then eased toward the wicker furniture. Three middle-aged women held the grass here. They were beautifully dressed and sunburned and they had been drinking. The booze hung around them. The nearest woman wore a white cotton dress which was printed in green leaves. Atop the dress was a collarless, violet jacket. She was a blonde.

I moved a little closer. Their voices were gently slurred and giddy. Should I introduce myself?

"She has them in her house too," said the blonde.

"I think that's exactly where she should keep them," replied a redhead wearing tinted glasses. The third woman, who stood between the redhead and the blonde, said nothing. She just swayed and clutched a tumbler of dark liquor to her chest.

The blonde nodded at the seven or eight pillows heaped in the wicker sofas (red pillows designed in hand-stitched yellow daisies). "They are just too tacky."

"Are there degrees to tackiness?" asked the redhead.

"Please don't be an ass, Phyllis."

I wanted to say something, to introduce myself, but decided I needed another drink first.

At the bar I ordered another scotch and soda. Now I don't know a lot about liquor, but the stuff they were serving looked pretty cheap—Mister Calvin bourbon, Frosty Marsh scotch and Floogle's gin. Where had they found this stuff?

The waiter was handing me the drink when it was intercepted in midair.

A bald-headed man stuck the whiskey tumbler to his lips, gulped, spoke. His accent was Southern, slow and thick as gumbo. "You Cody Walker?"

I extended my hand. I had seen him before. At Choir.

"Bob Sims," he said. His whole skin, even the skin of his head, was fish-belly white. He had little red veins in his pug nose and little blue bags under his eyes. "You're from South Carolina, right?"

"Glenn Springs. Yes sir."

"Oh yeah. Close to Aiken—you musta known Joe Beale. He was raised there." He staggered close and squinted. "Course maybe you were too young."

"Joe Beale?"

"They don't talk about him much up here. Everybody's kinda embarrassed, but they shouldn't be. He was the best thing Mallory ever produced. The best."

Sims clapped an arm on my shoulder, smiled tiny, yellow teeth. "Drinking's what really killed Joe. The hooch. And you know when it started—it started when they tried to Yankee-ize him. When they sent him to St. Georges. And it got even worse at Yale."

"He's dead now?"

"Yeah. Real dead. And you know something else . . ."

At that point a squat woman, wearing a pink satin muumuu, collared Sims and pulled him away. She shook her head. "He's a little tipsy. Sorry." She walked him toward the gate.

So Joe Beale *had* lived in Aiken. Attended St. Georges and Yale. So had my father. They must have known each other. Why had my father never mentioned Joe Beale? Why?

Doug entered the rose garden, saw me and came over. He had changed clothes and now wore a blue blazer and gray slacks.

"Listen," Doug said. "What do you think about my clothes?"

I didn't really hear him.

"I can't believe I came here dressed like I did. I know the family noticed. I know I'll hear about it."

From a door in the garden wall Bosey entered smoking a cigarette. She wore a mannish blue suit and her white hair seemed freshly washed.

I was still thinking about Joe Beale when Doug touched my arm.

"You should go speak to Bosey."

"What?"

"Mingle. Go say hello." He shoved me forward.

On the way over I ran into Lisa. She was serving white grapes and cheese. When I tried to speak she turned her back and walked away.

Bosey was leaning against the pink stucco wall speaking to a man who Doug had once identified as a senior member of the family, as well as the most skilled thumb surgeon in the world.

"We just bought a place down in Alabama," the doctor was saying.

"What's it called?" Bosey asked.

"Woosh . . . Wooshashee, I think."

"Indian?"

"Ya, and I think they still have some Indians around there too. Twenty thousand acres, you know. The house is the same design as yours."

The doctor was dressed in a pink wool sports coat, white

turtleneck and pink plaid pants, alligator shoes. His hoop stomach bulged behind his back and over his kidneys and caused the lower part of his pink sports coat to swell out like a round triangle.

"Ours has an Indian name also," Bosey said.

"Oh, what?"

"Can't remember."

"So I'm going to let Rocky manage the farm and the land for a year. What do you think, Aunt Bosey?"

"What happened to Yale?"

"He flunked out two years ago."

"Oh."

"We sent him to Middlesex, St. Lawrence, and then Arizona State. He likes the Arizona school."

"What's he studying?"

"Forestry. Let's see, I think it's forestry. He may have specialized though. Ya, he may be in milk management now."

"Ya."

"The dairy business has some potential for him. He seems to get along with cows. I've spoken to the president of the American Dairy Association. Don't tell Rocky though. He's a sensitive boy."

"How old is Rocky these days?"

"Thirty-one."

"Ya."

A small woman with gorgeous calves touched the doctor's arm.

"Chet? Excuse me, Aunt Bosey. Chet, you're wanted in the house. I'm afraid someone's smashed his thumb."

Chet excused himself. Bosey observed the crowd, glanced at me, then stepped through the garden-wall door.

I followed.

The air outside the party felt cooler. Bosey must have heard my steps.

"Congratulations on your sailing win," she said.

"Thanks."

"Chip is still a bit upset, I'm afraid."

"May I call you Bosey?"

She blew an agreeing line of smoke. "Are you a golddigger?"

"Ma'am?"

"Are you trying to get on here?"

I felt my face shrivel.

"It's perfectly all right if you are. I think I'd try to get on here if I weren't who I am."

Just then tires screeched and a vehicle sped past the house. Below the lone streetlamp we saw one word illumined on the van's side: "Ambulance."

The van wheeled down Chapel Road and veered into the dark.

"I have a feeling," Bosey said. She dropped the cigarette stub to the ground. "I have the oddest feeling." She pulled a white scarf from her suit pocket and tied it about her head. "Would you go with me?"

"Where?" I stuttered, still startled by her remarks.

Bosey gazed toward the black woods. "Mallory's."

We found her car and I drove to the back of Mallory Beale's house and sobered up fast.

A high plank fence surrounded the backyard. The access door was locked.

Bosey had taken a cane from her car. She pointed at the fence. "Over."

"I don't know."

"Afraid?"

"Maybe he doesn't want anybody here."

The cane swatted my leg. "Get over."

I took a hard run and jumped. Grabbed the fence top and kicked to the other side. I opened the gate.

We walked past the empty ambulance.

"I hate these doomish vehicles," Bosey said and bashed the windshield with her cane.

The screen door was locked.

"Hallo?" she called out.

No answer.

"Hallllloooo!" She looked at me. "Well, can you get in or not?"

I took her cane, punched a hole through the screen, reached for the lock.

"Better," she said.

We entered the house and stopped dead. A wheeled litter sat in the hallway, the kind which transports bodies.

Beneath a thick blanket lay a form.

27

Bosey breathed quietly. She unfastened her scarf and walked forward a few steps. She pressed two fingers to her lips and pondered the long shape beneath the blanket.

"Hallllowoo," she said once more, softly.

I stepped closer, but did not touch her.

Bosey drew her fingers below her cheeks. Her plucked eyebrows lifted and mussed white hair fell and framed her face. Her amber eyes softened.

"You know," she said in a bony whisper, "you know, I went with him once to meet Stalin. It was 1953. Mallory had put another deal together. But I just wanted to meet the nefarious Uncle Joe and Mallory said, 'Hell, yeah, sis, come along.' I remember we were wearing Russian bearskin coats that had otter linings and white mink hats which Mallory had bought for the trip. It was a holiday or something and Red Square was a million strong in Russians and the snow was falling and I was young and excited and snuggled in my fur next to Mallory atop Lenin's tomb. And when Stalin came out on the platform beside us, the crowd did not cheer at first, no. At first there was only steamy, breathy silence, and they waved at him. A million or more people, silent and waving in the Russian snow and cold. Then, way high there, on a cloud, I saw things building. Vast shapes. Slowly, they took form. The first was a color image of Stalin, himself banked upon the enormous snow cloud's summit. Stalin's face three or four miles wide and five miles high. Light then flurried upon a lower cloud as the second image grew as huge and tall and climbing as the other. I was shocked. The second image was—Mallory's. It was Stalin's gift to him. It lasted only a few seconds and then faded into the glowing cloud, leaving Stalin alone. And I remember Mallory looked at me and smiled that very tough smile and said, 'Naturally, I forgot my camera.' "

Bosey's hands opened upon her thighs. She waited beside the litter, her eyes round and sensitive and youthful. "Let me see him," she said.

I was appalled.

"Will you help me, Cody?"

I reached for the blanket and carefully pulled down the edge. I shut my eyes and opened them only when I heard her laugh.

Two large, green oxygen tanks lay upon the litter. There was nothing more. No body. No Mallory Beale.

Bosey laughed. The white hair showered her face as she dropped her head and embraced the tanks. "Mallloreee!" she whispered.

An attendant stomped down the stairs. "I just can't carry those tanks like I used to," he said. He wore a black bow tie and white jumpsuit. "It's easier to wheel them out."

"Have you seen Mr. Beale?" Bosey asked.

"Five minutes ago. Said he was taking a boat ride. You know, I saw him a couple months back. Didn't look too hot. But tonight, he looked terrific. What's he doing?"

Bosey crossed her arms. "I don't know. I really don't. But isn't it marvelous?"

It *was* marvelous, I thought, driving back to the party. (Bosey had told me to take her car. She wanted to walk.) The old man seemed to be recovering. Two months ago he could never have taken a boat ride. It was odd: As he became stronger, so did I. Finally I was getting to know the family.

The crowd at the Chowder Party had grown to sixty or seventy. They had packed around the door in the pink wall. As I moved toward the bar I heard whispers, broken conversations:

"The President's shot . . ."

"Shot?"

"Shot, meaning—on the rocks. Washed up . . ."

And:

"Nixon's a helluva thinker. Always has been. He shoulda burned the damn things. I just don't understand how he . . ."

And:

"You worked with him in the '59 campaign didn't you?"

"I don't care what they say, it was a good year. Joe Kennedy just outbanked us. Dick was a tough guy then, and he's a tough guy now. He'll make it."

"Fenwick says he's cracking up. Says this general's running the show."

I forgot about the drink, edged into the crowd. Then I saw seven or eight tall men wearing dark blue suits, small American flags in their lapels.

I moved closer.

In the men's ears were lodged clear pieces of plastic which connected to small wires disappearing into coats.

The side door to the rose garden opened. Applause. The men in the blue suits shuffled. Cameras flashed.

When I took a couple more steps someone violently bumped me backward: a big guy in a blue suit.

The applause intensified. Faces beamed. I heard "Hurrah," "Hang tough" and "We're behind you."

Then he stepped into the open. Dressed in a gray suit, black tie with small red polka dots, black English-cut shoes.

"Thank you. It's good . . . thank you . . . very much . . . it's good to see concentrated support."

Gray eyes in a ruddy, tanned face. Gold ID bracelet shaking on his left wrist. He opened his hands.

"We've bridged the gap. The tactics of the left-wing press have reached a point of deficient, low-level capability. At the White House, support systems are characteristically calm and functioning in a high-technocentric posture. All—is—well."

It was Alexander Haig. People closed around him, shaking hands, asking questions, giving advice.

I was determined to meet him. I ordered scotch number three, gulped two fireballs and worked through the crowd, three feet from Haig. I rehearsed my question.

His conversation was diligent and bright and dealt with Alexander Butterfield. He was drinking a Diet Coke straight from the can.

"General," I said.

His attention came swiftly. The gray eyes were cold and thick as the heads of rustless bolts.

"General, do you believe that in the event of a Soviet blockade of the Gulf of Oman that the proper American response would be a reflexive, unilateral military concatenation of alerts to signal our determination to keep those waters open?"

Haig did not even pause:

"I believe that such a response would prove effective, prudent, militarily correct and would counteroffense the Russian impaction."

We stared at one another until I grinned, turned.

Six feet away, I heard Haig ask, "Who is that young man?"

"A writer," said one voice, "a novelist."

"What's his name?"

A timid voice, shaking in booze, replied, "Don't you know—why, that was Thomas Pynchon."

I even felt like Thomas Pynchon. Slightly mysterious, swaggering a bit, burning in some kind of special, apocalyptic knowledge. The scotch was going down my throat smooth as wind. I was mean. I was tops. I drifted over to my three female friends, who were drunk. Hiccough drunk. The two conscious ones had turned from too pink to very red. Their hair was mussed, lipstick eaten, mascara smudged.

"Ladies, I just wanted to say that I agree with you about those pillows. They *are* tacky. Incidentally—my name's Cody Walker." I clinked my glass to theirs.

Suddenly Townsend was speaking. "Everyone! Everyone? It's time for you all to go. A lovely evening. Awfully much fun, but those of us having dinner should eat. I think a number of you are invited to our place for chowder. My chowder. Al

Haig will be there. As for the rest of you—well, I'm sure we will see you through the summer."

I felt an arm catch my waist. Doug and Marlow were walking fast for the gate.

"Where's Lisa?" I asked. "I want grapes."

Since we were all smashed, Doug left his truck and we walked through another house's yard, down rock stairs to the beach.

The sea was flat as a black stove lid. There were stars and a bright sliver of moon. Floodlights from the party above lit the beach. The sand was pocked and ribbed and big-grained. We sat down beside a clear tidal pool. Minnows flashed like sparks and the black surf touched the sand.

Doug had a glass tumbler of pure gin. He passed it to me. The liquor whistled down and the vapor burned my sinuses. Marlow drank the last clear inch, then set the glass in the sand. We sat there by the night sea, drunk and tired and close together. We had a spirit, a sense of camaraderie. I don't know, maybe it was something we gained from our experience in the rose garden. It was almost like going through a battle together.

We were so drunk that we hugged good night like Frenchmen. Marlow even went so far as to kiss me on the cheek, at which point my frosty, WASP reserve rose and I quickly climbed the beach stairs.

When I made the top Doug called out, "Cody, my girl's coming in a couple days."

"Who?"

"My girl. Parker. I love her, man. I really do. You have to meet her. I'm going to make her a partner in my fishing company. Maybe I'm going to make her more than that. Maybe she'll be uno numero with me. Hey, Cody?"

"Yeah."

"Maybe I'll marry her."

"Right, Doug."

Marlow began to chide and Doug laughed. Walking down

the beach, they started singing "Time Loves a Hero" and I listened until the song faded against the waves.

When I walked into my front yard I saw them. I think they had just discovered one another. They were sharply tense in the moonlight, each pair of eyes luminously fixed upon the other, and around them, or between them, there was a barely audible noise, a subtle whine or cry, a feral hissing. If they had had tails they could have been cats: Lisa and Harding.

I felt my drunkenness dissolve. "Well, hello, there—uh, ladies. I'm, I'm . . . uh—delighted to see you—both. It's a terrific time to walk at night—don't you think?"

"What is the bag doing here?" Lisa asked, glaring at Harding.

"Who?" I asked.

Lisa shot hard eyes at me.

"Oh, Harding. Over there, you mean. What is Harding doing here? Well . . ."

"I just came by to say hello, Cody," Harding said in her best blue-blood accent while staring at Lisa.

"See, she's just saying hello, Lisa. Isn't that sweet? Or, well, not sweet—but, isn't it nice . . ."

"What do you see in this guy?" Lisa asked.

"Please?" Harding clipped.

"Look, you got everything you want. Money, houses, cars. What are you screwing around with this guy for?"

"If I were tasteless I would ask you something similar."

"Hey, there's nothing between him and me. Nothing but pure biology."

"You're quite right, actually. I do have everything. Or almost everything. There's one possession I'm lacking. One I desire, ardently."

"Oh, yeah, what?"

"Cody Walker."

I closed my eyes.

Lisa came over and kissed me so violently that I felt my breath go. She turned to Harding.

"Let's divide him up. You take what's between his ears and I'll take what's between his legs. What do you say?"

"Cody, I'd like to meet you at the beach club soon," Harding said. "They make a smashing hot dog. You would fit right in—unlike others." Harding cocked an eyebrow and stepped away into the island dark.

Lisa crossed her arms. "Well, are you gonna meet her there?"

"Just cool down."

"Are you?"

"Probably."

"Good. I'm moving in with Chip. He asked me last week. I told him no for some dumb reason, but you can bet I'll do it now."

Lisa pulled back her small fist and punched from the shoulder, just like a guy. The blow struck my chin and I staggered. When she started moving toward me again, I tackled, threw her to the ground and pulled her over my knees.

"You know what you are? You're a little ghetto brat." I pinned her hands with my left and slapped her butt with my right.

She was scratching and wiggling. "Let go of me!"

"And you know what ghetto brats need?" Just as I delivered another slap, Lisa found my unprotected groin. She bit.

"Ouch!" I yelled. "Let go."

She wouldn't. I tried to pry her off. She only clamped harder.

"Lisa!"

She was growling and snorting.

To my astonishment, I started reacting in an odd way. Lisa sensed it immediately. The growling ceased.

"What is this?" she asked.

"Whatever you do, don't bite."

"What are you doing, Cody?"

"Rising to the occasion."

"You're a perv. A real perv," Lisa said and broke away and started laughing.

"No, I'm not. I'm a semi-perv. Real pervs want whips and chains. I'm interested in simple emasculation."

She kissed me and I reached a hand under her blouse.

"Your place," Lisa said.

"No, right here."

"Too dirty. Too dirty and there's crawly things."

"Crawly things?"

"Take me upstairs and do me."

Take her upstairs I did, but doing her was difficult. She wanted everything to start off in single beds again. I couldn't believe it.

28

Lying in bed in the dark, I could feel a rusty hangover building. The Chowder Party and the booze had exhausted me. Maybe because Lisa was near, I started thinking about Chip. I was determined to confront him about her.

"Hey, Comanche," Lisa said.

I lay still.

"Comanche leader?"

"Yo," I said, softly.

"Can we powwow?"

"No."

"Just a little?"

"Chip doesn't care about you."

Lisa left her bed and knelt beside mine. The room was dark. I felt her warm breath near my shoulder.

"Hold up your buddy's hand," she said.

"Stop."

"Do you love Harding?"

"I'm not sure."

"I don't want you to love her."

Lisa pulled down my sheet. I was naked. Using her nails, she lightly raked me from neck to ankles. She climbed into bed and kissed my ear. I palmed her back. Expertly, she slipped a condom over me.

At night, in the dark, a woman's back is a wonderful feel: lean muscles at the shoulders, soft lats beside breasts, stout erector muscles at the base of the spine. We were sweating now. I kissed her breasts, then her stomach. I tasted salt in her navel and tugged at small hairs below until she made a soft sound. We made love while the sea wind blew the gauzy white curtains into the room.

Later, Lisa was lost in a snoring sleep. I was surprised to find that girls snore, the sound somewhat clicky and squeally, like tearing nylon. I wondered if Harding snored. I was sure she did not, or if she did, it was a stiff-jawed hiss, elegant and reserved even in sleep. Lisa had propped her dark face on the inside of my forearm. Black hair covered her eyes, the sweet mouth open, the bottom lip arched and swollen and swarthy like a black cherry.

For two months I had been able to deal with Lisa and Harding quite separately. Now the matter was becoming tangled. When I looked at one I thought about the other. I knew I needed to make a decision, but I couldn't yet.

Later in the night I wondered again about Joe Beale. It seemed incredible that my father had never mentioned him, unless—unless something had happened between *them.* Not between Mallory and my father, but between Joe Beale and my father. It would explain everything.

I sat up with a realization: I didn't want to know the secret, if there was one. For the first time since my parents' death I didn't feel so lonely. I cared about the people here and slowly they seemed to be caring about me.

I had not seen Chip since the race and I was happy not to see him. My writing was sound. I liked Billy as a character and he was developing well. At first, he had been bumbling and callow. Now he was learning how to survive in the new land. Now he was maturing in the alien world.

Around two o'clock one afternoon the phone rang.

"Cody Walker, please?"

"Here."

"Pardon?"

"This is he."

"Lesly Combers calling."

"Hello, Mr. Combers. How's the Big Apple?"

"Young man, I don't want to get your hopes up, but I think you're going to be very rich very soon."

I listened to static.

"City Side Publishers has bought *Tiger River.*"

"You're kidding."

"Small advance. Very small. Three thousand five hundred, but our movie people are simply mad for it on the Coast. They say they don't want to wait for galleys. They want to Xerox the manuscript and send it around."

"Send it to whom?"

"Why, all the major studios. The president of Universal phoned today to say that it could be the biggest film since *Peyton Place.* His last line was—'Soon all Hollywood will be talking about *Tiger River.*' "

"Has he seen the manuscript already?"

"Oh, heavens, no."

"Well, how does he know . . ."

"Echoes, dear. They all listen for the echoes out there."

Lesly Combers went on about film rights, PR and the Texas-reared editor who was raving about the book. The editor's name was Thaddeus Cribb and he wanted me to come to New York and sign the book contract. Combers said to keep cool, not to be too excited. He said Cribb would call in the next few days.

I put down the phone. Calmly I walked into the bathroom and looked at myself in the mirror. Same brown hair and hazel eyes. There wasn't anything extraordinary here, or was there? I smiled. Sure there was. "You're going to be published. Why, Cody Walker, you're going to be a rich young man."

I yelled then and hooted and continued this wildness all the way to Doug's cabin, so that when he answered the door, awakened from his nap, wearing huge boxer shorts and no shirt, he looked at me and said in a horrified voice, "Christmas sakes, the market's crashed!"

I told Doug the news and he hollered louder than me and we scrambled and broke out rum and drank the stuff straight.

Doug acted out the way it would be when I was presented a five hundred thousand dollar check from Book-of-the-Month while I, bitten hard by the sweet rum, somberly accepted the Pulitzer Prize for fiction.

Now completely ecstatic and a little bit drunk, we jumped into Doug's blue truck and gunned through the center of the island heading for Harding's. I reached and hit the horn. Doug pushed my hand away.

"No. The family's napping. You'll wake them."

"They should be awake. The next Hemingway's here!" I tried to beep again, but Doug blocked me and I threw myself half out the truck window instead.

"All Hollywood's talking about *Tiger River!*" I screamed. "Hey, Mallory Beale!"

Doug was shushing and hushing and talking about responsibility and duty.

"You hear that, Mallory Beale? All Hollywood's talking about my book!"

When we arrived at Stone House, I bolted through the front door and sprinted the stairs. At the top I threw open the first door on the left, saw Harding lying in bed and rushed her.

"Come on," I said, kissing her quickly on the lips.

"Cody, you smell like liquor."

"Hold your nose and come on."

I jerked her from bed. She was wearing a Bennington College T-shirt and underpants printed in small giraffes. She jumped into jeans. When we made the truck we found that Doug had passed out. We picked him up and put him in the truck bed beside the winch. I cranked the engine and headed for Chapel Road.

"Where are we going?" Harding asked, frantically brushing her auburn hair. Somehow she had managed to snag a comb.

"To the lighthouse."

"What's happened?"

"I'm a novelist."

"You're a what?"

We skidded to a stop, I grabbed Harding's hand and we

darted inside the lighthouse, leapt the tiny steps and reached the glass summit where I turned to Harding, sat her on the soft semicircular pallet and said, "City Side is publishing *Tiger River.*"

Harding squealed and then kissed me. I think this was the best kiss so far, and we didn't want to break it, so both of us made small sounds that meant do not let go of me now, our soft eyes opening and focusing on each other, then closing again to hold the magic.

I told her the details about Cribb and the possibility of a movie and the whole time we kissed and hugged and somehow her jersey came off and so did my shirt and I kissed her breasts gently until she said to do it harder and I did and then we were naked and the late afternoon sun turned the sea pink and blue and in that harsh Yankee light she was beautiful and for some reason crying and smiling while I made love to her.

When we finished I lay down beside her and then I saw it—the blood.

"Oh, Harding, is it your time . . ."

"No," she said.

I put my arms around her.

"It was beautiful," Harding said. "You were beautiful."

"You mean . . . but you're twenty-six."

"I never found anyone. I wanted it to be special."

I wiped away the blood, then kissed her stomach. I felt sick. I put my hands over my face and felt her pull close.

"It's all right," Harding said.

"I'm a jerk."

"Just hold me."

"Sorry, sorry, sorry," I said.

"Shush now," she said. "Shush."

When I awoke the small pine and glass room was cooler and I kissed Harding's cheek and she stirred. I saw, carved on the white pine walls, initials and hearts: B.J. + A.K. and "California was never like this" and "careless love" and other initials etched and hacked into the wood. I took a broken piece of glass and scratched C.W. + H.W.

"You're sweet," Harding said, and kissed my shoulder.

Even though the lighthouse was chilly, we lay back down together and held each other and listened to the wind and the sound of the waves on the beach and watched in fascination as a brown wasp tapped the white plaster ceiling, swooped down and then rose and tapped again and continued to dive until an exit was found and then the black wings and red triangular head flew out into the violet twilight.

Doug was still asleep in the truck bed. We drove to New House and put him in the bed downstairs.

I wanted to take a shower with Harding, but she wouldn't let me. While she was in the bathroom I made some tea. She came out of the shower radiant. Her wet auburn hair was swept back and the blue eyes were large and soft.

Like a shuffling, blond, sunburned baby, Doug stumbled into the writing room. "I feel terrible."

"You look terrible," I said.

Doug set his fingers over his eyes, pretended to pry them open. "You guys look awfully chummy."

I squeezed Harding's hand. "Are we chummy?"

"I think so," she said.

"Parker's coming tonight," Doug said. "She's helping me set the lobster pots." He spread his arms like an evangelist. "The maiden voyage of the *Sasha.* I need a couple extra sailors. Just think, you guys have a chance to take part in the building of a fishing empire. How can you turn me down?"

We couldn't, and so, after hot tea, we followed him to the boatyard. The twilight was gone.

Three feet into the dark harbor, the *Sasha* sat on two braces. Green and blue paint mottled the wooden hull. Here and there new pine splices had no paint at all. The bow was gashed and several boards patched with tar and aluminum. She was a bona fide wreck.

"You're actually going to sea in this thing?" I asked.

"She's beautiful," Doug said.

"She's an American junk," Marlow said from the deck.

"Styrofoam is what she needs," a voice said from the dark.

Marlow lit a lantern and held it aloft.

The girl's hair was wild and wheaten. She was tall and wore paint-spattered khaki pants and a black slicker.

"Hey, Summers—how much you pay for this heap?" Parker asked.

A tangible coolness lay between Doug and Parker. As she languidly approached, Doug's disdainful slouch and careless demeanor increased so much that he looked as if he were going to expire from ennui.

"It's rented," Doug said.

"Oh, yeah? From whom?" Parker asked, her young skin red and chafed in the Coleman light.

"Chip."

"You're not dealing with him again?" Parker reached and brushed back Doug's bangs.

"How you been?" Doug asked and smiled and so did she and the air felt warmer.

"Why are we doing this tonight?" she asked.

Marlow leapt down from the *Sasha.* Island sun had stamped big freckles on his face. His wet-seal eyes looked tense. "Because not everybody around here is happy about a new fisherman."

"The hell with them," Doug said.

"You're taking money out of their pockets," Marlow said. His dingy waist-waders were streaked with yellow paint.

"I'm only setting out fifty pots."

"Chip told me they shot a fellow two years ago. Thompson machine gun. Blew him away."

"These guys are my friends. I've been talking to them for months. They even said I could have Todd's Cove over at Dover."

"*His friends* sent him this," Marlow said. He handed me a piece of cardboard.

Set out pots and you're dead, rich boy.

"Well, that's certainly to the point," I said.

"Just some rednecks," said Doug.

"I decided to bring this along," Marlow said. He flipped something from his back pocket, lost control. The big metal twirled in the air and Marlow jumped three feet.

The Walther P38 shone in the sand. I had seen one before. They were beautiful. Lying there, it looked like a blue viper.

"Good God," said Doug.

Marlow had his hands over his ears.

I retrieved the pistol and felt awkward and silly and just a little daring. "You know what I say, boys." I stuck the pistol into my belt. "I say full steam ahead."

29

At Dover Cove, Doug and Parker tossed in the first lobster trap. Doug jumped onto the side of the *Sasha* and pointed. "There's the first million! Right there, Uncle Mallory!"

Doug whirled, his face red and blue excitement, the nostrils of his fine nose opening and closing, black hair blown before his eyes, neck flushed and thick. "We must go for a dip!"

"No way," I said. "It's freezing."

Parker slammed her canvas shoes to the deck. "That's a roger, Summers."

"We're in the middle of the Atlantic," I said.

"I'll go if you will," Harding said.

I backed away toward the cabin.

Parker stripped off her slicker, advanced and cut off my retreat.

"Don't try to push me," I said.

"Now we're all going to jump in together," Doug said, dropping his jaw.

"No, we're not," I said.

"Be a sport," Marlow said.

"You're going," said Parker.

They were moving for me now.

"Listen, I'll bust some heads around here," I said.

"Hey, look," said Doug and pointed at the sky.

I looked up and Doug tackled hard and we flew over the side and down, breaking a black ground swell. The cold salt water shot through my sinuses. I kept my eyes shut. My heart contracted to the size of a cold turnip. Dog-paddling, I coughed and spat.

Parker was beside me. "Man, this is dynamite."

Harding stood in the boat. "Harding," I yelled. "Let's go. Get your buns in here."

"Too cold for me," she laughed.

Doug bobbed up wheezing air. "Hey, I swam all the way under the *Sasha*. I'm Admiral Byrd." He disappeared beneath the black sea.

"Oh, Lord," I said. "There he goes." Briefly I thought about sharks.

Suddenly Parker was yanked down. I swam toward the *Sasha*, felt a hand flick my calf, but kicked it away.

I made the ladder and turned around.

The sea broke beneath the stars. They surfaced screaming in laughter, Doug's arms around the blue-faced girl, slick hair plastered to their skulls, expelling steamy breath, mouths wide and laughing, lashes sparkling in water.

In a while we were all in the boat again. We set pots for two hours. Once I thought I saw a light behind the *Sasha*. I thought something flashed, then faded in the dark. This happened only once. Until later, I forgot it.

When the final pot was laid we clapped and whistled. From below, Doug brought up a camping stove. We stood arm-in-arm at the boat's stern and watched the luminescent pots bob in the dark sea.

Doug lit the stove and went below for some marshmallows. Marlow passed army blankets. The heat of work had gone. I was cold now and the blanket felt good. Harding and Parker moved close to the fire. The yellow flames shuttled in the dark and because of the flames the sea seemed even blacker, colder. I don't think I have ever felt as cold as I did at that moment. The stars threw hard light and the wind came and the sea held the boat like a fist, like a black hand that had no warmth.

Doug distributed sweet-smelling marshmallows on paper plates. "Got some news for you guys," he said in a soft voice.

He embraced Parker, who set her head against his chest. Doug then pulled the blanket around his face. The lantern light made his jaw stubble fire like salt crystals; his blue eyes were small pools and the black bangs touched his eyelashes. "Me and Parker are getting married."

I cast my eyes toward the fire.

Doug pulled the blanket from around his face. "Well, what do you think?"

Harding hugged Parker. "Marvelous," she said.

I cracked my knuckles, shrugged, gave an eye to the stars. "I think—well, I think—I want to be very clear—I think that if the first baby boy is not named for me that I will never dedicate a book to you."

Doug grabbed my foot. "Then it's okay with you?"

"Okay? Why, it's wonderful," I said.

"Our parents won't like it," Parker said, now sounding mature, logical.

"Tough," I said.

"After all," Harding said in lockjaw, "you do have your own lives."

"Harding, why is it at times like this you sound like the Baroness Boob?" I said.

Doug bit into a marshmallow. "They wanted me to marry somebody else, Cody. It's halfway set. I can't handle it. This is the girl. Right here. Besides, I have to marry her. She's my partner in the Summers Fish Company."

"Yeah, fifty-one percent worth," Parker said, cheeks red as winesaps.

"Forty-nine."

"We shook on fifty-one," Parker said, almost serious.

"When's the date?" I asked.

"Two weeks from today," Doug said. "There's one thing though. We have to keep quiet. Nobody can know but us, and I mean nobody at all."

"Need to get a preacher though," I said.

Doug pointed a finger.

"Not me," I said.

"Every Southerner's a preacher, Cody. You can do it."

"Doug says you're a writer," Parker said. "Come up with some words. Read from the Bible."

Harding crossed her legs and stared at me. "The Baroness Boob will say nothing."

I glanced at the sky again. "All right, I'll say some words on one condition—that I am not called upon for baptisms or funerals."

No one knew that at that moment we were closer to a funeral than anyone could have guessed.

I think I was the one who saw it first. Close to the boat, the buoy drifted and spun.

"Doug," I said, "there must be a real strong current here."

Doug leaned over the boat. He grabbed the loose buoy, which marked the pot.

Marlow jumped below and got a large flashlight.

Carefully, Doug put the *Sasha* in reverse.

The yellow light beam revealed the scattered markers circling away on the tide. All the pots had been cut.

The first shot whizzed from the left. A Coleman lantern exploded. We went down quickly. Somehow Marlow produced the P38.

"Those bastards," Doug said. He grabbed the gun from Marlow, stood up.

Four or five more shots hit the *Sasha*. The old wood splintered and cracked.

I slammed Doug's legs and flattened him. The girls were crying. Marlow was drawn up into a ball.

"Where are they?" I asked.

"Black boat," Marlow said. "There's a black boat out there. I just saw it."

I remembered the flash I had seen earlier.

"Marlow, let's move," I said.

Marlow only groaned, wheezed.

As soon as I crawled toward the engine Doug stood and fired.

"Liars!" Doug yelled. "You liars!"

The second time he shot, the gun kicked from his hands.

Then came the storm.

From the left, a hundred yards away, the sea shone as the machine gun fired and lit the night. I started the engine.

When the bullets hit the *Sasha* the air sprayed wood and metal. The burst was long. Then darkness, but we were moving.

I gave full throttle.

The second burst came and the night turned yellow and red and this time the burst was so long that I could see the small black boat and the silhouettes of figures. The bullets sang into the *Sasha.* Water and oil spewed across the decks. Suddenly a fire exploded in the stern. I couldn't see Doug.

"Harding!" I yelled. "Use the blankets. Put that out." I kicked Marlow. He finally scrambled to help.

The *Sasha* had moved three or four hundred yards now. Once more a blue-red arc cut toward us, but the bullets struck the water behind the stern. I left the wheel to look for Doug.

He was lying face down on the deck. I don't think anyone had seen him yet. They were still putting out the fire. I touched his face. There was blood. His eyes were closed.

"Doug," I said.

Parker rushed over.

She covered her face, then fell on him.

I embraced her, gave her to Harding and Marlow.

The remaining lantern offered light. I knelt down beside Doug, moved his head. His eyes opened. "Hey, boy," I whispered. "Hey now, boy."

On his forehead the blood was shallow, no bullet wound. It looked as if he had fallen and slashed his skull.

"Where are they?" Doug said and tried to rise.

I pushed him back. "They're back there. We're going home. They're not following."

Doug sat upright and Parker hugged him. Harding put her arm around my waist as Marlow drove back toward Black Island as fast as the old boat would go. Seawater was flooding the decks through exploded planks. The mast had been blown off. The air smelled like fire and burned oil.

When we docked, Doug had regained his balance.

"I'm calling the police," Marlow said.

Doug grabbed him by the collar. "No, you're not."

"Doug, we have to," Parker said.

"We tell nobody about this. Do you know what my father would say? We tell nobody. I'm starting over. I'll rerig, buy more traps, I won't give up. I'm gonna make it and no bunch of lousy Ricans are going to stop me." Doug broke away from Parker. "I'm gonna be free of this island. I'm gonna do it and nobody, nothing can stop me."

Doug stomped away. Parker wanted to go after him, but I held her back.

It was 11 P.M. and everybody was sleepy, so I brought them to New House and got them in bed.

I took a bottle of Chivas to my room. Harding lay in one of the beds, but she was not asleep.

I brandished the bottle. "Forgive me."

"For what?" she said. Her lips were trembling. The blue eyes looked red and rough.

I drank the Chivas.

"Cody," Harding said.

"I'm drinking."

30

For a couple of days no one saw Doug, but when we did he was sullen and aloof. Harding and Marlow pressed me to call the cops. I reminded them that we had promised silence. I told them that Doug was right—a police investigation would scuttle all his chances of independence.

I did not even tell Lisa about the incident when she came over one afternoon to tell me that she had moved into Chip's place. I tried to act unperturbed, but I wasn't. Later, I started spending more and more time on the script, even though I had not seen or heard from Chip. (Lisa said he was at a Gestalt training session in New York.) I got up every morning at five o'clock and drank two cups of coffee and watched the sunrise. For the first cup, and half of the second, I worried: about my position on the island, about Doug, about Lisa and Harding, the movie script, about the fact that I had not heard from the editor in New York. Then at the last of the second cup, the pressure to write drove these concerns away and I began to put down words.

One morning, when I sat down at the picnic table in the glass room, Chip walked through the backyard, opened a glass door and stepped inside.

Most of my resentment about Lisa receded when he extended his hand. Chip Beale looked ghastly. Black circles around his eyes, pallor upon his cheeks, a trembling in his hands. He looked as though he had been through some great struggle.

"Cody, I thought I'd come see you. I've been away."

He sat down and I made some coffee.

For thirty minutes Chip talked about his family, about his responsibility to them. He said that he had tried running the island but was resisted during his entire effort by the work crews. They had no respect for him. He then tried to oversee a few loans at his father's bank in Boston and for one reason or another that effort had failed as well.

Then, without transition, his thoughts shifted. His gold eyes looked fragmented and watery. Buck teeth hid behind his fibrous, black mustache. He was hurting. "Do you think I'm evil? I mean—do you think I'm an evil person?"

"I think everybody has bad parts," I said.

"Me?"

It was hard to answer him truthfully.

"Give me a couple of faults," Chip said.

"I don't know. I don't think that's up to me."

"Just one."

"Okay, I think you like power. I think you enjoy having people on a string."

"Like Lisa?"

"Maybe so."

Chip's face changed. A redness crept into his pallor, the gold eyes bulged. "I didn't plan the Lisa thing. It just happened. You're wrong about the power trip."

I said nothing.

"I mean, I've spent my whole life rejecting power, my family's name. You're real wrong there, man."

I sipped coffee, felt that I had lost the edge now. Chip delivered a speech about his hatred for power and how he had broken from the robber-baron mold that had founded his family. I felt like he wanted me to recant, wanted me to say I had made a mistake.

"So you see, I really think you misjudged me, man. Don't you think? I mean, don't you think I've totally beaten power?"

Somehow, I was able to look at him straight and not even blink. But I knew he had me and so did he. He stood up. He offered a great smile and the black beard perked and he reached and poured me another coffee.

"You need anything now, you come and see me." Chip opened the sliding door, stood on the steps. "Oh, yes. You're going to have to leave New House."

"What do you mean?"

"There's a cousin coming up from New York. Alice Pound, I think. She always takes New House. You've got another week or so."

"Where do I go? I mean . . ." I tried to control myself. "I don't have another place."

"Oh, we'll find something. Let me know when I can see that script."

For the rest of the day and into the night I felt something like panic. At 10 P.M. I called Doug, told him what had happened. He said it was typical. He said that once Chip had three people living on the island: a musician, a dancer and a painter. Chip had promised to back each in a project, then lost interest and simply stopped seeing them. Their houses were closed for winter repairs or simply rented to other family members. Finally all three just drifted away. Doug told me not to worry. He said he'd find me a house.

After the phone conversation I went outside. I sat and looked at the starless sea. The realization was horrifying: I was just a toy for Chip Beale, just like the others. And he would deal with me exactly the same way. He did not have the guts to cancel the movie project and order me off the island; he would just ignore me, allow me to fall into lethargy and finally atrophy, until someday someone would tell him that I had left the island quite voluntarily.

Somehow, I had to interrupt this process and I had to do it quickly. Miraculously, the next day I discovered the beginning of my connection to the only person who could save me: Mallory Beale.

I didn't get up until eleven o'clock. The previous evening was like a nightmare. I went downstairs, made some coffee. Standing at the stove, I had this sense of panic again. It was something I had never felt before. My stomach tightened; I felt dizzy and my heart raced. I couldn't breathe well.

I walked into my writing room. There was a new manila folder on the picnic table. I was relieved. Beale's memoir would help me forget things for a while. I didn't care who was leaving it or why. I didn't care if it was Mallory Beale himself.

Garbo. Garbo. Garbo. Garbo. I had seen her first two films. She wasn't Olive Thomas. She wasn't beautiful. In fact, she was like a guy. Big hands and big feet. A Swede. When I saw her on the screen I tried not to concentrate on those farmer hands. They seemed bigger than my own. They bothered me. But if I looked at her face—God, even in black and white her face was gorgeous, especially her eyes. They looked tired and gloomy. Maybe this is what fascinated me. Her sense of gloom and distance and despair. I liked these features in Garbo. When I saw her third flick I decided I wanted her in bed. Simple lust. Nothing more. I was determined, so I started a file. I followed her in the press for six solid months. One of the best clippings I had was written by Jim Tully. It defined Garbo:

"The Swedish film actress is phlegmatic, even apathetic. Of the fire that sets the white screen ablaze, only the ash is visible in ordinary life. She is broad-shouldered, flat-chested, awkward in her movements. Her figure is the seamstress' despair. She has no real beauty, but with clever lighting and photographing and good makeup that makes her lips more full and her eyes more narrow, she becomes graceful and fascinating on the screen. This affectedly sad, languid, indifferent girl is vibrant with inner life. She has a power to charm men and women. Thousands have been called the Sarah Bernhardt of the films, but Greta Garbo is one of the few who deserve to be mentioned in the same breath."

But what color were her eyes, Tully? Didn't anybody know? I wanted them blue. A certain blue, not light, but something close to violet. Something brooding, conservative. Something I could violate.

After reading Tully's piece, Garbo consumed me. I decided I had enough information. I needed to make the move. I couldn't go straight for her. Instinctively I knew that I had to go through friends. I heard on the news that the Barrymores had been collected to do a film: Rasputin and the Empress. *I knew them all—Lionel, John and Ethel. I had backed a couple of their movies, vacationed with them several times in Palm Beach. I decided to call Ethel. I was sure she could provide me the key for Garbo's bedroom. Ethel knew everyone.*

I reached her early in the morning. She was her usual witty self. We talked about movies and a few business deals I had going on the Coast. When I finally got around to Garbo, she laughed and said she knew there was another reason for my call. I just told her straight that it was lust, good old American lust and could she help. She thought awhile, then said that Jack Gilbert was a good place to start. He had dated Garbo for a year. She said she would call him.

It took Ethel two days to make the date between me and Gilbert. I went to the library, did some quick research. There were ten or twelve articles about Jack Gilbert and Greta Garbo. The following from a N.Y. newspaper was the best. It gave me a peep into Gilbert's soul:

"The Romeo of the films who wasn't going to marry again now engaged to Swedish actress. Handsome, dashing Jack Gilbert is defeated. Hollywood is on tenterhooks. His heart is riddled, he has begun to like things Swedish. Jack began to show signs of restlessness several months ago when his film work brought him into intimate contact with that desirable feminine gift from Sweden—Greta Garbo. What a couple! Both have been fashioned in the fire of love. Both are temperamental, stormy, beautiful."

So they were engaged. Good. It made things interesting.

31

The Pacific Ocean was soft and blue. I was sitting on a sixty-foot boat called The Temptress, *according to the Chinese mate who escorted me aboard. Gilbert had just purchased her. Teakwood decks, polished brass fittings, a double mast and two inboard engines. She was a beautiful creature. I sat at a small table. White gardenias floated in a bowl of water. I had read that Gilbert was big, boisterous, strong and nuts: my kind of guy.*

Beside the table, a phone rang. I waited for the mate to answer. Ten rings, twelve, fifteen. I finally grabbed the receiver.

"Hello?"

"Yes, hello. Who is this?"

"Mallory Beale."

"Mallory. Wonderful, or maybe not wonderful. I'm in a wee jam, I guess."

"Who are you?"

"Jack. Jack Gilbert. I know we were supposed to meet for lunch. I, uh, I got tied up here."

"At the studio?"

"Nope. Well—I'm in jail."

"Is this a joke?"

"Yeah, but I'm not sure on who. Look, I know we haven't known one another for a terribly long time, but I was wondering—could you come down and bail me out?"

When Jack Gilbert rammed his hand through the bars of the cell door, I saw he was huge, the fingers of the right hand like red knockwurst.

"Geez, how much is this going to set you back, Mal?"

"Mallory."

"Sure."

"Seven hundred bucks."

"Well, it's only a hundred more than last time."

"You've done this before?"

"Only twice. Last time it was Clara Bow. We got in a terrible row. She's a small-town bitch. Anyway, we were at the Brown Derby. She jumped in her MG. I had a Jag. She peeled off and I was right behind her. The cops caught us at Rodeo Drive right in front of that little Greek diner. They were going to haul us both in, Mal—both of us—Jack Gilbert and Clara Bow. You know what she did? She chucked one cop under the chin and then she flashed him a titty. He let her right off. Scot-free. Anyway, the cop had a partner and they're all kinds in L.A., so I unzipped and showed the flag. The guy belted me one and then booked me for reckless driving and flashing an officer. Can you believe it? Women."

I liked Jack Gilbert. He was like a big, mop-headed boy. A running back's neck and blue eyes and a dent in his square chin. The only thing that set him off bad was his squeaky little voice. "You might as well relax, Gilbert," a jailor said. "They called a judge."

"Is anything simple?" Gilbert asked.

"How about Garbo?"

"You like her?"

"Don't you?"

"Sure, even though it's finished, Mal. Even though it's all on the rocks. Yeah, yeah. I still like her, but I'm not *gonna marry her."*

"Tell me about her. Tell me what her normal day's like. What she does."

Jack Gilbert's face fell softly. The dark eyelashes touched his cheeks. He almost looked sweet.

"She's tough on herself, Mal. Hard. Like a man sometimes. She likes hot food—white pepper and paprika. She usually drinks a glass of vodka with dinner or sometimes just tea. In her whole house she's just got one place setting of blue porcelain. Hell, I'm a bachelor and I've got thirty at my digs. She likes to wear riding boots. She smokes. A package a day, but they're nicotine free. Isn't that like her? Isn't it really?"

"How does she dress?"

"You hooked on her?"

"I'm hooked."

"Well, she wears only cotton. Nothing else. Cotton blouses and cotton skirts and shirts. She hates silk. I remember I bought her a whole silk wardrobe and the next day she took it to the Salvation Army. She won't wear scent or creams. She always washes her hair herself and rinses it with lemon juice and mineral water. She's got a real swell place now on Laurel Canyon. Six rooms, warm, lots of wood. The only thing that's like a movie star is her swimming pool. It's heated. Every morning she gets up at six, has a swim. Fixes coffee and smokes those awful cigarettes. Then she goes to the studio."

"I want to meet her."

"You want to screw her."

"How, when, and where?"

"You're a cold dealer, aren't you?"

"And you're a washed-up matinee mannequin. Now, when and where, Gilbert?"

Jack Gilbert paused and thoughtfully observed the cell bars. He stroked the rusted metal.

"I could set you up a little rendezvous."

"When?"

"Easy, Mal."

"When?"

"Let's say three days from now at 6 A.M. Dawn. Soft light and lovely birds and the yellow cactus flowers just opening."

"How?"

He reached into his pocket, pulled a key from others. "This opens her backyard gate. She has a glass bubble over her pool. The heated water makes something like a fog. Sensuous. Lovely. You'll be waiting in the water just when she comes down. Greta likes these kinds of things. These little mysteries. I'll tell her about you. She'll do it. She'll do it for me because, see, Mal, she still loves me. She does. She loves my sweet Irish self."

I shook his hand. His hair was dirty and stank from scalp oil and gin. His halfback shoulders drooped and the boy had left his face.

"Lemme tell you something, Gilbert. Pretty soon the booze and the

dames are going to do you in. If you come to your senses before then, you call me. I'll help. I know the right people to sober you up. I can get you a decent job."

"I don't want to be decent."

Three days later I was treading warm water in Garbo's pool. Naked, I watched the sunlight polish the condensation on the glass bubble above. My heart was beating like a bad piston. Irregular, pound and skip and shudder. Visibility was eight inches. So was I. A vapor drifted across the pool.

Just then a door smooched open. A silhouette stepped into the pool. I swear I felt the water electrify.

It was Garbo.

For a while she made no movement. I saw nothing but the fog. I heard the soft water touch the pool's sides. Smelled the water—nothing sweet, nothing perfumed, just the fresh, hard smell of salt water from the sea.

Garbo.

I was going to say something, but now I knew she was playing. Now I knew she must like romance like Gilbert said, so I said nothing. I stopped treading water and laid my arms on the cool blue tiles and I smiled. Smiled at the fog and smiled at what was rising beneath the surface and smiled at this woman somewhere in the invisible distance.

Garbo.

I felt the water shake and rustle. She was moving toward me now. Palms gently cupped the surface and I heard the swoosh of feet kicking beneath the water and now I could smell it—acrid and sharp, faintly like hemp. The nicotine-free cigarette. I decided not to meet her, but just to wait. With beautiful women, you got to be tough.

"What you want from me, Mallory Beale?"

Deep voice, foreign and sexy, more German than Swedish.

"Time."

"What kind of time?"

"Sack time."

"Americans."

"What do you think I came here for?"

"Is this the way you approach a woman?"

"No, I usually wear my clothes."

I still could not see her, but the water was rough, alive.

"Jack Gilbert," she said.

"He says you still love him."

"Maybe."

"Do you still see him?"

"He sees Beatrice Lillie. She is a tart. Last month she was in a terrible automobile wreck, thank God. I'd been praying for weeks dat she would come into some disaster—and she did. But alas, she was not hurt bad. She stayed at Jack's place. A broken leg. This, at least, was good. Her legs were too nice. Now, maybe one will be shorter. Do you think?"

"Gimme a kiss."

"I don't kiss."

"No?"

"Well, I don't kiss those I do not know."

"Come over and we'll make friends."

She splashed and chopped the water. The moves sounded heavier, bigger than they should, but then she was a big girl, wasn't she?

About three feet away Garbo stopped. She laughed and the laugh was high and strained and wicked, almost unnatural. The cigarette polluted the air. She waited there, just a good reach away. I didn't move. I was determined to make this beauty come to me.

"Do you think dat Jack Gilbert is a great actor?" she asked.

"Jack Gilbert who?"

"Don't be cruel."

"Gilbert's a child."

"Dey say he makes a powerful lover."

"Well, does he?"

"Do you want to know?"

"Why don't you come a little closer?"

"You are jealous of Jack Gilbert."

"Perhaps."

"Perhaps he is more than you think."

Suddenly she leapt toward me from the fog and I saw then: the big angled jaw and thick curled hair and vulnerable blue eyes and a ruddy, hairless vault of chest. The laugh whined and cackled and Jack Gilbert caught my shoulders and lunged a kiss toward my mouth. I shot backward and leapt to the pool's side.

"You can't have everything!" Gilbert screamed. He swam forward. He wore eyeliner and mascara and the great red hands gripped the pool's side. "She's gone. Greta's gone. I sent her away. I out-thought you. Besides, I'm pretty as her. Don't you think? Come here, Mr. Tycoon. Let Jack Gilbert show you what love's all about."

I punched a hole through that plastic bubble. Easy as pie. I busted right through and made my car and put Garbo and Gilbert and Hollywood on my backest of back burners.

I sat back in the wicker chair. My body felt relaxed. The panic had passed. I chuckled a little about Gilbert.

I gathered up the last four or five pages—notes about bank mergers, a new oil business in Manila, an affair.

Then I saw a few lines scrawled at the bottom of one page:

I couldn't have made it without Bosey. Couldn't have.
December—the accident in Aiken—my son's death.

I felt myself take a breath. I read the line again: "December—the accident in Aiken—my son's death."

I stacked the pages neatly in the folder, sat and looked at them.

My father had been killed in an accident. A car crash in December in Aiken.

Was he talking about Joe Beale? Or was he talking about my father?

My mind began racing.

32

I walked outside, down the beach stairs. Climbed the big boulder. I tried to clear my head. I tried to slow down and think logically.

Joe Beale was raised in Aiken. My father was raised in Aiken. Joe Beale went to St. Georges and Yale. Joe Walker went to St. Georges and Yale. Joe Beale died in an accident in Aiken and so did my father—Joe Walker.

What was I saying? The idea was ridiculous, but so were the facts. I jumped from the boulder and went back to the house and poured a tea glass full of bourbon. I downed it in three minutes flat. I tried not to let the thought form, tried not to let the sentence take shape. It was useless.

Were Joe Beale and Joe Walker the same person?

For the next three or four hours I went over a thousand points, counterpoints, questions, assertions. Why had my father been so deliberately confusing about his early life? Why had he never mentioned Joe Beale? The memoir said that Beale's son died in an accident. Was it a car wreck? And if I wasn't Cody Walker, who was I? Cody Beale? I laughed out loud. How absurd. Who was my grandmother then? Why, the movie actress Olive Thomas, of course.

I laughed again. "Nuts," I said. "I sound absolutely nuts."

I drank two more tumblers of bourbon and thankfully passed out. I did not wake until six the next morning.

I had a headache, but I was more calm. My mind wasn't clattering. I took out the pages and studied the lines again.

It was an incredible coincidence—the accident. I had to believe that. I had to force that idea into my head until—well, until I could go see somebody. Sims. No, not him. I needed somebody with *all* the answers. Somebody like—yeah. Bosey. Beale had mentioned her. Obviously she knew about the accident, about Mallory Beale's son. Maybe she knew a lot of other things too.

Maybe she knew my father *and* Joe Beale and maybe she could tell me that they were too separate people who shared the same town, the same education, died accidental deaths the same month, but nevertheless they were two separate men—and then we would both laugh and say how bizarre, how impossibly bizarre and then we would have a drink and tell the story to our friends.

I made a promise to myself that I would wait a week before I went to Bosey. I would wait a week and cool down and try to think of a way to investigate the identities of these two men—right, two men, because Joe Walker was not Joe Beale. He couldn't be. He just couldn't.

The next day I saw Harding. She said there were several social events happening on the island. She said they were important, that I needed to attend. I think she could see that something was wrong. I told her that some cousin was supposed to take over New House. She said not to worry and that Alice Pound never came until the end of the summer. By then most of the family would be gone and I could stay with her. I did not speak about my discovery, my expectations. I couldn't.

For six or seven days Harding and I buzzed from one gathering to another. In the mornings we ate an early breakfast with Townsend. Took hardy walks on the beach with her and her black Labs. Listened as she told us how well Mallory was doing, that he seemed and looked ten years younger. Afternoons were spent having brunches with Dr. Westor (the thumb doctor) or Jean Talbot (the blond lady in my Chowder Party trio who just happened to own 20 percent of Time, Inc.) and Jean Talbot's friends George and Susan West, who had recently built their third hotel in central Florida.

In addition, Harding and I attended three island functions: the Canvas Party—held at the beach club—a gathering at which family and friends auctioned off summer paintings, carvings, renderings for anywhere from one dollar to thirty or forty bucks; the Night Skeet Shoot, where everyone got smashed on gin and tried (with the aid of an enormous World War II spotlight) to hit just one clay pigeon—I actually did; and the Ash Party, an entire day spent riding about on the island firetruck guzzling vodka gimlets.

I met almost everyone on the island at these events. They seemed more friendly, less reserved than I had ever seen them.

During these days I forced myself not to think about Joe Beale, Joe Walker. I kept myself dizzily busy and hoped that Chip's cousin might not appear until later. The hope was destroyed one morning when I was awakened by a workman pounding on the front door.

I ran downstairs, opened the door to a huge man wearing bib overalls, a trainman's hat and a small, gold earring.

"You Cody Walker?"

"Yes."

"Got orders to move you. Miss Pound arrives today."

I stood, trying to think. "Well, I don't have any place to go."

"Pardon?"

"Did Chip tell you where to put me?"

"He said to move you out."

I dressed, gathered my things. While the man shoved my brand-new wardrobe in boxes, I called Doug. He was there in five minutes.

Half an hour later, Doug and I loaded the last box into the blue pickup. The workman had already started scouring the upstairs shower. A second man arrived, began stacking chairs, rolling up rugs, pulling down drapes.

We were sitting in the cab of Doug's truck when the workman tapped on the window.

"You got the keys to a car?"

"Yeah!" Doug said. "That's where you can stay."

I handed over the keys. "No, Chip's taking the car too."

"The Garage," Doug said. "You can stay in the Garage."

When he turned the ignition there was only a rattle. He jumped from the cab, opened the hood.

I took the time to walk through New House. I remembered the meals with Doug and Marlow and the first night I had seen Lisa, naked and peering into the house. I recalled my first cup of Earl Grey tea in the kitchen and Doug trying his best to fry yellowtail, Southern style. I remembered getting smashed on Black Horse ale before a big fire while my first nor'easter whipped and lashed the house and Doug and Marlow lay asleep on the floor. I glimpsed all the nights Lisa and I had made love: the nervousness, the fun, the ecstasy.

In five minutes I had relived three months, and when I walked out the front door I turned and gazed at New House and promised that I would return and somehow, somehow—never leave again.

The Garage was not a garage. It was a small four-room cabin that sat behind Doug's parents' house on the north end of Black Island. The place was rough: a plywood floor, peeling yellow walls, naked bulbs in ceilings, no lamps, one single bed, an abused dresser.

I looked at Doug and he looked at me and we both managed a laugh. We unloaded the truck. Marlow arrived and the three of us swept the tiny house, dusted.

When things were more or less clean and ordered, I asked Doug how he was feeling and he said fine and that he was rerigging the *Sasha* and that Parker was getting excited about the wedding.

Marlow said that he was looking for a job. So far he had applied at the dog pound and city hall. The pairing of these two places produced a laugh. After a while the two of them left on separate errands and I made my narrow bed and lay down and then the thought rushed me.

I could call St. Georges and Yale. I could ask them if they had a listing for Joe Beale and Joseph W. Walker. I sat on the edge of the bed, looked at the phone. Nerves contracted my stomach. If there was a Joe Beale and a Joe Walker, then I would know for certain that they were, indeed, two separate people and I could forget my crazy speculation. I called Doug, got the main number for St. Georges.

It took me forty-five minutes to get the right person at the school. I told him the truth: that I was checking out the possibility of a double identity. The man's name was Clinkscales and he seemed amused at the idea. He said he would have to call me back.

I spent the afternoon by the phone, now and again taking a walk into the unkempt yard. I told myself how silly all this was, but that, thank God, I had found a way of checking things without seeing Bosey.

The call came at four-thirty.

"It was 1938, Mr. Walker. He attended St. Georges from 1938 until 1941."

"Who?"

"Joseph A. Beale."

"What's the hometown?"

"One second."

My heart fluttered.

"Aiken, South Carolina."

"Next of kin?"

"Mallory R. Beale. Same address."

"Okay. Now, what about Joe Walker."

"No listing."

"Let me give you the full name—Jos—"

"Joseph W. Walker. You gave it to me. We have no records of him ever having attended this school."

"Wait." I felt my breath go. "This is very serious. Can you double-check? Joseph W. Walker."

"I have double-checked. Joseph W. Walker never attended this school. Now perhaps you've confused . . ."

I mumbled thank you and hung up.

What were the possibilities? Maybe they had lost my father's records. Doubtful. Maybe there were two St. Georges. Possible. Perhaps my father had been lying and he, in fact, did not go to school there. But why would he lie? Didn't make sense.

At five-fifteen I called Mr. Clinkscales again, asked if he knew of another prep school named St. Georges. His answer was definite: "No. Not in the whole country."

I got an idea. I needed a picture of Joe Beale at St. Georges. If he was Joe Walker (even if he was only sixteen or so) I could see the resemblance.

"How about annuals or photograph books?"

"I thought of it, Mr. Walker. Checked. We didn't start a photograph annual until 1943."

33

I spent a restless night. No supper, little sleep. I tried to keep control, not think wild thoughts. One snuck in anyway. If Joe Beale was my father, then Mallory Beale was my grandfather. This sat me straight up and I did not sleep until dawn.

By ten o'clock I had called Yale, gone through the same process. I found out that Joe Beale had gone to Yale one semester. There were no records after that. No mention of him after the fall of 1941.

And Joe Walker or Joseph Walker, Joseph W. Walker—no trace. Not one. He had never attended Yale.

How about a yearbook?

They didn't take photographs until second semester.

It was 10:05 in the morning. I walked outside and heard a buoy ringing and it changed into my father's voice:

"Yeah. I went to Yale one semester and then, well, then I went to work for Mallory Beale. . . ."

I sat down on a wooden bench in front of the Garage. I knew the next step: Bosey. It was frightening. I couldn't seem nutty or prying. I had to seem interested in Joe Beale in a historical sense: "Someone mentioned his name at the Chowder Party; I thought that Mallory had only one son—Chip. I was just interested."

I became a little more calm. What was the main fact I wanted from Bosey? What would really convince me that Joe Beale and Joe Walker were the same man? Carefully I went over what I already knew.

1. My father was raised in Aiken. Joe Beale was raised in Aiken.

2. My father *said* he attended St. Georges and Yale. Joe Beale *did* attend the two schools.

3. My father said he quit Yale after one semester. Joe Beale did the same.

These points, combined with my father's impenetrable secretiveness about his early life in Aiken, the fact that there were no records of a Joe Walker at Yale or St. Georges, and the undeniable reality that my father had been very special to Mallory Beale allowed me to think that I had every reason to speculate about the possibility of double identity.

But what did I need from Bosey? What would completely convince me?

The accident. Sure. The accident. If Joe Beale had died in a wreck—if the details of Joe Beale's death matched the ones of my father's—then I would know.

I took a long walk on the north shore of the island. I told myself it was not true. It was too much like a fairy tale. And fairy tales didn't happen, did they?

I returned, showered. It was 12:30 P.M. I had to find Bosey.

I was sure she would be at the beach club. It was her custom to eat lunch there with other family members.

I walked down Shore Road. Even though it was early August, the afternoon air felt nipping and quick. I stopped and glanced down at my turquoise ring—it was a brighter shade of my father's eyes. I had to cool down now. I had to.

The exterior of the beach club was weathered boards and split shingles and long, empty porches. Brown weeds and ragged sea grass grew along the building's sides. Three outside showers, rusted clotheslines, stacks of wooden-cased Coke bottles. The sand, however, was immaculate. This was the ivory sand that Mallory Beale had hauled from Florida.

At the rusted and tattered screen door I stood and prepared for the entrance. Blue flies buzzed and bumped the screen. Probably imported from France, I thought.

Trying to look casual and cool and faintly bored, I stepped inside and yawned. The interior was composed of two large rooms separated by a walk-through kitchen. Thankfully, the first room was empty. I relaxed a little, let my eyes adjust to less light.

The floor was worn white pine and the walls brown fir. There were eight windows in this room and twelve in the next. The second room held around twenty-five people. Most of them seemed old. Lots of white hair, florid jowls, sagging earlobes and that peculiar click that dentures make when they are munching something that they should not. (It smelled like corn.)

So far no one had noticed me. In this room and the next, green Formica picnic tables supported neat rows of baleful plastic plates—the compartment kind you used in high school. Beside the screen door stood a Paleolithic drink cooler. I hadn't seen one like this since I was a kid. It was scarred and sweating and the lead door lay open. A sign plastered to the rusty lid read "Drinks 20¢. Pay Now! ! !"

From a walk-in pantry within the kitchen a man and woman emerged. They looked in their forties; both wore their brown hair in pageboy cuts. Standing side by side, they seemed to be twins, a rosy dimple beginning in her left cheek and finishing in his right.

I set my hands on the wooden counter before them and tried to sound jovial and confident. "Well, what's for dinner?"

"We don't serve dinner here," the woman said.

"Lunch, I mean."

"Luncheon."

"Yes. What's for luncheon?" I asked, feeling my confidence puncture and leak.

"On the blackboard," she said and stuck a prophetlike finger above her head. I glanced at her finger and then the nameplate she wore on her blouse—Mrs. Fick. The man's tag read—Mr. Fick. The Ficks, I thought. I studied the menu.

Today's Meal
Tuna Fish, Fresh Corn, Apple Salad, Ice Cream—Chocolate or Vanilla

"I'll have tuna fish, fresh corn, apple salad and ice cream," I said.

"Chocolate or vanilla?"

"Both."

"We hadn't got both."

"Chocolate."

"We hadn't got chocolate."

"Vanilla." I felt defeated.

In the next room someone banged a spoon against a glass. It was Bosey. Her amber eyes danced beneath the shoulder-length white hair.

"As you all know, Mr. and Mrs. Fick have been leaving their lovely little chalet in Boston and coming down to spend their summers with us for twenty years. Also, as you all know, I founded a small committee a couple of months ago to see what we could come up with as a reward for their generous service. I am happy to say that the committee and I finally agreed upon an expression of this family's gratitude."

Applause.

"We have passed the hat and we are happy to be sending both of you, at the end of this summer, to Paris for two weeks."

Mrs. Fick gasped and touched her face. Her husband emitted an "Oh, golly."

"The only thing we shall require is one postcard—and it must not be the Arc de Triomphe. Anything but that."

Bosey stepped into the kitchen and hugged the Ficks, who, teary-eyed and flushing, returned her affection, then entered the second room to thank the rest of the family. My lunch was forgotten.

Bosey saw me.

"Oh, Cody," she said and came over and grasped my hand.

Her skin resembled her brother's—tough and mottled. "What do you think of the trip?"

"I wish I were going," I said, surprised at Bosey's warmth.

"Oh, but Cody, you've seen Paris a hundred times. You wouldn't begrudge these good people their first introduction to Europe." A sudden smile seized her face. She wrinkled her bent, tough nose. "Cody, you are a writer, aren't you?"

"Well, yes."

"Good, because I just heard a wonderful story that I think a writer would appreciate. Do you have a moment?"

Bosey went to the drink cooler, grabbed two Cokes, did not pay and guided me to a picnic table.

"It's a story about Townsend which Constance Phillips told me just a few minutes ago. I was utterly spellbound."

I was finding that rich people loved the stories about themselves, as if even they couldn't believe their extraordinary fate.

Bosey tucked her sleek and surprisingly good-looking legs beneath her white tennis skirt. She wore a pale pink Izod shirt that was frayed and worn. Perhaps because of the shirt's color, I saw just at the right-hand corner of her upper lip—a pink imperfection, a small scar which resembled a tiny heart. For some reason this little valentine made me feel comfortable with her, as if signaling that she had a greater heart, one which might fully embrace me one day, if—if I was really related.

"It was the spring of 1943 and Townsend had discovered bridge. She was simply mad for it. She played morning, noon and night, particularly rejoicing in beating children and senile guests. To be honest, she was good, very good, and so set her sights on winning the Black Island Bridge Tourney, which had been initiated some ten years earlier. But here was her dilemma—if she loved her new pastime, then she adored, worshiped her old—baseball. A fanatic. Just crackers. So much so that in 1930 she bought a larger share of the St. Louis Cardinals. Her first cousin, Sally Smith, owned an equal share of the Boston Red Sox. At the beginning of the 1943 season Boston and St. Louis were to play an exhibition game at Fenway Park. Townsend was enraged at the date because it was to take place on the same day as the island bridge tourney, in which Sally Smith was a main contender. Now, as Constance Phillips tells the story, the family had all gotten together for the spring bash. There were cookouts and tennis matches and boccie tournaments and the usual holiday tents were up in the center of the island. Then Constance said she saw something unusual. Just beyond the tennis courts some workmen began cutting the grass very short. A couple of trees were felled, their stumps ripped from the earth and dirt tamped into the holes. Everyone supposed it was because Townsend wanted the area near the tents where the bridge tourney was being held to look as smooth and lovely as her rose gardens. At any rate, as soon as the second rubber started, a rather large bus rolled onto the new grass. Baseball players emerged—Boston Red Sox. Another bus appeared—St. Louis Cardinals. The Red Sox played the Cardinals and the Cardinals won, while Townsend watched from her L.L. Bean tent where she bid and won her first grand slam. Sally Smith was appalled."

Bosey sat back and laughed. Her yellow teeth gleamed and the pink heart at her lip spread. I noticed that the roots of her hair were red and thicker than the white ends.

I couldn't laugh because I didn't think the story was so funny, but I did grin—I grinned until my unscrubbed back molars felt the light.

Then I began carefully, "Somebody told me that Mallory Beale used to—uh, vacation in South Carolina."

"Ya, for some years. Ya."

"It's a great place."

"South Carolina?"

"Ya."

"Ya."

"Ya, ya." The conversation was beginning to sound like something out of a bad German movie. I had to move forward carefully. "Did he have, uh, well—did Mallory have—relations down there?"

Bosey's ripe face darkened. "Relations?"

"Well, yes. Did he have, you know . . . relations . . ."

Her amber eyes enlarged. "Are you asking me about my brother's sexual conduct?"

"G-G-G-God, no," I stammered.

"Are you interrogating me about Mallory Beale's sexuality?"

"No!"

"Relations with someone, you said."

By this time my face was burning. I had to set things straight. "Relations—in the sense of family. Look, Bosey, I know Mallory Beale had a son named Joe."

Her jaw stiffened. "Young man . . ."

"I heard his name mentioned."

"Where?"

"The Chowder Party."

"From whom?"

"And I've read some things. Other things. In his memoir."

"A memoir?"

"Somebody's been delivering sections of it."

"Rubbish. I've never heard of a memoir."

"Was Joe Beale killed in a car wreck?"

"Silence!" Bosey looked toward the other room. "We do not discuss—him."

"Look, I need to talk."

"Where is this—memoir?"

"I have it."

"Bring it to me."

"Tonight?"

"No. I'm going to New York this evening. Urgent business." She thought. "Come to my house at 8:00 P.M. sharp on Thursday. I want to see this writing."

Quietly I walked back to the Garage. I had not been cool. I had lost all of my finesse. But at least I could talk to Bosey and I was sure that she would give me the details of Beale's death, and maybe more. Maybe much more. Something was going to happen in five days. I could feel it.

The boxwoods which grew against the Garage's exterior had a spatter of red and yellow leaves. It was August 10, but I thought the air contained the first pulse of fall. I wondered where I would be when the maple leaves began to turn red and yellow. New House, I thought. New House, where I belonged.

Inside, the phone was ringing.

"Hello?"

"Wanna have sex?"

"Is this you, Lisa?"

"You got a minute?"

"Why don't you have sex with Chip?"

"He's got the droopies."

"The whatsies?"

"I'll be there in ten minutes."

34

She arrived in five, wearing a cerise velour jumpsuit, her hair black and sexy, eyes big as walnuts. She opened my door, slid down her front zipper.

"Aren't I shik?"

"Chic," I said. "Not shik."

"Oh, Mr. Know-it-all."

"Mr. Know-some-of-it."

"I got some news."

"What?"

"I'm pregnant."

I collapsed.

Lisa jumped on top of me.

"Let's do it," she said.

"Not with a mother, thank you."

"Stop squirming. It's not you."

"How do you know?"

"I know because I've decided. It's not yours."

She set a brown finger on my lips, then peeled away her jumpsuit. Her breasts were soft and round and the nipples stiff as thick stems. She raised and unfastened a small trap door in the jumpsuit's bottom.

"That's obscene," I said, but she sat on me suddenly and I shut up.

We had been going a couple of minutes when Lisa whispered, "Talk to me. Say something, baby."

"Do you think President Nixon should have destroyed the tapes?"

She stopped, screwed her mouth to one side and blew breath. After a moment she started again, black eyebrows scowling. While the twisted mouth relaxed and the wrinkles on her brow receded, I tried not to laugh. Sex was easier now, not so serious.

"Lisa, oh Lisa."

"Yes."

"What did the President know and when did he know it?"

A dark glower returned to Lisa's face and she pulled off and lay down beside me.

"Are you weird?" she asked.

"Why'd you stop?"

"I told you to say things to me."

"I did say things to you."

"Dirty things. You're supposed to say filthy, dirty things."

"Oh."

The black frown was still there. She studied me, then her chipped front tooth appeared and she laughed and so did I and we hugged each other and things started over and we were doing fine until I said the worst dirty things I could think of. They just sounded funny and we had to stop again, until we made love silently and it was good.

Soft and warm and spent, Lisa sprawled atop my chest. Sea wind chirped through the six window screens in my room. I could hear the sea rushing the rocks on the beach. I nestled my nose into Lisa's hair and breathed her scent, sweet and sharp. I wanted to tell her about my investigation into Joe Beale, but I held back. I couldn't tell any of them. Not Doug or Harding or Marlow. I could say nothing, not now, probably not ever.

"Tell me about the baby," I said.

"It's not a baby yet."

"Well, when it is a baby what are you going to do?"

"Marry Chip."

"Right."

"I will. You don't believe me, but I will."

Lisa rolled to the side of the bed, then stood and peeked out a window. She was more beautiful than Harding—at least today she was—broad shoulders, broom-straw waist, round calves.

"Have you told him yet?"

"Not yet."

"What will you do if he doesn't marry you?"

"He will."

"What will you do?"

Lisa turned, grabbed her jumpsuit and slipped into it. "You're looking at the future Mrs. Chip Beale." She stepped to the door. "You're looking at her."

I lay in bed for a while and then went to sleep. Around eight-fifteen I woke up. It was already dark. I could still smell Lisa. I wanted to hold her, tell her everything would turn out. Sometimes I felt the same thing for Harding. They had brought this out in me, these women. I owed them. I owed them both.

Every time I considered the meeting with Bosey my heart raced, so I buried these thoughts as best I could. Halfway through shaving, I noticed wrinkles at the corners of my eyes. Getting a little age on you now, I thought. I blinked my round hazel eyes and they still seemed boyish. The wrinkles didn't look that bad. Maybe they would bring me a little wisdom and I could figure out how to help Lisa. I knew Chip would never marry her.

As I pulled on a brand-new pair of khakis, I saw someone dodge from the front porch. I ran to the door, saw a stooped, gray-haired man disappear into the cedars. It was Johnny Day. The package lay beside the door. I picked it up. More pages. I looked toward the cedars. Day had been delivering the pages all the time, probably. Was the memoir being sent at Mallory Beale's direction? It had to be. But why?

I walked into the yard. The answer seemed obvious. Almost every section of the memoir had some reference to my father, so Beale was telling my father's story; he was telling me who I was—Cody Beale.

No. Not yet. You can't think this yet.

I returned to the Garage, began reading.

My fast-idle cam made the Beale carburetor something different. Something unique. It was light. Made totally from aluminum. The construction allowed the whole mechanism a perfect, reciprocating motion. I knew the guy who needed my carburetors, needed millions of them—Joe Stalin.

See, I'd done some smaller deals with the Russkis through Armand Hammer. Armand liked to make dough. I had worked with him three years earlier. Sold a hundred thousand trunk locks to the Reds. On this first occasion, I met Khrushchev in Moscow. I spent three days with him. He was a pig, a peasant and a brilliant politician. I liked him. I think he liked me. I told him I wanted to meet Uncle Joe. Khrushchev's bare, fleshy head crumpled.

The interpreter repeated, "Uncle Joe."

Then I just said, "Stalin."

Khrushchev laughed hard, slapped my back. He spoke quickly to the interpreter and the words got sharp and simple. "Mr. Beale, very few foreigners see Comrade Stalin these days. Certainly he would never see an American. He hates Americans. He probably thinks you want to poison him. He even thinks we want to poison him. It is impossible."

"Another time," I said.

So I studied Russian. I got pretty good at it too. I always thought that the Russian market would be a good one if I could break into it.

The Beale carburetor gave me my chance. I again went through Hammer. Made contact with Khrushchev. I had heard the Russians had a great need of parts, that everything was breaking down in the U.S.S.R. At any rate, I exchanged five or six telegrams with Khrushchev. In 1952 he had become a big shot. I sent three Vice Presidents to Moscow. They took diagrams and a good sales pitch. I didn't let them take the carburetor itself, though. Nor did I give the Russians a totally accurate diagram. I didn't want them to steal the idea and mass-produce the carburetor.

March 4, 1952, I got a telegram from Khrushchev. He wanted me to come to the Crimea. He said he had been impressed by my envoys and by the new design. Then came the shocker. Khrushchev said that dear old Uncle Joe wanted me personally to bring the carburetor and show him how it worked.

I telegraphed back, "You bet. Will arrive Sevastopol April 2. Beale."

In a week and a half I did some great research on Stalin. Collected a marvelous file. There was one thing I found absolutely fascinating. In almost every deal Stalin had made with the West there had been a gimmick, something which had caught his fancy. I spent another week listing his likes and dislikes, his favorite desserts, movies, games. (Candied beets in whipped cream, Stage Coach *and a Russian version of mumblety-peg.) Then I found something that he absolutely craved and rarely had. I made a call to Hawaii. I bought a bunch. I had my gimmick.*

At Sevastopol a committee greeted me. Khrushchev was not there. I had buffed my Russian and it was pretty good, but they gave me an interpreter anyway. I don't know about these Russians. Why do they all dress like extras from a James Cagney movie—crumpled fedoras, gray overcoats, yellowing white shirts, collective faces grim and gray.

Anyway, the four of us climbed into a black sedan and traveled for nine hours through the Russian countryside. I cracked a couple of jokes now and then about meeting Uncle Joe and noticed that each time I did my three companions went rigid and stopped breathing. I decided to spare them the anxiety and keep quiet.

In the heavy, Russian-made car we bumped through Tartar villages. I smelled dung and wood smoke and the sweet aroma of some flower like honeysuckle. Even though it was spring, the men in the villages wore round pigskin hats and the women light pink veils. Just before twilight we turned down a cliff and saw a beautiful castle. It was gorgeous and sat just above the blue Caspian Sea. We were near a town called Gaspra. The drive to the castle was lined by purple wisteria and yellow roses. One of the Russians with me said that this estate had belonged to Countess Panin, who had been a friend of Leo Tolstoy. He said that Tolstoy had spent several weeks here just before his death.

When the car stopped, a line of servants waited to greet me. The toothless women wore black kerchiefs, greasy aprons and brown fur boots. The air smelled like cypress. Just before the house ran a long colonnade which held black grapes. Communism looked pretty good to me, until we found Stalin's place.

The old boy lived behind the castle in something which resembled a ranch-style American home. Ten windows, then a plank door decorated with a hairy boar's head, then eight more windows. This my interpreter called the Lair. It was Stalin's and Khrushchev's hangout.

Khrushchev bounded from the front door like a chubby, red-faced kid. He wore a white Georgian shirt; the round collar was decorated with hand-sewn violets. He hugged me, gave me two kisses. His gapped teeth smelled like vodka.

"Tell me something," I said. "Why do you guys live back here when you have a castle over your heads?"

Khrushchev replied in pretty good English, "Comrade Stalin hates castles, Mr. Beale."

"Mallory."

"Mallory."

"Yeah, well, you and the rest of the crew ought to stay in the castle. Let Uncle Joe live down on the farm."

Khrushchev's big, wart head twitched. "Mallory, do not speak of the castle of the Countess Panin. Stalin does not believe it is there."

"He doesn't believe what?"

"For him the castle has no existence."

"That's crazy."

Interpreter, servants, my entire entourage jerked and shrank. Everybody but Khrushchev. He slapped his knees and laughed.

"Do you know the American actor Gary Cooper?"

"Yep, I know him."

"He is fearless?"

"Even in real life."

"You remind me of him. But beware, my friend. Here there is reason to fear. Be more—careful with your words." He opened a hand toward the house.

I walked into the place hoping for a truly Russian room. You know —animal furs nailed up on log walls and a big brassy samovar and a tin tub for a bath that some babushka *would pour. Nope, not at all.*

Everything had been ordered from a Sears and Roebuck catalog. Western-style bunk beds, a little ladder leading to the top level. A blue jukebox decorated in jitterbugging blond-haired girls and ducktailed, loafer-clad boys, a G.E. coffeepot, Maxwell House coffee, Lipton tea.

I sat in a chair and waited awhile. Fidgeted. Got a little sleepy. Then I gave up, took off my britches, hung them up by the cuff to keep the crease. I like creases. In my boxers, I lay down in the top bunk and slept.

A while later someone entered.

"Mr. Beale."

It was Khrushchev.

"Mr. Beale, let us go shoot."

"Shoot who?" I asked.

I don't think Khrushchev thought this was funny.

35

The Crimean air smelled salty and warm. I was walking alongside Khrushchev through a stand of cypress. He was decked out in tall leather boots and a long-sleeved rose shirt. I wore tweeds. We carried twenty-gauge shotguns. Two creeps followed us in the tree line. Khrushchev had been talking about the carburetor. He said that for some reason Soviet technology could not produce a reliable one. Theirs broke down a week or so after installment.

"Why do you think this is, Mr. Beale?"

"Let me tell you something, Nikita. Can you stomach honest answers?"

Khrushchev stopped. "Honesty has consequences."

"I'm not worried, are you?"

"Sometimes. Why does our technology fail?"

"One reason—I think we're smarter than you guys. In fact, I think we'll bury you one day."

"You think you are smarter?"

"Right."

"Why?"

"Because I'm in Russia selling you carburetors that you can't make. Uncle Joe will buy them and I'll be a richer man and that's why I think we're smarter."

Khrushchev looked at me coldly. "There's a Russian proverb. We like proverbs here. They say much quickly—the fox knows many things, the hedgehog knows but one."

"What does that mean?"

"But you are smarter, why do you ask?"

This time I laughed, slapped his shoulders. Out of the corner of my eye I saw the two guys following us. "Listen, why are those guys tagging along?"

Khrushchev did not turn his head but his eyes danced to the right. "They are shadows."

"Pretty noisy."

"Stalin sends them. They follow me always. They follow all of us."

"Why don't you tell them to beat it?"

"No use."

"Crap."

I turned around and went straight for these two little guys in the cypress. When I came close they ducked down behind some bushes. I laid the shotgun on the leaves, squatted down. I waited. Didn't do anything. I could hear them breathing fast, both of them. I just squatted there for a time and then stuck my hands through the bush, parted the branches and looked at the white faces.

I wiggled a finger toward one to come forward. He stuck his face closer.

"Do you speak English?" I whispered.

"Yes."

I nodded. He nodded. I looked at the other one, motioned him over. Both heads bobbed close to mine.

"I hear you Russians like proverbs."

"Yes."

"There's an old American proverb. We use it when people bother us. It goes like this. Get the hell away from me or I'll blow your ass off. You follow?"

When I rose they scuttled into the woods. I didn't see them the rest of the day.

Khrushchev and I hunted for two hours. I was a lousy shot. He was a good one as long as the birds weren't moving. He couldn't hit them on the wing, but he could blow them off fence posts. I told him Americans didn't consider that kind of shooting fair. Khrushchev said it didn't matter how the birds were shot, they tasted the same.

When we got back to the house Khrushchev wanted to see the carburetor.

"Nope."

"Did you bring it?"

"Look. I'm not showing this beaut to anybody but Stalin."

"You sound fearful."

"Not fearful, practical."

Khrushchev pulled off his boots. His bare feet gleamed sweat. They were pink and tiny. He sat on the floor. A smell seeped into the air, oddly sweet. Next he huffed and twisted and shucked off his trousers. Nikita sitting there in his undershorts, massaging his tiny feet with tiny hands. He pulled a vodka bottle from his pants pocket, swigged, offered me one.

"Not fearful, but practical?" he said.

"Yep."

"Maybe this is Stalin's plight. Maybe he is just being practical. Maybe he is not afraid."

"Afraid of what?" The vodka tasted cold and smooth as melted snow.

"Do you know he has his food analyzed now? Even here there is a small laboratory. Two chemists inspect everything that goes before him and even this is not enough. He makes us all eat with him. Beria and Malenkov too. Nearly every night. He loves sturgeon and when the fish is put before him he says, "Nikita, look at this beautiful fish. Please try some of mine, my dear friend." And I do. He does this, not out of friendship, but from fear of poison. He has just arrested his personal physician of twenty years. Why? Because he is a doctor and doctors know about poisons, yes? Beria and I, we call this the doctor's plot. Last week in Moscow, Stalin had eighty Jewish doctors locked away. God knows what he will do to them."

The vodka bounded from my belly to my brain. My face burned. "He sounds nuts."

"Stalin sane is a fearful man. Stalin crazy—" Khrushchev glanced at me, then slugged down the last of the vodka.

Khrushchev gathered his pants and boots. "We will eat with Stalin at six tonight. The dinner will be long and hard. Laugh some, but not too much. Do not play tough with him as you do with me. I think you are amusing; Stalin will not. Bring your American carburetor."

At the door Khrushchev stopped. "Do you know, Mallory, that the big toe and the second toe of Stalin's right foot are grown together. They are—I don't know the word."

"Webbed?"

"Yes, webbed. Webbed. The first two toes. This has significance in Russia—a superstition. Oh, I do not believe it, but there are those who do. It means that he is—the Beast."

I stretched out on the bunk, felt the vodka bore through my veins and arteries.

On the wall hung a poster—Stalin. He looked young and handsome. Swept-back long hair that curled over his fur collar. A princely nose, black and curving eyes. He sat at a desk looking out a window where blue snow was falling. He held a pen. The poster caption read, "Stalin in Exile."

The art was not bad. Then I saw something which lay on the pane of the drawn window. Something which made me shudder.

The falling snowflakes gathered to form a face. Something large and open-jawed which peered back at the smiling Stalin. Vaguely, almost imperceptibly, the snow had formed the face of a wolf.

36

A servant came to my room. A woman dressed in white, round and soft as an apple dumpling. I grabbed the carburetor, which I had carefully wrapped. She led me through a maze of dark corridors.

The dining room was the kitchen. No chandeliers. No candles and silver. Just a big, round table and straight-back chairs. Two Kelvinator stoves boiled pots at the room's far end.

The servant did something like a bow and went to the stoves. I sat at the table, looked at a picture of Lenin hanging on the wall. He looked like the devil himself—pointed beard, slant eyes, itsy-bitsy ears. I had this urge to take my pen and draw a couple of horns on that bald head.

I sat the carburetor right in front of me. Baby, do your stuff, I thought. We got to sell these boys the biggest bill of goods going.

Still nobody but me and I started thinking that maybe this was a Commie joke and Stalin and Khrushchev were all drinking up in the castle while I sat down here. My stomach grumbled and I turned my thoughts to dinner. I hoped at least dinner would be Russian. Probably not.

Finally, Khrushchev appeared dressed in a tombstone-gray suit. His face had lost the laughs. His suit looked like it had been sent out to be wrinkled.

He sat down across the table. "He is not in a good mood."

"How do you know?"

"He's laughing."

"That makes sense."

"When he laughs it is because he wants us off guard. He wants us comfortable so we will make a mistake."

"Why don't you stone-face it? Why don't you not laugh?"

"I like my children. Now Beria will be here and Stalin will try to get us all drunk. He does this often. But Beria and I have bribed the servants. They will pour us colored water. Only you and Stalin will have wine."

Both of them shuffled into the room then. Stalin first—short, his sagging face deeply pocked, the mustache brittle and the hair gray and complete, not having lost a follicle. Beria—short, bespectacled, cute as a weasel, teeth narrow and gray as matchsticks.

We had formal handshakes. The laughing Stalin embraced me, Beria did not. We sat. Servants appeared. All women. I felt my heart beating.

Stalin motioned Khrushchev over. He was to act as interlocutor between the old man and me. Khrushchev's whole countenance had changed. His face was red as watermelon and he guffawed at whatever Stalin said.

This was the way the conversation went between Stalin and me:

"So you've come to Russia, Mr. Beale?"

"Yes."

"Our Crimea is beautiful?"

"Very beautiful."

"Tell me, what do they think of us in America?"

I noticed his right arm looked stiff. A gray glove covered his right hand.

"We don't think much about you guys."

"No?"

"Oh, I guess some of us think about you."

A laugh. The black eyes slanted. The pocks beneath the chin spread. Below his right eye lay a broken capillary, red—like forked lightning.

"What do some think?"

I laid my hands on the paper-wrapped carburetor. "Do you really want to know?"

A great nod.

"They think you're unstable."

Nikita flinched.

Beria threw down a shot of colored water. Stalin sat back in his chair, slammed his left hand on the table and roared. A big laugh. Beria and Khrushchev paused, then slammed the table with their left hands and laughed too.

"I am *unstable," Stalin shouted. "I* am! *Yes, Nikita?"*

Khrushchev blanched.

"Yes?"

Khrushchev's little piggy eyes blinked in the crunch. He banged his hand down again and laughed, but said nothing. This banging and laughing continued until the food came.

I was not drinking much wine. My gut felt too tight. At every dish Stalin applauded and said, "Oh, how wonderful." Sturgeon or fresh bread or beets and each time he made Khrushchev taste the food first. Beria did not eat our food. For most of the meal his plate was empty. Midway into the dinner a servant dumped what looked like a pile of greens into the center of a bowl which sat before Beria.

At first Beria took small bites, using a spoon and fork. His transparent lips circled and the spectacles stood on his squenched nose. Then slowly he forgot utensils and simply stuffed the stringy vegetables into his mouth.

"Look at my darling," Stalin said. "You know what I call him, Mr. Beale? My cow. Beria, I call my soft cow."

Beria looked up from the greens and gently smiled.

Stalin ate quickly. I noticed Khrushchev was sweating. He ate little food. Stalin's eyes hit the brown package now and again. He pushed his plate aside and reached for the carburetor.

I saw the move coming and as he reached I put the carburetor beside me, away from his grasp.

The hate came from somewhere back in his skull. It rushed to the windows of his pupils and barely held there. His jaws and mouth changed shape. Then I remembered the face I had seen in the drawing and the face I saw now on him—the wolf. Long jaws and teeth and snout.

It receded quickly. The pocky smile returned. Stalin talked about FDR. How he loved his fake smile. Loved his ridiculous ebony cigarette holder.

"But do you know the President I admire?"

"Tell me."

"Your Harry Truman. I like him. He's a—a asshole. Like me. He is a big asshole. And do you know really, really why I admire him?" Stalin leaned forward, his good hand again edging toward the carbure-

tor. "Because I know that if I pushed the Korean affair he would drop an atomic weapon on me. Not on Moscow, but on me. Truman would have bombed me like Hiroshima and I knew this and so did he and I did not want this bomb on me. I liked him because he would have done this."

Poached apples and spicy tea and whipped cream. I was ready now.

"This carburetor will keep your trucks running," I began.

"Soviet trucks always run," Stalin said.

"This carburetor, Mr. Stalin, will keep *your trucks running."*

"How long?"

"Seven to eight years."

"Let me see."

As slowly as I could I peeled open the package until there she lay—brilliant in copper and plastic and aluminum, American technology.

Stalin's hand crept a little closer. I kept my hand on the base of the carburetor. Khrushchev kept poking my side, trying to move me away.

Finally the white hand, speckled in brown, touched the carburetor's highest part—fuel inlet. Then it caressed the idle speed screw, choke rod, idle mixture adjustment screw, throttle lever. His fingers balanced one eighth of an inch above my own.

He pulled the carburetor toward him.

I did not let go.

At last his hand retreated.

Beria sat unblinkingly. Khrushchev was soaking.

"I can get this from the Czechs."

"I doubt it."

"They are comrades."

"That's why they can't build a baby like this."

"How much?"

"How many?"

"Five hundred thousand."

"Seven ninety-five apiece."

"Capitalism will fall because of this kind of greed."

I knew it was time for the gimmick and so did he. "I could offer a little something extra."

"What is that?"

"Something you can't build and you can't make."

Stalin shrugged.

"Buy the Beale carburetor, Mr. Stalin, and I will throw in a thousand pounds of bright, sunny, fresh—pineapple."

Little smile, tongue cluck. The red lightning flicked under his left eye. A bear laugh and belly slap and "Yes! Yes! For pineapple, I will buy the Beale carburetor."

37

I found a bottle of Early Times, downed two shots, shuddered, and leafed through the pages again. There was no mention of Joe Beale or Joe Walker. Not one. There was no information about Aiken or the accident or anything else I was after.

Suddenly I said, what am I doing? Instead of wondering why Beale is sending this thing, I should just take it to him. Just say, look, what's going on here? Am I related to you? Mallory Beale! Am I your grandson? Of course not. Right. I just wanted to get it straight. Okay? Now let's get drunk, old man.

Yeah, that's what I should do. No way, though. Because right after that I'd be off Black Island for good. And I never wanted to leave this place. I saw that now. I wanted to stay on Black Island forever.

Carefully I collected the new pages and hid them in a box of clothes. Stalin and Khrushchev and Beria. What a life Beale had lived. I sat down on the bed, observed my room. Peeling walls, a naked ceiling bulb, cardiac-gray floor, six windows, five shades, three of which didn't work. Lovely. It looked like the kind of place migrant workers go to die. I took another belt and said, Now don't get depressed. You're staying on a beautiful, rich island, even if you are living in a two-room, field-hand's shack. You're dating two gorgeous girls; of course, one's pregnant and the other's preppy. You'll soon publish your first novel, a third-rate autobiography about insanity and incest. What more do you want?

I had another shot. There was a knock at the door and Harding entered. I dropped to the floor, doubled over, cranked one eye shut and lifted a hunchback's arm toward Harding's face.

"Rrrosssalinnn! Rrrosssalinnn!"

"Is Cody Walker here?"

"Rrrosssalinnn!"

"Shouldn't you be ringing the bells?"

"Dddrrruuunnnkkk."

"I see. Well, too bad. I wanted Cody to escort me to a party."

I straightened up. "Where?"

On the cliff, by the lighthouse, the red flames lit the night. The fire looked new, the flames stretching and straining as if to fry the white carcass of the quarter moon. I was bombed. Harding led me toward the red light.

"They were all here just a moment ago," she said.

"The bogeyman got them," I said.

Two brightly hissing lanterns sat near the big fire in which a black pot boiled and clamored its lid.

Then we saw flashlights blinking on the beach below.

I cupped my hands and yelled, "Doug."

A couple of lights danced my way.

"Hast thou seen the great whi-te wh-ale?" Doug shouted.

"I am the great whi-te wh-ale," I yelled back.

"Aha! It's Cody Dick!"

"What are you do-ing?"

"Trying to get la-aid."

I guffawed, stumbled and fell beside the fire. Harding had her hands on her hips, auburn hair flying, scar in her chin dimple turning burgundy in the cold breeze.

"Cody, I shan't endure this behavior."

I dropped my voice ten decibels and glared at the bubbling pot. "Oh, my, she's become the Baroness Boob."

I think Harding would have let me have it then, but Doug and the others strode up a path from the beach. They held things above their heads—black, creepy, spiderlike things.

"I wanted pot roast, but this will do," said Marlow. He raced toward me.

"Cody, look out!" yelled Doug.

"Cody, move!" screamed Parker.

They were dashing straight for me. They held living, moving, clawish creatures.

I balled up and covered my head. "Spiders! Spiders! I'll never drink again."

A rattle and crash. I peeped through my arms. Marlow backed away from the pot just as Doug tossed in a two-pound lobster, quickly followed by Parker's.

Doug opened a cooler, grabbed five Black Horse ales and handed them out.

"I propose a toast," Doug said. "Here's to the health and prosperity of Marlow's new profession."

"Wait," I said. "Hold it. Just slow down. What's Marlow's new profession?"

Face red as a strawberry, blond hair untidy and glowing, Parker came over and tapped her bottle to mine. "Good question. These guys won't tell."

"Just waiting for the proper moment," Marlow said.

"Do tell us," Harding said.

"Harding, your jaw's not working," Doug said.

"She's changed into the Baroness Boob," I said.

"Why don't you shut up, Cody?" said Harding.

"Baroness," Marlow said. "If ever the lovely passion which boils in your bones should ignite, call on me."

"Oh, no," said Parker.

"Yep," Doug said. "Marlow's become a fireman. A toast to towering infernos."

"Dear God," said Marlow, gazing at the night sky. "Please let something explode in fire."

With that, Marlow revealed that he was a volunteer fireman assigned to Cedar Point. He unclipped a plastic box from his belt.

"Look at it," Marlow said. "Just feast your eyes. I'm really an American now. I'm part and parcel of everything that smacks of Yankee Doodle Dandy. Do you know what this is? A beeper. My very own. Now I can be disturbed at any time. In the bath, in the yard . . ."

"You been beeped yet?" asked Parker.

"Still virgin," said Marlow.

"Here's to your first bloody beep," I said.

We drank the toast and then Doug opened the pot and pronounced the lobsters ready.

Doug placed the orange bodies on paper plates. Harding sat beside me and Parker beside Doug and Marlow held the center. Using blunt-tipped scissors and nutcrackers, we cracked and cut and split the scalding lobsters. The claw meat was a soft pink, the taste saltily delicate. We sucked the sweet juice from the legs. The meat here was white and we pulled wedges from the shell and dunked the white meat into a pot of yellow butter.

The lobsters disappeared quickly. Doug and Marlow gathered the plates, cleaned up. We sprawled before the dancing fire. From the land there blew a cold wind. I could feel the fall.

"Next Saturday," Doug said. "I've decided next Saturday for sure. Will you be ready, Cody?"

"For what?" I asked.

"To say some words for me and Parker."

"Really?" Harding said. "Are you really?"

"Of course," said Doug.

"Marvelous," Marlow said, rubbing his freckled nose. "I'll get the island fire truck. We'll ride you all around the island blasting the siren."

"This is supposed to be a secret," Doug said.

"I'm worried," I said.

"Why?" asked Doug.

"I haven't married a whole lot of people."

"It'll be great," said Doug.

We drank another round and Doug was the happiest I had ever seen him that night. He and Parker held hands, their heads cheek to cheek and their eyes beaming like blue stars and the smiles upon their rosy faces big and bright as the American dream.

It was a smile that I was not to see on Doug's face for a very long time.

The change in his skin began just before the wedding. The terrible thing that happened to his eyes came later.

Harding and I walked to the Garage. I crashed into bed and pulled her beside me. She was smiling and playful and I was bombed and wanted to play, too, but in a different way. I lifted her yellow football jersey and looked at her smooth stomach and below to the slightly protruding navel and started kissing there. She stopped me and she said not tonight and I said why and she said just because and I said okay, fine, and started again. When I popped open the bottom of her shorts, she stopped me. She was flushed. She pulled auburn hair behind her ears. I surrendered and sat back and looked at her. Small gold discs sat in her earlobes. The discs were engraved. There was a clean etching, then an onyx thread, then another line of gold and finally a round onyx stone. My dear God, she had style, even in a football jersey.

In my white linen trousers and blue knit shirt, I stretched out on the bed. I withdrew from her completely. As soon as she sensed my distance, she made a funny noise, a kind of soft squeak. When I didn't respond, the squeak intensified and her face scowled and the baby bottom lip protruded and finally she slid next to me and the squeak changed to a purr.

"I just don't need it," she said.

"I know."

"Sex."

"Yep."

"I mean I'd rather just cuddle and touch. It's as good as sex, don't you think?"

"Of course."

"Really, Cody? Do you really think so?"

I hugged her and settled my face against her warm neck and passed out.

Sometime later I awoke. Harding was pulling off my shirt.

38

I finished taking off our clothes. I raised her legs and laid them on my shoulders and made her place her hands beneath herself. Softly I twisted the pink nipples, kissed them. I was disappointed when they did not immediately turn hard. When I went into her we held our breaths. I moved and held back my full length.

"Does it feel good?"

"You make me feel so good," Harding whispered, her face scalding and red.

"Does it feel good, baby?"

"Do it, Cody. Do it hard, hard."

She opened and I went deep and she cried out a little which made me jump and retreat until she said, "No, no, it's okay. Come on, come on, come on."

I stopped now and again to make it last, my teeth scraping the hard tips of her nipples, pinching the interior of her thighs. The end was fast and hot.

We gently rocked one another and I felt empty and full, strong and weak, soft and for one molecule of this night—at peace, whole, included.

"I want to stay here, Harding."

"None of the houses have furnaces for the winter."

"You know what I mean."

"Yes, I know."

"Harding." I touched one blue eye and made it close. "You're my patron. Can't you help me?"

"I could marry you, I suppose."

"Marry me?"

"So you could have my house, my position."

"I might not need your position."

"Oh?"

Naked, I rose from bed, leaned against a wall, looked out a window, then turned. "Because maybe, just maybe I'm Mallory Beale's grandson."

Harding laughed like a barmaid—loud and phlegmy and so hard that when she finished she burped. I had no idea she could do something so uninhibited. Drunkenly, I stood there and grinned. People just don't know what to make of you when you grin—are you confident or mocking or sly or are you just crazy? The more I grinned the more Harding paled, until finally she said, "How appalling."

She then spat questions at me: How could I say such a thing? Was I insane? Where did I get the information? Was there a secret will or had I made an incredible discovery and how ridiculous this was and she was not interested anyway, in fact she was bored, utterly bored, because this was obviously a child's fantasy; but was there any truth in it at all and if there was, could I possibly give her Stone House?

I put on my pants and did not elaborate. Harding was still sputtering questions when I walked her to her beautiful yellow Jag and kissed her good night. Dizzy and fuming, she drove away.

I stumbled back to the cottage and got into bed and thought, Bosey, come through. Some kind of connection. No, more than that. Something undeniable. Something which proved that I was—Cody Beale.

For the next three days I reprimanded myself for having confided in Harding. What a stupid mistake. From now on I had to have only two drinks. Keep my mouth shut. Wait and see.

Tuesday morning I rose early and took a walk up Beale Street and turned right on Chapel Road. Beside the black tar road, plum trees held red fruit and below the plum trees ferns cast spiny arms that sprawled upon the brown leaves of the forest floor. On the rim of the deep woods stood the birches. The birches—so Yankee, so white and prim and cold, so perfectly in control, as if, even now, they held the first frost, which would shatter summer and burn the whole woods, strike down every leaf and offer only blue sky and white moon and air, Yankee air—cold and thin and sharp as a pane of ice. I stopped at the chapel. On the red brick walls the ivy was heavy and thick.

I sat down, my thoughts turning to Lisa. I wondered if she had told Chip. I wondered if she was all right. Suddenly I saw her. We lay in bed making love, touching, holding. Something hurt. I tried to switch my thoughts to Bosey, to the meeting, which was only two days from now. Lisa's face wafted through again. In my head I shifted my gaze, blocked the painful space in my chest. Lisa and I could never make it.

Near the violet sea at Chapel Road's other end, the blue Ford truck chugged and huffed. When I saw the yellow fog lights and the rust crane rising over the cab, I felt my heart warm: Doug Summers.

He parked the truck. His hair was black and shaggy. His eyes were the thinnest of blue.

"Hi," he said listlessly.

"Where've you been?"

"Had to leave the island a couple days."

Then I saw the odd color of his skin. No longer tanned and youthful, but rather like a thin mustard spread over rust. Somehow the texture seemed to be changing as well. Suppleness had departed. Around his face and across his big forearms and over the backs of his hands a tension and brittleness spread. He looked used and dirty and tired.

"What have you been doing?" I asked.

"Working."

"Rerigging the *Sasha?*"

Doug stuffed his mustard hands into his jean pockets. He turned a perfect Eagle Scout profile to the woods, his long lashes blinking, and placed one ragged Brooks running shoe over another, balanced, sighed.

"I tried, Cody. I caulked the holes. Worked thirty-six hours straight, no sleep at all. Doing black beauties and Nescafé. I set the pots out near Cutty Hunk. Next day, they were gone. Cut. All of them. Somebody cut every last line."

Doug swept his hands through his hair. "I borrowed the money from Dad. Fifteen hundred bucks. I borrowed money—and I lost it. Every cent and I haven't told him yet. I haven't even told him."

He was still looking at the woods, still propped on one foot. I did the same. I surveyed the woods and balanced on one foot and reached a hand to touch his shoulder, but he shrugged.

"It's all right," I said.

"Don't tell me that. It's not all right and don't you tell me that it is because I lost the money. I was stupid and I lied to my father and I lost every damned dollar and it's not all right!"

I kicked a few leaves.

While Doug's eyes were averted I studied his complexion. Maybe some of the orange-mustard color came from working on the *Sasha* in sea air—some, but not all. The change in his skin was too radical, too deep. Something else had happened, as if he had been dyed by some extraordinary chemical, stained by some secret process, and in the soft tissue below his bottom eyelashes another tint was building—purple.

"But I'm going to make it back. Every bit that I borrowed and I'm going to be independent. I have plans. They're cooking. Right now I got things lined up."

Doug glanced at me. He swept an open hand at my chin. "Oh, yea. Something else. I'm getting married today."

"What?"

"Parker and Harding are decorating the chapel right now."

I looked over my shoulder at the silent building.

"You said next week. I'm not ready. Marlow's working. I . . ."

"I'm not waiting anymore. I've got to get my new enterprise off the ground. You saying the words or not?"

I looked at him. "Your father's going to kill you."

"Probably."

"Your father's going to kill me."

"Probably."

"I'm not a preacher."

"Oh yes you are," Doug said.

When we walked into the chapel we became very quiet. Maybe it wasn't a ceremony at St. Bartholomew's, but it was still a marriage. The aroma of early fall flowers filled the interior. The black slate floors had been mopped. The wooden benches sat perfectly ordered and the tiny American flags which stood above each window frame looked crisp and new; even the pickled oak paneling appeared dusted and clean.

Doug and I hesitated and slouched in the entrance. Looking toward the front of the chapel, we saw a large semicircle of clay pots and washtubs and old wine bottles and from these common holders radiated the flowers: tall, white cattails and thin goldenrod and red sea roses and snappy black-eyed susans and blue and pink wildflowers and all these connected by a green fern chain. When the sun dashed through a cloud and touched the flowers, the colors leapt and joined and swirled together, making the whole chapel like a palette of pastels—light blues and golds and reds—a gentle tapestry of light.

"It's beautiful," I said.

"Looks like a wedding," said Doug in a trembling voice.

"Well, it is, isn't it?"

"I just wanted a couple words, you know? Something like love each other and don't write bad checks."

I think Doug would have left then, but from the old vestry room Parker entered. She had her blond hair pulled back and the curls seemed round and sunny. Island tan was her only makeup, except for a small rouge rim at her lips. She wore a navy blue dress with white buttons.

"Parker," Doug said, as if something was wrong.

"I just wanted to look nice for you," she said softly.

"I look like a bum," Doug said and blushed.

Harding stepped from the vestry room wearing the same style dress, though a different color—yellow cotton, light green buttons. Her auburn hair was brushed from her face in wings in which you could still see the brush strokes.

"A shower. I need a shower and suit and tie," Doug said and tried to leave, but I caught him.

"Too late," I said.

"Oh, Cody," said Doug. "Oh God, Cody."

Harding handed me a Gideon Bible. The outside cover bore a red brand—Holiday Inn, Hartford, Connecticut.

"I selected the reading," Harding said.

She and Parker walked toward the semicircle of flowers.

Doug put a hand over his eyes. The mysterious stain had turned his knuckles chocolate. "For Christmas sakes, Cody, let's go drink a beer."

I pulled his hand down. "Now look, you can't hurt this girl."

"I'm not dressed."

"Doesn't matter."

"Oh God, oh God, oh God."

"You have a ring?"

"Nope."

"No ring?"

"I just wanted things simple."

"You got things simple."

Doug dropped lower, bending his knees and leaning toward me whispering, "Listen, just one Black Horse ale. One apiece. Me and you, buddy. Let's just get the hell out of Dodge and drink one. I'll come back, I promise."

I caught Doug's arm. "No sir," I said in nasal redneckese. "No sir-ree. I'm abinding you and atying you in holy wedlock 'fore the sight a God Almighty."

Doug almost fainted. Somehow I weaseled him to the altar. Still blushing, slicking at his black hair, hands stuffed in his khaki pockets, white tennis shirt thin and wrinkled, he slumped beside the prim Parker.

Harding and Parker were smiling. Doug and I were shaking.

The flowers were radiating. I opened the book to Harding's marker: Ruth.

Before I started reading, I felt impelled to speak. I cleared my throat. "Well, here we go. I guess we'll all hang together."

Everyone relaxed a bit.

"Doug, I recall the first day I met you. You raced into the backyard of New House and jerked me out of a chair. You remember?"

"I thought you were a hick."

"And I thought you were a prep school punk."

"You were both right," Parker said.

"I remember early on, we rode out toward Cedar Point. You didn't say much," I said.

"I was checking you out."

"Same here."

Harding made a noise, raised plucked eyebrows.

"Anyway, maybe you two should hold hands or something," I said.

Parker took Doug's hand.

I read the underlined words: "And Ruth said, entreat me not to leave you, or to return from following after you for wherever you go, I will go; and where you stay, I will stay. Your people shall be my people and your God my God. Where you die, I will die and there I will be buried. The Lord will do this for me and more also and nothing but death will part you and me."

Well, everyone became teary then. I shut the Book. All eyes were cast down. "Oh, for God's sakes, Doug, kiss her."

When he did, something violently shocked, thumped the right-hand side of the chapel. We twitched, thinking we'd been found out, then laughed.

The others went ahead to Straw Hill. Outside, I looked beside the chapel. The noise had been too loud, like a hurled rock or a distant bullet impacting in the wood.

I saw the creature lying beneath a window—a beautiful wild canary. The eyes still blinked, but the brains had exploded through the tiny, yellow skull. A lower windowpane was shattered. I held the warm body and watched the blue eyes finally shuttle still. The heart turned once or twice and then the warmth began to leave. I felt the incredibly small heat ascend to the fine feather tips and then depart. Using the heel of my shoe, I dug a hole and buried the pretty little bird. I wondered if this was a sign or omen.

Doug's cabin was bare—linoleum floor, ashy wood stove, lanterns and a big mattress, which sprawled in the corner. There was no water and no electricity, but the view was beguiling. The front windows looked down upon a bushy island hill and then three blue tidal pools and white cattails and sea grass, then light brown sand and the blue sea flooding the sandbars. Beside a green Coleman stove sat a case of Black Horse ale. I had chugged half a bottle when the others clomped onto the porch. They had walked. I had driven Doug's truck. I popped open three bottles, made the first toast.

"Here's to lots of kids," I said.

"Christmas, not yet," said Doug.

"Perhaps you should plan on just two," Harding said.

"Six at least," I said, winking at Parker, and we clanked bottles and drank the beers.

We traded island stories about our first days together. We lit the lanterns as the dark came and drank for hours. I guess I would have drunk more, but Harding said that we must bid good night.

I hugged Doug, then Parker, and then we all embraced. Doug said to take his truck.

Halfway down Straw Hill I turned and yelled, "Thrive and prosper, children! Thrive, thrive, thrive and prosper!"

Harding clamped a hand over my mouth.

At the Garage, Harding and I showered separately, then climbed into my narrow bed. The sea wind was blowing cold air. The cedars and scrub oak rattled and creaked and the channel buoys were ringing. Pine needles tapped the roof, sounding like sleet.

Slurry drunk, I pulled Harding to my ribs. "See Bosey tomorrow night."

"How did you find out about this? About you and Uncle Mallory?"

"Seeecret."

"Why?"

"I ain't a Beale. I ain't nothing, and I don't want to talk no more about it. . . ."

Harding held me until I passed out.

39

It was something I heard. I thought the sound was Harding: a wheeze, a whistle in her nose. I listened. The sound grew into a singing, though this quickly diminished to silence, and then a low grumble held the air, a small tenor growl that chewed and hacked, and turned into the singing, the whining.

When I rose from her, Harding opened one eye. "Too early," she said.

Barefoot, the brown beach felt cold. I was following the noise. It was familiar. Something I had heard as a boy. Something like a wooden yo-yo whining on distended string.

I stepped around a large sand dune riddled by cattails and reeds. They murmured, but my sound was not them.

When I cleared the dune I saw this handsome man and I knew the sound. He held a deep-sea spinning rod and the line was singing out into the sea. My father had fished and used a big cam-driven reel and the song of line zipping through blue water had never left me.

The man worked the rod well. He possessed rare handsomeness, a star quality. His flesh was youthful and brown and the bending rod pumped the veins in his forearms. Even from where I stood I could see jade eyes flashing as quickly and brightly as the water of the flats. He wore brilliant red canvas Bermudas and stood calf deep in water. He was shirtless and from his skin there radiated something like light.

The nine-foot rod was bending, the line cutting the sea like a black ray, zipping fifty yards out into the flats, where the water grew deeper, more blue, but not blue enough to hide the tremendous shape of something that glided and tracked through the water. A monstrous black shadow, a dark presence that stirred sand and flashing minnows and passed to the man's right, paralleling the beach so gracefully, then spreading out into the sea, the big reel burning, whizzing line and the thing heading out toward deeper water, not to go but rather for the turn, the sweep, and then completing a great arc, once more paralleling the beach and passing down below the man's left and the man holding the shadow as much by his eyes as by line, the jade eyes implacable and solid and relentless in their surveillance, the jade eyes commanding this black creature to accommodate the frail line, until suddenly the man's face bore a smile, his cob teeth gleaming yellowly in the sun and the smile grew larger and bigger and I thought childishly that maybe the man did not have a creature at all but that somehow he had caught the heart of the sea. That he had thrown a line into salt water and hooked the darkest part.

With a soft swish and several vibrations the rod suddenly relaxed and the line lost life. The man's face became a complete smile now, the skin cracking in wrinkles and the teeth bared and even the skin on his nose washboarding and flushing purple-red.

The shadow retreated toward the horizon. At the edge of some great drop it stopped and hovered, then disappeared into darkness and depth.

As the man reeled in line he still smiled, showed no sign of disappointment. When the big spool was full he looked toward the sea and tucked the reel under his arm and laughed. He laughed and kicked water and threw the rod and reel over his shoulder and sloshed through the flats and—I knew him. Mallory Beale.

I squatted down on the beach. He had disappeared behind a line of sand dunes. I wanted to follow, but couldn't. What had happened to him? He looked years younger. The lesions seemed to have left his face. The jaundice had vanished. He had power. Maybe it was somebody else. No one could change so completely in four months. No one could undergo such a startling rejuvenation—could he?

I sat and waited. I was hoping one of them would return, Beale or the shadow. I looked at the distant water, but saw no movement. I thought about walking toward the dunes, but what if Beale was sitting there? I wasn't ready to face him yet. The time was not right.

Rising, I glanced back at the sea and, incredibly, I saw the thing or at least part of the shape again, a great black fin or flipper sweeping above the drop, gliding the edge of the darkness, so that I ran down into the water, splashed waist deep and the creature skimmed the drop's edge until by degrees it once more disappeared.

I had probably been standing in that freezing water five minutes when Harding's voice called:

"Cody."

I waved her silent.

"Cody!"

"Quiet."

"What are you doing?"

"Do you see anything?"

"Do I *see* anything?"

"Near the drop. Is there something there?"

"You're going to die of pneumonia. Now, out. Right now."

In the blue pickup, I was halfway to Stone House before I dared say anything.

"Have you seen Mallory Beale lately?"

"I haven't."

"He's years younger."

"What?"

"Maybe fifteen years younger."

"Are you stoned?"

"I can't believe it. I can't believe it. Something's happened to him."

"Something's happened to you."

I yammered about Mallory Beale and the creature and asked

Harding if she had ever seen anything huge swimming in the waters around the island. She said there had been whales and large sharks, even great whites off the beach. I thought of my own shark encounter early in the summer.

By the time we arrived I think she had decided I was a little nuts, so she gave me a blue Valium and a glass of cognac and sent me to steam in Grover Cleveland's bathtub.

Drugs always work. My chill was gone. My mind was Valium and Courvoisier, though I still wondered at Mallory Beale's inexplicable rejuvenation and, too, what had wrestled upon the black line's hook.

Two hours later I drove back to the Garage. I had to be alone, had to prepare for Bosey. I took a long run in the afternoon, and then a nap. I knew that after tonight, no matter what happened, no matter what Bosey said, I would not be the same.

Around six-forty-five in the evening I returned to the cottage after a walk down the beach. My cheeks were red and cold and the joints in my fingers ached. The fall was coming. I could sense the cold waking in the ground, piercing the rocks and striking the lowest branches of the island trees. Quickly I stripped off my damp jeans and slipped into the red and blue velour robe which Harding had picked out at Burberry's in New York. There was a knock at the door. Deciding not to answer it, I waited. Another series of knocks, fevered and persistent, as if something was wrong.

The door opened and Lisa entered, her face red with sea wind and the black eyes leaky and wild, ecstatic.

She raced into the room. "Did you hear yet? Did anybody spill the news to you yet?"

"I guess not."

"I'm getting married."

"To whom?"

"Take a guess."

I sat down on the bed. My heart was beating wrong. She wore her white maid's uniform. It was covered in dust and soot and the hem of the dress dangled small dust tails which floated above her red scrub-floor knees.

"You're not marrying Chip Beale," I said.

"Yes," Lisa said. She threw herself on my lap. She touched her stomach. "Me and sweetpea here are finally gonna have a home. A home? We're gonna have the whole island and I've already started planning. I'm gonna get Chip to throw Bosey out of the Big House 'cause I want it. In five years, I'll be top dog."

I sat and listened to Lisa making plans for herself and Chip and the baby.

"What do you think?" she asked.

"I suppose I'm rather surprised."

"You know, you talk funny. You're starting to sound like the rest of these people."

"When is the marriage?"

"Real soon. Chip didn't want nothing fancy. At first I was gonna make him do it in the biggest church in Boston, but I decided not to. I'm gonna be cool. We're having it on the island as soon as possible."

"You have to give the family time to gather."

"Gaatthurr. You say it just like Harding. Listen, Cody, marry them but don't sound like them. Yeah, next week. Chip's not inviting the family. It's just him and me and a preacher. He wants it quiet, but I'm telling my buddies."

Lisa gave me a kiss on the cheek and sprang from the bed. "Got to call my ole man. He'll be outa his head. I'll get Chip to give him a house too. He can move his pizza joint up here. I can see it up in lights—Kraskawitz's Black Island Pizza." She clapped her hands and ran out the door.

I didn't move. I sat and stared at the dingy shades in the dingy room. How had this happened? How had she accomplished this?

The clock read seven-thirty. I had to meet Bosey at eight. Sluggishly I opened a drawer and pulled out Beale's memoir.

I was walking up Beale Street, feeling blue. I felt like there was a pot of luck and it held just so much and no more. Lisa had gotten to the luck first. There wasn't enough left for me. I tucked the memoir under my arm and trudged ahead.

Bosey's house was a modern bungalow standing by the sea. Tonight the small windows were brimming gold light. When I rang the doorbell she appeared quickly, her face not doom and tension, but open and warm and her white hair amazingly neat.

She asked if I wanted hot chocolate and I said sure and sat down in a room lavish in couches and big pillowed armchairs and several fat ottomans. The only hint of the usual Beale bareness lay in the floor, which was unvarnished, unwaxed maple.

From the kitchen Bosey asked about my movie project and then about Doug and Marlow. I watched her from my position on a turtle-green couch. She wore a black Chinese suit and red sash. Through the steam her mottled skin looked moist and fresh. When she came back into the room she carried the hot chocolate in big white cups, but her face had changed. The change grabbed my stomach. The small heart-shaped scar at the right corner of her mouth was hidden in hemmed lips. She was looking at the memoir.

"Is that it?" Bosey asked, her eyes fierce and yellow.

"Would you like to hold it?" I offered her the pages.

"Hold it?"

"To read some, if you like."

"I will have it, if I like."

Bosey took the pages, then from her black suit pulled a pair of reading glasses. She flipped through the first section.

I couldn't swallow and my ligaments felt tight and drawn. Maybe the pot of luck was not empty.

Bosey leafed through a few more pages, then put them down and sat her elbows on her knees.

"Why you?" she asked.

"What do you mean?"

"Why should he give this work to you?"

"Maybe he wants to say something to me."

"And what's that?"

I circled the rim of the cup with my fingers. "I need help, Bosey. I need to know about—Joe Beale."

Bosey rose and drank some hot chocolate and touched a finger to the side of her spotted, patrician nose. The little heart laid out on her lip.

"I'll have this discussion with you once. Only once and that because Mallory—the old fool—for some reason has confessed to you a grievous hurt. I will briefly tell you about my brother's other son on one condition—that you give *me* the memoir."

"Ultimately."

"Ultimately?"

"I will give it to you ultimately, but I want to keep it awhile."

"I want it tonight."

"No."

She swept at her white hair and drank some hot chocolate and sighed. "Olive Thomas was a beautiful creature. Red hair and blue eyes and the figure of a princess. Mallory met her somehow in his business. He loved her. Perhaps she was the only woman he truly loved. They went to Paris and had a child. Olive died there. So did Mallory, or at least the youthful Mallory—the prankish, wisecracking boy. He brought his son back to the States. He wanted to raise him in some distant place. Some place in which the rest of the family could not discover him. But more important, Mallory wanted Joe far away so that he would never let him into his heart, never love the boy the way he had Olive. Despite all his precautions, Mallory did love him. A great deal. And then, Joe died. Suddenly. And Mallory turned cold."

"But Bosey, did Joe die in Aiken? In a car crash?"

"I will not answer any more questions even if the answers are simple. I will not. I am Mallory's sister."

"Bosey, I . . ."

"Why are you so very interested in Joe Beale?"

I looked at the floor. "If I told you, you'd think I was crazy."

Her yellow eyes surveyed my face. The small pink heart was moist upon her lip.

"Time for you to go," Bosey said. She walked me to the door. "You may keep the memoir for a while. Discover what you must."

I stepped into the dark.

"Cody," she paused. "There is someone on the island who knows more about Mallory Beale than even I. Someone who is *not* related."

"Who?"

"Johnny Day. He's served Mallory for fifty years. I think if you asked him, he could tell you—everything."

According to Bosey, Johnny Day lived in three rooms off Mallory Beale's kitchen. In the Garage, I called Beale's house and spoke to the maid, Molly. She told me that Day had gone to Providence and that he would return on August 23. Over a week away.

The wait was hard, but not as hard as seeing Doug and the horror of his eyes.

40

Some days later, at twilight, I was sitting on the paint-peeling steps of the Garage. The last red glow of the sun was upon the blue ocean and the sea magnified and threw the red light into the ravaged pine by my house and the green pine tossed the last of the light from the tips of its needles into the lowering dark. It was cold.

I saw Doug at a distance. He had been gone four days now. Both Harding and Lisa had been asking about him. When I saw him I didn't call out. I could tell something was wrong. He moved differently. He had no energy. Life was weak in him.

When Doug walked into the edge of porch light, I was stunned. He looked pounds lighter. His usually fresh, black hair was matted and dirty and even in the small light I could see that the color of his skin had become furiously red, though below this immediate redness lay the mustard tint which was so deep that even the fingernails of the bony hands seemed stained. Even worse, I could smell him—a rancid, rotting smell, a sickening odor of sweat and filth and neglect.

"Got any food?" Doug asked. His voice was parched and shallow.

"Doug, you look . . ."

"You got any food?"

"Crackers. In the house."

He walked inside.

In the good light and from behind he didn't look too bad. He wore yellow linen trousers and a blue flannel shirt and polished Weejuns, but the bones of his big body stuck against his clothes like wooden knobs. He walked straight for the lamp and turned it off. Then he switched off the ceiling light. Only a small night-light burned beside the door. Fragilely, he sat down on my bed. His sour odor was filling the room.

I moved to turn on a lamp.

"No," Doug said.

"Why?"

"I want it dark."

I sat down in a chair near him.

"You want the crackers?" I asked.

"What time is it?"

"Doug, what's wrong, man?"

"What time is it?"

"I don't know, around nine."

"Yes, I want crackers."

I brought him saltines and a glass of water and when I cut on the light I saw them—only for a second. The bloody spheres which sat beside each pupil. The eye sockets looked bruised and purple and wrinkled. Doug cried out and covered his face. Quickly I snapped off the lamp and grabbed him.

"Tell me."

He shrugged me away and stumbled from the bed.

"Tell you what?"

"What have you got?"

"Stay out of my life, Cody."

"I'm not staying out of anything. You look like hell. What is it?"

"I'll tell you, but not now. I'm halfway done. I got another week left, then I'll be all right. I got to go down there one more time."

"Are you getting some kind of treatment?"

A pause.

"Yeah."

"Just tell me what it is—what disease?"

"I hate it down there. Valladolid's too hot, but I have only one more week. Then I'll be back. Then I'll tell you. But you keep quiet. You don't tell anybody I'm gone. I sent Parker to her parents. She doesn't know about it."

Doug rose, reached out, grabbed my head in both hands and then he left. No good-byes, no handshake. He just walked out of my room and into the night.

I sat in the dark and listened to the wind twist and pop the pine tree beside my house. I kept seeing Doug's ruined eyes, the bloody wounds that gleamed beside his blue irises. When I rose and turned on the lamp the word flashed: Valladolid.

In the other room I found a world atlas in the bookcase: Valladolid was an Indian village in the southern tip of the Yucatan Peninsula.

At two o'clock in the morning I was still awake, my mind buzzing between Johnny Day and Doug.

Maybe I shouldn't see Day. Maybe I was pushing too far. All these similarities between my father and Joe Beale were coincidences. Nothing more. On the other hand, I knew I had to press forward because there was the chance, the incredible chance that it was all true.

And Doug. What about Doug? Why was he being treated in some godforsaken place like Valladolid? Then the thought shivered into my consciousness. Loss of weight, change in skin color, the horrible red wounds in his eyes—cancer. My God, maybe Doug had cancer. I had heard that Mexico allowed the use of new drugs. Maybe that's why he was there.

This notion roused me from bed and sent me for the bourbon bottle. I had two shots and finally at 4:30 A.M. drifted off.

Wednesday arrived. At precisely six o'clock I called the Beale house. This time Day himself answered the phone. When I introduced myself I sensed his tension. After all, he had been delivering the memoir for months. Of course I said nothing about this. Carefully I came to the point.

"Johnny, someone told me you could help with a problem I've got."

His Irish voice was edgy. "I'd be delighted to be of service."

"I'm interested in Joe Beale."

"Sir?"

"Joe Beale. Mallory's son."

Silence.

"He was . . . a friend of my father's. I . . . I think they might have been . . . close. I wondered if we could meet and you could tell me what Joe was like."

A long pause.

"I didn't know him that well."

"But Bosey said that—"

"He was in Aiken and I was in Boston. You'd have to talk to someone else, I'm afraid."

I tried to convince Day, but he would not see me. I called Bosey, told her the problem. She said she would help.

An hour later Day called back. He was hesitant, but said that we could meet at Beale's house at nine o'clock the next morning. I could tell he wasn't pleased.

I went outside and sat on the wooden bench and listened to the sea wind. I had to be delicate with Day. I had to be jovial and friendly and subtle. At the same time I had to find out about the accident. Joe Beale's accident. If I could discover the details of Joe Beale's death, then I would know about Mallory Beale and my father and me. Then I would know for sure, wouldn't I?

Lying in bed, fluttering on the edge of sleep, perhaps I felt the fire first. As if the distant flames touched my eyelids, then retreated, touched and retreated once again. When I fully opened my eyes I saw a red pulse beating upon a pane of glass in the window: scarlet, then yellow, scarlet, now blue. It made no impression until I heard the siren far away but approaching. I lay still and waited and the siren grew closer and the blinking upon the windowpanes intensified.

I leapt from bed and jumped out onto the freezing porch. Over the trees toward the north I saw bright flames torch the bellies of black clouds. Something massive was burning. In the distance I heard a fire truck lug and grind, its siren screaming.

In two minutes I was dressed and running up the causeway road. The fire had grown so much that a kind of weak day illumined the black woods. I ran toward the first gate, turned right and then stopped. I could see now—it was Mallory Beale's house. Mallory Beale's house was burning.

I could barely even breathe. I felt all my muscles rivet, weld. The huge, dry house sputtered fiery ash and the red light grew and bloomed. I made myself take a breath and then I raced through the unnatural, twilight woods.

Two fire trucks sat in the yard. One from Cedar Point, the other the ancient Black Island truck. Eight or ten firemen dashed around. Suddenly two silver currents of water hit the growling yellow flames. Huddled against the Black Island fire truck were Bosey and Townsend. They wore nightclothes and their faces were stiff from fear.

"Bosey, what happened?" I asked.

Bosey tossed her white hair and motioned me closer. "It was like a bomb. Ten minutes ago. It went up like a bomb."

I touched her and she was cold. Beside her sat Townsend, all in a crumple. She had bared her teeth and her rough skin seemed hard and redder than usual. "We couldn't find him. We couldn't find him. We tried," Townsend said.

"Who?"

"Mallory."

I knelt down and brought Townsend's face from the fire and toward me. "What do you mean?"

"Mallory's somewhere in the house."

I turned toward the fire. The roiling flames wrinkled and scurried and suddenly the flames seemed like faces. A thousand faces flickering and winking and contorting and howling. The fire seemed to be laughing at me as if it had consciousness, as if it knew that all my dreams were burning. Then I heard it—some place deep in the boiling pyre of the house—a scream. Then a call for help and a scream again.

Several firemen stumbled from the burning front door. Two of them wore no masks. The other had oxygen tanks and a white asbestos suit. One more man emerged, coughing, his face scoured red and black. It was Marlow. I grabbed him.

"Why didn't you get him?"

"Tried. Second floor. Too hot, man. Too hot."

Again, another scream from the flames. I looked toward the second floor and I saw him through flames, a dark form, hands covering his head, screaming, "Fire! Fire! Fire!" The form rushed toward one window ripped blue and red by flames. It seemed to be nearly out the window, but stopped halfway in the scorching bubble and then blazed and sizzled so that for an instant the singed face was lit, the mouth agape and terrified, then the form fell back into the house.

Marlow sank to the ground. The other fire fighters did not move. I spotted the oxygen tanks, grabbed one and slung it over my shoulder and clamped the mask to my face. When one fireman tried to catch my shoulder I kicked him and ran through the front door and into the flames.

Inside, I felt the hair on my face burn and pop. The maple staircase shimmered and shot flames, the staircase glowing and intact, though now only red coals. I felt my way around the corner and into the kitchen. Less smoke, heat. I scrambled through the kitchen and the dining room and made it to the back porch. The door to the back staircase was shut. Quickly I pulled the handle and when the hinges opened a blast of smoke and heat hit me.

A few seconds later I could see. I looked into the back staircase and heard the roaring of the fire, the howling. It sounded like something alive, it sounded like some kind of animal roaring. I breathed the good oxygen from the tank and looked at the stairs. There were no flames there. I took a deep breath and then another and climbed the steps.

The entire front of the house was afire and the heat was like a wall—solid, scalding, impenetrable. When I tried to go forward I felt my flesh begin to burn and so jumped back.

Then I turned to the left and I saw him, Mallory Beale. He had retreated to a corner in his bedroom.

"Mallory!"

He was on his knees. There was no hair left on his head and his clothes were gone and the skin was black except where fissures of blood and water seeped.

"Mallory!" I yelled again.

He reacted, shook and trembled. The voice was weak and gurgling. "Fire," he said. "Fire."

I tried to walk toward him but the lane of fire was too strong. I would have to run through. It was the only chance. I breathed deeply and dropped the tanks and the mask and leapt forward, felt the flames suck me, pull me into their furious heat, and suddenly everything beneath me fell.

There was no sensation of falling. Only noise and heat and impact. I lay on the back porch. The fire was eating it too. I got to my knees and saw Beale. I kicked through burning timber and grabbed the curled, smoldering form and jumped for the outside.

I dragged him toward cool trees. Halfway there, hot, soft stuff was coming off in my hands and the smell was ghastly. I fell and so did he. He was curled like a fetus. His skin was black except for the blood that ran from huge sinkholes in the chest or trickled down from the hole that had been his nose and stumps that had been his ears.

The others rushed toward me then. Someone threw a blanket over Mallory Beale. Marlow had his arms around me. Someone was feeding me oxygen.

I watched them carry off the body and then watched the fire gobble the rest of the house. Marlow was asking me questions and Bosey put her cool hand on my head and then there was a voice from the dark. We stopped. All of us.

The prep school drawl, the marvelous, long, sinusy slur. "Good God. Is everyone all right?"

41

When I saw Mallory Beale I gasped. Townsend rushed to him and so did Bosey and Marlow. I lay on the ground and did not move.

Beale walked over then. In the firelight of the burning house he looked so young. His silver hair was shining and the jade eyes looked wet and strong. He stood and looked at me, hands upon his hips. He stood for some seconds and then his big, square jaw stuck out and he smiled and said just one word: "Wallace."

A fireman touched his arm and told him that Johnny Day was terribly burned. Mallory Beale turned away then and walked to the ambulance where they had carried Day. He entered and closed the door and the ambulance drove away.

It was the name he had called me the night I stood outside his room. Surely he knew my name was not Wallace?

Marlow took me to the hospital. They checked to make sure I was okay. I had a few burns and had swallowed some smoke. I had a large bruise on my hip from the fall. They wanted to keep me for the night.

And I wanted to stay. Because somehow I had to see him. Somehow and even though he might be dying, I had to ask Day about the accident.

A doctor gave me a shot and for two or three hours I was almost unconscious. About 3 A.M. I woke. It took me a while to think right and I was incredibly sore. My hip throbbed and my right index finger had a large, white blister. I could still taste smoke.

Painfully, I slipped into my jeans and sweatshirt.

The hall smelled like stainless steel and Mercurochrome and medicine. It was half dark. From the shadows I watched a nurse answer the phone behind a white desk. When she left I quickly stepped forward.

I located the patient chart, found Day's room number. Three twelve, seven doors down from me.

On bare feet I moved soundlessly, opened his door. It was an intensive care room. Five machines flashed dials and lighted graphs. Day lay on a strange silver contraption which erected his burned arms and legs so that only the center of his spine touched anything. Several plastic tubes pierced his body. I could hardly recognize the face. No hair, half a nose, blisters, black and red flesh. The smell was awful, as if he were already dead. The stench of a corpse.

When I touched his right hand he moaned, opened one black, swollen eye.

"Johnny. It's Cody Walker. Listen, we have to talk. All this is—is terrible, but I must talk to you. This is going to sound nuts, just nuts. Look, I think—I think I may be—related to Joe Beale. Yeah, I may be related to him and you're the only one that can help me find that out. You understand? Can you hear me?"

The eye blinked, the hand squeezed mine a little.

"Okay, okay. Now I know that Joe Beale died suddenly. An accident. But was it a car crash? Did he die in a wreck?"

Almost imperceptibly, Day nodded his head.

"Is that yes? Are you saying yes?"

His voice was thin, watery. "Car crash. Aiken."

For a few seconds I couldn't say anything. I walked away from him, closed my eyes. Then I returned.

"Johnny, I know you're hurting. I know. Look, I have to tell you this. I think, I think Joe Beale was my father. Sounds crazy I know, but it may be true. Is there any way you can help me? Is there anything that you know about him?"

The eye closed. Silence.

"Johnny. Don't go. Please. Don't—go to sleep. You're the only one. Johnny . . ."

"Birthday."

I leaned close to his mouth. "What?"

"Birthday. Mallory Beale."

"Tell me."

"Mr. Beale gave Joe on his birthday—a turquoise ring. Mr. Beale's turquoise ring."

I looked down at my hand and raised my fingers into the dark light. My ring shone, the turquoise ring that my father had given me.

"This?" I asked, and held the ring toward his face, but his eye closed.

Someone grabbed me.

"Get out of this room. Mr. Day is gravely injured. Get out."

The nurse hurried me to my room, closed the door, snapped off the light.

Surrounded by the dark, I said it:

Mallory Beale is my grandfather.

About nine o'clock the next morning Marlow came to the hospital and drove me back to the Garage. He offered to stay, but I told him no.

I was in bed most of the day. Lisa came by in the afternoon and Harding toward evening. When Harding asked about my conversation with Bosey, I told her that so far things still were vague.

About nine-thirty that night Marlow called to say Johnny Day had died. I hung up the phone and swallowed one of the Darvons the doctor had sent along. I went to sleep.

The realization began sometime in the early morning when everything was black and still. A pain in my hip had awakened me, then I started thinking.

Why had my father changed his name from Beale to Walker? Was it so he could live on his own, cut out an individual life far from Mallory? And what had happened between them anyway? Why had Dad been so close to his father, so involved in business and then suddenly left?

More and more questions. I wanted to learn about my father's early life in Aiken. I wanted to know about his business deals and his rise to power and his fall. And what about money? Maybe Joe Beale had some secret trust fund which Mallory had set up. Maybe my father had been worth a cool ten million himself and I only had to discover it.

By six o'clock in the morning I was a wreck, a shambles. I knew I had to stop these questions, shut them off or they would devour me. There was one way to do that. It was obvious. I had to confront Mallory Beale. I had to see the old man and tell him my discovery and let him answer everything.

I decided to wait, to move slowly. I had to find the perfect time. And when I did I would go to him and say, "Grandfather, I know who I am."

Around noon I rose from bed. My body hurt. It felt as if the fall in the fire had bruised everything. I took a shower, managing to keep my scalded index finger out of the hot water. I thought about Johnny Day, felt grateful and sad.

When I was drying off the phone rang.

"Hello."

"Hey, there, boy."

A voice soft and sibilant and Southern.

"Who is this?"

"I would say your sugar daddy, but we don't know each other that good—at least not yet."

"Who is it?"

"Thaddeus D.—for discover—Cribb. And I done done my middle initial proud. You know why?"

I didn't answer.

" 'Cause I discovered me a writer. A real, bona fide teller. You."

I knew who it was then. Thaddeus Cribb, the editor.

"Mr. Cribb, I'm sorry. I—"

"Don't you be sorry, boy. Especially after writing a book

like *Tiger River.* Naw, don't you be sorry. Course it needs fixing. Yeah, the patient has got to have an operation. Minor surgery. A snip here and a tuck there. But it won't be much. He's healthy, though a little bit on the puny side."

Thaddeus Cribb continued talking in his soft and curious jargon about the minor surgery and the sutures and the bandages and how he was convinced that the patient would fully recover. Then he asked me to come to New York and sign the book contract.

When I stuttered, hesitated but finally agreed, he rushed the end of the conversation and said, "Don't it feel great to be up here with the victors?"

Everything was breaking right for me. I felt like Midas. I felt like nothing, nothing could go wrong in my life again. But I knew others were in trouble. I had not seen Doug in a couple of days. Did he really have cancer? And if so—was the treatment in Valladolid any good? And what about Lisa? I still didn't believe Chip would marry her.

I lay down and slept until it was dark. I dressed, combed my hair, decided to see Chip Beale.

Riding over in the blue truck, I thought about *Tiger River.* Wondered if it would sell. It didn't matter. If it sold only five copies it was fine with me. I didn't need money now—and what's more, I probably never would.

I knocked on Chip's door and he opened it and I was startled.

42

He looked terrible. His usually regal beard had been trimmed down to something that resembled a burr patch. Along his jaw, bald spots revealed gray flesh. His gold eyes seemed sunken and hard and moistureless. To satisfy manners, he asked me about my injuries, said the fire was terrible and he'd miss Day. Then he returned to his concerns.

"Want some ginger tea?" he asked.

"No, thanks."

"I'll put a teaspoon of bee pollen in it."

"Bee pollen?"

"Yeah, I've had to go back to it. No energy. I don't know. I just got no energy, man."

I finally agreed to bee pollen and tea, and when Chip stepped away I noticed that he had cut his hair again. It was a mess. The red strands around his collar were ragged and uneven and too much had been shorn from the top.

He brought the tea and sat down on the floor. He wore bib overalls and scuffed combat boots. We sipped tea and I noticed his exposed ears. I had never seen them before. They were huge and fleshy and the interior ledge was wild in gold bristle. I was faintly repelled.

"I've decided to take care of Lisa," Chip said.

"I heard."

"She told you?"

"I think it's the honest thing to do."

"I'm no fool, Cody. I know she did this deliberately. But I'm a generous man. I'll give her my name."

"When's the ceremony?"

"Soon as I can get it together."

The ginger and bee pollen tasted terrible. I looked at Chip and suddenly his big, buck teeth protruded. He touched the nub of his ring finger to his chin. The minus sign glowed.

"I want you to be the best man."

"I should make it a profession."

"What?"

"Nothing. You know, I saw your father at the fire. He looked incredibly younger."

Chip seemed somber. "It's strange. Ever since you came to the island—almost four months ago—ever since then, he's grown stronger." Using an index finger, he touched the gold bristle in his left ear. "I'm glad he told me to write you that letter."

His words connected things.

Chip flipped a switch by the bay window. An outside flood-lamp shot a funnel of light onto the black lily pond. I stared at the light and the dark.

"I thought you wrote the letter," I said.

"Oh, I physically wrote it, yes. But frankly, I'd never heard of you, Cody. Father said that your family were distant friends and he wanted you up to see the island. He was intent upon having you here. Finished with your tea?"

Inside, I was glowing.

"Well, you'll have to go now." He offered his hand. It was his usual dismissal—polite and formal and insensitive.

He escorted me to the door, his hand in the small of my back. "The ceremony will be brief. No one knows about it except Lisa, you and me. My decision may seem cold, even hard, but what I am doing and the way I am doing it is the best thing for Lisa and the child. One thing more." The half-dollar gold eyes glimmered and the buck teeth retreated. "You have to move out of the Garage. I want you to stay in the cabin at Straw Hill. You can really get into the fall there. Doug's already out. Can you dig it?"

I forgot I had driven the truck. Walking down Beale Street, walking through the heart of the island, walking in complete dark, the words felt warm: "He was intent upon having you here."

It was clear now. Mallory Beale had summoned me. It was not the caprice of Chip, but rather the will of Mallory Beale that had brought me to Black Island.

Under the new moon, under the new, clear, glorious moon, I made my way to the lighthouse. Its white body towered in the dark and I leaned against the cold stones and looked out toward the black sea.

My grandfather had called me home.

The next morning I collected my clothes and other belongings, set them in the back of the truck and moved to Straw Hill.

I should have been furious at Chip for forcing me to move again. I knew why he was doing it: power. He wanted me to feel that he controlled my life. But he didn't. I had finally, if secretly, discovered my position in the family. I was a Beale as much as he and I relished my secret.

When I stepped into the cabin the air was cold. A gas stove corroded in one corner. Beside the stove sprawled a mattress dressed in squalid sheets, no pillows, a ragged quilt. Three green lanterns hung from dusty rafters overhead. In one barren, planked corner stood yellow hockey sticks, peeling skates and two fishing rods—the remains of Doug's habitation. A window looked down the hill toward three blue tidal pools, a brown sandbar and then the sea.

I was jubilant. I had no electricity and no water and no bathroom. Wonderful. Marvelous. I looked like a pauper and I loved the irony. Having little, I possessed all. The forest and the tidal pools and the beach and even the sea—it was mine now. Or at least partly mine. I was certain that my grandfather —I stopped. Yes, he was my grandfather, my grandfather, the one whom I would love and serve the rest of my life—I was certain that my grandfather would give part of everything to Chip, to Doug and to me. To me!

I hung as many clothes as I could, then grabbed a towel and set off for Chip's house to take a shower. I saw, hanging on the back of the cabin, Doug's waders. I did not stop to fret or worry about him now. I knew, I absolutely knew, that even if he did have cancer, he would be all right. Everything would be all right. Lisa would marry Chip and Harding might marry me and Doug would recover.

As loud as I could, I yelled, "Hallelujah." I ran down the rutted, dirt road, made Beale Street and raced along the bumpy tar surface. And I kept shouting "Hallelujah" as long as I had breath and until I saw the startled faces of the crew who were working either side of Beale Street. Carrying scythes and shovels and rakes, they straightened and stared. Even though the air was cool, they wore no shirts, backs white as birches, arms brown as ash. On their heads sat Boston Red Sox baseball caps; on their feet, Wolverine boots.

I flung the towel over my shoulder and spread my arms. "Fellas, I know I'm acting a little weird, but I've had some good news. I've had some incredibly good news."

A car pulled behind me. The beautiful Harding was driving the yellow Jag. She opened the left car door and I got in.

"Cody, you look rather odd," Harding said.

"You look wonderful."

"I can't look wonderful. I just finished a grueling game of squash."

"Wonderful, wonderful, wonderful."

"You sound like Lawrence Welk."

"Thank you."

"Have you heard something from Bosey?"

I wanted to tell her so bad that my toes curled and my right calf cramped.

"Ow!" I yelled.

"God, what?"

"Ow, ow, ow!"

"What?"

"Yank my foot!"

Harding grabbed my ankle. She pulled and I straightened. The cramp began to release.

I hugged her and we kissed. She relaxed and sank against me and then asked if I had seen Doug. I said that he was doing something for his father and might not be back for a few more days. Harding said that she was worried about him and that his color was bad. I told her it was probably from working on his boat.

She started the car and we rolled along the rugged road. Cool air made the afternoon light thin and hard. The sea grass and reeds beside the road were losing their vibrant green, fading in the cooler season. Sand the soft color of brown eggs piled itself to either side. Short telephone poles stood in sea grass and looked gray and dented and lonely. The whole island —rugged and rent and plain—the whole island looked beautiful. Once I had thought they should bury the telephone wires and pave the pocked road and trim the ragged weeds, but now I saw the beauty of careless simplicity.

"Let me out on Bloop Street," I said.

"Chip?"

"Bath."

"Please?"

I grabbed my towel. "I'm staying at Straw Hill for a while. Chip said I could use his place to bathe." I reached and touched Harding's warm face. "Unless we could use your shower."

"I'm rather busy today. But maybe we could have luncheon tomorrow."

"Deal."

"Quite."

Quite, I thought. I loved the way Harding spoke. I loved her style, her properness. In fact, I loved Harding. She seemed to think I was something special. Lisa had never thought so; she had not and she would not. Lisa needed only herself, but Harding needed me. It made the difference—quite.

As I walked through a stand of blue fir I saw Chip sitting on a hill that faced the harbor. He held a phone book in his lap.

"Cody," he hollered, "I need your help."

I went over and sat down beside him. Beneath tree light, I could see his cruelly cropped beard had patches of new, gray hair and just across the tip of his bent nose lay the beginning of a deep wrinkle.

"Who should marry us?"

"You're looking through the Yellow Pages?"

"Under 'Ministers.' "

"She's probably a Catholic."

"Wouldn't it be freaky if I flew in a cardinal?"

"I think she would like that."

"No, we need something simple."

I looked at his gold eyes. They seemed dim and milky, without energy.

"How about a Congregationalist?" Chip asked.

"What are they?"

"Not Catholic."

We looked up several churches and several names and finally Chip decided on a Congregationalist minister—a Rev. E. R. Huck. Chip still sounded cool and rather mysterious about the ceremony. Then he said something curious. He said that I must not hate him, that what he had planned was infinitely generous though it might not appear so and that the ceremony would be held in the next day or two. I said I could not be there tomorrow because I had to go to New York. He asked me why and I told him about Cribb and the novel contract and he jumped from the ground and clapped his hands.

"Out of sight, man. Wow. You've really got a contract?"

"I think so."

"Well, this renews my interest in everything. Maybe we'll still do *Billy Browning.* Me and you. Yes, we start back to work on *Billy.* There are some heavy people we can meet in the city. They can help us get this flick off the ground."

I was cool as a melon. "Fine."

"I've got it," Chip said. "You'll meet my friends in New York and then I'll meet your editor. Help me pack."

43

The next day as we flew toward New York City a different personality visited Chip. There was a complete change in him. The farther we got from the island, the more his hippiness diminished. He omitted from his vocabulary words like "far out," "vibes" and "karma." Even "dynamite" somehow was left trailing behind the gooselike New England air commuter. The Big Apple was barely in sight and Chip was becoming cosmopolitan. He talked about Capote and Warhol and Bernstein—all of whom he claimed as dear friends.

When we arrived at La Guardia, instead of renting a budget car or catching a cab, Chip acquired a black Cadillac limousine.

The driver extended a mahogany table in the back of the velvet car. The crystal glasses rattled as I said:

"I need to go straight to the Algonquin."

"Not now," Chip said. "Potsy Delano's waiting."

"It's six-thirty. I want to be a little early."

"I said, no, Cody."

I looked at him, then reached for two small glasses and a bottle of Stolichnaya. I poured two shots, handed him one, downed mine.

I touched the driver's shoulder. "The Algonquin, please."

Driving to the hotel, Chip was silent. The blue ice had risen in his face. I set mine just as cold. I had studied summer ice on the island. I knew how to affect the countenance. When the chauffeur opened the car door Chip and I agreed to meet for dinner. He gave me his phone number. Eyes distant and disaffected, we bid good-bye through perfectly clamped jaws.

I checked my watch—seven o'clock. Cribb was not due until seven-thirty. I entered the hotel.

Two clerks were talking at the hotel desk. One wore a red wig, which was slightly askew upon his head. His face was as white and round and seamless as an unbaked pie shell. He was speaking to a shorter man, who was young and dark. ". . . and, darling, when they found that body in the East River, why Jesus, Mary and Joseph, the crabs had eaten out everything but the gold in his teeth."

The clerk turned, "Sir?"

"Cody . . ." I stopped, smiled at myself. ". . . Walker."

The clerk thumbed a set of cards. "Ah, yes, Mr. Walker. You may just sign any bill—City Side."

"Pardon?"

"Your publisher."

"Oh."

I advanced further into the hotel. An older man took my light bag, gave me a key.

"The lounge is to the left," he said. "Do you wish to see your room?"

"Not just now."

The lounge was like a living room. Wingback chairs sat beside round tables. I sat down. In the table center was a small bell. I pushed. A cheery chime. The room was fusty and faded and there was a sense of distinguished dust. This was the place for a Beale, I thought. For some reason I sat straight and began to peel off a pair of imaginary white gloves.

First, I unfastened the two yellow ivory buttons on each hand, then carefully, casually, yet with grace, I tugged and removed the cashmere gloves finger by finger and stacked them invisibly upon the table.

An eye glimmered across the way: a bald-headed old man in pinstripes and purple cravat and an engraved ring which hung on his little finger. His gluey-blue eyes surveyed me, then he nodded.

A waiter appeared in a gray felt suit. "Yes?"

"Glenlivet, straight up."

When he left I stood and went into the dining room. A rose carpet covered the floor and the tables had white, thick cloths and rose mats and the knobby silver shone by the plates and the rose stem glasses. The place was lovely and worn, as if the sun had been allowed to shine and beat upon the linen and silver and wainscoting until the proper, dull patina had been evoked. When I presented myself to my grandfather—to Mallory Beale—I wanted, when we became close, as I hoped we would—I wanted to lunch with him here.

The Algonquin was made for Beales and we for it.

Halfway through my cloudy scotch whiskey a bearded man in red and green tweeds appeared. He stuck out his hand and said in a sharecropper's brogue, "Hey, there, boy. What you drinkin'?"

"Glenlivet," I said, rising to shake Thaddeus Cribb's hand.

Above the beard, the rough face scowled. "No kidding."

"It's very good."

"You don't talk like a Carolina boy."

"You do."

The brown crowder-pea eyes watched my face. "You should be drinking bourbon."

The waiter came over and Thaddeus Cribb ordered Wild Turkey neat.

When we sat down there was no idle talk. Cribb went straight to business.

"Now I want to cut out about two hundred pages."

"Great," I said.

"What the hell do you mean?"

"It's your business. You ought to know it."

"Listen, you're supposed to fight me."

"Why?"

Cribb snatched the drink from the waiter, gulped it down and ordered two more. "One for him and one for me." His neck was turning in his collar and he was making swallowing sounds.

"Did you say—why?"

"I said it."

"Because it's your soul. Because writing is everything you are or hope to be. Because, as Faulkner said, you should be willing to murder your grandmother for your art."

"Isn't that a bit pretentious?" Cool, cool, I was so cool. Like something that never melts, like the very heart of Black Island.

Cribb pushed a red finger against his turkey-tail nose. "Ooohhh, I seeeeee," he said. "You think, you think you're one of *them*, don't you?"

The waiter served the bourbon. I pushed the drink away. "Glenlivet," I said.

"You ain't them, boy."

"Do you know Mallory Beale?"

"The *world* knows Mallory Beale. Did you meet him at a party?"

I smiled.

"He's different. Mallory Beale is different. But most of them ain't worth nothing. They've never worked, never strived, never failed. Let me tell you something." Cribb twisted his neck and chin as if trying to swallow a bone, grimaced, leaned close in sour-mash breath. "I could take a knife and a sack of rice and I could survive anyplace in the world. Anyplace. That's what matters. Only that."

He hovered, swallowing and grimacing, then slumped down in the purple wingback. The new drink came. We said nothing and turned our whiskey glasses on porcelain coasters. His fingers were slick as peeled, red crayons. The nails were chewed to the blood-line quicks.

"We need to go to the office. Sign the contracts."

"I wish you'd travel to Black Island. It's beautiful. Thirty huge houses. A beach club, a—"

"I've seen those places. We called them fish camps."

"This is no fish camp."

"See, my daddy did an emergency appendectomy for a rich

Yankee down yonder in Georgia. They got to be friends. We used to go up in the summer to his fish camp in Maine. It ain't nothing. It ain't nothing to me at all."

We turned our glasses some more.

"Don't you know how many books I've turned down this year?" Cribb said and his voice went raspy and soft as wool. "Three or four hundred. I even rejected André Malraux's autobiography. Rejected it. Camel trains and tinkling bells in the desert. All that romantic crap. I chose you. I took your book. Don't you know how much I love you, love your work?"

I didn't. Over the summer I had become separate from my novel. *Tiger River* was like a college project. At the time I was writing it the work was painful and as important as the world, but now . . . it was nothing more than some distant assignment. I was a Beale.

"Maybe we should change the title. It's too slick. We need something more corny. Remember what Fitzgerald said. 'We have to face it. America's heart is corny.' "

"I'm not changing the title."

Cribb's crowder-pea eyes lidded. "I'm gonna change the title," he hissed.

"It's my book. You don't change anything."

Cribb rose from his chair, crept toward me. "*I'm* changing it."

"No."

"Get hot, boy."

"What?"

"Feel something for your work. Get hot, damn you, you little redneck."

His rough, red face pushed only an inch from my own, his breath reeking of bourbon. "Fight me, redneck. You scared? You scared? Come on, come on, come on, you little piece of—"

I swung at him.

Cribb dodged and hooted.

"I knew you could get hot! It's your blood, boy. Your blood ain't blue, it's red. Writer red and hot and dicey. You ain't cool like them. You're part fox and you're part trash. It's your damn blood and it's sweet as wine."

From the direction of the desk several white faces floated into the room. The faces mumbled and milled until Cribb assured them that we were just working out the last scene of a new Papp play. He ordered more liquor.

After a fourth scotch my temper receded. Cribb seemed less manic. We left the Algonquin and hailed a cab for the publisher's. I was soused.

The cab worked through the flash of city streets. Whores in red and lavender hot-pants catcalled from corners. At a stoplight one whose hair was white and wild rushed my window and smooched an orange lipstick kiss against the glass. We moved through Times Square, the neon blasting open the night, the sidewalks jammed, vendors selling squares of red meat that bubbled and smoked over burning charcoal while barkers screamed at the crowds to see "naked gals, girls, women, naked down to what you want to see, live, live, live flesh before your very eyes." In every place here the neon was quick and ebullient, jacking up the night, climbing the canyon buildings, scalding the alleyways and, when the neon touched flesh, fusing and riveting and rending it, transforming the crowds, the walkers into smaller electric imps of a beautiful, jagged, onanistic Jordache billboard above the whole neon and flesh ballet below.

I suddenly missed Harding. In this cannibalizing light and action, I missed her badly. I wondered if she was thinking of me and missing me, back on Black Island.

Driving through Times Square's last braying lights, I saw it: Everything was mine. A beautiful woman, the Beale family, the island, New House, *Tiger River.* I was Midas and the whole world had turned to gold.

I had hoped the publisher would, indeed, be one like Random House, which I had heard was a homelike dwelling located sweetly among the tall pilings of Manhattan. But City Side was three floors in a bleak building that would not even make the steps to a skyscraper.

Cribb's office looked just as grim. No walnut wainscoting, no huge desk, no view—except for an awful neon sign across the street which balefully blinked "The Ruddy ass." Apparently the letter "L" had burned out of the last word. I felt ill.

Contracts signed, I called Chip. Cribb and I went outside to wait on a street corner. His hiccoughs had now become almost violent and his neck twisted and wrenched as if he had swallowed some sixteenth-century poison.

I had to ask, "What's wrong with your stomach?"

A few gulps, mucus gasps. "Bad books," Cribb croaked. "I've been reading bad books. Harvey Wolf's last novel sent me to the hospital. They thought I had cancer. I knew what it was. It was that awful book, that terrible, terrible book. They fed me intravenously, discovered a hiatal hernia. A nurse found out I was an editor. She felt sorry for me, brought me a little present —white paper, pink bow. Something to read. I opened the package—*My Father's Toes* by Harvey Wolf. I vomited for an hour."

Soot granulated the New York air. Horns pierced the streets. Somehow, I felt sorry to leave this man, his odd anatomical convulsions. He was my editor. My first one and, instinctively I knew, your first editor is like your first real lover: overwhelming, possessive, magical, deadly, sweet and as deeply involved in you as any one person can possibly be in another. First editors *are* first lovers and in all your life you will never again have an affair so honest and vulnerable, so brave.

"Don't sacrifice sense for sound," Cribb was saying.

"I won't."

"You already have, but I'll cut that out. The patient is traumatized, but not dead, not yet. Remember less is more."

A bashed Datsun scooted to the corner. It bleated a horn. I made out Chip inside.

"Less is what?" I asked.

"Less is more."

"Less than what?"

"Don't play the innocent with me, Walker."

Chip was beeping the horn.

"Who the hell is that?" yelled Cribb.

"Chip Beale."

"Just like those guys, always driving beat-up old cars."

The horn shrieked. Cribb leapt toward the Datsun, pounded the hood. "Damn it, I'm not finished yet! Just knock it off, just pipe down!"

Cribb whirled back. "Don't romanticize so much. Remember this . . ."

Many horns screamed now. Cribb brandished his fists at them. "I'm giving a lesson here! I'm giving a lesson!"

Back to me:

"Remember—subject, verb, object. That's all. That's all in the world a good storyteller needs, got it?"

"Got it." I was laughing.

Cribb jerked open the Datsun door and threw me inside. Cab drivers and bus drivers and ordinary Chevy drivers were all hollering now. As we pulled away Cribb scuttled beside the car. "Remember one thing, Walker. Remember the only thing you must do is develop the narrative line. Develop the narra . . ." but we were beyond him now, the perfect Jap gears whining down Second Avenue.

I hung out the car window and waved at him as long as I could. He was still running. A cranberry face in flapping tie and black suspenders and baggy tweed pants, hands funneled at his mouth, screaming advice and admonitions and love, Thaddeus Cribb, and love.

44

Black Island at 12:40 A.M. We had taken a cab from the Cedar Point airport. Chip's face was pouting and dark. He was still muttering about Cribb and angry with my defection.

At the third island gate he managed to crack these words: "Why don't you hike to Straw Hill, Cody? You can work off the bad vibes."

Walking down the night road, a long mile and a half toward my new and dismal abode, I was thrilled. Never had Black Island felt more like home. The cold sea air was hospitable and the wind sweet and sharp as I came to the narrow planked door of the shoddy cabin, whose windows held no light. When I rolled beneath the soiled sheets I felt Black Island slide beside my heart like a lover. She pulled me close and whispered, "Welcome home, baby. Welcome home."

I awoke about seven. Buoys were ringing in the sound. Gulls keened the morning air. Wind rattled the screens. The wind grew louder. I opened my eyes a little. The wind was scratching, then raking and finally punching the screens. The racket stopped and then the whistling began, a bad imitation of a beginning gale.

"All right," I said. "Who is it?"

Lisa sprinted through the door and hopped onto my bed. She kissed me.

"God, you're sexy," she said.

Lisa's black hair had been styled. The part lay exactly along the center of her head and the sides had been razor cut, feathered and the back a dovetailed shag. She looked rather boyish, she looked good. Her black eyes dazzled with light. Beneath her left eye I saw a butterfly scar. It seemed faintly blue and I had not seen it before.

She drew a finger down my naked chest and stopped at the navel. When she smiled, her chipped bicuspid shone white as a Sunday plate.

"Got you a surprise," Lisa said.

She pulled an envelope from her back jean pocket, plopped it on my chest. "Cody Walker" was printed in living pink.

"I did fifty of them. Worked for twelve hours." She presented her hands. They were stained black and red and green and blue and yellow. "Open it up. See what you think."

"Lisa . . ."

"Just open."

I sat up in bed, opened the envelope. There was a small piece of tissue and then the card. Within a carefully drawn green rectangle lay these words, printed in pink Magic Marker:

Black Island
requests the honor of your presents
at the marriage of—
Lisa Stanislaus Kraskawitz to
Charles Cabot Beale
Saturday the 18th of Sept. 1973
B.Y.O.B.
two o'clock at the lighthouse

I covered my face. "Oh, Lisa."

"It's not engraving, but it's got personality, you know?"

I didn't know whether to cry or laugh, so I just reached and hugged her.

"You can't do this," I said.

"I know I can't send them. I just wanted to have them. Something to remember. But you know what? I ought to do it anyway. I ought to tack an invitation on every door on the island."

I hiccoughed.

Lisa laughed.

I hiccoughed again.

"You know what's good for hiccoughs?" She threw back the covers and went for me.

I rolled away. "You're getting married."

"Not until two."

"Two? Two when?"

"This afternoon at two o'clock."

I grabbed the invitation. It was true.

I doubled over. "We can't."

"Oh, yeah. We got plenty of time," Lisa said and started tickling me.

I laughed and fought and then gave up. The laughing went away slowly. We both got quiet and then serious. This was the last time. It had to be and we knew it.

Carefully I pulled her Black Island T-shirt over her head. Her tan was fading. The summer had left her. I grabbed her waist and pulled her toward my face. I reached and kissed one breast while I squeezed the other. Her hands caressed my hair and scratched my scalp. She slipped down, so that her face lay beside my own. She was silent until I slipped my hand into the jeans, fingers gently parting, then entering and we both gave the first little gasps.

"Do me soft today."

"Okay."

"Do me real easy."

I spread her across my chest, then pulled down and off her jeans. While she was lying on me I caressed her, and then entered, and she was warmly wet and I felt the blood making her bloom. I arched my back and drove, smelling the scent of lovemaking, hearing the loving bash and brawl of two bodies as they near the flash. I cried out and so did she until the last of it was finished, and we lay within each other, hearts and lungs and blood swollen, vital, hammering.

"Hold me," she said.

I circled her in my arms.

"Hold me."

"I am, babe."

"Just hold me."

We were quiet for a while. I felt her finger tapping my cheek. We exchanged a couple of kisses and I told her about my visit with Thaddeus Cribb. I noticed her considerable lack of interest in the world of publishing. In fact, she asked only one question about the book:

"Do you think it can make a lot of money?"

"It doesn't matter."

"Why not?"

"Something else has worked out for me."

"Tell me."

"I will, in time."

"Time. What time is it?"

I looked at my watch—twelve thirty-five.

Lisa gave a little scream. "Oh, my God. I've got to get dressed."

She jumped into her clothes, smacked me a wet kiss and dashed.

I stayed in bed, staring at the ceiling. A hockey mask hung there. Doug had been gone for days now. Maybe when he returned he would be better. Maybe those secret treatments would do some good. If he was not better when he returned, I would do something. Send him to the Mayo Clinic or Sloan-Kettering. I would take care of them all—Doug and Lisa and Harding and Marlow. I would make sure nothing would ever harm them. My grandfather would be proud. This trait of running the show, calling the shots—it had come from him, and from his son, my father.

Soon I had to see Mallory Beale. I decided to start looking for an appropriate time. I had to plan carefully.

I made it to the lighthouse around five till two and just in time to see Chip leap from his Ford. He wore a gray cutaway, gold vest and carried a gray top hat.

The Congregationalist minister and Lisa and a man in a

black suit waited beside the lighthouse. The grass was green and the sea blue and the thicket brambles beside the lighthouse held white sea roses. Lisa was wearing a short, pleated white dress; atop her head sat a white veil. Her shoes were scalding red leather. Her black eyes were shining and I could see her smile thirty yards away.

Chip greeted Lisa and gently took her hand.

I came forward, kissed Lisa's cheek. "Good luck."

"We'll knock them dead," Lisa said and gave a salacious wink. I was surprised to feel myself blush.

Chip introduced me to the preacher—Mr. Huck. He wore a rumpled brown suit which seemed lopsided. The right shoulder was low and exposed his white shirt, while the left suit collar touched his ear. He smelled like peppermint.

Next was the fellow in the black suit. Chip said he was the witness, but this introduction was not true. He was someone else. Someone who would change the course of two lives present—Lisa's and the child's.

I do not remember his name, only the way he looked. He looked ink, everything about him stained and black. Black hair and black eyes and even his tiny set of teeth seemed to have black borders. He was a lawyer.

Reverend Huck pulled from his right suit pocket a rough cabbage of a Bible. "Mr. Beale, do you have the ring?"

Chip fished his gray cutaway and produced a small box. When he opened it Lisa gasped and so did I.

It was the gaudiest wedding band I had ever seen: a flat gold band having around the circumference six different-colored stones. The first was a blue diamond, the second sapphire, the third aquamarine, the fourth a ruby. I could not make out the others.

The minister set the ring on the worn pages of the Bible and the ceremony began. It was done in five minutes.

When Reverend Huck said, "You may now kiss the bride," Chip leaned and pecked Lisa on the cheek.

We were all walking back toward the car when it began to happen.

Chip's face was blue. First, he bid good-bye to the minister and handed him a white envelope. He sent the inky lawyer to escort Reverend Huck to his nearby Nash Rambler. When the two men were twenty yards off he smiled at Lisa, who was hugging him close; he said, "Could I have that back?"

Lisa looked at her hand. "My ring?"

"It's my mother's ring actually. It's all I could find at the moment. Oh, I'll give you another if you want."

"Chip, this is mine."

Chip stopped and looked at her. "Oh, all right. I'll give you that too. You know I like that word—'give.' It sounds good. It sounds sweet. It is what I have tried to do for you today, Lisa—give. A lot of guys would have ordered you to have an abortion. I think you know me, my feelings about life, the holiness of life. I could never do something so cruel. Now, I want you to know that I will make sure that there are plenty of houses for you to clean every summer. You will always have a job on Black Island. You and the child are welcome here anytime—anytime in the early summer. The later summer and fall, we are a bit crowded. I have also seen to it that both you and the child will be covered by a family health plan and you will receive five thousand dollars a year until you remarry. Lastly, I have given to you the greatest gift possible. For the rest of your life, and the child's, you may bear my name. Beale. I give it to you, Lisa. It is yours."

With that Chip Beale walked away into the woods and the lawyer appeared at Lisa's side. He offered a fat, black pen and a piece of paper.

"Could you sign this, please?"

45

"What is it?"

"A decree of divorce. Everything has been done. It has been signed by Judge Lowell, witnessed and notarized. Your rights have been scrupulously observed. Please sign." Bordered in black, the sharp face and tiny teeth grinned.

"Wait a minute," I said. "We need time to think about this."

"*We* don't need to do anything. *She* must sign."

"I won't," Lisa said.

The lawyer's black eyebrows touched, frowned and then happily ascended. "Your father, Mr. Wojaska Kraskawitz, owes several loans to Boston Bank. Presently, he is behind on two of them. Mr. Charles Beale sits on the board of Boston Bank. If business is not concluded forthwith, the loans will be called due. We will sell your father's business, attach his home, repossess his car, destroy his credit and order an audit by IRS. After that, we get tough. Sign."

Lisa paused. The lawyer stuck the pen into her fingers. She gazed at him and then at me. She turned and looked at the lighthouse and then far, far out into the sea.

In five seconds she signed four times. It was over.

I took her to Straw Hill and we built a birch fire in the wood stove. When the fire was burning I opened two Buds and we lay down on the mattress and looked out the window toward the blue tidal pools. We held hands and drank the beer.

Lisa finished her beer and got up and went to the shelf and brought back two more. She knelt on the mattress and popped open one can and then the other and her onyx eyes held no tears, though her lips were parted and I could see the cute, chipped tooth. She still wore her cheap bridal dress and the red patent leathers. It hurt to look at her.

She handed me a beer.

"He's a bastard," I said.

"I hate this place anyway, you know?"

"I know."

"I mean, I just hate it."

Lisa took a sip of beer, then set the can down and put her hands to her face. She started crying and turned her back and faced the brown sea grass in the marsh below.

For a long time I let her cry. I tried to sip my beer but her crying hurt too much so I put my arms around her and felt her tremble and I squeezed her until she made a small noise. She cried a little more and I said nothing. I just held her and put my lips against one soft ear.

"I need to go," Lisa said.

"Spend the night here."

"No."

"You need somebody."

"I need to be by myself. I got to think, get my head straight."

"You sure?"

"No."

I tried to walk her home but she stopped me when we reached Beale Street.

"Look at me," Lisa said. "It's kind of funny if you think about it. The maid in her red shoes and bridal dress. The maid walking home after the master jilted her. If you really think about it, it's kinda funny."

I watched her walk down the rough road.

I drank a couple more beers. Chip Beale needed a good punch in the mouth. What I really needed to do was go over there and not say a word, just open his door, walk in and plant one right on his nose.

I thought about this and got up and acted out the scene. Me storming into his room, no, not storming, me coming in real quiet, soft, and Chip's big, gold eyes getting bigger and me saying nothing—well, maybe one line, like "You jerk"—then just letting him hold one right in the gut, a long pole-driver to the diaphragm. Then lighting a cigarette and dropping the smoky match on the floor and watching him squirm for air while the cigarette burned halfway down, then walking out, me not saying anything.

I turned and belted the cabin, jumped around and cradled my hand.

My first two knuckles were skinned, but I managed to open another beer. I was looped. I lay down on the mattress, nursing my hand and my beer and said, "No, the way to get him is to be quiet, act like business as usual and then when Mallory Beale puts me in charge, then nail him. Kick him off the island, or if not, if not that, just harass him. Throw big island parties and always invite him. If his pipes bust in winter, make sure the work crews don't get there for days; give Lisa one of the island's biggest houses; name her son after him . . ." The list rambled on until I went to sleep.

The next morning the interior of my head felt like a bucket of rusted metal. The cabin was cold. The sea blew daggers through the thin walls. I wrapped myself in a blanket, hopped and hobbled toward the shelves in the corner, grabbed a beer, opened it and drank. Horrible, but wet.

I reclined in bed, watching red leaves fall from the ash and maple trees. In the tidal pools below, a blue heron hunted while in the white cattail stands a bevy of quail shuddered gold and black. I thought about Lisa, worried about her. She needed help. Chip would do nothing. Exactly then I decided. Sure it would be wonderful to find the right moment to see my grandfather, but I couldn't wait. People needed my help. Doug, Lisa, probably Marlow and Harding in some way. I had to move now. I decided to see Mallory Beale in three days.

I prepared.

During the next three mornings I rose at five-thirty. The air was bleak and cold. I shook the embers in the stove and added dried birch and oak, which Doug had stacked under the porch of the cabin. I did not use the lantern but preferred to sit in the dark cabin and watch the sun light the India-ink tidal pools at the base of Straw Hill. When the sun rimmed the horizon the sea became pink and then red and finally black-blue, and then the softer blue. I drank coffee. I wrote notes to myself about the way in which I would approach my grandfather. I wrote down what I would wear—pinstripes, black wingtips, black- and red-stripe tie, white button-down oxford. I sorted through the memoir and wrote down all the clues which led me to my deduction. After the writing I dressed in my old gray sweats and ran the island: down the dirt road, onto Beale Street, turning onto Shore Road, then cutting by the beach club and heading north by the tennis courts and the huge island houses. Just beyond the houses I turned east and glanced up at the blackened remains of Mallory Beale's house and ran on past birches and oaks and small roads which led into other island homes and, nearing the first gate, took a right, sprinting down Honk Hill and then finally racing up Straw Hill.

In the cabin I stripped down to my jock, stoked the fire hot and pumped out as many push-ups as I could: the first day only fifty, then seventy-five, then one hundred. After push-ups I did jumping jacks, sit-ups and then, discovering an old seventy-pound barbell, curls and finally some presses.

On the afternoon of the third day I decided that I would spend the night at Chip's bungalow. I gathered the clothes I had chosen for the meeting with Mallory Beale.

46

Ten minutes later I was standing in a cold, red twilight beneath Chip's creaking windmill. The bungalow was quiet and apparently empty. I reached and touched the green lattice which formed the windmill's base. Twenty feet high in the air, the blades were squealing in a light wind. I reached and placed my hands on the moist latticework. I studied the rusted and turning axle, which depended from the wind vane. I could feel the wind trembling the wood, making the wood purr. I thought back when I had first seen the windmill, back in May, so long ago. I held the wind in wood and suddenly felt futile and alone.

I am a Beale, I said. A Beale. It didn't feel right.

I knocked on Chip's front door, and when there was no answer I entered. The place was the same mess: Natural Farm Vitamin bottles (a company Chip had purchased when I first arrived), stacks of letters postmarked London and Zurich and Rio, jazz albums, snowshoes and hip-waders and several tennis rackets and desiccated bags of golf clubs.

I went into his kitchen and opened a cabinet where he usually kept wine. It was empty. On the pine counter sat jars containing yellow sunflower seeds, brown pebbly lentils, black beans, brown rice and a glass Buddha filled to his eternally smiling mouth with amber honey.

In the living room I crossed the elaborate and beautiful Persian rug: it was sienna sand dunes and blue sky. I sat down on the old mattress, still covered by the green and yellow tie-dyed sheet. I turned on the floor lamp and felt seventy-five watts strike my face. Several dead yellow jackets lay on the fir-wood windowsill. Their eyes glinted in the lamplight. Even in death their bodies looked beautiful: striped abdomens, black stripe, then yellow, then black. Wings folded against the abdomens and the fibrous cells of wings pure and inviolate. But it was their faces which fascinated me. Each triangular yellow and black head was turned toward the windowpane, turned toward the invisible wall which separated them from the world they sought. Small heads, seed-shaped amber eyes, now flooded by an unnatural light which they never desired and never understood. When I touched one he crumbled.

Lisa spoke softly. "Hey, cowboy." She was leaning against the front door. Even from where I sat I could see the black eye. She put her head down and came and sat beside me.

I touched a finger to her chin and raised her face. Her eyeball was red. The black and blue welt was speckled with blood.

"What happened?"

"Chip."

"Chip did this?"

"He ordered me to get an abortion."

I put an arm around her shoulders.

"He said he'd changed his mind. He said he wouldn't have a bastard son walking around the island. He said I was a liar and a manipulator and I needed a lesson. He hit me, Cody. He hit me hard."

She began to cry.

I rocked her in my arms. "I want you to call your daddy."

"I did."

"Did you tell him about the baby?"

"I told him I wanted to come home, but I don't have the money."

"I'll get you the money."

Lisa turned to me. The luscious summer tan had eroded from her face. There were sharp lines at her eyes and her cheeks seemed swollen. She looped both arms around my waist and shivered. I pushed my head against hers and smoothed her soft hair. I wanted to say something simple and direct: Lisa, let me marry you and we'll raise that baby together. This was in my heart, but I could not say it.

"Where's Chip?" I asked.

"In the bed. I made him some noodle soup, took it to him. He threw it on the floor, Cody. He threw my soup right on the floor and said, 'Get hosed out.' Then he hit me."

I raised Lisa's cheek, spoke softly. "I'm going to put on some hot water. Lay out a tea bag. You're cold. The tea will help. Will you drink it?"

"I just wanted to be somebody," Lisa said and slid her fingers between mine. "You know I didn't want to be nothing like my family. I wanted to be somebody special."

I rose and ignited the gas flame beneath the teakettle and set a Sleepytime tea bag beside a white cup.

I opened the ramshackle door to Chip's bedroom. The sharp smell of joss sticks cut the air. Chip had moved a stone Buddha close beside the mattress. The tub-bellied god was surrounded by blue stone vases holding dead chrysanthemums.

Chip lay back against two pillows. He had pulled a red and black blanket to his neck. His face was hollow and waxen above the black beard. The gold eyes were sunken.

"I'm going to Idaho," Chip said. "I'm going up to my land and get away from this place."

I closed the door. "I want a thousand dollars."

"I'm broke. I don't get my allowance for two more weeks."

I sat down on the side of his bed. On the dusty window ledge beside him stood five empty jars of something called Mundi. I took one of the jars, smelled it. "What's this?"

"Mundi, man."

"What is it?"

"Earth, soil. I started taking it a couple weeks ago. I eat a jar a day."

"You're eating dirt?"

"Not dirt, the earth. I'm taking the living planet into myself. It's what I want to be—the earth, the good, clean earth that never kills or partakes of killing. It just grows, man. It just grows."

I grabbed him by his shirt collar and pulled him halfway from bed. "Listen to me. I want you to have a thousand dollars cash waiting at the bank for Lisa."

"I'm broke."

I slapped him. "You get out of the bed and call the bank and have the money waiting."

Chip held his face between his hands. "She's a servant. She's nothing."

I slapped him again. "Get out of bed. Call the bank. Get the money. Do it now or I'll beat your brains out. Do you understand?"

I hoisted him from the bed and threw him toward the phone. I whispered to him. "Don't ever speak that way about Lisa again. Not ever. Now dial."

When Chip punched the first two numbers I left the room.

Lisa was sitting on the couch. She had tidied her black hair. She tried to give a big, brave smile. The butterfly scar beneath her eye was black from the blow.

I knelt before her and kissed one knee. "Chip's getting you a thousand. That will get you home and give you a little living money. I'll help, Lisa. I'll help as much as I can."

"My family will throw me out."

"Maybe not."

"They will."

"I'll have Chip send some money along. For now just go home and wait. I'll be in touch. A bus leaves the Cedar Point depot every two hours. Let me have your phone number at home."

Marlow bopped his way through the front door holding a map. His big seal eyes seemed soft and relaxed. The handsome nose was losing freckles.

"Got my trip planned, folks. Down the eastern seaboard to the Keys. You know I—"

"You have another trip first," I said.

I told Marlow to take Lisa to the bank and then the bus station. He was surprised, concerned. I told him I would explain.

I walked Lisa and Marlow to Chip's car. As usual, the keys sat in the ignition.

"You need to get away. I'll call you. Things are changing very fast now. I'll be in touch with you soon."

Lisa embraced me and kissed my neck. "Ever since that day we played ball, I've been loving you, Cody."

"I'll call you," I said. I opened the car door and put her inside. "The bank first," I said to Marlow, who looked stricken.

"My God, the place feels like it's falling apart," he said.

"No, it's coming together, Marlow. All the points are ready to connect." I opened his door and he climbed into the driver's seat.

The car rolled away. I waved and said quietly, "I love you, Lisa."

In his cedar bedroom Chip knelt in a red caftan before Buddha.

"Did you call the bank?" I asked.

"Yeah, the money's waiting. I've been talking to the Lord Buddha."

"What's he saying?"

"Do you think I'm a bad man?"

"Is that what Buddha says?"

"I just wanted to destroy power, my own power. I wanted to be free from power and corruption and lead a good life. I wanted to bring order and light to my family, to Black Island. I hate manipulation. I hate those who abuse others. I have grown in that way, Cody. Don't you think? Isn't it clear that I'm free in that sense at least? I don't use servants. I don't spend money. I live simply, like a warrior. I'm not bad, am I?"

I stripped off my shirt, kicked off my shoes.

When Chip turned his gaunt face to me, I was naked. He seemed to recoil at my flesh.

I felt the smile flush my face and pry my mouth open. "I want you to go to Straw Hill. Live up there a few days. Freeze at night. Stink for a while, and when you smell bad enough, you can come down here and ask me to use the shower."

"I have to consult the Lord Buddha."

"You can take him with you. While you're up there, make some provisions about Lisa, and don't think five thousand a year lets you off the hook. Her family's poor. You and Lord Buddha come up with a figure for Lisa, and when you do, bring it to me. Then I'll double it and that's the way you can *begin* to repay her."

I left him and turned the shower sterilizing hot and scrubbed myself for half an hour. I dried and entered Chip's room again. He was gone and so was Buddha. I took the small stone vases and dead flowers and heaved them out the window. I stripped the bed of sheets and found clean ones and remade the bed. I opened his clothes-crammed closet and put on a purple terry-cloth robe. It was eight-fifteen and full night.

I looked in the shaving mirror on Chip's mahogany highboy. Two brushes with silver handles lay on a bronze tray. I combed my brown hair straight back. My face was strong, the hazel eyes confident.

A knock at the front door. When I opened it the shadow lit a cigarette—Mallory Beale.

I didn't even shake.

47

"Chhiiippp?" Mallory Beale's slur sounded sweet and magic.

"Cody," I said.

"Oh. I was looking for Chip."

"Up on Straw Hill."

"What's he doing up there?"

"I think he's meditating."

"What a lot of crap. Don't you agree?"

"Yes, I do."

"Are you recovered from the fire?"

"I just had a few cuts."

"Too bad about Johnny."

"I'd like to see you tomorrow, around ten in the morning, if I could," I said.

"What for?"

"Business."

"Business?"

"Yes, business."

The cigarette breathed in the youthful face.

"Shall I have the maid make coffee?"

"Coffee would be fine."

"Very good. Ten o'clock tomorrow then for—business."

"I look forward to it," I said.

"So do I," said Beale. "I'll be in Townsend's house across from the tennis court."

He walked away.

It was a sleepless night of stars and planes of black space seen through the windows by my warm bed. The last leaves of Japanese maples hummed and rattled. There were no insects or peepers or owls. The night was pure. Like a prince, I lay in my purple robe beneath the heavy blanket. In the darkness the stars were trembling and vibrating like a swarm, like a sterling swarm in space and I saw the stars as I had never seen them and they were bright and living.

Up and coffee. Little sleep had made me round-eyed and curiously strong. I ripped off one hundred push-ups. From the closet I grabbed jeans and old running shoes and ran the bright, cold, salty island in twenty minutes flat. I yelled at the sea and yelled at the trees and the boulders and the air itself, "Hey, you! You guys! Hey, you!"

In the bungalow again, I boiled water for tea. I crunched one hundred sit-ups until my muscles burned and cramped. I was sweating. I fixed the tea and went to the stereo. I wanted to hear something Southern. I wanted to blast the island awake. I put the two big speakers outside the door. I sorted through the sloppy record stacks looking for the right sound, then found it: The Band. "The Night They Drove Ole Dixie Down."

I flipped the record onto the turntable, twisted every dial as high as possible and then let The Band blast open the morning.

The second time the Sony got started, Harding stormed toward the front steps dressed in a violet flannel robe, barefoot, her auburn hair piled and pinned, without makeup, eyes wide and flashing a dangerous blue.

"Cody, you have aroused the entire island."

"At last."

"Aunt Bosey fell from her bed and Townsend's new spaniel has gone into premature labor."

"Reveille!"

"You're drunk."

"I'm sober." I jumped over the speakers, caught and kissed her.

"You'll awaken Uncle Mallory."

"Time for his rusty, blue-blood self to be up."

"It's 6:15 A.M., Cody."

"He's got a hard day ahead of him."

"What kind of day?"

"Why don't you come to bed and I'll tell you."

"I thought you'd never ask."

In bed Harding rolled over on top of me. The dawn light outlined her jaws: rather full at the top and tapering to a dimpled point at the chin. Her auburn hair fell in wedges and wingtips before her eyes and when she threw her head back to manage the hair, her throat looked rosy and full.

"You're awfully cocky," she said.

"Today is my day."

"What's happened?"

"You have the softest legs in the world."

Harding slid her long legs between and across mine. I caressed her warm shoulders and slim back and waist.

She kissed me, using a soft suction and satin tongue, her lips somehow pushing mine apart and sucking my gums.

I was ready, but she wanted to play. I was stroking her gently beneath, but she pulled my hand away. She nuzzled my ears, blowing and teasing. She bit my neck and then moved down my chest. Her left hand plucked my right nipple until it went hard, while her tongue circled my other nipple and I heard myself say what Lisa had said to me. "Do it hard. Real hard."

And Harding bit, stung like a wasp, so that I found myself moaning like a woman, throwing my head back, bucking my hips to move into her, which she still would not allow. She kissed my abdomen, her hands beneath my buttocks, and when she found me higher than she expected, she just touched my tip with her tongue.

I flipped her, going slowly at first, not giving length, just minute circles, using a hand to hold myself back and now *she* was making the pleading sounds until I pierced deeper, pumping in short, quick time, and her hands jammed my buttocks until I finally thrust the whole thing into her and felt her slam against the bed and then we went against one another hotly, lost and beyond ourselves and our breaths and the noises which rumbled from our throats and the coming was long and, for the first time, perfectly simultaneous.

Delightfully, we lay entangled in arms and legs and tresses of hair. I propped an arm beneath my head and looked at the misty sky and the white scoop clouds and, below the clouds, the last maple leaves and red oak leaves and in the distance the hard, white trunks of birches. The air looked cold and spangled, and the light in the air was so hard that I could almost see the salt from the ocean, granular and whirling like bright, big atoms in the wind.

"Cody, something's happened. Tell me." Harding's voice was the wonderful, clenched, upper-class snip.

I looked at the blue gem on my finger. "I talked to Johnny Day before he died. I learned some things."

"Don't be obscure. Is it true or not?"

I didn't want to say it. I backed off. "I'm going to see Mallory this morning. We have to talk."

"Frankly, I think you've gone around the twist."

"Really."

"Mallory Beale's grandson. The more I've thought about it the crazier it seems."

"Of course, if I offered you Stone House this afternoon, you'd probably accept."

"Oh, probably."

"That's my girl."

"Am I your girl?"

"Do you want to be?"

"Oh, yes."

In the cold autumn light I stood before Townsend's house. The two rough cedars which guarded the side door seemed green and virile and unapproachable. The wind pushed through the branches and the whole yard smelled of evergreens. I was wearing my pinstripes and white oxford shirt, my careful, striped tie.

I was a little nervous, but they were good nerves, the kind you need before a speech or a good performance. I tugged at my shirt cuffs. The oval onyx cuff links snapped light. I had found them in Chip's highboy drawer. I looked at my turquoise ring, took a steadying breath. My heart chugged faster. I reached and touched the cedar needles. They felt cold and simple and deathless.

Without a knock, I opened the door and stepped into the hallway. Suddenly bells went off, vibrating, screaming somewhere above my head. I jumped and just as I did Townsend came around the dining-room corner.

"They got you," Townsend said. Her rough face was friendly. She wore a red plaid hunting shirt and blue wool skirt with brown L.L. Bean overshoes. She had mascara on her stubby eyelashes.

"What was it?" I asked, the bells still jarring my head.

"Mallory's out of the shower. He rings the bell when he enters so no one will turn on any hot water and freeze him. He rings it also when he gets out to let us all know we can wash a pot or something. Isn't it absurd?"

"Odd," I said.

"Mallory says you're here for business."

"I am."

"Baby boy, you're not going to ask him to invest in some crackpot idea, are you?"

"Nope. I'm going to invest in him."

"How marvelous. He loves investors. Now, listen, we're having a private birthday celebration this morning and I wanted you to be part. Just Mallory and me and you. The big bash will be this evening. You don't think he'll get drunk, do you?"

"Today is his birthday?"

"Didn't you know?"

"Incredible."

"I just hope he doesn't drink."

"I'll watch him."

"He's doing so well. I'm just afraid he might hit the booze again and it would ruin him, Cody."

"Depend on me."

Townsend patted my face. "I've got to get more candles for this evening. My God, he's lived a long time."

In the living room the bay window radiated sunlight. Duck decoys sat on the simple walnut coffee table and the large oak bookcases. The ducks' flat eyes felt heavy on me. A few more huddled in the living-room corners. There must have been twenty or so. They seemed awfully smug. They seemed superior. I went over to a beautifully carved duck and thumped it on the faded beak.

The room was so simple. A Shaker-design coffee table, two bookcases, a backgammon table with two cedar chairs, a stuffed armchair and a yellow pinewood straight-back, which had a cracked pine footstool to match, the two high-backed sofas covered in beige muslin that faced each other before the fireplace and, beneath them, the bare oak floors, not a rug in sight.

I stood by the fire and tried to compose myself. Behind me, the floor popped and I turned.

Mallory Beale looked like a king: a royal-blue suit and dark red tie and black shoes, brilliant green eyes, new and imperturbable. He offered a hand. His grip was tough.

"Happy birthday," I said and heard my own voice; my accent was exactly like his: Haappy Buurrthday.

"Where's Townsend?"

"Went for some candles," I said.

"I guess that's for tonight?"

"For the party tonight. Yes."

"Well, shall I go ahead and ring for the smaller cake?"

"Certainly."

Mallory Beale pushed a wall buzzer. He went over and sat in the stuffed armchair. He had a gambol to his gait, like a young man. He offered a hand toward the pinewood straight-back. I sat down.

Suddenly my mind was empty.

Mallory Beale reached inside his sleek suit and pulled out a Lucky Strike package. He offered me a cigarette. I took it. He pulled out another for himself, slipped the package back into his coat pocket. He thumped the cigarette on his left thumbnail. He lit mine and then his own.

We sat and smoked. He blew the smoke through his nose. I just puffed. The time was magic. Immaculately attired, there we sat, two businessmen in smashing suits, waiting for the other to play the first card.

Somehow I began.

"Grandfather . . ."

I waited for a response. I looked at his face. Nothing.

"Grandfather, you were behind the invitation to Black Island."

Molly pushed in a wooden cart bearing a small white cake, a cake without candles. She pushed the cart exactly between us. Steaming coffee and ivory white cups and glittering teaspoons and milk and brown sugar sat beneath.

Mallory Beale's nod dismissed her.

"Have you seen the cake?" he asked, and his gin and jade gaze shifted toward it.

The icing was white and crystalline, but in the cake's center was an outline, a design. I leaned forward. It was perfect; that is, the symbol was perfect. The drawing was clumsy and inaccurate; nevertheless, I discerned the shape of Black Island. A triangular daub of red marked the lighthouse.

"Damn fine cake," Mallory Beale said.

His face revealed no surprise.

"You sent me your memoirs," I said. "It took me a long time to understand what you wanted."

"But now you do?"

"Yes."

I crossed my legs and sat back in the chair. "I know who I am—Dooley Rice Codell Beale. I am your grandson."

It came then, it flooded his face like a rolling wave of sunlight, a great breaking smile which opened his green eyes and spread the matron lips and exposed his teeth and his deep and dark and black interior.

48

"Who do you think you are?" Mallory Beale asked, the smile holding his face.

"A Beale," I said.

"A Beale. A Beale," the old man said. He poured a cup of coffee, offered it. I declined. With an embossed silver spoon, he took one-half teaspoon of brown sugar.

"Why?" Beale asked.

I felt calm. I felt cold as slate. I placed my elbows on my knees, joined my hands, studied the boiling blue of my ring.

"My father was secretive about his younger years. Until a month ago I didn't know where he had been born, what had happened to his parents. All I knew was that he was raised in the orphanage in Aiken. Then when he was fourteen he met you."

I leaned forward, closer to Mallory Beale. "My father's name was not Joe Walker. It was Joe Beale. His mother was Olive Thomas and you were his father. You raised him in Aiken, sent him to school and took him into your business. For some reason he left, changed his name to Joe Walker and moved back to South Carolina. In 1968 he was killed in a car wreck. In 1973 you sent for me."

Beale set a bony finger upon his bent, brown nose. The jade eyes glimmered. He cut a heaping wedge of cake, set it on a saucer. He left the chair, stood by the bay window and ate a mouthful, swallowed coffee. "What a story. Beautiful, beguiling, but—crap. Half truth, like any good story. Here are the facts. Olive Thomas was Joe Beale's mother. I did raise Joe

Beale in Aiken. There he met your father, who was living with his alcoholic mother in a dump. The boys became friends. I felt sorry for your father and sent him with my son to prep school —that is, I sent Joe Wallace—his real name—to prep school. In 1941 I sent both boys to Yale. That winter my son—Joe Beale— was killed in a car crash in Aiken. Funny that your father died the same way in the same town—twenty-five years later. I let Joe Wallace fill the hole in my life, but that was a dreadful mistake."

"But the ring," I said, and took it off my finger and held it for him to see. "The turquoise ring."

"Yeah, so?"

"Johnny Day told me that you gave your ring, this turquoise ring, to your son on his birthday."

Mallory Beale laughed. He reached a hand toward me, then retracted it. "I did give the ring to my son, and then when he died I gave it to your father."

I sat back in the chair and held my burning cigarette.

Mallory Beale finished his cake. "You see, your father was a thief from the beginning. He would come to Pink House on the weekends to visit Joe. And every time he left, something went with him—a silver letter opener, a watch. Yeah, he was a thief. Rotten apple, no good, a bum—but my God he was charming. And handsome. As I said, I sent him to Yale and he cheated and got thrown out and I endowed more dough and got him back in. I remember the second time he got ousted I said what are you gonna do now, Joe, and he said I don't know. I'm broke and got no dough, you got an extra job around? I did. I put him in the steel company, but I already knew what he was doing—sizing me up. I saw the cutthroat ambition. It was damn clear but I still kept him around. Maybe because I liked the challenge; see, I was getting old. Things weren't ticking right in me. Things were getting rusty and so this kid, this greedy kid who had great brains and classy style and a weasel's heart—he became a whetstone for me. I trained him, oh, not directly, through the managers in the company. I told them to give him every job they could—from working band saws and pipe cutters to mechanical drawing. In two years he went from a junior exec to vice president of the steel company.

"It was 1943 and we were doing cracker-jack business and retooling and making the best tanks and flattops and planes in the world. We did 1.6 billion in the steel company that year. A lot of that profit was due to him. He was a boy wonder. He was great at cutting corners. His natural ability at cheating worked perfectly for Pentagon contracts. Look, he started off on a Sherman tank design by refusing to use the required thickness for armor plating. I remember he knocked off a quarter of an inch, which made the tank about as safe as a paper bag, but—and this is how luck always saved him—the lightened armor made the tank fast. Faster than anything the Nazis or the Japs had. They could fly. It's the reason Patton nearly took Germany by himself—speed. Think about it. We kicked the crap out of Germany because your father just wanted to make a few more bucks.

"Finally he was setting his sights on me. I let him head up three other businesses—the Cumberland Hotel chain and the Southwest banking system and a new airline I was planning to create made out of B-47s when they started coming back. He was terrific. He learned everything fast. He made friends, allies in every business I put him in. He had such charm. Some of those guys still love him. I was feeling better and better. I could feel him coming on, feel everything in him tuning up and burning and priming. I got rid of my doctors and all their pills and diets. Yeah, I dumped them all. The more leeway I gave your old man, the more he grabbed and the stronger I got. Then in 1950 he made his move. I knew it was coming. He had power in four or five companies. I kept him away from the guys who had real power—Truman, Kennedy, Mellon. I never let him link with those guys. But he had connections, see he had friendships with these two-bit company execs. He built a network. I admired him. He tied the major companies together. He pulled them under the steel business. What he was building really was a conglomerate, a kind of Gulf & Western. He wanted the steel company, which he now controlled, to buy the others. He wanted to drive me out and set up his own little empire. Except it would have been pretty big. Oh, I'd say he could have been worth two billion on paper, something like that. But like I said, I never let him have the big boys, Rockefeller, Lodge, etc. I made sure he couldn't tag those guys. Kept him out of the bank too. That was important. You know, sometimes I've wondered—if I had let him into the bank, maybe he could have done it. Maybe he was so smart he could have brought me right down.

"But like I was saying, he made a move in 1950. Bad move. Showed me he was a bad man. He had a casino in Vegas, got in with the wrong crowd. He made what he thought was a big friend—a thug called Statz, Bugsy Statz. A nobody who thought he was big guns out West. I had ears out there. I knew what was being said. Statz wanted in on your father's big takeover. Like all thugs, he gave bad advice. Statz said, now get this, Statz said in a meeting they had in the Sands Hotel—Statz said, 'Why don't you just put the old man's lights out? Knock him off. I got friends in banking. We'll take the whole ball of wax.' Well, I didn't fall off the tree yesterday. When I heard about this 'business' meeting, I knew what I had to do. Now I have to say, your father didn't say yes, but he didn't say no. He wanted to think. I don't know. Maybe he wouldn't have tried. Maybe he would have gone back to Statz and said forget it. No dice. But I didn't want to wait, so I went straight to Vito Genovese. I'd done him a few favors. We were pals in a way. We had dinner in a nice little joint on Mulberry Street in the city.

"I remember I was eating chick peas, and Vito, he was on his diet, white spaghetti—just olive oil and pasta. I told him about Statz. I left your father's name out. Vito had dealt with Statz anyway. He didn't like him. Vito was having problems too. Luciano was fighting to get back in the country and had paid out a lot of dough. A lot of bribes. He had a good chance to come back, which would have been very bad for Vito. I had some muscle on the Senate committee that was investigating Luciano. I had senators in my pocket. So I said I'll keep Lucky in his hotel in Palermo if you take care of Statz. We shook hands on it just when they brought out the cheesecake. It was the best cheesecake I ever ate. Two weeks later Bugsy got his brains shot out. Then I personally went to all the little companies your father ran and fired the top men. Replaced them with the guys three levels down. I remember I went into Joe's office at the steel company in Boston. I could see the city behind him. It was sleeting. Everything was gray. I said to him, 'You're finished, Joe. There's nothing left. Everything's over for you.' And you know what he did? He laughed. He looked at me hard and laughed."

Mallory Beale stuck his small hands into his suit pockets. The jade eyes were flat and hard and terribly green. The thin-boned face and owl nose coursed blood. "So you see, all this stuff you dreamed up—it's a story. Nice fiction. I brought you here to see if you were worth a damn. To see if you had guts, ability. I think I know the answer now, but you don't belong here. The island's changed. It used to be hard and clean, but now it's gone soft. Everyone here has blue blood except two guys—me and you. Me, I'm gonna die. You, you're gonna get out. Leave. You don't belong here."

Behind Mallory Beale I saw fog moving toward the window, sifting through the evergreens, reaching for the house. I had no feeling. "Why did you give me the memoir?"

There came that smile again, so big and vital, so powerful that it seemed to radiate heat. "You know, I could do deals. I could see when to move and how to move. I could figure out a guy's hand in two minutes flat. I did that for the first twenty years of my life and then—I got bored; it wasn't fun anymore. So I started taking notes on all these big shots. Recorded conversations. I deliberately went out of my way to meet big names—Churchill, Roosevelt, Stalin, guys like that. Some I had business with, but I wanted something else. I wanted to catch part of them somehow. I wanted to preserve them. That's how it all started and then one day I knew what I really wanted, maybe what I was, maybe what I desired more than any deal I had put together—I wanted to be a writer. A writer. Do something that would last. Yeah, I sent you a letter. And then you got here and I discovered *you* were a writer. For some reason Harding gave you some of my stuff. I found out about it, followed suit."

"Why did my father change his name from Wallace to Walker?"

"I destroyed him completely. He couldn't buy a pair of shoes on credit. He had to start over."

Upon me there was the gentlest calm, a placid and imperturbable pall. I reached for the package of cigarettes, lit one.

"Look, I want to be remembered. I want a piece of eternity. Writing can secure me that. I have good ideas. I want to secure them like stock. I want them underpinned. Words can do that. Words can hold everything. All the men and women I have loved. All the deals and the handshakes and the power. If I can write them down, if my work is any good, then as long as there are libraries, as long as man thinks and reads and communicates, *I AM*. My world will never die. If my words are any good, I can have it all, everything that I have done or dreamed or thought. Words can afford me what money never could—immortality."

I pulled the last smoke from the cigarette. I set the stub into an ashtray. I just set the stub there. I did not smash out the fire. A line of smoke rose between us, between Mallory Beale and me.

I blew at the smoke and it disassembled and the breath caused Mallory Beale to blink.

I rose, began walking from the room.

"Do you think I'm any good?"

I entered the bright, maple hallway.

"Do you think I'm any good at all?"

I stopped at the door that led to the outside.

"Yes," I said. "I think you're pretty good."

"Where are you going?"

"Back."

"We have business to discuss. I'm working on some things. It will take me a while. Come see me in three or four days."

I kept moving.

"Wallace. We have business, do you hear? We have . . ."

The next two days were fragmented. I came down with a fever of some kind. I was delirious. I stayed at Chip's place. Harding came over, but I insisted on solitude. Everything seemed to be cracking apart. I took the small Sony radio by Chip's bed and slept with it. I listened to music. I kept seeing all the days I had spent on the island. They continually presented themselves in blues and reds: my first night on the island, *Ole Blue,* my first vision of Mallory Beale, my first sex with Lisa and Harding, the good times with Doug and Marlow and even Chip.

The vomiting started at some point in the second day. There was nothing in me, so only clear water issued. After four or five convulsions I was completely empty. I began drinking water. It was something that my father had said: "If you are sick and nothing comes out, then drink water."

For hours I continued reliving every moment of my stay, examining every word that I had said or thought, recalling in exquisite and excruciating detail—my first bowl of chowder, the wonderful groans of Lisa as she worked toward ecstasy, the deep pleadings of Harding, the brilliant colors of my new clothes, New House, the Yankee spring. Each image came quickly and sharply and I lived through them as if for the first time, until finally at the end Mallory Beale's gigantic, mottled face arose, not his new one, not the younger man's face, but rather the first one I had seen—skin broken by lesions, temples frail as paraffin, eyes desiccated and dry and the smile working his face until his mouth opened and the smooth, cob teeth glowed and then I was somehow in his mouth and everything went black around me and I heard a beating, like a drum beat in the blackness, a long pulse, slow and vibrating, which became louder and finally thunderous, as if I had been swallowed by a pulsating and cavernous black heart.

Harding withdrew a cool cloth from my forehead. "Why didn't you call me?"

Through the bedroom window the sun lit the tiny scar in her chin. I reached to touch her face. My arm was willow weak. I felt a sweat suddenly stand on my body, rise from my skin. The sweat started hot and then turned cold. I shivered and Harding threw blankets over me.

Harding fixed me soup and fresh juices. She never left the bungalow. I slept a lot. She told me that Chip had gone to his place in Idaho.

It was September and the wind was blowing black clouds. Harding said she felt snow in the air. Early snow. The soup made me stronger. The images, the past months on the island, did not return.

I was awake when the phone rang.

49

Harding said, "Doug, how are you, darling?" Then her expression changed and she said, "Georgia? Well, of course. I'm sure Cody knows . . ." She turned away and there were a few more words I did not hear. She hung up the phone.

"Doug's been shot. He's in Georgia. Some place on the coast. Parsonsville or something. He doesn't want anyone else to know. He wants us to come."

I pulled back the covers. Shakily, I sat on the mattress edge. "How bad is he hurt?"

"He sounded dreadful. His breathing was bad. He said to go to Savannah, then Parsonsville."

I got up, felt my head spin. I sat down again, this time rose more easily. "I'm going to take a shower," I said. "Get us everything we need."

"I have credit cards," Harding said.

The shower burned away the sweat. I used Chip's peppermint soap. My legs felt silly and weak. Toweling off, I didn't have the strength to dry my hair, so Harding did it.

We booked a plane flight. Three hours later we were leaving Black Island. The black clouds touched the tops of branches. White birch trunks gleamed in the sudden cold. We bumped and twisted down Beale Street. In the woods many ferns had turned brown. They looked like rusted wire. Leaves two feet deep held the forest floor. Harding inserted a card into the first gate. The wooden arm squeaked and rose. We drove down the long causeway. On the right the sea was gray and unmoving. On the left the reeds were dun-colored. I saw the first of it then. I was surprised. Snow. It began falling from the black clouds. I turned in the seat as we neared the second gate at the end of the causeway. The island was barren and gray and immobile. The white snow was falling heavily now. It fell straight down and did not blow and it came so quickly that Straw Hill disappeared and the distant docks became obscured and I could no longer see the shores of the island so that everything here became lost, everything except one light on the island's highest hill: one lamp burning in the second floor of Townsend's house where the old man was staying. Suddenly in a white swirl and silent avalanche, even this feature faded, became only a hollow glowing until the snow covered everything and Black Island disappeared from my eyes, beneath snow, forever—or so I thought.

Cedar Point to Atlanta to Savannah.

When Harding and I stepped off the Delta jet, the sun was huge and rectangular. Temperature seventy-eight degrees. Harding saw to our clothes while I rented a Ford van.

In twenty minutes we were rolling through downtown Savannah. Ancient three- and four-story homes, their exteriors blue and pink stucco. Yellow marble steps. Wrought-iron gates and fences surrounding yards of oleander, azalea, honeysuckle, banana and palm trees.

Vaguely I remembered Parsonsville. It was thirty or forty miles down the beach.

Harding reached over, touched my face. "Want me to drive?"

"I'm okay. What was the name of the landing?"

"Butcher's, I think. Yes, Butcher's and ask for Spot."

We drove for forty minutes. The sea was on our left—shanties and mobile homes, occasionally a new, plastic motel. On our right lay merciless flat land, jade pine groves, swamps and crusty palmettos. White egrets hunted in the black water. Vultures carved the air.

The sign surprised me: Parsonsville, Georgia. Population 493.

I pulled into a gas station.

"I'll get us some sandwiches," Harding said.

She left the car. A restaurant stood beside a liquor store.

The gas station sold Budweiser and fishing gear and bait. The interior air felt heavy and cool, like earth. Crickets screamed from mesh cages and minnows formed black clouds in glass tanks. A big orange and jade parrot sat on a pine stand. Its black tongue curled from the banana-yellow beak. "Welcome back. Welcome back. Welcome."

A sign hanging over the cash register read "Alfbender's Gulf. Marriages performed. No cash—no gash!!"

The owner walked out. He was playing something that looked like a piccolo. He had long black hair, balding forehead, apelike jaws.

I asked directions to Butcher's Landing. Easy—two miles down take the second right, then the third left, over a draw bridge, next left and then through a "holler" and at the second or third stop sign turn left and you can't miss it.

When I got back into the van Harding offered a greasy, black-chili, country hot dog. I wasn't hungry.

At Butcher's Landing I asked a skinny gas pumper for Spot. The gas pumper shouted "Hey" and he appeared—a black man with cruel white spots covering his face and hands. When I asked about Doug, Spot glanced down at the docks. Sitting in the water was the forty-foot blue Hinckly. The same one Doug and I had raced.

Spot touched my arm, pointed to a shack behind the marina. It had a rusted tin roof, bleached pine boards, drying fishing nets.

The porch reeked of dead fish. Heads and bones collected in one corner.

Inside, in the dark, an orange hammock was holding a body.

I saw Doug and entered. His big hands were crossed on his chest. His eyes were half shut. When I squeezed his hands they were cold.

I touched his face. Stubble here. Cold. He was shirtless and the bandages were a bloody mound on his left side.

"Oh, God," Harding said behind me.

I pressed Doug's cold hand harder. Nothing.

Harding sat down beside the hammock. She was crying.

I leaned close to Doug's face. His complexion was still mustard. Purple welts swelled beneath his eyes.

I swept back the black bangs.

The long lashes blinked, opened.

"Got here pretty quick," Doug said, weakly.

Harding staggered from the floor. "Doug. Oh, Doug."

I found Spot, asked if there was a nicer place around. He scrawled a note on a piece of paper.

Thers a haus nex dore.

Mine your welcome to it.

It was a little prefab job. Windows and light. Clean. The windows faced the harbor and the blue Hinckly.

I carried Doug over. Harding grabbed his pack. I called a doctor.

An hour later Dr. Mullins arrived. A squat man with one fiery mole on his cheek which presented a single red hair. He opened Doug's bandages, worked on the gun wound. He applied gauze and said there was no infection, but he wanted Doug in his office in the morning.

"Parasites," Mullins said. "They've given him jaundice."

When he held a penlight to Doug's eyes, I saw that the bloody wounds had disappeared, but the whites were still inflamed and puffy.

Mullins gave him a shot. Harding walked the doctor to his car.

I pulled a chair beside Doug's bed. I said nothing.

He shrugged. "It was cocaine. One haul, Cody. One haul and I could have been free. I don't know—it all went to hell. Mexican cops busted us coming across the border from Guatemala. They started shooting. I ran. I heard the shot and felt my ribs sting and there was all this blood. The cops got everybody but me and two other guys. One of them sailed me here and then split. I just gave out."

"How'd you get into it?"

"You know that guy, that guy we met in McDonald's? That creep? Valance. That was his name. Yeah, Valance. When my fishing business fell through, I went to him and he told me about this big haul he was going to make from the Yucatán but he needed a boat. He said the stuff got sidetracked and he had to have a boat. I didn't want to be stupid, Cody, so I flew down three times to check things out. The second time I went to Honduras and met Valance. He had the cocaine stored in a diving shop. I came back to Black Island and swiped the Hinckly. She could handle four hundred pounds. Everything went fine at first, then Valance heard on the radio that the spicks had found out something. They were talking out loud on the radio. They were searching for us by air and sea. We decided to pull back down to Guatemala and then come up with mules across the Yucatán. Valance . . . he didn't get caught. He disappeared just before . . . the . . ."

Doug was out.

I sat down by Harding on a dilapidated couch. I reached for her hand.

"Are you all right?" she asked.

"I'm fine."

"I love you."

"Me too."

I left her, went into a small bedroom. There was a phone. I pulled Lisa's number out of my wallet, began dialing.

Just before connection, I put the receiver down. I couldn't talk, not yet. For the first time in years I said a prayer. "Oh God, please take care of Lisa."

The next morning I tried to take Doug to the doctor but he wouldn't budge. He said he wanted to rest, then go.

"Where?" I asked.

"South."

"We are South."

"Honduras."

"Doug, you're hurt."

"Lemme sleep awhile. We'll talk. You won't believe the plans I've got."

He slept for the rest of the afternoon and into the evening.

50

Around six o'clock I fed Doug Campbell's chicken noodle soup. I asked him about the parasites the doctor had discovered and he said that he had gotten them from swimming a river with Valance in the Yucatán. He said that Valance had contracted the same worm and had nearly gone blind.

Perhaps we heard them then. In the twilight—the engines. We looked out the windows, beyond the Hinckly, toward the harbor.

She motored into view. Gray and white, two tall masts, destroyer angles. *Ole Blue.*

A large light shuttered and flashed from the deck.

Doug sat up. "Must be Pop."

"How do you know?" I asked.

He pointed to his pack. "Hand me that flashlight."

I gave him the large, battery-powered lamp.

Quickly he blinked signals.

Silence. No light. Then suddenly the deep horns of *Ole Blue* blasted the dark air.

"Hah." Doug smiled.

"Thank God," said Harding.

I touched Doug's shoulder. "I can get you out of here. Jump in the van. You don't have to go back."

Doug was flashing the light, sending code.

I grabbed the flashlight. "He'll have you. He'll find out everything. You'll never be free."

Doug jerked back the light. "No, no, no. We'll just go back home, Cody. Me and you and Harding. We'll ride back on *Ole*

Blue, catch up with Parker. We don't have to tell them everything. I just had, yeah—I just had a gun accident. We were shooting sharks and I had a little accident and got nicked. Nothing else."

I leaned against the wall and looked at *Ole Blue.* Men scrambled across the deck. In the stern the *Boston Whaler* was being lowered into the sea.

"You can rest, Cody," Harding said. The scar in her chin glowed like a spark.

"Come on," said Doug. "Look, we'll go home, play a little ice hockey, maybe go down to the Caymans with Harding. Then we can make the break."

"Make the break for what?" I asked.

Through the darkening air the *Boston Whaler* sped across the sea.

"Honduras. We can buy five or ten thousand acres and plant coffee. We'll start our own plantation, Cody. What do you say?"

The speedboat landed. Lights searched Doug's sailboat. He flashed our position. Three men walked up the hill.

"Listen, coffee would be great. I know we can make it work. Me and you, buddy. Why, we'll be rich. Absolutely rich and free as air. Free. Are you with me?"

The men stomped up the steps. The room was dark. From across the sea only the light of *Ole Blue* made anything clear. I looked at Harding, at Doug and then at myself.

"Sure," I said.

"All right," yelled Doug.

"Mr. Summers," a voice called.

"I never imagined you guys as coffee magnates," Harding said.

"In here," Doug said. "In here."

The men entered. Doug knew one of them—Riley.

Riley asked if we were okay and Doug said he was hurt a little.

Riley went over, picked him up. Politely, he asked if Harding or I needed to take anything.

"A seltzer," Harding said.

At the docks everybody climbed aboard the *Boston Whaler.* Everybody but me.

Doug was wrapped in blankets, lying in the stern, his head propped on a pillow. Harding sat in a deck chair beside him. Incredibly, someone had fixed her a drink.

Riley extended his hand. "Please, sir?"

I backed away.

"Cody, let's go," Doug said.

"You go on ahead," I said.

Harding came forward. "Don't do this, Cody."

"Riley, just grab him," Doug said.

The big man actually moved toward me.

"I've—I've got some business in South Carolina," I said.

"Business?" said Doug.

Harding's eyes were tears. "Please don't."

"Yeah. A few things."

"When you coming up then?"

Harding set her drink down.

"Couple days, Doug. Couple . . ."

The boat's engine cranked. It was leaving.

"We'll make Black Island in three days. Call me," Doug said.

Riley had settled Harding into her chair. Her face was wet. The deck lamps filled her eyes. They were blue water.

"Honduras," Doug yelled. "Honduras. We'll be rich. We'll be rich—and free. And free. And . . ."

They disappeared into the dark of the night and the dark of the sea.

I held my hand aloft until I saw the speedboat raised and lifted into *Ole Blue.*

The enormous engines groaned. The lights flashed upon the masts and portals and decks. Her horns blew and blew in the moonless night.

I got into the van and drove a half mile to a small bar. I drank a few beers and tried to think.

An hour later I was going down the road that ultimately led back to Glenn Springs. Ahead I saw warning signs, flashing lights: "Caution, Drawbridge Up, STOP."

I pulled the van over. Before me the huge drawbridge towered into the night. I saw someone standing by the bridge. I got out and walked toward the man. Below, in the river, I saw a motorboat.

"How long's the bridge usually stay up?" I asked.

There was no answer and no moon and the night was dark.

"Do you know anything about these bridges?" I stepped forward.

The old man lit a cigarette and breathed and the ash glowed and lit his jade eyes, silver hair.

Disbelieving, my eyes strained and I took some steps.

"You left this." He reached out and pushed something across the pavement. "I gave it to him. He took good care of it. So should you."

I squinted and made it out—my father's suitcase, the one he had taken to Yale and beyond.

"Why did you leave?" he asked.

"You told me to leave."

"I said you didn't belong on the island. You don't. It's no good there. It's soft."

I could hear the marsh: katydids and green leopard frogs and the night itself warm and dark and living.

"Look, there's a position in Boston International Bank. The directorship of a fund I started twenty years ago. It offers grants to musicians, painters, dancers. People I don't understand really. It's a good position. You can see the whole business from there. The bank, the steel company and newspapers."

I could hear a mockingbird singing in the dark.

"I have a house in Boston. Three stories, brick, wrought-iron fence. It goes with the job. Do you know anyone who'd be interested?"

I didn't answer.

"Do you know anyone at all?"

"Maybe."

"Bosey's birthday is October the second. The family always gets together at the Beacon Club. The house could be ready by then."

Below the stars, below the towering bridge, Mallory Beale stretched out his hand.

It was there, in the dark, everything. I looked at it and then I looked at him and for a moment I did not see his face, but rather the face of another—black hair and blue eyes and a Gable mustache—and then beyond him, down the winding, black river and out into the sea, I saw *Ole Blue,* shining with a light which I had never seen, shining.

It was then that I heard the melody. Maybe it came from the van or from the motorboat below or maybe it came from the soft and black and infinite sea—the song I had heard all summer:

> Well they say, Time loves a hero,
> but only time will tell—
> if he's real, he's a legend from heaven;
> if he ain't he was sent here from hell. . . .